The Simple Life

The Simple Life

Ruth Porter

Photographs by the author

BAR NOTHING BOOKS

Montpelier, Vermont

Published in the United States by
Bar Nothing Books
100 State Street
Suite 351, Capitol Plaza, Box 3
Montpelier, Vermont 05602
802 223-7086
bnbooks@sover.net
SAN 256-615X

Grateful acknowledgment is made to
New Directions Publishing Corp. for
permission to reprint
"Brotherhood" by Ocatavio Paz,
Translated by Eliot Weinberger,
from *Collected Poems 1957–1987*,
copyright © 1986 by Octavio Paz
and Eliot Weinberger.
Reprinted by permission of
New Directons Publishing Corp.

Design: Glenn Suokko, Inc.
Typeset in Caslon
Special thanks to Brita Bergland, Annex Press
Printed in the United States

ISBN 0-9769422-5-9 (hardback)
ISBN 0-9769422-6-7 (softcover)

FIRST EDITION

Library of Congress Control Number
2005935852

Brotherhood

Homage to Claudius Ptolemy

I am a man: little do I last
and the night is enormous.
But I look up:
the stars write.
Unknowing I understand:
I too am written,
and at this very moment
someone spells me out.

Octavio Paz

I

"I really can't believe you thought there was something going on between Susan Brownmiller and me."

"Well, I wasn't the only one."

"Honestly, Is, you just make things up. You only see what you want to see. I haven't even said two words to her for twenty-five years. You just make up this whole *thing*, and then you believe it."

Isabel hunched a little lower on the seat. She looked through the windshield, but she didn't really see. That was the convenient part about driving around while they had a fight. At least they didn't have to look at each other when they hurt each other.

"It's not the first time," she said, but she didn't say it very loud. She felt too miserable to make an effort.

"What did you say? I couldn't hear that."

He looked around at her then, as much pain on his face as she could feel on her own, and she was suddenly sorry. "I said I knew it was a dumb idea to come to the reunion."

That was when the car bogged down and stopped. Jeff stepped on the gas, and the engine whined, but they didn't move.

"God damn it! Now look what you made me do. I should have been watching this stupid cow path. Why in hell can't they pave the roads in Vermont? They're too stingy, that's why." He squeezed the steering wheel until his knuckles were white. He even tried to shake it.

Isabel looked away in embarrassment. Beyond the muddy road, set back from it, was a white farmhouse. Not particularly beautiful or particularly neat, it sat at the center of its own universe with its barn beside it, in a circle of fields, ringed by wooded hills, ringed by blue, more-distant hills. There were no people around, but Isabel could see that the ones who lived there lived in peace and harmony with nature, a life of simple, basic things, the kind of life she had always yearned to live herself, only she didn't know how.

The only sound was made by the spring peepers, still occasional because it was still daylight, although night wasn't far off. The light was transparent with that purity that comes in the early evening in early spring.

She looked around at Jeff and smiled and said, "I guess that's why Vermonters always talk about mud season. I remember now." Too late she realized that she had forgotten all about their fight, assuming, without even thinking of Jeff, that he was seeing what she was seeing.

"It's just like you to laugh. How *could* you think it was funny? We can't even get out of the car. There's mud everywhere. You probably haven't noticed—you're so damn unrealistic."

She could feel him trying to reel her back into the fight, but it was as though she was suddenly on the other side of the window, out there with the peaceful farmhouse. Watching Jeff from that distance, it was different. It didn't matter.

"Let's get out and look around."

"We can't! There's no way to know how deep it is. It's horrible."

"It's only mud."

"You never care what a mess you are anyway."

She felt the sting of that. "I'm as dressed up as you are. Look at my shoes. They're much more delicate than yours. And I have stockings on, *and* a new dress. I'm just braver, that's all."

"It's not *your* class reunion, so *you* don't care."

"I'm going to push us out, and then we can go back to the motel, and I'll clean up." She didn't even look at him or wait to hear what he had to say. She opened the door with determination.

She didn't want him to see any hesitation, so holding her breath, as though that would keep a little more of her out of it, she poked the toe of her shoe at the satiny, brown surface of the mud. Her shoes were new, high heels of wine-colored suede. She had looked down at them often and with pleasure while Jeff was talking to his classmates. It was hard to see that delicate and stylish foot disappear. The mud clutched coldly at her ankle, and she still wasn't touching bottom. She gasped.

Jeff was leaning over the steering wheel so he could see. "Now you know what I mean." His smile was bitter.

"It surprised me, that's all. I'm still going to push us out. Just wait." She put the other foot in and slid off the seat until she was standing, gasping a little and trying to hold up the skirt of her new dress with the mud halfway up her shins. "Wow. It's cold."

She started walking toward the back of the car. She moved in slow motion, pointing her toes because the mud was trying to take off her shoes. She wished she had thought of taking them off herself. If one got lost at the bottom of the mud hole, she'd never find it again. When she got to the back of the car, she had to let go of her skirts, which were long and full. The bottom of her dress slid slowly out of sight into the mud.

The car was Jeff's, a dark blue Honda that was small and light. One good push would do it, the way it did sometimes when the snow was deep.

"I'm ready whenever you are." She waved at the back of his head through the rear window.

He raced the engine, and she reached down to get a good grip on the bumper, prepared to give it everything she could all at once. She could feel the jerk when he put it in gear, and she could hear the engine revving. Mud sprayed everywhere, but that was all. Maybe she hadn't started to push at the right time.

"Try it again." But even as she called, she knew nothing would happen. And nothing did.

Jeff turned the engine off and stuck his head out the window. "It's no use, Isabel. I told you so. I'm going to get out. Maybe the people in that house will let me use their phone."

"I'll do it. You can stay there."

"Don't be ridiculous. Look at you. They'd never let you inside."

"By the time you get out, you'll be just as bad."

"No I won't. You watch."

When Isabel looked through the back window, she could see Jeff climbing laboriously into the passenger seat. He was so long-legged, and his car was so small, that it wasn't an easy maneuver. She walked in slow motion around the side of the car, although she didn't want him to think she had come to see him fall in the mud. She held out her hand to help him, but he jumped past her, turning his body slightly, refusing her help. She looked down at her outstretched hand and saw that it too was covered with mud. She wiped both hands on her skirt and followed him across the front yard to the farmhouse feeling secretly disappointed. He was right about that much anyway. He had jumped almost over the mud, so that nothing got dirty except his shoes. Isabel looked down at her dress. The whole thing was splashed with mud, and there was a heavy band of it around the bottom.

Jeff went up onto the porch and rapped smartly. The glass in the door made a loose, rattling sound. "They ought to do something about that before next winter," he said.

Isabel stayed at the bottom of the steps. In his dark suit, tall and thin and precise in front of that old-fashioned door, he could have been a salesman. With his neat tortoiseshell glasses he looked as though he would be selling something intellectual. He knocked again and then paused, listening. When he didn't hear anything, he cupped his hands around the sides of his eyes and looked in.

"What do you see? Tell me."

He turned to look at her, blinking in the light. "I don't think anyone's in there."

"What's the room like then?"

"I don't know, just sort of dark. I think it's a hall. I saw some stairs."

"Why don't we try the back door? Maybe they're in the kitchen and can't hear you."

"Maybe."

Isabel went first along the path through tall bushes which were just getting their new leaves. She was sure the kitchen door would be on the same side of the house as the big barn, but she didn't say it out loud. Jeff hated it when she was so positive about things she couldn't possibly know. When she got to the small back porch, she stood aside to let him be the one to do it.

The back door was half open. Jeff pushed it a little farther and stuck his head inside and said, "Anybody home?" He tilted his head, waiting for an answer, but there wasn't one.

Isabel said, "I guess nobody's in there. That's too bad."

"I don't see a telephone, but I could go in and look for one. What do you think?"

"Maybe they're in the barn, doing chores or something."

"We could look."

"I wonder what kind of people live here."

"All I want to know about them is whether they have a telephone or not."

He came down the porch steps and crossed the driveway to the barn. Isabel followed trying not to feel annoyed. Their fight seemed to be over, and she didn't want it to flare up again.

They went through a door that creaked, into a dusty, low room with old work clothes and bits of harness hanging on nails around the walls. A bare bulb hung from the ceiling in the center of the room. It was lit, but it gave off a dim light through the thick lattice of cobwebs around it. It was much warmer now they were out of the wind.

Jeff crossed the room and went through a low doorway on the far side. When she saw him ducking under the large beam that went over the door, Isabel thought of Alice in Wonderland. She stopped to laugh and then had to hurry to catch up. On the other side of the door was a dark passage, spidery and empty. She felt an irrational stab of fear that lasted until she almost walked into him around the bend of the passage.

The hallway was suddenly wider and higher with light coming in through big open barn doors at the end. It smelled of fresh sawdust and animals, a smell of the circus. There was a radio playing faintly somewhere, but no people. They walked down the hall looking into the empty animal stalls on each side.

"I wonder how far it is to the next house. I can't remember seeing any houses before we got stuck. Can you?"

"I guess I wasn't looking. There must be somebody around here though, or they would have turned off the radio."

"Maybe they leave it on all the time to fool people. Damn this god-forsaken place!"

Isabel walked to the open doorway and stood there looking out. The early evening light was as clear and pure as water. Beyond the black barnyard mud was a fence and then a wide field just starting to turn green. In the center of the field was a huge, gray mound of rock, like a monument. On its far side was an old stone wall and beyond that a steep, wooded hillside. The trees were getting bright young leaves that shimmered with delight and foolish hope for the new year. She stood there looking and looking, overflowing with the beauty of it.

"Come on, Is. What are you standing there for? We've *got* to do something."

"It's so beautiful. I was just looking."

"We don't have time for that now. It's almost six o'clock. We're going to miss the dinner for sure, and we paid for it too."

By the time Isabel turned around to follow him, he was already near the bend in the hallway.

"It's going to be dark before we can get a tow-truck out here. I bet they'll have to come all the way out from Severance. I'm going to go into their house and use their phone. Let them sue me."

Isabel had gone a few steps before she turned back for one more look. Something moving had caught her eye just as she turned away. Coming out of the woods toward the gap in the stone wall were two people looking very small compared to the two huge cows that walked behind them. She had to blink to make sure she was really seeing what she thought she saw. Framed by the dark doorway, the bright field with the tiny figures was like an N. C. Wyeth illustration for a book she had read long ago. Now she could even hear a ghostly jingling of chains.

"Jeff, come back. Here they are."

"What?" He stuck his head around the corner. He looked exasperated.

"The people. Come and see. These must be the people who live here."

He said, "Where? I don't see anybody." But he came back and stood beside her in the doorway.

"Isn't it beautiful? That's a team of oxen, isn't it? You don't often get a chance to see something like this. An old man and a boy. The boy's the one holding the stick. Do you think he's telling the oxen what to do?"

"I don't know, and I don't care, but I tell you, I wouldn't walk right in front of them like that. They're not even looking back to see how close those cows are getting."

"They're trained to do that."

"Well, *I* wouldn't walk in front of them, no matter what. You couldn't be sure. You never can tell about animals, even dogs. It's always a mistake to trust them."

"Don't you feel as though this is a magic place, Jeff? Like maybe we fell into a fairy tale?"

"What—the wicked witch of the mudhole who snatched our car?"

"I don't mean *that*. It's just so beautiful here, and strange. I mean it's so different from home and the bookstore, even from the reunion...."

"I agree with you about that. It sure is different. I'll be glad to get back to where things are normal."

"No, I mean, it's so beautiful that it seems enchanted, like in a story. That's what's different about it. I mean it's not really surprising that we could look out there and see those people with oxen. Don't you feel that way too?"

"No."

"Not even a little?"

"Not even a little. It's very scenic. Sure. But I want to get back to the reunion where I can be comfortable."

"Oh, I wish..."

"What?" He sighed. "You're never satisfied with the way things are, that's your trouble."

"Well, *I'm* not the one that minded about the car getting stuck. I'm even glad it happened."

"Oh for God's sakes. The things you say. It's because you don't think. You'll probably be sorry before we get out of this mess, even if you don't know it now."

"I bet I'm not."

"We'll see."

"Jeff, this is serious. Please listen."

"What is it now?"

"When we sell the bookstore, we're going to move out of Abingdon, aren't we?"

"Probably."

"I mean, I know we've talked about it a lot, about where we'd go."

"There isn't any hurry. We'll probably go from place to place for a while. Until we see....Florida, Palm Springs, Arizona. We can try them all."

"I have a much better idea."

"What's that? Look, they're getting close. God, are they big! I bet they're dangerous. Look at those horns!"

"Let's take the money and buy a farm like this one, around here some place."

He looked around at her. "You have *got* to be crazy."

She met his look of amazement. She could feel her jaw getting tight. "No I'm not. I'm completely serious."

"Well, it's a crazy idea then. Here, look out! We need to get out of this doorway." He grabbed her by the upper arm and pulled her into an empty stall.

The clanking of chains was much louder, and suddenly the light coming through the large doorway was blocked, and the huge team rolled into the passage filling it completely. The old man walked nonchalantly right in front. He held the whip up before the noses of the oxen and said, "Whoa." His voice was surprisingly deep for such a gnomelike person.

Isabel stood beside Jeff in the doorway of the empty stall. The gigantic, horned heads were right on the other side of the opening. Isabel had never been that close to really large animals before. The smell of them, a rich smell of fruity fermentation, filled the air. They turned their heads slowly and in perfect time with each other, and four enormous brown eyeballs rolled slowly around to look at Isabel with stately and detached curiosity. She felt small and very vulnerable standing there, wondering if they were going to object to her red dress. Did oxen hate red the way bulls were supposed to? Maybe they only minded bright red, not the dark wine-red she was wearing.

The old man was standing in front of them, unfastening something on their yoke. When the oxen turned to look at Jeff and Isabel, the old man looked in their direction also. His gaze was as calm and unsurprised and slow as that of his cattle.

Jeff cleared his throat nervously and said, "Hello. My name is Jeffrey Rawlings. I was wondering if I would be permitted to use your telephone."

The old man nodded and turned back to the yoke without speaking. He had to stand on tiptoe to reach the top of it.

Jeff turned to Isabel and gave an exaggerated, clownlike shrug, as though he wanted to say, "Okay, so what do I do now?" There was no way he could leave the stall.

The huge beasts were chewing in unison, with great sideways, rolling, jaw motions. Isabel could hear their teeth grating against each other. She felt herself slowed to their time. She let her eyes roll around the way theirs did to see who was going to make a move next.

Jeff shifted from foot to foot and then said, "Our car is stuck in your mudhole. I believe we need a wrecker."

The old man's eyes flicked across Jeff's face and then back to the yoke. He reached in his pocket and took out a big metal pin, put it through a hole in one of the bows and hit it with the heel of his hand to drive it into place. Without looking up from what he was doing, he said, "I'll come take a look."

Jeff looked surprised. He opened his mouth and took a breath, as though he was about to speak. Then he closed his mouth again without saying anything. He flapped his arms at his sides several times, but there was nothing he could do either.

The old man picked up the whip which he had propped on the floor in the doorway. He made a flourish in the air with it, and said, "Come up," one soft gulp of a word. Then he turned and marched down the hall with the whip resting on his shoulder like a rifle. With heavy dignity, with a ponderous swaying of bodies and clanking of chains, the oxen moved forward after him.

Jeff and Isabel peeked out the door to watch. Isabel whispered, "But they're going the wrong direction." Jeff frowned and shook his head to shut her up.

The old man stood at the end of the passage, pointing with his whip to the stall on his right. The oxen walked heavily toward him, rolling the way fat people do when their feet hurt. When they got near, the old man said, "Haw," and the oxen disappeared into the empty stall. Isabel could hear them shuffling, clanking, and creaking as they moved around in there while the old man stayed where he was at the end of the hall. After a minute their heads appeared in the doorway again. The old man was pointing down the hall with his whip. They turned out into the hall and down it. Isabel and Jeff had to step back as the oxen swept past filling the hall with their bodies. They blocked the light again as they went out of the barn in a rich cloud of animal scent. The old man walked out behind them.

Isabel and Jeff looked at each other. The barn seemed much emptier than it had before the oxen came in.

"What's next?" Jeff said.

"I think they're going to look at our car."

"Well, I hope he doesn't think I'd let him touch my car with those things."

"Jeff, they're amazing. Didn't you think it was great the way he turned them around?"

"Cause I'm not, and that's all there is to it. I'm going to call a wrecker."

"They looked plenty strong enough."

"That's just what I'm afraid of. There's no telling what they would do to my poor car."

Isabel started out the back door after the oxen. She didn't want to miss any of it. The barnyard mud was soft and black, and every place the oxen had stepped was a round hole filling with water. She hesitated. The light-colored mud on her feet was already caked and dry.

Jeff called to her from the other end of the passage. "Come this way, Is. You don't want to walk through that muck. We can get back to the car this way."

Isabel followed him back through the barn the way they had come in. When she stepped outside, the air was clean and sharp and smelled of ice. It was colder, and the spring peepers sounded louder than they had when she stood at the other end of the barn. The sky was still luminous, but the first stars were beginning to prick through. The dark, peaceful hills made a safe circle around the fields and buildings. Isabel felt like bursting from the beauty of it all.

Down the road, the oxen were just getting to the car. The old man was right beside them, and Jeff was trying to catch up. His arms were swinging and his suit jacket flapping with the awkward, scarecrow way he had of walking when he was in a hurry. Isabel followed slowly, trying to take in everything beautiful around her, refusing to be drawn into Jeff's anxiety. The lights were on in the kitchen, and the door was shut. That was where the boy had gone.

By the time she caught up to them, the old man and Jeff were standing side by side where the deep mud ended, looking at Jeff's car. The oxen stood back a few feet, facing the car and chewing thoughtfully.

"It looks pretty helpless, doesn't it?" she said, as she stopped beside Jeff. "Like a wounded animal caught in a tar pit with its door open like that."

The old man gave no sign that he noticed her arrival, and Jeff looked at her as though he had never seen her before. He turned to the old man.

"You really don't think I need to call a wrecker?"

"You do whatever you want." He picked up his feedstore cap by the bill and resettled it on his head. "It's your car that's stuck."

"You really think you can pull it out by yourself?"

"With my team."

"I don't know what to do. It would save a lot of time and money." He ran his hand through his hair. "But they could hurt it, and it's only two years old. It doesn't even have any serious scratches on it yet."

He looked over at the old man, but the old man stood there tapping the toe of his workboot with the end of his whip, as though he hadn't heard a word.

Jeff looked around at Isabel. "What do you think we ought to do?"

"What can happen? There's nothing for the car to bump into. I don't see what we're waiting for."

She caught a quick glance of appreciation from the old man.

Jeff said, "Well, okay, but remember, Isabel, this is your idea. I just hope we're not making a big mistake here."

The old man had moved in front of his oxen and raised his whip, but he hadn't started them moving. He was looking at Jeff, waiting for the word to go.

Jeff nodded to him. "Yes," he said. "My wife says to do it."

The old man said, "Gee-up," softly, and walked his team in a wide circle so that when he halted them, they were standing in front of the car with their backs to it. He ducked under the yoke, took down the chain that was draped over it, and laid it out on the ground between them with one end hitched to the large iron ring that hung from the center of the yoke. Then he peeked out over the back of the ox that was nearest to Jeff. He was so short and the ox so tall that the only parts of him that showed over the ox's back were his eyes and the top of his head in the faded red cap. "You might want to steer your car," he said to Jeff, and then he disappeared, not waiting to see what Jeff was going to do.

Jeff didn't move. Isabel said, "Do you want me to do it?" She was excited.

Jeff looked down at her legs and the bottom of her skirt where the mud was flaking off in dried chunks. "No thanks," he said sourly. "I'll do it myself." He went to the edge of the mudhole and gave a great flapping jump into the open door of the car. He closed the door and climbed into the driver's seat. Isabel watched him trying to maneuver his long legs in the narrow space.

When she looked at the old man again, he was crouched under the front end of the car trying to find a place to attach the chain. He seemed indifferent to the mud. In a minute he stood up and walked stiffly around to where Jeff was sitting by the open car window.

"Take it out of gear, but don't turn on your engine. Just keep your wheels straight."

He picked up his whip and walked to the front of his team. Holding his whip high, he said, "Come up," softly. He walked backwards away from the oxen, and they walked slowly, steadily toward him while the car slid silently behind. There was no straining, no drama, no loud noise, only the soft sucking of the mud and then the gritting of the oxen's feet on the dry part of the road. When the car was out of the mudhole, the old man lowered his whip so that it hung in the air in front of the huge noses. "Whoa," he said in a deep, but quiet voice.

Isabel spun around and around in the road, saying, "Hooray, hooray," until her muddy skirts were flying out in a circle around her. When she stopped, she almost fell over with dizziness, but the others didn't notice. The old man had already unhitched the chain from the car, and Jeff was walking toward him with his hand outstretched and a big smile on his face.

"Thank you very much Mr....uh...."

The old man looked at Jeff's hand coming toward him. Then he looked down at his own hand. He wiped it up and down on his trouser leg, looked at it again and gave it to Jeff to shake.

"Thank you. What do I owe you?"

"It wasn't nothin. I didn't even have to yoke 'em up." He walked over to his team, and Jeff followed. Isabel joined them.

"But don't you want some money?"

The old man watched the toe of his boot kicking at a little ball of mud on the road. He said nothing.

"I would have had to pay the wrecker."

The old man didn't seem to feel any responsibility for the awkward pause.

Finally Isabel said, "It's amazing how strong they are. I wouldn't have believed it. I don't think I ever saw any oxen up close before."

The old man smiled and grabbed the horn of the ox nearest

to him. He jiggled the huge head back and forth affectionately. "Yup. They're good boys, all right. They know their job."

"Do they have names? I mean, what are their names?"

He smiled at the huge head he was holding on to. "This here is Buck. He's my nigh ox. That'n over there is Ben. He's the easy-goin one. He just takes life as it comes. Buck 'n Ben, that's them." He jiggled Buck's head, making him nod in agreement. Then he turned to Isabel. "Where are you folks from?"

Isabel was just opening her mouth to say Massachusetts when Jeff said, "We went to Green Mountain College. I'm up here for my twenty-fifth reunion. Boy, time sure flies. I guess I'm getting old." He chuckled a little.

Isabel didn't smile, and neither did the old man. She said, "You live in a beautiful place."

"It'll do." His voice was gruff, but he tilted his head toward her in gentle acknowledgment. She felt they understood each other, although she couldn't have said why. They were all three silent, looking at the ground. Then Jeff cleared his throat.

"Well, thank you very much, Mr.....I'm sorry I didn't catch your name."

"Trumbley. Sonny Trumbley."

"Well, thank you so much, Mr. Trumbley. If you're sure you won't take anything for it. Come on, Isabel. We'd better get back to GMC before they send out a search party."

Sonny Trumbley spoke to his oxen, and they all three started toward their barn, walking companionably side by side. Jeff got as far as the door of his car, and then he stopped.

"Mr. Trumbley," he called, "Oh hey, Mr. Trumbley. Could you wait a minute?"

The old man stopped and turned to look back. The oxen continued on their ponderous way.

"I have to go back the way I came. Could you just wait until I get across this place again? In case I get stuck."

The old man shouted to his oxen to whoa, and they all three stood where they were, waiting without interest while Jeff and

Isabel got into the car, and Jeff turned the car around and drove it back through the mud, making the engine rev much too much in his nervousness.

When the car was safely across, Jeff honked the horn, and kept on going. Isabel looked back. She just had time to see the three of them walking off side by side again before the car went around a bend in the road.

It had gotten much colder since the sun went down, and Isabel had left her coat at the motel. Now that she was in the car, she realized how cold she was. She turned the heater up as high as it would go.

Neither one of them spoke for a few minutes, and then Jeff said, "It's twenty of seven. You know we might even have made it to the dinner after all, except that we're going to have to go back to the motel so you can change."

"Oh." She thought for a minute. "Do you want me to go like this?"

He looked around at her, as though trying to see if she was serious, but he didn't ask.

"I could probably knock off the worst of the mud. And most of me will be under the table. I mean, if you want me to."

"Isabel. Don't be ridiculous. It would be too embarrassing. We'll have to miss it."

"Well, okay. It's up to you." Now that they had left that magic spot, she could feel the disagreeableness settling over her again.

"You don't ever care about anything, do you, Is?"

"Maybe I'm just different than you."

"Hah!"

"That was a great place, wasn't it? And an amazing old guy."

"I would have rather gone to the dinner."

"Did you see? He had on suspenders *and* a belt."

"I wasn't really looking at his clothes."

"Well, he did. I wonder why."

"He probably didn't want his pants to fall down. Who cares?"

"You know, Jeff, I'm serious about this subject. You don't pay any attention to me when I try to talk to you about it, but...."

"How an old man holds his pants up?"

"No. You know that's not what I mean. I'm serious about what we do when we sell the bookstore."

"Let's wait and see how much money we get for it. That old guy you liked so much would probably say, 'Don't count your chickens before they hatch,' or something."

"That's okay, but what I mean is this—I think you and I have kind of different ideas about what we're going to do with that money, and I think we ought to talk about it. I mean, I think you think I'm going to go along with what you want to do, and I might not."

"Just what do you mean by that?"

"There. I've said it, and I'm not sorry. You always think I don't know what goes on in the real world, and I always have my face in a book, and I don't know how to take care of myself, and I suppose it's all true. But there's another part of it that you haven't got right. That's going to be my money too, and I have some ideas about what I want to do with it, and even if they are dumb ideas, I have a right to try them out."

"Not if it's going to waste the money, you don't."

"Look, I don't want to start the fight up again, I just mean we have to talk about some stuff. I've been looking around at the reunion. When you were talking to your friends, there were some times when I didn't have anybody to talk to. And I've been wondering why we got married in the first place. I can't remember any more."

"Because we loved each other."

"Yeah, but I'm not sure what that means—what we meant by that."

"Well, it just...."

"And more important, I'm not sure what that has to do with now."

They were looking straight ahead again, both of them being careful not to see what effect their words were having on each other.

"Well, at least we made it back to the paved road. I guess we don't need to talk about this any more. Let's go to the motel, so you can clean up, and then we can go into Severance for some dinner. Okay? We can be back in time for the party."

"Sure. Fine. But we're going to have to figure this out some time. It's not that being at that farm tonight changed my ideas about what I want to do with my life...."

"Isabel, you sound like a child. You're forty-four years old. Remember?"

"I know. But I feel like I haven't done anything yet. I don't feel old."

"That's why I want to get out of the bookstore now, while we're still young enough to enjoy ourselves."

"I don't want to just have fun. There is something I want, something I need to do, and being at that farm made me think it wasn't just a dumb idea."

"Those things always sound better in books than they do in real life. That's your trouble—you read too much. Look at Thoreau. He talked a good game, about how cheap it was to build his cabin, for instance. But the truth was that he didn't know anything about building. There were bent nails that he wasted lying all around that cabin. And nails were expensive in those days."

"I know, Jeff. You've told me that a million times, and I always used to believe you, but not any more."

"I don't know what you could possibly mean by that. It's a fact, for God's sakes. Sometimes I don't understand you at all, Isabel."

"It doesn't make any difference. That old man we saw tonight doesn't care about stuff like how many nails Thoreau used up. He's living his life simply, the way he always has. I don't see why I can't live like that too."

"Oh for God's sakes, you're the simple one. I just wonder if that old geezer was up to anything. There's something funny about the way he wouldn't take any money."

Isabel couldn't think of anything to say to that. She shivered and hunched a little lower on the seat, but she felt a new determination, and she resolved not to forget it.

"He never would look me in the eye either. I hope we've seen the last of him."

"Well, I haven't," Isabel said, but she didn't say it out loud. It could wait.

2

IT WAS SUNNY and warm for early May, the day Isabel drove into Severance. It was almost exactly a year since she and Jeff went to his class reunion and got stuck in the mud. She stopped at the traffic light where Main Street crossed Merchants Row. Everything seemed different, smaller and shabbier, less prosperous than it was then. But she was different too. So many painful things had happened, all the fighting with Jeff, and then the divorce, and even more fighting over who got what. And that was still going on.

So here she was, about to begin this new life that she had dreamed about for a whole year, and she was scared and not at all sure she could do it, even though she had to make a new life for herself now that the old one was gone. Well, she had to try anyhow, and before she could do anything else, she would have to find a place to stay.

She parked on Merchants Row and went into the Severance News to buy a local paper. While she was handing her two quarters to the woman behind the counter, she said, "You don't know of any rooms for rent, do you?"

The woman took the money. "No dear," she said. Then she looked at Isabel more closely. "For you? No, nothing like that. Check the classifieds."

"That's what I meant to do. I just thought you might know. I want something cheap, really cheap."

The woman looked at her doubtfully. "Well, there's always Roxy's, but...." She thought a minute. "Oh well, I guess you ought to know what you want. Roxy's cheap."

"That's good."

"She mostly rents to men. But that's Roxy for you. Still, it's not like you were real young. I mean, you're old enough to have been around. I guess you can choose for yourself."

"You make it sound bad."

"Well, not really. Roxy is good-hearted. Her place is just a bit run-down—a certain clientele. Probably because she's so cheap."

"I guess I need to take a look," Isabel said. "How do I find her place?"

"I'll tell you what, dear...." The woman glanced over at a man who stood in front of the rack of magazines. Then she leaned toward Isabel across the counter. "I'll give you directions, and you drive over there. Okay?"

Isabel nodded.

"It's the best way. You just look at the place before you decide."

Isabel thanked her and left. She thought she would drive by Roxy's house and then get a cup of coffee and think about it while she checked out the classifieds. She had never pictured this part. In her fantasies of herself in her new life, she always already had a place to live and a job.

She took a left off Merchants Row over a bridge and then

another left at the end of the bridge onto River Street, the way the woman told her to do. On the other side of the bridge everything was unfamiliar. When she was at Green Mountain, she used to come into Severance with her friends to go to the movies or to the stores, but none of them ever went to this side of the little river. Here all the buildings were old and run-down. There were large empty sheds on both sides of the street. No one was around. It would be scary to go through here at night, even in a car.

Everyone who knew her thought she was crazy or very brave to try to remake her life in the middle. A few days ago, her friend Nancy told her how brave she was to throw over the past and start a new life. Nancy said she didn't know anyone else who would have the nerve to do that. She, Nancy, wouldn't dare, and she really respected Isabel for being so brave. Isabel didn't think she was brave or crazy either, just determined to do something different, even though she wasn't sure how she was going to do it.

On the left at the end of a long brick warehouse was a tiny parking lot, just big enough for two cars. It was overshadowed by a huge tree whose roots had buckled the sidewalk. This was the place. Isabel pulled into the parking lot beside a two-story brown house that tilted away from the street. When she stepped out of the car, she saw how close the water was. The bank dropped steeply down to the wide stream. The house seemed to be leaning out in order to see down into the water. Isabel was enchanted—to be in the center of Severance, right across the river from the downtown, and to feel as though you were out in the country—this was a promising way to begin. It could even be an omen. What did it matter that she would have to drive by a few dark buildings to get here?

She went up the steps and rang the doorbell before she remembered that she had meant to drive by and look at the place and think it over before committing herself. She could leave now and come back later, but she didn't want to. She wanted to see what the house was like inside.

All the windows were closed, even though it was a bright, warm morning. She couldn't hear enough to be sure, but she had a feeling that the doorbell wasn't working. She pushed it again and waited some more. Her heart was beating fast. A toilet flushed inside somewhere. She knocked once and then again. Finally, she heard shuffling footsteps. Then someone was fumbling with the lock on the door. It jerked open.

"God-damned door." The old woman looked Isabel up and down. "Well, okay, then. What do you think *you* want?"

"Roxy?"

"What do you want to know for?" She had pouches under her little eyes. The orange scarf which she wore like a turban made her skin greenish and blotchy. If she was in her sixties, they had been hard years. She didn't seem good-hearted at all.

"I heard you rented rooms," Isabel said, wishing she had been more cautious.

Roxy pulled the door toward her so that not much besides her head was sticking out. Isabel couldn't see in at all. "Sometimes I do."

"I was thinking about renting a room."

"Who sent you?"

"What?"

"Who sent you over here to try and get a room?"

"Oh....I don't know her name. She was selling newspapers at the Severance News downtown."

"At the Severance News?" Roxy looked surprised.

Isabel said, "I asked her where I could find a room to rent."

"You did?"

"I could describe her. She was nice. She acted like she knew you."

"That's okay. Most everybody knows me." She opened the door all the way and stuck out her hand. "Rowena Fox, but everybody calls me Roxy. It's kind of my nickname."

Isabel took her hand. It was soft and damp. "Mine is Isabel Rawlings. Some people call me Is, but I don't like it when they do."

"I thought you was like some kind of inspector or somethin."

"You did?"

"Sometimes they send out a woman, just to trip you up."

Isabel would have liked to ask what they were inspecting for, but she didn't want Roxy to get suspicious again.

"I knew you couldn't be local. You look different some way. That's why."

"I do? And I was just wishing I had on a skirt, or at least, something nicer than blue jeans."

"They do that, you know—dress casual so you don't suspect. But I'm right. You ain't from around here, are you?"

"I'm from Abingdon, Massachusetts."

"And you want one of my rooms?"

"Yes. I might."

"For more than one night?"

"Yes. I mean, I think so."

"I don't usually rent out just for one night, you know what I mean? Unless it's somebody I know pretty well." She gave Isabel a sly look. "Now if you wanted it for as much as a week...."

"Well, I do....that is, I do if I like it. You have a room I could rent then?"

"Yes, darlin, I do. I didn't realize what you had in mind. That changes things."

"Can I see the room then?" It made sense to look at least. She wouldn't have to take it.

"You can." She stood aside so that Isabel could come into the house. "This here is the hall. My room is right there." She pointed to a partly-open door at the foot of the stairs.

"I was hoping you could rent me a room that faced the back—looking out over that beautiful little river. I know I would want one if it looked out over the water."

Roxy's little eyes were intent, as though she was trying to find the secret message. She seemed to shake her head a few times, but it might have been involuntary. "I'll be right back, hon," she said, and she went into her room, leaving Isabel in the dark hallway.

There was linoleum on the floor and heavy wood on the bottom half of the walls. Above the wood, the walls were covered with flowery paper. At the end of the hall was a dark, closed door.

"That's the kitchen down there," Roxy said. "Let's go upstairs."

Isabel thought Roxy had gone to get a key for the room, but she wasn't carrying anything but a lit cigarette. She started up the stairs, pulling herself along on the banister.

Isabel followed uneasily. Maybe she was crazy to do this. She could just hear what Jeff would say about Roxy. He wouldn't want to have anything to do with her. But Jeff was narrowminded. Things were more complicated than he thought. And anyway, as Isabel told herself, this was no time to shrink back. Roxy represented real life, and that's what she was looking for.

Roxy stopped at the top of the stairs. "Whew, I got to catch my breath." She took a deep drag on her cigarette and blew smoke past Isabel down the hall. "Okay, hon, this room looks out the back." She opened the first door at the top of the stairs. "You're right. You got more privacy that way."

The room was small and bright. It was on the corner of the house. There were two windows. Isabel went straight to them. The one across from the door looked out on the parking lot and her own old, white station wagon, but the other window looked over the little river, as she had known it would. There was a wide, rockless pool in the stream. She could see down through the water to where in the shadows she thought she saw a fish. She was delighted. This made up for any shortcomings.

Mrs. Fox was sitting on the bed with an ashtray in her hand. "If you're a smoker, I got no problem with it. I put ashtrays in all my rooms."

"I don't smoke."

"Well, okay. So, what do you think of it, darlin?" She waved her hand around the room. A trail of smoke followed her gesture. "I always loved flowers, and I really went to town in here. More suitable for a woman. But then some of my men guests.... you'd be surprised."

"It's very nice," Isabel said absently. She was worrying about the way the whole house smelled of cigarette smoke, wondering if she would be able to get rid of the smell in the room by leaving the windows open.

"I had to search the stores to find the right patterns. See, on the linoleum there and in the wallpaper. It's not the same colors, but it's the same kind of flower—cabbage rose. My favorite. See how it goes. It's over here on the bedspread too. A lot of people might not notice."

"I think I'd like to rent this room, Mrs. Fox. How much is it a week? And can I rent it by the week?"

"Sixty a week. No, seventy. That's what it is." She put out her cigarette and stood up. "Of course if you took it by the month, I could make it a little cheaper."

"How much then?"

"Sixty a week—only you'd have to give me the whole $240 up front. I wouldn't ask you for a deposit."

"I see."

"Because you look trustworthy, hon. Now, some people...."

"What about the bathroom?"

"I'm glad you asked me that. I was just about to show you anyway. It's very convenient—right next door."

Their feet made a crunching sound on the buckled linoleum, and the noise echoed down the hall. Roxy looked at the closed doors. "I only got one other renter right at the moment. Gene Mooney. He lives in the front room there, but he keeps to himself. You might not see him at all. And he's real quiet. The only way you know he's there is you hear his radio sometimes. He likes a country station." She knocked on the bathroom door. "I tell him to leave it part way open, so we can tell if he's in there or not, but he forgets." She shrugged and opened the door.

The room was clean but dreary. There was a tub with a shower in it, a washbowl and a toilet. The bottom half of the window was covered with a plastic curtain.

"I'm goin to put in some new linoleum soon as I find some I like. And maybe a countertop here. It's kind of cracked around the washbowl, ain't it? And I'd like some of them light fixtures with the bulbs all around like movie stars have."

Isabel nodded.

"Then you can see to put your make-up on." She looked at Isabel's face. "If you decide to wear any. How old did you say you were, hon?"

"Forty-five. I'll be forty-six in a couple of months."

"You don't look that old, hon. You must have good skin. It's real smart of you not to wear make-up. Of course when you get to be my age, you'll have to, if you want to look good at all."

Isabel tried not to notice how uncomfortable she felt. She hoped she could learn to ignore Mrs. Fox's personal remarks.

They walked out of the bathroom and stood at the top of the stairs. The door to the room—Isabel was already thinking of it as her room—was open, and the clear spring light made a bright rectangle on the floor at their feet.

"I've decided I would like to rent your room."

"Well, that's good, hon. You won't be sorry."

Too late Isabel remembered the words of the woman at the newstand. She meant to look around and think it over. She hadn't even checked the ads in the paper. Jeff would call it another example of how she rushed into things, but then he thought the whole idea of moving to Severance was stupid. "I'd like to take it for a week," she said, thinking that was sensible. She could take her time looking at other places, and it would be a lot cheaper than staying in a motel.

"So, I guess you're takin a little vacation for yourself. Come to get away from it all in Vermont, have you?"

"No, actually, I'm planning to move here, and I probably will be renting the room for a long time, but I have to figure some things out."

They started down the stairs together. Then Isabel went back and shut the door to her room. Roxy waited for her. "Is there a key for the door?"

"I never lock the rooms, hon. It's only Gene, and he wouldn't bother nobody. There's a latch inside for when you're in there, if you care to use it."

"Oh."

"Of course you could get a lock for the door if it would make you feel better. I don't think it would cost you too much to rig somethin up."

"Okay. I'll think about it."

They reached the bottom of the stairs. "Come in, hon, and I'll give you a receipt, and a key for the outside door. I always keep *that* locked up good and tight."

"I'll just go out to the car and get my purse."

"Well, hon, now *that's* where you want to be careful. This ain't the best neighborhood in town. You ought not to leave your valuables alone out there. In here it's different. Old Gene and I ain't goin to rob you."

Isabel had to jerk on the door to get it open. "I'll be right back, so I'll just leave the door open. Okay?" She didn't wait for an answer. The air was clean and sweet. She felt like a child let out of school as she ran down the steps. Maybe she was making a big mistake to take this room—not that a week would matter except in a symbolic way, as an example of how she always did things that everybody already knew it was a mistake to try—like starting your life over when you were halfway through your forties. But then she looked up at the huge tree, so old and gnarled, and its leaves were still so small and new that they didn't even shade the parking lot yet. She heard the water splashing over the rocks, and there were her own windows looking out on these things, more her own because nobody else would understand why she wanted to live here. And for that minute she was sure she knew what she was doing.

She grabbed her bag from behind the seat and went back in to pay the seventy dollars. The door to Mrs. Fox's room was part way open. When she heard Isabel close the front door, she called, "Come on in, darlin. I'm in here."

Isabel pushed open the door and took a few steps into the cluttered sitting room. All the blinds were down, and the air was full of cigarette smoke and cheap perfume. It seemed particularly like a burrow after the sunshine outside. Everybody that came in there probably made the same silly joke about Mrs. Fox's den.

"Come on in and have a seat, hon."

"No, thanks. I can't stay."

"Well, I got to get you a key." She pushed herself up out of the sagging armchair. "And I want to make you out a receipt." Her little eyes fastened on Isabel's face. "You are goin to pay me now, ain't you, darlin?"

Isabel rummaged in her bag a minute, pretending to look for what she already knew wasn't there, and then she pulled out the folder of traveler's checks that Jeff had insisted she carry instead of cash, and said with more assurance than she felt, "You don't mind if I pay you with traveler's checks, do you?" She held the folder out so Mrs. Fox could see it.

"Aw hon, I don't know what to do with them things. I ain't had any experience with 'em."

"I guess I'll have to go to the bank to get some cash." She wondered why she had listened to Jeff. She didn't have to any more.

"You do that, hon. I'd like that much better."

"All right." She turned to go.

"Here, hon, take this so you can get back in again." She handed Isabel the key and shuffled back to her chair.

Isabel had just gotten to the door when Mrs. Fox said, "Oh say, I'd like to know somethin personal, since we're goin to be livin in the same house and all. Okay?"

"I guess so," Isabel said.

"Well, I seen you ain't wearin a weddin ring, and I was just wonderin how come a nice little lady like you are....well, why ain't you married?"

"I'm divorced." She paused. Mrs. Fox was waiting to hear more. "I just got divorced a few months ago. I guess I'm trying to start over again."

"Well, darlin, you've come to the right place then. There are some real good men around here."

"That's not what I mean by starting over."

"I know, hon. It *seems* that way when you're still hurtin. I never had to go through divorce myself, but I...."

"I can't imagine doing it all over again. I want to live my *own* life now, the way *I* want to, not the way somebody else tells me I should." She spoke more vehemently than she meant to.

Mrs. Fox put her hand over her mouth to suppress a smile. "Don't be mad, darlin. *I* know what a woman has to put up with in this world."

"You don't have to be concerned, Mrs. Fox," Isabel said, sternly. "I'm not going to bring any men back here or anything."

"Hey hon, don't mind me. We ain't exactly children, and this is 1991. You do what you feel like. Don't mind me. I like a good romp as well as the next one. So long as you ain't makin a livin that way, I got no problem."

"Well, you don't have to worry. I can guarantee that I'm not going to bring any men to my room. My intentions are completely different. I got married when I was twenty. I've never really had a chance to be on my own, and that's what I mean to do now."

"How old are you now, hon?"

"Forty-five. I know that's late to be thinking of starting over, but...."

"Let me see now. You was married for twenty-five years. Am I right? To the same man?"

Isabel nodded.

"I really feel sorry for you, hon. I been through enough myself. My husband was a...."

"I'd better go get your money for you."

"Sure, hon, sure. Don't mind me." But she looked hurt.

Isabel pretended not to notice. "I'll put a few things in my room before I go to the bank. All right?"

"Sure, hon. Whatever you want to do. After awhile I suppose you'll get a house so you can bring all your stuff up here, huh?"

Isabel didn't say anything.

"You probably had some real nice dishes and furniture and all like that down there in Massachusetts, didn't you? You'll be wantin to have it all up here, I suppose."

"No. I have everything with me."

"I was talkin about your furniture and dishes and all like that."

"I don't have any of those things. Jeff kept all that stuff."

"What? You poor little thing. It must've been a real bad divorce."

"Not at all. It was very friendly. We agreed on everything."

"He took all your stuff."

"It wasn't like that. I'll tell you about it sometime, but right now I ought to get to the bank."

"Well hon, I want you to feel at home right here. Use my kitchen any time you feel like it, just like it was your own."

"That's very kind, Mrs. Fox. Thank you."

"Call me Roxy. Everyone does. Mrs. Fox sounds like a old lady." She smiled a flirtatious smile, looking sideways at Isabel. "I hope I'm still a long way from that."

"Okay....yes....I'll be back with the money in a few hours, if that's all right."

"Sure hon, sure. I'll see you later, okay?"

Wednesday morning after she had breakfast at a coffee shop on Merchants Row, Isabel knew she couldn't put off calling her mother any longer. She stopped at a pay phone on the street.

"Hi Mom. It's me."

"Isabel? Is that you?"

"That's what I just said," Isabel said, wondering how the conversation could have gone wrong before it had even started. "Why do you sound worried?"

"Where are you, Isabel?"

"I'm in Severance, Mom. I got here yesterday. I told you that's what I was going to do."

"Oh Isabel, I wish you wouldn't go to Severance. It's crazy."

"I know, Mom, but I'm already here, and it's fine. How are you?"

"I'm all right, except for worrying so much about you."

"Don't worry about me. I've got a really nice place to live. I can look out my window at a little river. I'm looking for a job that...."

"Why can't you go back to Abingdon and work in the bookstore? It's your bookstore. I don't see why...."

"But, Mom, you know we're going to sell it, and anyway...."

"What does Jeff think of this crazy idea of yours?"

"It's none of his business. We're not married any more." She thought briefly about trying to tell her mother even less about what was going on in her life. These conversations were always so painful.

"Don't get mad at me, Isabel. I just want you to be all right."

"I'm not mad, but Abingdon is over, and Jeff is over, and I wish you could begin to accept that because it's the way it is."

"Isabel, that's just what Dianne and I have been talking about."

"How is Dianne? I haven't talked to her lately. Is she okay?"

"She's fine. But she's worried about you too."

"That's just because she hasn't heard from me for so long. Tell her I said hello and that I'll call soon."

"Dianne thinks you need to get some counselling."

"For God's sakes."

"Don't swear at me, Isabel. I'm just telling you what your sister says."

"Okay, but...."

"She says you don't realize how emotionally difficult a divorce is, particularly when a person has been married as long as you have."

"I know, but...."

"She says you need to start healing, and part of that is grieving, like when someone dies. I remember when your dad died, I...."

"I know, Mom, that's what I'm doing here in Severance, I want to start a new life for myself. I want to...."

"Isabel, where are your boys?"

"You know. I've told you. Joey's on Cape Cod for the summer, and Nicky's driving to LA."

"See. That's just what I mean. If you would go back home instead of chasing off after fantasies, Nicky wouldn't be chasing off across the country. It's dangerous."

"Mom, let's not talk about this any more. You've told me all this before. I'll call you in a few days. Maybe I'll have a job by then to tell you about."

"At least give me your phone number before you hang up."

"I'll have to call you with it tomorrow. I'll get it from the landlady. I don't think I'll have a phone of my own for a while. I'll talk to you tomorrow. Okay?"

"I suppose so. But, Isabel...."

"What?"

"You be careful."

"I will, Mom. Don't worry. I'll talk to you tomorrow." She hung up the phone and walked down the street, struggling not to cry. The conversation had made her feel like a child again.

By Thursday night Isabel was settling in. She hadn't looked at any other places to live, but that was because she realized that she liked it where she was. She went to sleep with the windows open, the smell of damp earth and moss in her room, and the sound of the water in her ears. She hadn't seen anything of Roxy since the day she moved in, and that was all right too. She told herself that she had finally arrived in the country and that she was beginning to feel at home.

The last few days had been full of ups and downs. She had had no luck finding a job. Every time someone turned her away, she felt awful. It made her realize once more that she was all alone, that there was no one here who cared whether she made a new and simple life for herself in Severance or not.

She had checked out every bookstore within twenty miles. She was a little less homesick when she was in a bookstore. But none of them were looking for employees, even though Isabel would have been glad to compromise and keep at least that much of her old life.

Interspersed with these bleak moods, there were periods when she dared to hope, when she hugged to her heart what Nancy said to her. The part Nancy didn't understand was that Isabel didn't really have a choice. The old life was gone, over, finished. It was no longer hers. and even though she wanted the divorce, she was still rejected, banished, exiled. So she had to go back to West Severance. It was where the farm was and also where she had met Jeff and married him. Because if that had been a wrong turn in her life, it might be important to go back to the same place to start over.

At the same time, she didn't want to think of her marriage as a mistake. It sounded as though she thought her boys, her dear, dear Nicky and Joey were a mistake, and she didn't mean that. It was confusing, because she missed them both, and yet, she had to try this new direction without them. They were almost grown up, busy with their own lives. She needed to have her own life too. She *would* make it work. She would because she had to.

Friday morning was dark. A cold drizzle was falling, and spring seemed like a distant memory. Isabel had walked downtown to get some breakfast without nearly enough clothes on, and she was freezing. She hurried back to her room, where she turned on the overhead light and the one that she had put on the table under the window. She put on a sweater and some tights and curled up on her bed under the covers to wait until she could stop shivering. She wouldn't ever get used to this place. She wasn't ever going to stop being lonely. She could never find anyone who would want to hire her, who would see that she knew how to work. She would always be cold and alone.

The next thing she was conscious of was the toilet flushing and then a light knock on her door. It was almost noon, and she had been asleep. She sat up and pushed her quilt off to the side. "Come in. It's not locked." She felt disoriented, bloated with too much sleep, and embarrassed about it.

The door opened a little. Mrs. Fox poked her turbaned head inside. After she had looked all around the room without saying anything, she opened the door the rest of the way and stood leaning on the knob.

Isabel said, "I moved the furniture around some. I hope you don't mind." But she was thinking that the way Mrs. Fox looked around so curiously meant that she hadn't been in to snoop while Isabel was out, although she might be trying to make Isabel think exactly that.

"Don't mind me, hon. I want you to make yourself at home."

"I like the bed over here by the window. It's nice when the window's open. And I can't hear the noises from the bathroom over here."

"I see you put the refrigerator on the floor."

"Yes. I wanted the table under the window. I can use it as a desk and a bedside table too."

"I was just thinkin you wouldn't need to turn that little refrigerator on if you wanted to use mine in the kitchen. I don't usually let people use my kitchen, but since we're both females and all...."

"That's okay. I don't know what I'm going to do about cooking for myself. I haven't figured it out yet. I thought I might buy a hotplate and a kettle so I could make coffee in here. I probably won't know until I find a job."

"What is your line of work, hon?"

"I worked in our bookstore—Jeff and I owned it together. It's for sale now, but we're still keeping it open, of course. I was working there until I left to come up here."

"Well, I better get back downstairs. I need to get goin. I'm terrible about gettin dressed in the mornin. I'm a night person all the way."

"I've got to get going too. I've been to a lot of places looking for a job, but I haven't found anything yet."

"There's lots of people out of work around here, hon. It's real hard to find anythin."

"I know. Everywhere I go, people tell me that. I'm getting worried. I don't have any references. I mean, I can't ask Jeff...."

"I should ask Leroy for you. Leroy would know. Leroy is amazin."

"Leroy?"

"Leroy LaFourniere. Don't that name sound familiar?"

"No."

"Well, it will soon. Everyone around here knows Leroy. He's a real important person, plus he's my cousin."

"Oh."

"Leroy would know where you should look for work. Leroy knows everythin."

"What does he do?" Isabel asked, without much interest.

"He's in the real estate business, but he does a lot more than that. I don't think Severance would run too good if Leroy wasn't around. Why he knows all the aldermen and the chief of police. He's tight with the mayor—he's been to his home lots of times. You name it, Leroy LaFourniere is goin to be on the inside track. He could really help you out."

"Well, thanks, Mrs. Fox, but I don't want to bother your cousin. I'm sure he must be much too busy."

"Oh he's *busy* all right. Not much goes on in Severance without Leroy's a part of it. But that don't mean he's too busy when *I* ask him to do somethin. Me and Leroy grew up together. We're

almost like brother and sister. And we're French. The French
don't never forget their families. That's just the way we are."

Isabel nodded to be polite.

"Leroy grew up without nothin. But he's done good. They
don't want for nothin now. Marie—that's Leroy's wife—I don't
know her too good. She keeps to herself. They could have any
house in town, even one of them new condos out on Prospect
Heights. But they still live where they always did, not too far
from here. Leroy has his office right there in his home." She
paused for breath and looked around the room. "Well, I guess I
better be gettin downstairs. I ain't even got my cigarettes with
me." She stepped out into the hall and began to close the door,
but before it was completely shut, she stuck her head back in.
"Say, I know what I came up here for. I seen you come in a while
ago. You looked half froze."

"I was. I came back to get more clothes. I certainly wasn't
dressed right for the weather, was I?"

"You had ought to have had your raincoat on for one thing."

"I don't have a raincoat, but I'll be fine."

"You *got* to have a raincoat."

"I have a sweater and some tights, and I'm going to get some
warmer shoes. That'll be plenty."

"Well now, hon. You're goin to take mine, and that's all there
is to it."

"No, I couldn't."

"I won't take no for a answer. It'll be hangin on the post at the
bottom of the stairs there. You be sure you take it when you go
by."

"Well, no...." Isabel began, but the door was already shut.

Later on, when she went downstairs, the raincoat was there, a
bright red plastic, strongly scented with dime-store perfume.
Laid carefully on top of it was a map drawn by Roxy's unsteady
hand. It showed River Street, the bridge and a few streets on the
other side of the bridge. There was an X marking Leroy's house.

Underneath the map it said, "Be sure you stop by to see Leroy and tell him who sent you."

Isabel thought about taking the note and leaving the raincoat. She didn't want to touch it. It was so intimately Roxy's. But Roxy could be in her room watching out the window. She might even come running out to insist. Isabel sighed and put on the raincoat and stuck the note down into a pocket. "All right," she said to herself. "I'll go and see this cousin then. But this is the only time I'm going to let her tell me what to do. I've got to start standing up for myself."

3

THE BIG BLACK car cruised smoothly up to the curb. Leroy thought how it was just the way a deadly shark would nose silently up underneath a boat. His car was like a large animal, only better, because it was always clean and obedient. It did everything he asked without hesitation or rancor. He would have been embarrassed if anyone found out that he imagined he knew the feelings and personality of his car, but in the secrecy of his own thoughts, he felt the big Lincoln's presence.

He was just turning off the key when the office door opened, and a woman in red came out. For a second he thought it might be Roxy, but right away he saw that he was wrong. This one was younger than Rox and very different, old-fashioned maybe, with brown hair and nice legs, what he could see of them. She came down the sidewalk from his door without really seeing him or his car, although her eyes slid across his face as she turned at the corner of the front yard.

He went inside. On his way through the hall, he hung his Stetson carefully on the coatrack. In the office Renée was standing in front of the mirror. Her handbag was open on the desk beside her. She was making up her face.

"Hey, Leroy. I was just getting ready to leave."

He said hello. Renée's skirts were a little shorter than everyone else's, and her legs were always worth a look, especially when she was wearing high heels.

"You don't need me for anything, do you? I didn't know you were coming back." She was combing her hair now.

"No. I don't have anything. Who was that who just left?"

"Some woman who's living over at Roxy's. Did you see her?"

"She was coming out when I pulled up."

"I don't know what the deal is. She sure doesn't look like she'd be living at Roxy's."

"What did she want?"

"I'm not sure. Maybe she was looking for a job. She wasn't real clear about it."

"Did Roxy send her over?"

"I think so. I told her you weren't hiring anyone."

"Maybe I'll go over to Roxy's and see when she's planning to pay back that loan."

"She's not your type at all, Leroy." Her eyes in the mirror looked him over hard, willing him to obey.

He moved to the desk, out of her line of vision. "Anything in the mail today?"

"Nothing important." She dropped her arms and turned toward him, still holding the comb. "I take good care of you, don't I, Leroy? Even if I am your niece and not your mother?"

He stepped over to her and caught her hands in his own and looked into her face. With her sharp features and high cheekbones, she was very French. He loved the way she looked. "You are the best, Chérie. It's too bad we are related."

"Leroy, I'm serious."

"Well, so am I." He took the comb out of her hand and set it gently down on her bag.

"I don't know if Roxy is up to anything or not, but I know this woman is not for you. Okay? I mean I do know what's best for you. You already admitted that."

"I saw her. I was just teasing you. I was on my way over to see Roxy anyway. It's always good to catch her on a payday. You know that."

He sat down at his desk and flipped through the mail. Renée hadn't bothered to open the junk. Neither of them said anything for a minute, and then Renée said, "There's something I've been wanting to ask you."

When he looked up at her, she faltered.

He said, "Yes?" but he put an edge into it.

"I've been wondering...."

He knew what she was planning to say. "You think I'm in trouble for money, and I'm going to Roxy to get some help?"

"Of course not, but...."

"Chérie, what do you think? That Roxy has cash sewn up into those filthy old mattresses of hers?"

"Oh Leroy, it doesn't have anything to do with Roxy. But I can't help noticing...."

He cut her off. "The money is fine, Chérie. You leave that up to me."

"But, Leroy...."

"Don't you know I'd tell you before I told anyone else? By the way, I think if I go over to Roxy's, I'll check that woman out."

"I don't see why." She had put everything back in her handbag, and now she picked it up and slung it over her shoulder.

He saw he had said just the right thing to keep her from thinking about money. And he definitely didn't want her to start paying too much attention to his business. He said, "Well, I've been thinking. If we hired somebody, maybe part time, to do the paperwork, we, you really, would have to spend less time in the office. The more I think about it, the better I like it."

"I don't know....besides she's not right for you. And now might not be the time to have to start paying somebody extra."

"You let me worry about that. I'll tell you when there's something to worry about. You know that, don't you?"

She was smiling at him now. "Yes, I know."

"And about getting somebody, it doesn't need to be this one. She's not my type. You already said so. And you are always right, Chérie."

Still smiling, she said, "It could be good. I would like help with the office work, especially now the weather is getting so nice. Or maybe it's just you, Leroy. You could sell anything to anybody." She went over to the closet and took out her coat, but she didn't put it on. "I'll be in tomorrow morning for a while." She blew him a kiss and left. He could hear the clack of her heels down the sidewalk and then the slam of her car door. He sighed and left the room, locking the office door behind him.

He stopped by the coatrack to leave his leather jacket on a hook right under the hat. He stepped back to look. If the hall was dark, someone might think he was standing there facing the other way, tall and thin and dressed in black—not a guy you'd want to tangle with. He liked that.

He went down the hall and into the kitchen. Marie was standing at the sink with the water running. She was singing to herself. The weather was brightening, and the clear spring light came through the window and shone gold on the neat circle of braids around her head. She was exactly his age, almost sixty, so it was amazing that her hair had no gray. It was still the same light brown that had made him think of a sparrow when he first met her, when they were young. She always made him think of sparrows, although she wasn't particularly small. Still, there was something quick and sharp and neat that made him think of those humble and cheerful birds.

"What's for supper, Chérie?" He wanted her to know he was there; he didn't want to startle her.

She shut off the water and turned part way around, still holding her hands over the sink so they wouldn't drip on the floor. "I'm cooking you some trout. Jerome brought them over, two of them, nice big ones from out at the lake."

"Did he have any news? How are the kids?" He sat down at the kitchen table. There were two places set. A discontent passed across his mind, a brief cloud shadow. She always said the food was for him, as though she didn't need to do anything as physical as eating. He pushed the silverware just a little bit crooked as he listened.

"He and Tammy want to bring them over on Sunday after church. Will you be here? I told him you would be. But I could.... and there's something else too. The bank statement came the other day, and I opened it."

He felt like swearing. "What is this?"

"I don't know why—I opened it by mistake."

"Have you been talking to Renée?"

"Nothing but hello. What do you mean?"

He believed her. "Nothing Chérie. Forget it." He didn't want to get paranoid.

"But, Leroy, I couldn't help noticing that...."

"You've forgotten our arrangement, Chérie."

"No, of course not."

"Well, what is it then?"

"I take care of the house, and you take care of the money, and we don't interfere in each other's business. And you're right, Leroy. I'm sorry."

"That's a good girl, Chérie. And of course I want to be here on Sunday. The grandkids are just as important to me as they are to you."

She looked doubtful, but she didn't say anything, and after a minute she smiled to show him she wasn't doubting him.

He said, "Don't worry. I won't let anything get in the way. That's a promise." He thought about getting up and walking over to her to give her a kiss. She looked sweet with the evening sunlight behind her head, but she might think he wanted something. She might think she had to buy his promise, and he hated that idea. Better to change the subject. "Trout sounds good. I don't want to be too late because I want to go see Roxy, and she's probably going out for the evening."

"Roxy," she said flatly, and then, "Would twenty minutes from now be all right?"

"That would be fine, Chérie."

"All right, twenty minutes it will be. But now, go out and let me work."

4

THE WEATHER HAD changed back to spring again by the evening. The sky outside the window was a pale green, shimmering through the thin branches of the trees. Isabel leaned out so that she was looking almost straight down into the water. It gurgled in a playful, teasing way, carrying on a secret conversation with itself, or maybe with her. A voice on the edge of sound was saying "Isabel" over and over, as though the little river was speaking her name, calling her to come down to take part in some wonderful, secret ceremony of spring. She didn't know how many times she heard the voice before she realized someone was calling. She pulled herself back into the room and went to the door and opened it.

Mrs. Fox was standing part way up the stairs with one hand pressed to her heart. She was panting. "Whew, darlin, I thought I was goin to have to come all the way up after you."

"I'm sorry. I didn't hear you. I was looking out the window."

"Well listen, hon, I want you to come down to the kitchen. There's somebody that wants to meet you."

"Me?"

"Yes, darlin."

"Your cousin?"

"How'd you know?"

Isabel walked over to the banister and looked down. "I forgot to tell you. I stopped by his place, but he was out. I was going to tell you when I left off your raincoat, but you weren't there."

"That's okay, hon."

"Thanks for the raincoat. I hope you didn't need it."

"Come on down, hon. I don't want to keep Leroy waitin."

"I'll be there in a minute."

"Good." She turned slowly, holding onto the railing. She took a few steps down, scuffing her feet to keep her high-heeled slippers from falling off. The little red corkscrew curls on top of her head quivered with each heavy step.

Isabel leaned over the banister, watching her. "You look nice. You're all dressed up," she said, realizing it was the first time she had seen Mrs. Fox in anything but nightclothes, or her hair without curlers.

"Thank you, darlin." At the bottom of the stairs she turned and went down the hall toward the kitchen. Her loose slippers slapped the linoleum with each step.

Isabel went back into her room and looked in the mirror. She combed her hair quickly and knotted it with a twist at the back of her head. She was wearing an old pair of shorts, but she didn't feel like changing. She wished she had said she was busy. She went to his house. That should have been enough. She put on her sandals and went downstairs.

The hall was dark and smelled of cooking grease. When she opened the kitchen door, the light was so bright that it made her blink. The first thing she saw under the lamp which hung over the table was the back of Mrs. Fox's head. Under the light her curls were an electric red. She was talking in a steady stream, and her curls trembled. Facing her across the table was the cousin, a man with a long sad face. His dark hair was mixed with gray. He looked at Isabel and smiled a tight, thin-lipped smile, and his eyes rolled very slightly. He could have been acknowledging that they both understood what Mrs. Fox was, or he could have been amused by what she was saying.

Mrs. Fox stopped in mid-sentence and screwed herself around in her chair. "Well, here you are, hon. Come sit down with me and Leroy. This here's my cousin Leroy, that I told you about."

Leroy stood up and reached out a hand. He was so tall that he had to stoop to keep from bumping his head on the light. His fingers were bony, cool and dry, and he gripped her hand so tightly that it hurt. She was surprised and confused. She looked up and saw that he was watching her intently. She sat down without saying anything.

Mrs. Fox reached out to pat her shoulder. "Look here, Leroy. I told you Isabel was real sweet, didn't I?"

"Don't mind Roxy," he said. "You'll get used to the way she talks." He raised his hand as though he was going to caress Isabel's shoulder, the way Roxy was doing. "None of us pay any attention to old Rox." He waved his hand instead, and put it back down on the table. Isabel sat silent and uncomfortable, planning to get away as soon as she could.

Roxy took her hand away from Isabel's shoulder and said, "Aw, come on, Leroy. Don't go gettin stuck up on me now." She looked at Isabel and spoke firmly, darting her little eyes in Leroy's direction every so often to see how he was taking it. "He listens to me. He can say whatever he likes, but he always comes over here and asks me what he ought to do when he's got a problem. You can't deny it, Leroy." She batted her eyes at him coquettishly. "I give you good advice too." She turned to Isabel again, "He's always sayin he don't know what he would do if he didn't have me to ask when things come up. Ain't that true, Leroy?"

Leroy said, "Rox, why don't you get Isabel a cup of tea?"

Roxy jumped up. "Oh sure, Leroy. Thanks for remindin me. I didn't mean to forget my manners like that."

Isabel was going to say she didn't want any tea, but no one asked her. Roxy already had the kettle from the stove and was heading for the sink to put some water in it. Her tight pink slacks sagged at her knees and bulged around her little pot belly.

Isabel thought that maybe she didn't mind staying for a while after all, because she was curious about Leroy. He was so different from what she had expected him to be. When she turned around, she saw that he was leaning on his elbows watching her. Between the crisp, white wings of his open collar, Isabel could see his adam's apple in the shadows of his shirt. When she looked up at his face, he was smiling at her. His eyes were black and deep.

"Isabel," he said. "That's a beautiful name."

"My grandmother was Italian. I was named for her."

"It's a French name too."

"Is it?"

"What are you doing in Severance, Isabel? What are you doing in Roxy's house?"

"I'm renting a room here."

Leroy picked up her left hand and looked down at it. "Tell me about yourself, Chérie." He toyed with her fingers, depressing them one by one. Isabel felt silly, but she liked it too. He acted as though he had known her for a long time. She knew that he noticed that she wasn't wearing a wedding ring, and she couldn't help seeing that he was.

Just then Roxy set the cup of tea down with a bang, catching herself on the corner of the table and shaking it so that everything on it rattled. Isabel pulled her hand out of Leroy's.

"Damn these old bedroom shoes. I got to do somethin." She looked sorrowfully down at her feet. "They are *forever* trippin me up." She lowered herself into her chair with a sigh. "I ain't had 'em more than a year. You just can't buy decent stuff no more." Her droopy eyes focused on Isabel. "Here, hon, put you in some sweetener." She pushed the sugarbowl across the table.

Isabel put a spoonful of sugar into her tea and stirred it around. No one said anything. The sound of the spoon was loud in the silence. She put down the spoon and took a sip. The tea was weak and soapy. She looked at Leroy's shirt front, at the starched white cloth which moved in and out as he breathed. She didn't raise her eyes to his face. "I went to your office today," she said.

"I know."

"Hey, Leroy, I told her you might know where she could go to find work. You know who's hirin. Ain't that so?"

"Jobs are hard to find right now. What do you do, Chérie?"

Isabel saw with surprise that his eyes were not deep after all. They were quite flat. She couldn't see through the surface. It disappointed her, although she couldn't have said why. Leroy confused her. He wasn't handsome, but he was a very attractive man. She hadn't expected that. In fact, she had planned for a new life without sexual attraction in it, and that confused her still more. "I've always worked in a bookstore," she said.

Leroy folded his hands on the table beside his empty cup and looked at her politely. "As a clerk?"

"Well, sort of....I guess." She wanted Leroy to understand, and in fact, she felt somehow that he would understand, if she could be clear. But it was complicated, and she didn't think she should waste his time with a long explanation.

He frowned, "I don't think I can help you with a job like that. There are some bookstores in Severance, but I don't...."

Just then Roxy cut in. "Hey, hon, you don't mind if I smoke, do you? I'm tryin to cut down, but you know how it is."

Isabel shook her head, but Roxy wasn't looking. She was already striking a match. Leroy smiled at Isabel, while Roxy blew a blue stream of smoke at the lamp.

"I don't particularly want a job in a bookstore. I mean I'd really rather do something different. I worked there for almost twenty-five years, but you see, we owned it."

"Oh, I see," he said. "And all of a sudden you decided to leave,

Chérie?"

"It wasn't sudden. I think it came up slowly until I was more and more sure about it, but it's hard to say. Sometimes it seems different when I remember it...at least Jeff says I remember things wrong." She was making it more confusing. Somehow she needed to explain what she was doing here so that he could understand. He wanted to help her. She could feel that.

"And how does Jeff know so much?"

Roxy got up and shuffled over to the counter beside the sink where she put down her empty cup.

"Jeff's my husband. We owned this bookstore in Abingdon, Massachusetts—that's where Jeff was from, and we ran it together." She paused and looked at Leroy, but she couldn't see into his eyes.

Leroy picked up her left hand again. He appeared to study her fingers for a minute and then looked up into her face. She could feel that he was interested in her.

Roxy had the radio on and was turning from station to station.

Leroy said, "You aren't wearing a ring. I noticed that right away."

"Hey, here's 'Your Cheatin Heart.' I used to love that song." She took a few dance steps and then stumbled. "Damn."

Leroy turned in his chair to watch, but he was still holding onto Isabel's hand. When she said, "We got divorced," he turned back to look at her and gave her hand a squeeze. He was so sympathetic that Isabel was ashamed of herself for feeling embarrassed by so much attention.

"Recently?"

She nodded. "It was final last winter. I stayed on at the bookstore for a while."

Roxy said, "Remember that roadhouse you used to take me to, Leroy? The one outside of Jerusalem Corners?" She started to spin around and tripped. "Damn these old house shoes anyway. I got to sit down." She shuffled over to them and sat down holding onto the edge of the table. "I got to catch my breath. That was where I first saw Ralph LeMay, that roadhouse." She lit another cigarette.

"I understand why you want to start over, Chérie, but why Severance? Why are we so lucky?"

"Aw, Leroy. Ain't he sweet, hon?"

"It isn't just because of the divorce," she said. "It really goes back long before that. I mean, I think I've always been a country person, even though I've never had a chance to live on the land, to live the simple life—I don't know what else to call it—something besides living in town anyway. I know that's naive since I've never done it. But I have always been fascinated by country life, and I know a lot about it just from reading."

"She was at Green Mountain College, Leroy. There's a lot of them hippie-type people over at that school. Ain't that right?"

"Now, Roxy, don't talk about what you don't know about. It looks dumb."

Roxy sat back in her chair. She folded her arms and shut her mouth tight. Her eyelids drooped.

Isabel said, "In a way it's because of GMC that I decided to move here." She was sorry for Roxy, although she was glad to have Leroy on her side, and Roxy would try anyone's patience. She looked from one to the other of them. Leroy was waiting for her to say more.

"That's where she met her husband, Leroy. At that school. Ain't that right, hon?" She sat forward in her chair. She had already forgotten Leroy's reprimand. She looked at Isabel. "Men don't ever understand them things, do they?"

Isabel sighed. "This is what happened last year," she said. She turned toward Leroy. "My husband and I were up here for his class reunion. We were out driving around, and we got stuck in the mud at a farm way up in the hills. It was so quiet and peaceful there. God, I never saw any place as beautiful as that. An old man pulled us out of the mud with a team of oxen, if you can believe it."

Leroy was looking at her intently. She could see that he understood how important that moment was to her. Even Roxy was waiting to hear more.

"I realized right then that that was what I was looking for—that I wanted to live the way those people did—in harmony with the earth and the seasons, as a part of nature, or something. We were already planning to sell the bookstore. I tried to talk Jeff into taking the money to buy a farm in Severance, but he thought I was crazy."

She looked from one to the other of them. Nobody spoke. Finally she said, "Well, that's my story. I decided to go ahead without Jeff." She shrugged. "There were other reasons too."

Leroy smiled at her. "So you divorced Jeff and moved into Roxy's house, and now you are trying to find a farm to buy. Am I right, Chérie?"

"Yes, that's my long-range plan. We haven't even sold the bookstore yet, so I don't have much money. That's why I need a job for a while, but eventually....what do you think? Is my plan crazy? I'd like to know what you think."

Now it was his turn to shrug. His eyes dropped to the table where he watched his own long, thin fingers pulling at a hole in the tablecloth. "I couldn't say, Chérie. Where was this beautiful farm that you saw?"

"Oh, if I knew that.... It was way out of town, but I don't know which way. I wasn't paying enough attention while we were driving. I'm planning to get a map. Then I can drive the back roads until I find it."

"Who owned the farm?"

"I think that old man must have."

"What was his name then? I want to help you, Chérie."

"I can't even remember that. I've tried to think. He told us, but all I can remember is Sonny....and that his oxen were Buck and Ben."

"Hey, Leroy, that could be Carroll Trumbley. He's always got a ox team, don't he?" Roxy leaned across the table. She was eager.

"Well, Rox, you could be right. There are lots of guys around called Sonny though." He turned toward Isabel. "Does Trumbley sound like the man's name?"

"I'm not sure. It could have been...."

"We'll have to check it out for you sometime, Chérie. I could take you out past the Trumbley place, and you could see if that was the place you remembered. Of course, there are a hundred hill farms around, but that's a nice one."

"I'd like to see it. That would be great."

Leroy stood up. "Well, I better get going. I was supposed to be out in West Severance at eight o'clock."

"Don't rush off, Leroy. You ain't hardly had a chance to talk to Isabel here." Roxy bored into his face with her little eyes, waiting for him to get the message.

He looked down at her, unperturbed.

Finally she dropped her eyes and said, "You ain't talked about where she could go for work and all."

Leroy looked over at Isabel and smiled. Everything about him was tall and thin, black and white, but his smile was generous. "Come over to my place tomorrow, Chérie. We'll find you something to do. Unless you would rather start on Monday?" He walked over to the kitchen door where his black leather jacket and hat were hanging on a hook. The heels of his boots clicked across the wavy linoleum.

"Hey Leroy. That's nice. I told her you'd help her out." She looked over at Isabel. "Didn't I, hon?"

Isabel nodded, but she was turning in her chair, watching Leroy, and thinking, "Could he really mean it? Maybe I didn't need to be worried after all."

Leroy put on his cowboy hat and then took it off again and put it back on, rearranging it slightly as he settled it on his head. Finally he tilted it back and reached for his jacket.

Isabel said, "But you don't even know what I can do."

"You can show me tomorrow, Chérie."

She was afraid of talking him out of it. Still, it could all be a misunderstanding. "But...."

"Perhaps you don't want to work for me?" He didn't wait for an answer. He opened the kitchen door and stood with his hand on the knob. "So long, Roxy. We'll talk about that other matter tomorrow or the next day." He touched his hat with two fingers. "See you tomorrow, Chérie."

He was just closing the door when Roxy rocketed up out of her chair. "Wait up, Leroy. Can I get a ride downstreet? I won't be a minute gettin ready." She hurried past him down the hall without waiting for an answer.

Leroy looked at Isabel and then rolled his eyes toward the ceiling. "Roxy," he said loudly into the hall, "I can't wait while you get dressed. I know how long that takes."

"It's just my shoes, Leroy. I'm all ready." Her voice was muffled.

"She's in her closet. I should sneak out while she's hunting for her shoes. I was already late."

Isabel took her tea cup over to the sink. She was holding the tea bag, trying to decide where to put it, when Leroy said, "Roxy keeps her trash basket under the sink."

"Oh, thanks."

"So long. I better go light a fire under her. She's probably got a big night lined up."

Isabel pushed the chairs straight and turned off the light. The kitchen seemed empty now that he was gone. When she got to the bottom of the stairs, she saw that the door to Roxy's room was not quite closed. She pushed it open and went to Roxy's window where she pulled back the curtain just enough to see out.

Roxy was clumping down the front steps, trying to balance herself on her spike-heeled shoes, hurrying to catch up with Leroy, who was already standing by the open passenger door of his huge black car. Roxy was saying, "Next week. Okay, Leroy? Somethin came up."

Isabel couldn't hear what Leroy said. He slammed Roxy's door and went around to his side, stopping to brush something off the sleek hood of his car. Standing in his black clothes beside his black car, he was like a character in an old movie. Isabel was glad she was going to see him again tomorrow. She would find out then if it was true about the job. And even if he didn't want to hire her, it meant he wanted to see her again and without Roxy around. She went up the stairs feeling happier than she had in quite a while.

5

Roxy wiggled down into the seat with a sigh of pleasure and then shifted to another position right away. Before the engine had a chance to turn over, she had moved again.

"Sit still, Rox. Can't you?"

"Damn, Leroy, I love your car."

"Yeah. I know."

As the car slid out into the street, he saw the curtain in Roxy's room swing shut. So Isabel was watching them leave.

"Where are you going, Rox? I'm in a hurry."

"I know. It ain't out of your way. I'm supposed to meet Ely Singleton down at Vincent's."

He looked over at her. She sat there perfectly satisfied. She probably didn't even remember that he had told her to stay away from Ely Singleton. She'd never had any more sense than a child.

"Don't look at me cruel like that. We probably ain't goin to stay there. It's just a place to meet."

"What are you doing with Ely Singleton?"

"Nothin," Roxy said, crossing her arms firmly across her chest. "We're just friends, is all."

"Well listen, Roxy...."

"I don't tell *you* what to do, Leroy, and anyhow, I ain't doin nothin....Ely's just a friend, that's all."

The car pulled up to the curb across the street from Vincent's Bar and Grill. "I'd take you right to the door, Rox, but I'm going out to West Severance, and I'm already late."

"That's okay, Leroy. I don't care." She opened the door and got out. She was as affable as a child too.

Leroy bent his head so he could see her face as she stood outside. "Hey Roxy," he said. "You be careful."

"Well thanks, Leroy, but I could say the same to you. Neither of us got where we are by bein careful. Look at you—hiring that woman, and you don't even know can she type."

"That was your idea. I was counting on *you*. I figured you thought she could do good things for me."

"I don't know about that, hon. I just wanted you to give her some names, is all. But if she's workin for you, she'll be likely to stay on at my place. That would be good. She seems nice enough."

"I think it'll work out."

"Sure, but that's what I mean. We both take chances—you more 'n me. And I like Ely Singleton. Besides there ain't that many guys around to choose from these days. Thanks for the ride."

Leroy watched her in the rearview mirror as she walked behind the car, wobbling a little on her spike heels. When she started across the street, he stepped on the gas, and the car accelerated smoothly, headed for West Severance. He looked at his watch. It was already eight-twenty. He told Carol Ann he would be out there around eight, but it wouldn't hurt to get her a bit worried. He pushed the button, and the passenger side window slid down, blowing out Roxy's cheap perfume, which might attract Singleton but certainly didn't turn *him* on.

The spring night smelled of icy water and damp ground—exciting after the long frozen winter. Out of town the stars were beginning to show in the sky, and a mist was rising from the low places because of the rain. It was a beautiful night to be driving in the country. A night like this would make a lot of sixty-year-old guys think of their youth, but not him. He didn't have such great opportunities when he was a young man, not anything like the ones he had now, and age hadn't slowed him down, not yet anyway, so instead of dwelling on the past, he was still thinking in terms of the future.

Queer how she was talking about Sonny's place the very day he was on his way out there. Of course he thought of it as soon as she started talking, although maybe that was because it was on his mind already. Anyway, he wouldn't have mentioned the Trumbley name, not so soon. But he didn't think either of them thought he had much interest in the whole thing, which was good. The only thing he could do was play his hunches and be ready to rake in the chips. Things had a way of coming together when they were supposed to. Here she was looking to buy some time in the future, and Carol Ann was looking to sell. Who could tell what would happen, especially if a guy kept his eyes open.

The big Lincoln smoothed out all the mudholes and corduroy patches on the Trumbleys' road. He pulled to a stop between the house and the barn behind Raymond's ratty sedan. The light in the barn probably meant Sonny was in there. It made sense to say hello to him first. Carol Ann would look out the window and see the car, but since she probably wouldn't have heard him pull in, she wouldn't know how late he was, and he wouldn't have to apologize for it.

He tried to be extra quiet when he shut the car door, but even so, all the spring peepers stopped singing. The night was full of them, all waiting for one to have the nerve to start up again. Finally, there was one questioning peep, and then several answering ones. Before he got to the barn, they were all at it again. They were just like people—nobody wanted to stick his neck out; nobody wanted to be the first to take a chance. He wondered if that first peeper had an advantage with the females, or if he just stuck his neck out for nothing.

He opened the barn door and went in. It was much warmer inside and dusty-dry. There was no one there, only some old jackets and bits of harness hung around the walls. He ducked through the low doorway and went down the passage between the empty stalls. In the last one, Sonny's oxen were eating their hay. Leroy stood and looked at them, wondering where Sonny was and feeling he was nearby somehow, when one of the oxen shifted, and he noticed what he hadn't seen before, a workboot and a bit of green trouser leg. He took a few steps into the room around the huge team, and there was Sonny, sitting in a lawn chair, just taking it easy.

He looked up when Leroy came into view, but he didn't seem surprised. "Leroy," he said, "what can I do for you?"

"Not a thing, Sonny. I just stopped in to say hello." He looked at Sonny to see what he made of it, but it was impossible to tell. Sonny's face was as impassive as his oxen. "I told Carol Ann I was going to drop by. Perhaps she mentioned it?"

"No, I don't recall that she did." Sonny's voice was as calm as his expression, but Leroy picked up on how he dropped his eyes for a minute at the mention of Carol Ann.

"Your team is lookin real good, Sonny," Leroy said. He moved a little further into the room and stood close behind the off ox, resting his elbow on its back. It was so tall that his arm had to angle stiffly up. He patted the huge haunch. "How does a man your size get 'em yoked up, anyhow?"

Sonny grinned at him. "Oh, I got it worked out bit by bit. I raised 'em from calves, you know. They wasn't always this big."

"I'd like to watch you yoke 'em sometime. I bet it's a sight. Are you going to take them to any fairs this year?"

"Well, I don't know. I might. They don't really care for 'em that much. Too many people. They prefer to work in the woods."

Leroy thought to himself that he wouldn't let any dumb ox be the one to decide whether or not they went to the fair, or anywhere else for that matter, but out loud he said, "Well, I'd go to the pulls just to watch you work."

Sonny raised his faded feedstore cap and scratched his head, while keeping his eyes fixed on the sawdust floor. Still, Leroy could see that he was pleased, even if it embarrassed him a little.

The ox he was leaning on shifted his weight, and Leroy was tempted to move his elbow, but he didn't. Sonny might think he had made so much money that he wasn't comfortable around cattle any more. He wasn't one of those developers from Connecticut who'd never been out in the country before he started dividing it up. That was his great advantage.

He said, "Well, I guess I better get in there and see Carol Ann. I'm a whole lot later than I thought I would be."

Sonny looked up at him. "She won't like that." His eyes were bright.

Leroy grinned back at him. "The women like to keep us on the move, don't they? Are you coming in?"

"Not right away. I'm too old to hurry because Carol Ann tells me to. Tell her I'll be along in a minute."

The ox Leroy was leaning on slowly raised his tail. Leroy knew what that meant, and he stepped back. The manure dropped onto the sawdust floor, splashing one of his cowboy boots. He let Sonny see that he noticed and didn't care, and he could tell that Sonny liked him for that. He said, "Nice to see you, Sonny," gave the ox a quick pat and left. As soon as he was in the passage out of sight of Sonny, he stopped to clean off his boot, first with a handful of sawdust from the floor and then with a corner of his white handkerchief. It made him uncomfortable to have dirt on him. When his boot was clean again, he went up to the house.

Through the glass in the back door, Leroy could see Carol Ann and Raymond sitting at the kitchen table. Their teenage daughter was washing the dishes. When he knocked on the door, Carol Ann shouted, "Come on in," without turning around in her chair to see who it was. That was how he knew she must have seen his car. She probably figured out that he had gone to the barn to see Sonny first.

Leroy shut the door and walked over to the table. "Sorry I'm late," he said when no one said hello. "How're you doin, Raymond?"

"Oh, I can't complain. Have a seat, why don't you?"

Leroy looked down at the table. It was small and not level. A pack of cards and piles of pennies sat in the middle between the coffee cups. On the side nearest him was a stack of dirty plates and bowls. He walked around to the other side of the table and sat down without taking off his jacket. There didn't seem to be a good spot for his hat, so he set it carefully on his knees.

Carol Ann hadn't said anything, but she was watching him, and he knew he didn't really have to worry. She would come around when they started to talk.

"I don't want to break up your game. What're you playing?"

"Aw, we were just foolin around, playin blackjack for pennies. It don't mean nothin." Raymond picked up an empty jar as he spoke. He started to drop pennies into it. Raymond's fingers were long and finely shaped, scrubbed pink on the surfaces, but with black lines marking all the creases and outlining the curve of each fingernail.

"You're goin to break that jar, Raymond."

"It don't matter. One thing we won't run out of around here is peanut butter jars." He grinned at Leroy. The triangular piece broken off his front tooth was what gave Raymond's smile its saucy, devil-may-care look. He said, "She hates it when I beat her."

"I do not! You didn't beat me anyhow." She looked daggers at Raymond and ignored Leroy completely. "We weren't countin that first hand. You said so yourself."

"Oooo, temper, temper," Raymond said to her.

Carol Ann turned to Leroy then, and trying hard to hide her anger, she asked him if he wanted some coffee. When he said he would take a cup, she stood up and turned toward Raymond. "How about you?" she said, and her voice had a knife-edge to it.

Raymond didn't look up. He shook the pennies in his closed hand so that they made a loud rattle. Leroy couldn't hear the beginning of what he said over the noise of the pennies. Raymond ended by saying, "I know you want me to get it out of there." He put the pile of pennies into the jar and then looked over at Leroy. "Still, it ain't every day we have company. It's kind of a surprise to see you out here, Leroy." It was almost a question.

Carol Ann picked up the stack of dirty plates and took them to the sink. Leroy watched her stump stolidly across the room. She was short, like Sonny, but she was thick where Sonny was thin. Carol Ann was almost square. Her face went with the rest. Everything about her was chunky and solid. Leroy wondered what Raymond saw in her. It wasn't as though they got along extra well. And Raymond, with all his black curls and his crazy grin, was a good-looking guy. Raymond probably could have his pick of lots of women. The funny thing was, they had been married for a lot of years, but Leroy couldn't remember ever hearing any talk of Raymond stepping out behind Carol Ann's back. It was a mystery. Leroy couldn't imagine that Raymond would be crafty enough to do something like that and get away with it.

Carol Ann set his coffee down in front of him. Carol Ann's hands always took Leroy by surprise. They reminded him of the hands in a television commercial—hands that ought to belong to a woman who was very different from the dumpy Carol Ann. And how could she live on a farm and manage to keep them looking that way?

She sat down heavily in her seat. "I asked Leroy to come over. I met him downstreet the other day, and we got to talkin about real estate. I thought we ought to find out just exactly what this place is worth."

The teenage girl stopped washing the dishes and shut off the water. She half turned toward the table so she could hear more without being too obvious about it.

"Whoa, wait a minute, honey." Raymond looked over at Leroy. "No offense meant," he said, and then he turned back to Carol Ann. "It ain't any of our business what the place is worth, cause we don't own it, and the guy who does own it don't want to sell."

"Oh, come on, Raymond. We've argued about all this for years. All I'm tryin to do is get us a few facts so we know what we're arguin about here. Every time we talk about sellin the place, we end up in a big argument about what it's worth. I thought Leroy could give us a few facts, so we know what we're talkin about. That's all."

"Does Gramps know you asked Leroy to come out?"

Leroy cut in. "I stopped off to say hello to him on my way in, so he knows I'm here." He looked Carol Ann squarely in the eye. "He said to tell you he would be in in a little while."

Carol Ann gave a stiff, little nod. "I know what that means. Alison, go out and tell Gramps I said to come on in so he can hear what we're talkin about."

"Okay, Ma." She wiped her hands on her blue jeans and ran out the door.

Leroy set his hat carefully on the floor and pulled his chair closer to the table. The coffee was thin and bitter. "Your coffee is very good, Chérie," he said.

Carol Ann stared at him without taking in what he said. "Look at that child, Raymond. It's a wonder I don't have to tell her when to breathe. She never wears a jacket unless I specifically tell her to. She's almost fifteen years old, and she still can't figure that out for herself."

"Aw honey, she don't need a jacket just to run across the dooryard. She won't have time to cool down."

"It's not that anyway. It's the *principle* of the thing. She ought to be able to think of her jacket without me tellin her, that's all."

Raymond ran his hand through his black curls and looked over at Leroy. When their eyes met, Raymond's widened in an expression of surprise. Leroy sipped his coffee and registered nothing. He could feel Carol Ann watching to see if he was going to sympathize with Raymond. It wasn't a difficult choice, although he liked Raymond a lot. There were no consequences to ignoring Raymond.

The door opened, and Alison came back in. She was a tall girl, thin, with dark hair and pale skin. She looked a lot like Raymond. She was out of breath. "Gramps says he'll be right in, but you can go ahead and talk about whatever you want to without him. That's okay." She went back to the sink.

Carol Ann said, "Thank you, but I hope that doesn't mean he won't show up here until we're all done, and that'd be just like him."

Alison turned around from the sink where she had just picked up a plate. "No, Ma, he's comin right up." She put the dish under the running water and scrubbed it with her hand. "He said so."

Leroy watched her at the sink. Without any clothes on, she would be unformed, all square bones and no soft places, but sweet in her innocence. Some day when she filled out and knew what she was, she would be good-looking, like Raymond, only more restrained.

"How's the real estate business goin these days, Leroy?"

"Pretty good, Ray. I've been busy. Marie says I've been too busy. They talk about Act 250, and how all these other new regulations are going to hurt us, but I don't see it. Or put it like this, I haven't seen it yet. It may come, but...." He looked over at Carol Ann. She was listening intently. "Right now there are still a lot of people who live in New Jersey and Connecticut. It seems like they all want to move to Vermont, and they all want to own an old Vermont farmhouse. They don't know how much work it takes to live in one, how much upkeep." He and Carol Ann smiled at each other. Her eyes were on his. "They don't find out about that until later, and they don't tell...." She gave a little snort of laughter. "....because then they might not be able to sell. So they just keep on coming, and I stay too busy." He looked at them both. Their faces were serious, but he could tell how eager they were. "Of course, no one knows the future. The market could change at any time." They were looking at him with round eyes, two solemn children waiting for him to tell them more. He glanced at Alison, but she seemed intent on her dishwashing.

The door opened with a rattle, so suddenly that it startled them all. Sonny stepped inside. Leroy who had been very hot for quite a while, noticed right away that Sonny didn't have a jacket on.

Sonny nodded to him as he came over to the table. He stopped by the empty chair, but then he walked on around the table to the woodstove. Leroy heard him lift the lid. He stood up and turned to watch Sonny poking the fire. Sparks swirled toward the ceiling.

Leroy had been waiting for such a pause in the conversation. He took off his black leather jacket and hung it carefully over the back of his chair. He was conscious of his hat on the floor and stepped neatly around it. "Nice clear night out," he said to Sonny. "It'll probably get down there tonight."

Sonny was easing a stick of wood into the fire through the round hole on top. "Yup. We'll get some frost tonight for sure. That guy Holden out on the County Road is likely to lose some corn tonight."

"He plants early, does he?"

"It seems like he's earlier every year. Always in a hurry to beat everyone else on the market. He'll get caught one of these days." He gave the fire a final poke and put the lid back on. "Maybe tonight. He's a nice young fellow, but he's got a lot to learn. There's a right time to do everythin. It don't pay to be in too much of a hurry."

He walked around behind Raymond to the empty chair, and both he and Leroy sat down together. Leroy was mulling over Sonny's words about being in a hurry. You always heard what to do if you were willing to listen hard enough, or maybe if you were willing to believe and act on what you heard. Leroy could see it would be a big mistake for him to be in too much of a hurry over Sonny's place.

Raymond stood up. "Well...." He paused. "I think I'll step outside for a minute." When he got to the door, he looked back at Carol Ann. When he saw she was watching, he took a jacket the color of used motor oil off a hook by the door and threw it across his shoulder as he went out.

Carol Ann said, "He's gone out to smoke. Ever since I quit, he don't smoke around me."

"He's a good boy. That's for sure."

Carol Ann looked at him sternly. "Yes, he is, Gramps, but that don't mean he ain't ever wrong. You can't always take his part."

Leroy looked up to see Alison coming over to the table, wiping her hands shyly on her hips. When she got near and Carol Ann looked up at her, Leroy could see her eyes widen and darken and her lips tremble from the pain between her and her mother. "I'm goin to leave the pots to soak, Ma. I got a lot of homework."

Carol Ann looked past her at the sink. "I guess that's okay," she said grudgingly. "There ain't a whole pile, is there?"

"No, Ma, there's only three of 'em."

"Just so you don't forget. I won't have time to do 'em, and anyhow, it's supposed to be your job."

Alison's face was dark and her mouth twisted. "I was just goin to do my homework for a while. I'll come back and do 'em later."

"Well, I guess it's okay," Carol Ann said with a sour face. "I know what *that* means."

"I *said* I'd do 'em, Ma." She spoke sharply, but as she spoke, she left the room, so Carol Ann couldn't answer her.

Carol Ann shrugged and grinned at Leroy, but her grin had

too many teeth in it and no humor at all. "You tell me what's the hurry to do homework on a Friday night."

None of them looked at each other for a minute, and then Leroy turned to Sonny. "I saw Carol Ann in town the other day, and we got talking about the real estate business, or I guess you could say we were talking about the price of houses, and mostly what she wanted to know was what this house, your house, would be worth on today's market." There, he'd said it straight out, and he wasn't sorry, because he'd been hanging around long enough, picking away at the edges of the subject. And besides that, he wasn't going to let Carol Ann think she could run him like she apparently did everyone else around here. And as a practical matter, there wasn't a whole lot of sense in trying to sell a place which wasn't even for sale, so he might as well find out what was going on. No one could say he was one of those downcountry types who barge in and start talking about business without even being polite first. He was a country boy and local, and he knew how to act. He'd been here for about forty-five minutes if you counted the time he spent out in the barn with Sonny, and he'd been listening and smiling and making polite conversation the whole time.

Carol Ann was talking to Sonny. "What I want is for us to know what kind of money we're talkin about. Just so we know, see. Cause every time we get into a argument about sellin the place, we don't really know how much we're talkin about."

Sonny picked up his feedstore cap and scratched his head with the same hand. The hat flapped back and forth in time with the scratching. He looked worried. "Honey, I don't mind if you find out what this place is worth, that is, if Leroy don't mind figurin it out for you."

The door opened just then, and Raymond came in. He hung up his jacket and walked over to the table, bringing a rush of icy, clean air mingled with cigarette smoke. Everyone looked at him.

Then Sonny went on. "You *should* find out about it. That's

good. You're goin to have to figure out what to do when I ain't
here no more."

Raymond slid into his seat. "Where you goin, Gramps?"

"I ain't goin nowhere until I die. Then I guess I'll go wherever
I'm told to go. Do I look like a good candidate for heaven?" He
grinned at everyone.

"You ain't goin to die, Gramps. You shouldn't ought to talk
like that. You'll probably outlive everybody, even Al."

"Raymond," Sonny said, "I appreciate the thought, but we're
havin a serious conversation here. And what I'm tryin to say is
that it's okay by me if you and Carol Ann, and all the rest of
'em, want to talk about what this place is worth. I ain't stupid. I
seen enough to know that the world's goin to go on without me
in it."

One of Carol Ann's plump and dimpled hands was lying on
the table. Sonny reached out his gnarled fingers and gave her
hand a clumsy pat. "I know you think a new house'd be easier
to take care of, and maybe it would. And I know you got your
heart set on a new, modrun kitchen with all the trimmin's. But,
honey, I was born in this house, and I intend to die here also,
and that's that."

Carol Ann looked serious, but she didn't say anything. Leroy sat there and was glad he hadn't really come on strong. For
just a little while, because of the way that woman named Isabel
had been talking about Sonny's like it was some magic place,
and him on his way out here and all, it had seemed like a hand
waiting to be played, the hand that was going to come along
just when he needed it to bail him out. But it was good that he
hadn't moved too soon. He could have talked about what a great
price you could get these days for an old farmhouse with ten or
so acres. Any one of those downcountry types would have come
on that way. That was just one of the reasons why he always had
the edge on guys like that, that and the fact that he wasn't in it
just to make money. These were his neighbors, in a manner of
speaking, and he really cared about them. He wanted what was

right for them. In this case, it certainly meant leaving Sonny, who was a real sweet guy, to die in peace. You wouldn't catch old Leroy trying to sell Sonny's house out from under him just because there was money to be made, not even because he, Leroy, was in a spot and had to get his hands on a good lump of cash. No sir. Anybody could see that would kill Sonny, and Leroy cared more about the old ways than that. That wasn't Leroy's kind of deal at all, although there were people around who said it was. But those were mostly people who were jealous of what he'd done, of how he'd come up the hard way and still managed to make it big.

Leroy smiled at Raymond and Sonny to let them know he was on Sonny's side, and then he turned to Carol Ann. "Chérie," he said, "this is what I would like to do for you." He felt sorry for her in a way. She seemed to control them all, but it was only show. When it came to real power, Sonny could deal her a body blow without even breaking stride to do it. "I will send you some descriptions of houses that have sold recently—some pictures—that way you can compare those houses with your own. Then you will have an idea of what price is possible."

He looked over at Sonny to see if it was all right to go that far, but Sonny dropped his eyes to the table. Carol Ann sat very still, a lump of flesh. She wasn't very smart. Perhaps she didn't understand why descriptions of comparable properties would be useful to her. Or perhaps she was smarter than he thought. Perhaps she saw that he had come out to see how the land lay, and he had found out what he needed to know.

"This way, Chérie, I won't have to tramp all over your house, looking at beams and inspecting your closets. You know the house already. By this means, you will be able to figure the price range." He looked around the table. "Would it be all right with you, Sonny, if I sent over that stuff for Carol Ann to look at?"

"Oh sure, Leroy. I ain't got any problem with that at all. Like I told Carol Ann, I think all of 'em *ought* to know what they're goin to do with this place when I'm gone. I'd like it if it stayed in the family, of course I would, but I ain't goin to write it into my will either."

Leroy stood up and reached for his jacket. "Well, good. I'll send it along then." He drank the last few swallows of his coffee and set the cup back down. "Thank you, Chérie. Are you still working over at the Texas Café?"

Carol Ann nodded. "From six in the morning until three-thirty, except on Sundays."

"Maybe I'll drop the packet by there tomorrow. I could leave it with May if you weren't there."

"Sure. May'll be there. She just about lives there since Frank died. She says she has to have somebody to do for."

"She used to be in there just about all the time when he was alive too," said Sonny. "Back then what she said was that she needed to get out of the house for a while."

Leroy reached down to the floor for his cowboy hat. Even at his age, he didn't have any trouble reaching over that far. "Well, give her my regards in any case. She's a great cook."

Sonny and Raymond nodded.

"Now I'd better get on home before Marie begins to wonder what I'm up to." He grinned at Raymond, trying to get something started there, a little man's joke about the wives. Raymond grinned back. He was always ready with that crazy, lop-sided smile, but he didn't act like he got the joke at all. "I'll see you around, Raymond. And Sonny, I hope I'm going to get a chance to see you work your team this summer."

"I appreciate it, Leroy."

"So long, Chérie."

He settled his hat onto his head and stepped out into the bright night. The air was sharp with the smell of ice and mud. The world seemed huge and clear and still after the stuffy kitchen. He thought he'd handled it all pretty well. He'd managed not to get drawn into the argument on either side, and he was in a good position to take advantage of whatever happened next. It was too bad that it wouldn't be useful for a while, although who could tell, a man Sonny's age could go any time. He pushed his own worries out of his mind and got into his car. Something would turn up. When you looked down, that was when you got scared. You had to trust it and keep on climbing.

6

THE NEXT DAY Carol Ann tried to explain it to May at work. It was after the breakfast rush was over and not yet time for the crowd that came in for mid-morning coffee. May did all the cooking, but they still split the cleaning up. May was fair about that. Saturday was always different than the weekdays anyhow.

There were only three customers in one booth dawdling over their breakfast. May had scraped down the griddle, and Carol Ann had the coffee urn loaded and perking away. So they had time to sit down and put their feet up for a few minutes. They always sat in the last booth, the one farthest away from the door, and May always brought a damp rag with her, so each of them could put her feet up on the other one's seat, and May could wipe down the seats before they left. Back in the corner the way they were, if any of the customers came toward them, they could take their feet down before anyone saw. May was fussy about that. It was surprising that she let them put their feet up at all, except that they were both heavy-set women, and working in a diner is hard on anyone's feet.

"Leroy LaFourniere came out to the house last night."

"He did? What was *he* up to?"

"It wasn't his idea. I asked him to come out."

"Well, what'd you do that for?"

"I know you don't like him, May, but...."

"It ain't that I don't *like* him, honey. He's *likeable* enough. It's just that I don't trust him. You got to watch the man."

"Oh, May. Come on."

"Say, I almost forgot. Janet wanted me to ask you if you would stay on tonight. She has somethin she wants to do."

"I wish she'd asked me sooner. She's always waitin until the last minute."

"I know it. Well, it's easy enough. Just tell her you got plans, and she's too late."

"It ain't anythin definite. I was goin to see if I could get Raymond to take me out some place, but he don't even know about it yet."

"Well, you tell Janet whatever you like. *I* don't care. What does Raymond think about Leroy LaFourniere comin out to your house?"

"You know Raymond. He probably didn't think about it one way or the other."

"I guess Leroy is so crooked, he probably sleeps in a round bed."

Carol Ann laughed, although she had heard May say the same thing about other people.

"When he ain't out tomcattin, that is."

"You don't know that for sure, May."

"Well, I ain't never run with him, if that's what it would take to know, but I've heard enough talk over the years."

"Talk is cheap, like they say."

"Honey, I'm just tryin to warn you. Likeable as he is, Leroy don't take care of nobody but Leroy. You're in trouble if you ever forget that."

"I know. You don't have to tell *me* that."

"So what'd you ask him out to your place for then?"

"It's hard for me to make them at home understand, but you ought to be able to see it."

"I hope so." May pushed back some wisps of grey hair that had worked out from under her hairnet. She gave the table a swipe with the damp rag while she waited for Carol Ann to get the words right.

"It's hard to explain. Gramps understands what I want better than anybody, but he don't want to do anything." She looked down at her hands lying on the table. She loved the way they looked. She worked hard to keep them soft and smooth. May had a cup of tea, but Carol Ann was waiting for the fresh coffee. "It's just impossible to take care of that old place. Gramps don't know. I could sweep from now until the fourth of July, and there'd still be more dirt. And to keep the cold out—why you plug one hole, and it comes through some place else. We could sell it and build us a new place, real nice and easy to take care of."

"Your grandpa don't want to sell the old homeplace. Is that it?"

"You sound like you're on his side, May."

"Honey, there ain't no sides about it. I'm just listenin to you."

"Gramps says it's all right to find out about what the place is worth, but he was born there and he intends to die there, which is not very smart, because supposin he's got to go to the hospital. I don't see how we can do it. It costs so much to heat the place. Raymond and I have to pay for the furnace fuel. Gramps gets in the wood we need, but he don't have any money. What little he gets has to go toward the taxes. It was all we could do to pay the heatin oil bill last winter. We ain't got it paid yet, and probably won't until midsummer. So what'll we do if it's a real cold winter, or the price of oil goes up? We just won't make it at all.

See what I mean?"

"Well, listen here, Carol," May said, and her voice had such an edge to it that Carol Ann looked up in surprise. "If I could give you any more money than I'm givin you now, you know I'd do it, don't you?"

Carol Ann was annoyed, although she tried to keep it from showing in her voice. She wanted May's sympathy and her understanding of how hard it was. She didn't want May to immediately relate it to herself. Just because May didn't have any life outside of the Texas didn't mean that everybody lived that way. "I wasn't talkin about what you *pay* me, May. I wasn't hintin around for a raise, if that's what you mean."

May said, "I know that, honey," in a softer voice.

But Carol Ann knew better. For just a second there, May had been ready to protect her precious diner against anyone. They could both pretend it wasn't so, but that didn't change anything. May had to fight for her place, and Carol Ann had to fight for hers. That was the way the world was. Finally, after thinking it through, Carol Ann said, "If someone was makin it harder and harder for you to keep the Texas in operation, you would get real upset, wouldn't you?"

"You *know* I would," May said emphatically. "I wouldn't let *anybody* stand in my way."

"Well, that's just what I feel like, and that's why I got Leroy LaFourniere out there—to tell them that we could sell that old dump and build a new house with the money."

"Did Leroy say that? I mean could you really get enough to build a new house with? Did he tell you how much he thought the old place was worth?"

"Well....no....not in numbers exactly."

"Carol Ann, you better be careful. You hear me?"

"He said he thought we could get enough, or at least he said a lot of downcountry people want to buy houses like that."

"He didn't tell you what your place was worth." She said it flatly. It wasn't a question.

"May, how could he? With Gramps sittin right there, large as life, sayin he didn't want to sell. I figure he said all he decently could. And he's goin to send me a lot of literature about other places, so I can compare. Otherwise, he said he would have had to tramp all over the house lookin at closets and beams down in the basement. You know how they do." She looked at May to see what she would say, but May just nodded thoughtfully and said nothing. "And I really didn't want him goin upstairs and all over. I mean, I ain't had a chance to pick up in weeks. I didn't even *know* what it was like up there."

"Well, just you be careful, hon."

"I know, May, I know. I may be a hick, but I ain't dumb, you know. I saw how fast he got out of there last night after Gramps came in and said he was plannin to live in that house til he died. Maybe nobody else saw it, but *I* sure did."

The door opened. May was facing that way. Before Carol Ann could turn around to see who it was, May said, "Get your feet down. Here comes Ralph Merrill."

Ralph was tall as well as wide, and he rocked from side to side when he walked. He came rolling toward them with a grin on his wide face. "Don't get up, ladies. If I'd knowed you was takin a break, I would've waited. If you got some hot coffee, I'll just help myself." He went past them around the end of the counter.

May said, "Well, there ain't no help for it. We better get the last of them dishes done up. Ralph's just the first." She waited until he had his back toward her, helping himself to the coffee, and then she carefully wiped off both seats where their feet had been.

Carol Ann got her empty coffee cup that she had stashed back in a corner, so she wouldn't get it mixed up with the customers' cups. She went over to the coffee urn. It was quite a squeeze to get by Ralph who was coming back the other way.

"So how's it goin, Ralph?"

"Oh, I can't complain."

She filled her cup without saying any more. She was planning to talk to him while she straightened the counter, but just then the door opened, and a whole crowd came in, and when she got unbusy again, Ralph was gone—not that it made any difference because he would be in again on Monday, and she would pass the time with him then.

7

It was nine-forty in the morning when Isabel closed the outside door softly and went down the steps. She had tiptoed downstairs expecting Roxy to come out of her room with words of advice and offers of clothing, but there was no sign of her. No doubt she was sleeping off the effects of last night. Isabel felt pleased by her escape and then guilty for feeling pleased.

At the bottom of the steps, she started toward her car. Then she noticed what an incredible color the sky was, luminous, washed clean by yesterday's rain. She couldn't remember the sky ever looking like that over Abingdon. And there were millions of birds. The air was full of their excited voices. Even the unhealthy little trees which grew along the brick wall of the warehouse next door were reaching as high as they could toward the sky. Isabel decided to walk to Leroy's. She wanted to be a part of the excitement.

By the time she got to the bridge, she felt the way she used to feel when she was a child and got a day off school. Time stretched out ahead, filled with possibilities. She stopped in the middle of the bridge and picked up a few loose stones and leaned over the railing to drop them one by one into the stream below. She watched each little explosion of water and then the stone as it spiraled down out of sight in the murkiness. There was something white gleaming through the water just inside the shadow of the bridge. If she could land a stone on it, it would mean Leroy was going to give her a job. She tried three stones, but each one veered off differently. After a while, she gave up trying. If she didn't get the job, she'd go somewhere else. In the spring sunlight, she felt she could do anything. She was eager to see Leroy again. Maybe he wouldn't be as interested in her as he had seemed last night. But, it was possible. Anything was possible. She walked on.

Just as she got to the corner, a low, red car pulled up in front of Leroy's place. Its little door popped open, and two legs wearing high-heeled shoes poked out and felt for the ground. In the second before the rest of the person was visible, Isabel remembered the awful woman in Leroy's office and how she had practically pushed her out the door. Still, today was different. She had a reason for being here today.

The woman had to reach down to slam the door of her car. She walked up the sidewalk to the office. Isabel tried unsuccessfully to catch her eye and then followed her up the walk. The sign stuck in the front yard said, "LAFOURNIERE REAL ESTATE Your Neighbors Are Your Best Friends."

Isabel followed the woman onto the porch and stood waiting for her to unlock the door. The woman still didn't know she was there, so she coughed a few times to let her know, and when the woman turned around, she held out her hand and said, "Hello. I'm Isabel. Isabel Rawlings. I was here yesterday."

The woman didn't seem surprised, and she didn't say anything. They both looked at Isabel's outstretched hand, but the woman made no move to take it. Finally Isabel let it drop to her side. She said, "Leroy....I mean Mr. LaFourniere told me to come in this morning."

The woman went inside without saying a word. Isabel followed her. She said, "I saw him last night. I guess he hasn't had a chance to tell you yet."

The chair the woman had set out for her yesterday was still in the same place, so Isabel sat down on it. The woman took off her jacket and went into the closet with it. Then she came out again and stood in the middle of the floor staring coldly.

"Do you think he will be in soon?" Isabel asked out loud. Under her breath she said, "All right. I don't know what I've done, but if you want to fight, you aren't going to scare me."

The woman shrugged in an exaggerated way. "I don't know," she said. "You never can tell." She walked out of the room.

Isabel thought she had gone to call Leroy down from upstairs, but in a minute the woman was back with a pile of mail which she put on her desk. She sat down and started sorting it into two piles. "Every day he has a different schedule. He's...." She looked at Isabel then, and a little smile twisted the corners of her mouth. "....unpredictable. That's what. Leroy does things Leroy's way." She turned back to the mail.

"Well," Isabel said, "I suppose I ought to wait now that I'm here. Maybe I'll get lucky. I feel lucky this morning."

"Luck," said the woman. She rolled her eyes toward the ceiling, but she seemed more friendly.

"Mr. LaFourniere didn't exactly say what I would be doing, but...."

"You don't need to be so formal. No one ever calls him anything but Leroy. You might as well call him that too."

"Okay."

"And I'm Renée." She put the last piece of mail into one of the new piles and stood up.

"Okay."

Renée rummaged around in her purse and brought out a comb.

She began to fluff up her dark blonde hair. "And listen. You don't need to tell *me* what Leroy told you. I know Leroy a lot better than you do." She sighed and dropped the comb into her purse again. Her hair didn't look any different.

"Okay."

She looked sharply at Isabel and then sat down. "I know all there is to know about how Leroy operates." She took up one of the letters and opened it, using a nail file as a letter opener.

Neither of them said anything after that. Isabel was sitting right in front of Renée, but she tried not to look at her too much. And Renée seemed absorbed by the letter she was reading. She acted as though Isabel wasn't in the room. If she thought Isabel would get discouraged and give up, she was mistaken. This idea of starting a new life, the simple life she had always wished for, was not just a passing fancy, and she wasn't going to be scared away from any piece that might be useful to her.

Finally Renée sighed and set down the letter. She looked directly at Isabel. "Listen, you can wait as long as you like. It's fine with me."

Isabel looked back just as hard. "Okay," she said.

"I'm going to finish looking over the mail, and then I've got to get going myself."

"Okay."

"If he hasn't come in by the time I leave, I suppose I could show you how to lock up."

"That would be great."

Renée took a breath as though she was going to say more, but she must have thought the better of it, because she turned the breath into a sigh and picked up the letter again.

Isabel felt pleased with herself. She had stood her ground. After a minute she reached into her bag and brought out her new blank book. It was new only because she hadn't used it. She had bought it in the bookstore months ago. She had paid for it because it was important to start off clean, and she knew as soon as she saw it that she wanted it for her new life, although it wasn't until later that she decided to keep a journal like Thoreau's.

She glanced up in time to see that Renée was actually leaning across her desk so that she could see over it to the book on Isabel's lap. Their eyes crossed, but neither of them acknowledged the other, and Renée leaned back hurriedly and pretended to be absorbed by her letter.

Isabel opened the journal to the first page. She hadn't written anything yet, but she had been meaning to begin ever since last Tuesday when she moved into her room at Roxy's house. She wrote Saturday, April 27, 1991, at the top of the first page and then under it, 'Dear H.D.'— Thoreau's initials. She had had that much planned for a long time. She didn't know what to say next, and she could feel Renée waiting. She couldn't write anything with Renée there.

That was when her luck kicked in again because just when she thought she might have to put the journal away and maybe even give up waiting and leave, Leroy walked in.

"What a surprise. I wasn't expecting either of you, and here you are, all cozy together."

They both looked up at the sound of his voice, and their eyes caught on each other's before they turned to look at Leroy. Isabel shut the book on her blank first page. Leroy smiled at her. It was odd of him to say he wasn't expecting her when he had told her to be here.

"I didn't know you were coming in today, Chérie," he said to Renée. "But I'm glad you were here to show Isabel what to do."

Renée shrugged. It was very French, and it committed her to nothing. "I wasn't planning on working this weekend. I have to take those Schneiders from New Jersey out to see the old Booth place. I wasn't going to do anything else." She looked up at Leroy with her face set and her eyes narrowed into slits.

"Chérie," he said, and there was surprise in his voice. "Would I ask you to do more?" He walked over to her and stood behind her with his hands on her shoulders, kneading them with his long fingers. She moved back and forth under his hands like a cat. "You work too hard, Chérie. I always tell you that. Have a good time today. You deserve it."

"Hah," thought Isabel. "She's in love with him, and she thinks I might try to take him away. That explains everything. Well, she doesn't have to worry about that, not from me anyway." She didn't feel disappointed either, even though he was attractive. She wasn't here to get involved with anyone. She was glad she had seen this exchange. It would make a good story to tell Nicky when she talked to him on the phone.

Leroy was smiling at her over Renée's head. "So what do you think? Did Renée make the job sound good, Chérie?"

"He's showing off," Isabel thought. "He wants me to see how much power he has over her." Out loud, she said, "Well no, she didn't tell me much. I guess we were waiting for you." Below his head, between his hands was Renée's face looking at her with great coldness.

Leroy looked down at the top of Renée's head. "You haven't started Isabel on any little jobs, Chérie?"

Renée stood up abruptly, twisting out from under his hands. She walked across the room to the closet, her heels striking little hammer-blows of irritation.

Both Isabel and Leroy watched her, forgetting their conversation with each other. They were still looking dumbly at the closet door when Renée came out again, holding her jacket.

"I need to get going," she said. "I just stopped in to see if there was anything in the mail. I'm supposed to take those people out to see the Booth farm."

"Was there?"

"Was there what?"

"Anything in the mail."

"Oh no. Nothing important. I needn't have bothered to come in."

"I guess Isabel and I are glad you did."

Renée went over to her desk and got some papers out of the top drawer. She folded them and put them carefully in her purse. "I don't think I'm the one to tell Isabel what to do." She kept her back toward Leroy as she spoke. "*I* don't know what you want."

"Chérie, what I want, what we both want, is someone to do some of the clerical work, so we can be out doing what we're supposed to be doing, selling property. Okay?"

Renée closed her bag and put it over her shoulder. She turned around to face him and said, "Leroy, I just don't understand you at all." Her voice was low, almost a hiss. "I have to go. I don't want to be late. I'll see you on Monday." She left the room without looking back or saying goodbye. The outside door slammed.

Leroy went into the hall and then came back to stand in the doorway while he settled his black hat onto his head. He looked at Isabel thoughtfully, but he didn't say anything. Then he went out too.

Through the window Isabel could see them standing beside Renée's little car. Renée was talking, gesturing with her hands. She was frowning.

Isabel could plainly see what was going on. The more Renée felt that she might lose him, the more angry she got at him, and the more she showed how angry she was, the more inclined he would be to leave. Renée must have felt that too, which of course made her even more angry. Isabel was sorry for her. It was easier for her now with Leroy there for Renée to be mad at. It meant she could be in the background just watching them.

Leroy came back inside and sat down on the corner of the desk. He shrugged. "She's French—hot blood—you know. She'll come around. Give her a little time."

"I'm afraid I've caused trouble."

"No, Chérie, *I* have caused the trouble, and I'll take care of it. It won't last." He stood up.

"I'm sorry she's angry. I don't think she likes me."

Leroy reached forward and picked up her hand which was lying on her lap. He looked into her face as he leaned close. "Not like you, Chérie? That's silly. It'll work out. Trust me."

Close up he smelled cold and clean—sharp, like rubbing alcohol. He was so formal in an old-fashioned way, and yet she felt as though they had known each other for a long time. She liked the way he made her feel. Still, she didn't intend to get involved with anyone. That part of her life was over.

She pulled her hand away and sat back in the chair. "Why don't we wait until Monday. You and Renée could decide together if you have any work for me." As soon as she said it, she was sorry. She could see that it hurt his feelings.

"I thought you wanted to work for me," he said.

"Well, yes....I do."

"So why....?" Suddenly all his swagger was gone.

She wanted to offer some comfort, although why would he care what *she* thought about it. Still, it appeared that he did, and that touched her. "I think you would be a good person to work for," she said, feeling a bit shy.

"Thank you for saying that, Chérie." He smiled at her. "You have no idea how much that means to me."

"And I'd like to learn about Severance. I mean, if I'm going to stay here...."

"I have been wondering if you liked to ski."

"No, I've never....I don't think I'd like it. What made you say that?"

"People usually move here because they like to ski."

"That's not why I came. Are you sure you want me to work here? You don't really know anything about me."

"Chérie," he said. He started to reach for her hand again, but he must have thought the better of it because he sat back on the desk and folded his arms across the crisp front of his shirt. "You did the clerical work for your bookstore?"

"In the beginning I did it all. Then later on, it got bigger."

"I would say you are overqualified. You could get a better job than I have to offer."

"I worry about it. If someone asked for recommendations—I mean, no one knows what I can do but Jeff, and I don't know *what* he would say."

"Your husband?"

"My ex-husband. I don't think I could ask him for a recommendation. At least, I wouldn't want to."

"Jeff's not a skier either?"

"No. I guess we never had time. We were always working on the bookstore. We hardly ever had time for anything else—except our two boys, but they are grown up now."

"My children are grown up also, but now we have the grandkids."

"I guess it's an accident I'm here—in a way it's literally an accident, because I wouldn't be here if we hadn't gotten stuck at that farm." She looked at him sitting on the corner of the desk. "Don't you think sometimes things happen just the way they are meant to?"

"Yes, Chérie, that happens to me a lot."

"Because that's the way it felt when we came to Jeff's reunion—I told you about that."

He nodded.

"Ever since, I've had that place in my mind, and how I want to live in harmony with nature the way those people did, I mean, do."

"What has that got to do with me?" He was smiling.

"That's the strange part—I mean how things fit in that you don't even know are going to—like a plan, sort of."

He slouched there on the corner of the desk with his long legs stretched out, his arms folded and his eyes part-way shut. He didn't seem to be paying attention, but she knew he was.

"I'm not talking about God, or anything like that, but there's some place I'm supposed to be now. In my life, I mean." She paused, but she could see he was waiting for her to say more. "And this job is part of it, I think. It's perfect for me to work in a real estate office, so I can learn about the land around Severance, only I never would have thought of it. It kind of happened by itself in a way, didn't it?"

He smiled again. He was so thin, so black and white, so two

dimensional, but his smile was full of promise.

"The hard part is to know what the plan is. I think I'm supposed to have this job so I can learn about Severance. But you can't really tell what's what until later, if you see what I mean. I'm trying to let it happen the way it's supposed to, without thinking I know how it's supposed to be. I guess that sounds sort of dumb." She was so sure that she had said too much, that she could feel the color rising in her cheeks. She felt him lean forward, but she didn't look at him.

"No, Chérie, I know exactly what you mean. When you fight it, nothing is any good. You have to go with it. When you do that, amazing things happen."

"Oh, I can't believe you know what I mean. That's just what I think. Only sometimes it's hard to say what's what. I can't always tell."

"You have to go with what feels right. That's what I do."

"I'm trying."

"And it feels right for you to work here."

"Does it?"

"To me it does. You can trust me, Chérie."

"That's wonderful. I haven't ever tried to explain this to anyone before. I'm surprised that it makes any sense."

"It's exactly what I feel myself, Chérie."

"You don't know what a difference it makes to have someone who understands."

"So it's settled. And you won't worry about Renée any more? It will be fine about Renée."

"I hope *she* thinks so."

"Don't worry. She's never met anyone like you before. It makes her nervous. She thinks you're a hippie. She'll get used to it."

"A hippie? I wouldn't have thought that. I suppose I was a hippie years and years ago—although I never dropped out or anything."

"There were lots of them at Green Mountain College. They made everybody nervous in those days."

"That was so long ago."

"It's not a problem any more." He stood up. "Renée will have to show you what work there is. I leave most of that to her. I'm sure the two of you can work it out so that it suits everybody."

"I hope you're right. I wish I felt as sure of that as you seem to."

"Trust me, Chérie."

"I'd like to. It's so nice to have someone who understands."

"Good," he said smiling. "Now." He stood up. "I have one little job I need done. Can you run a Xerox machine?"

"Oh sure."

"Great. Take a look at this one, will you? I need some copies...." He watched her walk over to the machine.

"All right," she said. "This is easy."

"Then we're all set." He opened drawer after drawer of Renée's desk, taking out papers, whistling tunelessly through his teeth. "Here," he said, handing her a handful of loose pages. "Make two copies of every one."

"Okay." She had to do the first one over, but after that, she did it right.

A few minutes later, Leroy came over to watch what she was doing, leaning in close to her. "Chérie," he said, "let's try it out this way: I'll pay you $200 a week, and you do up to twenty hours work. If it turns out to be more, I'll pay you more. I don't think it'll even be that many hours a week, but I'll still pay you $200, even if it isn't."

She took a step back so she could see his face. He looked serious. "All right," she said. "I didn't...."

"And, look, Chérie, I can pay you in cash. That'll simplify things for both of us."

"That's fine with me—better maybe."

"Let's try it out then. That's not much money."

"I don't need much. Your cousin's place is very cheap."

Leroy shook his head. "You may have to change your mind. It's not easy to have so little." He walked over to his desk. "There's so much you can't have." He sat down and opened the top drawer and took out a manila envelope.

Isabel started the Xerox machine on another page and then turned to look at him. He was writing an address on the envelope. She liked the way he understood what she was trying to do. "One of my goals is to get rid of all the unnecessary stuff in my life. There's too much trivia. I want to simplify things."

"I don't know, Chérie," he said, shaking his head. "I think you don't know what it is to do without."

She turned back to the machine without replying. There was no reason to suppose he would understand *everything*. Still, she was disappointed, and knowing it was unreasonable didn't make it less so.

Leroy put the envelope down on the pile of finished pages. He reached in his pocket and pulled out a roll of money held together with a wide rubber band. He didn't flash it around, but he let her see it, and she knew it wasn't an accident. He took off the rubber band and pulled two five dollar bills off the roll. "Put one copy of everything in the envelope and drop it by the post office, will you, Chérie?" He laid the money on top of the envelope. "Send it first class. This should cover it. You can put the other copies on my desk." He put the rubber band around his money roll and put it back into his pocket. "I'll fix the door so it'll lock when you leave."

"You aren't going to be here?"

"No, Chérie. I have business up above St. Johnsbury today." He went out into the hall and got his jacket and hat. Then he came back as far as the doorway to set the lock.

"I'll get you a key of your own next week. See you on Monday, Chérie." He touched one finger to his hat and was gone.

When Isabel looked out the window, his big black car was sliding down the driveway, and then it was gone, and it felt too quiet in the room. She finished the stack of pages and turned off the machine, and it was even more quiet, more empty. She wondered if Leroy's wife was upstairs, but she couldn't hear anything.

She took the finished pages over to Leroy's desk and sat down to separate them. Part way through the job of sorting, she decided to look for some paper clips. The desk was large and old-fashioned, with long drawers. There was very little in any of them—envelopes in the front of one, and in another, loose pencils which rolled loudly across the empty space. She pulled one drawer all the way out just to see how long it was, and there in the back, lying naked and alone on the floor of the drawer was a squat, black pistol. She was so surprised that she had to look at it for a long time to be sure it was real. Then she picked it up. It was cold to the touch and much heavier than she expected. She was afraid to keep it in her hand, or to raise it above the level of the desk, even though there was no one around to see.

It flashed into her mind that maybe Leroy wasn't the way she had pictured him—upright and honorable and old-fashioned. Then she scolded herself for being so suspicious. Country people had a different attitude toward guns. That was something she would have to get used to. It was wrong to think anything bad about him when he had been so kind. It was mean-spirited of her.

She shut the gun away in the drawer and finished sorting the pages. She was just putting them into the envelope when she looked up and saw Leroy standing in the doorway. "He's come back for his gun," was her first thought. And then, "What would he have done if he had come in when I was holding it?"

"Don't look so frightened," he said. "I won't eat you." He laughed and tilted his hat back on his head. "It's a beautiful day outside. It wasn't very nice of me to leave you stuck in here. Get your things together and come with me, Chérie."

"But...."

"You don't have plans for today, do you?"

"No. I thought you might have some work, but...."

"Bring that envelope. We can drop it off at the Texas. That'll be better anyway. Come on, Chérie. This is an order from your new boss."

8

WHEN SONNY CAME into the kitchen, Al was at the sink doing dishes.

"The cattle are ready. We're goin up in back to get that maple from the other day. You comin?"

"I want to, Gramps." She shut off the water and turned around, wiping her hands on her blue jeans. "I got to do these pots before Ma gets home is all."

"You can do 'em later. She won't be home until this evenin. I ain't goin to be up there all day."

"Ma'll really kill me if she comes home, and I ain't got 'em done."

"It's up to you, honey."

She looked around at the pots and then back at Sonny. "You know how mad she gets."

Sonny knew. Carol Ann would really go on the warpath if she

got home on Saturday night and found Friday's dishes still in the sink. Out loud he said, "Your ma is a good girl, honey. She can't help it if she's got a lot of worries on her mind. Where's your dad at anyhow?"

"I think he's in the front room. Why?"

"I got to ask him somethin, and then I'm goin to go on. I got Buck 'n Ben all yoked up out front, so I can't wait around."

"What'll I do, Gramps?"

She looked at him so seriously, trying to be good. He was glad she wanted to go with him. He loved to work in the woods with her. They fit together. An old man and a young girl, but even so, they made a team. It was always better when she was there.

"Come on with me, honey. I'm just goin to skid out that bit of firewood. We'll be back long before your ma gets home."

"Okay, Gramps," she said, and her face got less solemn.

He patted her on the shoulder. "I got somethin to say to your dad, and then I'll be ready to go. I'll meet you out there. The saw's all ready. I gassed it up and sharpened it both."

"Okay, Gramps. I'll just put some water in my pots."

Sonny went into the front room. Raymond had moved the couch out from the wall and rolled up the rug so that he could spread one of his engines out on newspapers while he rebuilt it. He had brought it in in pieces, and he would have to take it out the same way, but he had been able to work on it during the cold days of winter.

Sonny stopped in the doorway. "Well, Ray, it ain't like it's real cold out any more."

Raymond looked up and flashed one of his crazy grins. "Don't I know it! Carol Ann tells me often enough. But it's goin out of here today. I already promised."

"I was thinkin we might get on the cattle truck—get the brakes straightened around—maybe after noon, if you could see your way to it."

"Oh sure. I ought to be done with this here by noon."

"Me and Al are goin to skid down that maple, but we'll be

done before noon, barring accidents." He rapped his knuckles on the wood of the door frame. "But if you got somethin more pressin, my truck could just as easy wait."

"Hell no, Gramps. It don't matter. Just so I get this thing out of the front room."

Sonny could see that Raymond wanted him to notice what a good boy he was being. It embarrassed him to see that, and he dropped his eyes to the floor in front of his workboots. "Well, okay. I guess we'll go on then. See you later."

Sonny went outdoors. Al was already there, getting everything packed up. She had looped the heavy logging chains up on the ox yoke, so the oxen could carry them without the chains dragging and getting caught on rocks or stobs in the road.

"We ain't goin to need gas for the saw, cause I just filled it, and we ain't got a lot to cut."

"Okay, Gramps."

"But we'll need the ax and the peavy too."

Buck rolled his eyes and looked around when he heard Sonny's voice, but Ben didn't move. He always counted on Buck to make the decisions for both of them.

"Where's the tools for the chain saw?"

"I got 'em in my pocket, so we don't have to carry 'em." She shifted her weight and stuck out her hip, grinning slyly at him. He could see the wrench and the file sticking out of her back pocket.

"Good girl. Let's go. You want to drive?"

She smiled at him again and went over to pick up the whip. She raised it beside the oxen and said, "Git up," and both of them heaved forward without hesitation. The first few times Sonny let her drive, the oxen had been surprised and doubtful, rolling their eyes toward Sonny for an explanation. But they were used to it now and accepted her orders. She was the only person besides Sonny who had ever even tried to drive them.

Sonny picked up the ax and peavy and chain saw and followed. The road went around the machine shed beside the barn, through all Raymond's junk machines, and past the big rock, across the back field toward the hill. It was going to be a fine day—warm, but not too warm to work.

What was it about spring that made even an old man get excited about the promise of new life? He loved to walk behind his oxen in the rich cow smell that was the combined smell of them both. Buck's own personal smell was dry and dusty, and Ben's was more like over-ripe fruit. Sonny thought he would be able to tell which was which even if he couldn't see, although he had never put it to the test. But there was a third smell, which was distinct and was the smell of the two of them together. He walked along in this smell, in the clear, morning light, feeling how everything he didn't like was smoothed away because he was there behind his team and on the way to the woods with Al.

She was walking close beside Buck, and every once in a while she would forget and reach up to hold onto the tip of his bow. Then she would remember and let go again. It was a bad habit she was trying to break herself of. When she first tried to drive Buck and Ben a few years ago, she was so small that she had to hold onto the yoke to keep from getting left behind. She was a lot taller now, already taller than Carol Ann, and she didn't have so much trouble keeping up.

On Al's head was a faded red feedstore cap, just like Sonny's. In fact, it had been one of his, until she had taken it over for her own. It would have been too big for her, except that she stuffed all her hair up inside it so that she looked like a boy. That drove Carol Ann crazy. Carol Ann wanted Al to be more feminine.

They came to the far side of the field. As soon as Al waved the whip, before she even said, "Whoa," the oxen stopped. Of course, they knew what to do, the same as anyone. Sonny put down the tools and went to open the gate. He left it open and went back to get his tools. When everything was through, he set the tools down again and closed the gate.

There was an old stone wall outside the fence, and then the

woods and the steep grade began. It was still quite sunny along the road in the woods because the trees hadn't really leafed out yet. The birds were making quite a racket. This was their big time of year, and they were getting all the mileage out of it that they could.

Sonny was puffing a bit as he went up the steep part. Still, it felt nice, and you'd have to say it wasn't bad for a fellow who was seventy-eight. He'd go as slow as he had to, but he damn sure wouldn't quit altogether. There wouldn't be any point to anything without this. In a way, being in the woods was like being in church. In fact, you could even say it was better. In church you might think about God, but you could also think about lots of things that you weren't supposed to think about—thoughts connected with neighbors that you weren't getting along with, even thoughts about other people's wives. But being in the woods was almost like praying, you almost had to think about God and His goodness. It just came up. It was right there before your eyes. You couldn't avoid it.

The maple was about halfway up the hill and on a road off to the side. Al and the oxen were getting ahead, but it didn't matter because they knew where to go and what to do when they got there. It was fine for him to take it easy and enjoy his walk. That was why he and Al got along so good. It was okay with Al if he took it easy and worked slow, and it was okay with him if Al was in a hurry to see what she could do.

When he came up with them, Al had already turned the oxen around and taken the logging chains off their yoke, so they would be more comfortable. Those chains were heavy, and Al wasn't very big, but she never shied away from anything hard. Sonny loved her courage.

He went over to where the maple tree lay. The last time he was up here, he had put the tree down, but he hadn't done anything to get it ready to skid. He set down the tools and stood looking at the tree. Al came over and stood beside him, waiting to hear the plan.

"It ain't that big. I think we might could take it down in three loads. What do you say?"

"Sure, Gramps."

"See, we'll take out the butt first. We can walk Buck 'n Ben right up to here where we're standin. And we won't cut it too long, cause that's goin to be a pretty good load. We don't want 'em to bottom out goin through that low place in the night pasture."

He glanced over at Al, but she didn't say anything. She just nodded and looked serious, so he would know she was thinking about everything he said and agreed with all of it.

"Then we'll have a clear path to the middle part, and we can cut that longer."

He wanted her to know how to come to these choices, as well as how to do the actual physical work of driving and hitching, although if he had thought about it much, which he didn't want to do, he would have had to admit that there probably wasn't much sense in her learning any of it, since hardly anybody logged with oxen any more, and she would probably grow up and get married and have babies and forget everything she had ever learned. Still, it was also true that it pleased them both to have him teach her.

"Then I thought we could take down the top pretty much like it is. We'll probably have to trim it before we go through the barway, but we can see when we get there. Okay?"

"It's okay by me, Gramps."

"Well, let's get at it then."

Sonny took off the old plaid wool shirt he was wearing on top of his other clothes. Then he started up the chain saw. Al got the ax and began to trim up the top. The roar of the saw was good, and the way the sound changed when the saw was biting was even better. Lots of guys wore things over their ears to keep them from being damaged by the noise, but Sonny figured you were a lot safer if you could hear what was going on. Besides, his ears were good considering his age, and he guessed they'd probably hold out for the time he had left. He might ought to get some for Al though.

He cut the trunk into three sections and took off a few branches as he went by. Then he shut off the saw. For a second there was the shocked emptiness that was always there when the saw stopped. Then the small sounds began to pour back into the vacuum. He always had the feeling that everything, the animals, the trees, the earth itself, was holding its breath to see if he was going to start the saw again. Everything was waiting but Al, who was still taking out branches with the ax. He liked to watch her swing. She didn't look all cramped and awkward and scared of it like most women. She really knew how to work. He had taught her himself. Neither of her parents had ever had enough time for her, although Raymond always liked it when she wanted to hang around. People were always in too much of a hurry any more.

He went and got the small chain. The chains were lying near each other but separate, not all tangled up together the way some people would have left them. He found the place to put the chain around the log. He dug away at the leaves and litter on the ground so that he could see that he would need to roll the log over part way to get the chain around. As soon as he put his hand on the peavy, Al noticed. She put down her ax and came over. She crouched down, working the chain under the log while he rocked it back and forth for her. They didn't have to say anything for each of them to be in the right place to help the other. She hitched the sliphook over a link and gave the chain a few jerks to see if it would hold. He stabbed the peavy into the ground where it wouldn't get run over.

"That looks like it, Gramps."

"Okay. Do you want to drive?"

"Yes, please." Her eyes were hidden under the bill of her cap.

"Good girl. I'll hitch for you."

"Thanks, Gramps."

She brought Buck and Ben over, turned them around, and

backed them up a bit. Sonny got the big chain and hitched it. The oxen stood patiently. They were sleepy with all the warm spring sunshine, so they didn't even start up when they heard the chain clank into place. They just watched Al through half-shut eyes. When she told them to get up and stepped to the side, they moved smoothly forward onto the road and down it. Sonny walked along in the good smell of the woods dirt dug up by the log, the chink of the loose ends of chain as the oxen swayed, the warm sun, and best of all, the way Al and the oxen were all doing their jobs just as he had taught them.

The second load went almost as well as the first. Everybody did everything just right, and the work rolled smoothly along. Then they hitched up to the top. Sonny took over driving right at first to see how it was going to go. Sometimes a top could fool you and roll over when you first started out with it. You could get into quite a mess if you weren't watching out for it.

So Sonny took over until they got off the side road, just to see how it was going to ride, and it did fine. It didn't shift at all. He stopped the oxen, and when Al came up beside them, he handed her the whip. He could see she was having a good time with it.

She smiled at him as she took the whip, and then she started them up again, and the three of them walked down the road side by side. Sonny stepped off into the trees to give all the branches a chance to clear him since the thing spread out at the top end. They hadn't taken much off because the more branches they left, the more wood they got down in one load, and limb wood was always a nuisance to handle.

They were about halfway down when it happened. Sonny was walking behind and carrying the tools. He thought he was looking at them, but maybe he wasn't, because it seemed like the first thing he noticed was a loud crack, almost like wood hitting wood, and at the same moment he saw Al go down. Then everything speeded up and got slower at the same time, the way it always does when something like that is going on. He either dropped the tools or set them down in the road because the next thing he knew, he was crouching beside Al trying to see her face which was mostly buried in the dead leaves that lay along the edge of the road. Her cap was off, and her dark hair was spread in every direction. He held his hand out in the air over her head, but he was afraid to turn her over.

"Al, honey, can you hear me?"

She gave a small groan and turned her head.

"Thank you, God," was what he thought. He could see her open eyes looking at him through the tangle of her hair.

"I let 'em get away from me, Gramps. It ain't good for their trainin."

He looked down the road. Buck and Ben and the load were already out of sight. He couldn't even hear them. "That don't matter. They'll stop at the barway and wait for us. They won't even know what they done. Are you okay is the main thing."

"I think so," she said. Her eyes looked around. She reached up and pushed some of the hair out of her face.

"What happened anyhow?"

"I don't know. Somethin must've spooked 'em. One minute they were goin good, and the next thing I knew, they both took off at once."

She sat up slowly and carefully. Sonny wanted to brush off the leaves and twigs that were stuck to her face and tangled in her hair, but he didn't. His hands were too rough. Instead he stood up and went over to pick up her hat. He knocked it off on his leg and handed it down to her.

"Thanks, Gramps. I'm okay."

"The top must've clipped you when it came by."

"Yes. I think so. Somethin sure gave me a good smack."

"You got to watch out for a wide load like that."

"I couldn't help it, Gramps. It happened too fast."

"Yes, I know, honey. It wasn't your fault."

She had picked most of the leaves out of her hair. It was when she pulled it back so that she could stuff it all under the hat, that he saw the dark blood. It lay across her right temple and into the hair above her right ear. Just as he saw it, it pooled up and began to run across her cheek. Before he could say anything, she made a gesture to brush it away, as though it were a fly. When she took away her hand and saw the blood on it, she looked surprised.

Sonny reached his handkerchief out of his back pocket. He wished it was a clean one, but it wasn't. Still, it would have to do. "Here, honey, hold this on there real tight until we get down to the house. Then we can see what we got. Can you walk?"

"I'm okay, Gramps. I can walk."

She stood up slowly while he hovered around. He didn't want to help her if she didn't need it. She seemed to be doing all right, so he went over to where he had left the tools, thinking he could carry them down at least as far as the barway, so he wouldn't have to come back after them later. He must have just dropped them when he saw Al fall, because the chain saw was upside down, and the gas had run out onto the road. He tightened the gas cap, picked everything up, and turned around just in time to see Al take a few steps and stagger, catching her balance against a tree. When she took the hand holding the handkerchief away from her face to grab the tree, the blood poured out over her cheek.

Sonny dumped the tools on the edge of the road and put his arm around her. "Come on, honey, let's take it slow."

"I'm okay, Gramps, honest. I was just dizzy there for a minute. I think I can do it."

"We'll do it together, honey. Don't worry. You're goin to be all right." He said it to her, but he realized while he was still saying the words that he was the one who needed reassurance; he was the one who was scared.

They walked down the road with their arms around each other, awkwardly, clumsily. Neither one of them knew how to walk so close. Buck and Ben were waiting by the closed gate. They were chewing calmly. They didn't look like they knew they'd done wrong.

"Here, Al, let me help you to sit down until I get them started through the night pasture. Then I'll be back to help you."

He expected her to protest, to say she didn't need any help, but to his surprise she said, "Okay," quite meekly and sat down under a tree to wait for him. Her face was streaked with dirt and in shadow, but even so, he could see how pale she was.

As he was walking away from her, he said, "By God, I hope that top's goin to go through the gate." He didn't know whether he was talking to her or to himself. He sighted from behind, looking past the top and the team to the width of the opening in the stone wall. "It might could go, but it's goin to be close. I guess I'll have to try it, cause I left the saw back up there. I sure would hate to have to go after it right now."

It wasn't until he had opened the gate and was ready to start the oxen that he realized he hadn't seen his whip since the accident. It didn't matter. He would look for it when he went up after the tools. He didn't like to ask Al about it because she always took everything so seriously, and he didn't want her to feel bad.

Buck and Ben never noticed that all he was using was a small branch he broke off a brierbush which grew up between the fence and the stone wall. They were intent on getting the job done. They seemed to know, the way they always did, that this was the last load, even though it wasn't noon yet.

He got them up pretty easy and held his breath as the top started through the gate. It was close enough so that one branch rattled a loose stone on top of the wall and bent the fence post way over as it went by, but it did clear and without doing any real damage either—a bit of luck just when he needed it.

When the oxen were started across the pasture, he went back and helped Al up. They walked through the gate, and then Al turned around to pick up the handle to the electric fence.

"Leave it open, honey. I'll close it when I come back up. Let's get you down to the house."

"But, Gramps...."

He wouldn't let her reach for the gate. He didn't say anything. He just made her walk across the field. He was thinking the sun might make her feel worse, and he wanted to get her the rest of the way there before she really started to feel bad, although Al was as good as a boy, and strong. She probably would have kept on going no matter how far it was. Still, they didn't even know how bad she was hurt. And in spite of how strong she was, she felt so light and thin under his arm. She wasn't very old, and she wasn't very big, and that was the simple fact of it.

When they got to the other side of the pasture, the oxen were waiting at the gate. He had hoped Raymond would be out there getting some spare parts from one of his junk cars, but he wasn't. Sonny didn't want to frighten him by shouting to him to come and give them a hand. He managed by himself to get the gate open so the oxen could go through. They headed toward the woodpile, and he steered Al toward the house.

"We better unhitch 'em," she said in a weak voice.

"Now, honey, you leave that to me. They ain't goin anywhere. They know they're all done, and they're satisfied. I told you they wouldn't know they done wrong. I'm goin to set you down and wash your face, like I used to when you were a little girl. Remember?"

Al nodded and almost smiled.

"Then when I get you all fixed up, I'll come out and unhitch. You leave that up to me."

When they got to the kitchen door, Sonny opened it and then stepped back to give her room to go through. She steadied herself on the door frame and stepped shakily into the kitchen. Raymond was just coming through the other door from the front room. Over Al's shoulder Sonny could see the surprise and fear spread across Raymond's face.

"Hey, Al...." he said.

"I'm okay, Dad. I just got hit with a branch. It ain't nothin."

Sonny stepped into the kitchen and shut the door. It was dark after the sunshine outside. "We got to clean her up and take a look, Ray, but it don't look too bad."

Raymond said, "I'll just put this stuff down." He started back into the front room with the engine parts he was carrying. Then he came back and walked across the kitchen. "I'll be right back to give you a hand." Sonny opened the kitchen door for him, and he went out.

Sonny shut the door. "Now, honey, sit down there while Gramps gets a basin of water and cleans you up."

Al sat down at the kitchen table while Sonny bustled around. He turned on the overhead light and filled one of Carol Ann's biggest mixing bowls with warm water.

By the time he got a clean washrag and a cake of soap, Raymond was back. He stood in front of Al running his hands one after the other through his dark curls. "How'd it happen, Gramps?"

Sonny dipped the rag into the water and lifted it up. The drips splashed back into the bowl. Al had been sitting with her elbow on the table, her head propped on the hand that held the handkerchief. She opened her eyes and looked at Sonny. His first thought when he saw her look was that she couldn't be too bad if she was worried about not getting the oxen in trouble. Of course nobody was thinking of what Raymond would say, but that if Raymond knew something, there was a pretty good chance that Carol Ann would find out sooner or later. So Sonny squeezed out the rag and gently took the blood-soaked handkerchief out of Al's hand while he figured out how to tell what happened. The blood ran down her face when she took away her hand.

"We was bringin down the top with the branches all on. Al didn't leave enough room for it, and it went by her and clipped her," he said, counting on the fact that Raymond wouldn't picture it precisely enough to see that there wasn't any reason for the top to go fast enough to do damage unless the oxen were acting up.

Al closed her eyes again. Sonny thought she was satisfied with the way he'd handled it. He glanced over at Raymond who looked as though he might not have heard anything anyway.

Raymond said, "Wash it off, Gramps. Let's see how deep it is."

He reached past Sonny to push Al's hair out of the way, but just before he touched her, he pulled back his grease-covered fingers. "I can't help you unless I wash up first, and that would take too long."

Sonny touched the rag to Al's cheek, wiping away some blood which had dripped down and then dried there. It was hard to begin on the cut itself. He would have washed the rest of her face first—she had a big streak of dirt that went clear across her cheek to her mouth—but Raymond was watching impatiently, so he dabbed at the cut, timidly at first, and then a little harder. It began to bleed again where he touched it. He rinsed out the cloth and kept on. "It's bleedin a lot, but I don't think it's deep. A head wound'll always do like that, and that's good when it does. What's it look like to you, Ray?"

"I don't know. It's kind of ragged and messy, ain't it?"

Al opened her eyes. "It's okay,' she said. "It don't hurt."

Raymond said, "Al, you'd say it was okay if your arms and legs was pulled off. We can't ask you about it."

"But it's *true*, Dad." She looked upset.

Sonny was still wiping, trying to get a good look at the whole cut at once. "It's okay, honey. We know it's true." Then to Raymond he said, "It's raggedy, but it ain't deep. I don't think she needs stitches, do you?"

"I don't know, Gramps. You know lots more than me. Can you get her cleaned up enough?" He was pulling at his curls again, standing them up all over his head. "How are you goin to get a bandage on that? Where her hair is and all?"

"That'll be a bit tricky."

"We don't want to do nothin wrong. I mean...." He stopped, confused.

Sonny felt sorry for him. "You don't have to worry, Ray," he said. "She ain't hurt very bad. We'll get it fixed up just fine."

Al opened her eyes again. "If my hair's in the way, why don't you cut it off? I been wantin a haircut for a long time anyhow."

"Cause your ma would skin us alive if we cut your hair, that's why."

"Oh, Gramps, you could tell her you had to, so you could bandage me up."

"I'd a lot rather not have to."

"It'd be too late for her to do anythin about it by that time."

"That wouldn't stop your ma if she decided to go on the warpath."

He cleaned the rag again in the now-brownish water and wiped over the length of the cut. "There, Raymond, you can see the whole thing. It ain't bad. It ain't nice and straight like a knife cut, but it'll heal okay. You still feel all right, Al, honey?"

She nodded.

"Here. Don't move your head. Hold this rag up there, while I go find somethin to bandage you up with. Your dad can't do anythin with them dirty hands of his."

Sonny went into the bathroom. Over the washbowl was the large old-fashioned wooden cabinet where they kept the medicines. It had always been there. Carol Ann hated the way it had glass doors on the front so you could see everything inside and how messy the shelves were. She was always threatening to bust it up for kindling, so she could replace it with a modern cabinet with a mirror on the front. Sonny dreaded the idea of watching himself while he washed and shaved.

He got the first aid box and started back to the kitchen. Carol Ann had bought a special kit, thinking they ought to be more safety conscious. It had been a fancy kit with all kinds of things packed inside. But that was several years ago. Now all that was left were a few tongue depressors and some poison ivy medicine—things they had no use for. Carol Ann had forgotten the safety business. She didn't notice that they were back to dealing with things the way they always had. She used the box to store Band-Aids in. Sonny found a couple of gauze pads among them. Al's cut was going to take something larger than a Band-Aid.

Sonny set the box down on the kitchen table. "We can use this gauze, but we're goin to need some tape. I thought there was some in here the last time I looked."

"I used it a few days ago, but I put it back," Raymond said.

Sonny was looking at him, but thinking about whether there was anything else they could use instead of adhesive tape when Raymond got a sneaky look on his face. His eyes dropped away from Sonny's, and he said, "No. Wait a minute. I know where it is." He left the room.

Sonny had to go back to the bathroom to get the bottle of iodine. The whole thing was taking a long time. He knew Al was wishing they would hurry up and get done fussing over her. And he had to get outside and tend to Buck and Ben. By the time he got back to Al, Raymond was there with the roll of tape.

"By God, Raymond," Sonny said, taking the tape and looking it over before he set it down on the table, "we don't need to ask who borrowed that."

"You can peel off the outside, for God's sakes. It's clean enough underneath."

"Well, I guess I'll have to." He took the lid off the iodine bottle. "Now, Al honey, give me that rag, and I'll put some of this here on it, and then we'll get you all done up." She handed him the rag. "Keep your eyes shut, honey. Here goes." He hurried to get the iodine on before the blood started flowing again. He couldn't tell whether it stung or not. She didn't flinch, but then she was pretty tough. He didn't like to ask if it hurt.

He took a last look at her cut. It was wide and crooked. He wouldn't want her to have a scar. He was just thinking they might do better to get her in to the emergency room after all, when he remembered an old trick of his mother's. He put down the rag and went over to the sink. Carol Ann had a basket of eggs on the counter. He got one out and broke it open in a cup. He ran some water over the largest eggshell and started to peel out the membrane that lay inside it. It was thin, almost transparent, hard to get a hold of with his stubby fingers. This was the kind of job he usually got Al to do for him.

"What's goin on, Gramps?" Raymond was staring at him with

a scared look on his face, like he thought Sonny had lost it completely, and it was going to be up to him to take over.

"Relax, Ray. I ain't crazy. I'm goin to put this over Al's cut. When it dries, it'll draw the sides together, so it don't make a scar."

"God, Gramps, that's weird. How'd you know to do that?"

"I remember my mother did it when someone got cut real bad. I can remember a couple of times."

"Do you think it'll work?" Raymond ran his hands one after the other through his curls. Al's eyes were open, watching them. A little trail of blood went from the cut across her cheek again.

"I don't know, Ray, but I think so. It can't hurt anyhow. We'll be done in just a minute, honey."

"It's okay, Gramps."

"That's my girl. I'll get this thing straightened out in a minute here."

Finally he got two pieces of the membrane smoothed out. He ran them under the water and sent Raymond for Carol Ann's sewing scissors.

"Here you go, Gramps. I'll take 'em back when you're done with 'em."

He cut the pieces the right shape. "Hold still now, girl, while I get these on. It's such a long gash, I got to do it in two pieces." He wiped over the cut one last time and spread the membranes over it, trying to smooth them down. It was worse than saran wrap. He'd get it all laid down in one place, and there would be a wrinkle in another. His eyes were too old, and his fingers too thick, and Raymond was breathing over his shoulder trying to see everything he did. Finally he got it more or less in place and laid gauze over it. Al never moved. It was hard to get the tape to stick in her hair. He had to use more than he wanted to.

"There," he said at last. "I hope that's not goin to give Carol Ann too much of a fright."

Raymond said, "I think it looks real good, Gramps."

"We don't need to tell Carol Ann about the egg. What do you

say, Ray? There ain't no sense gettin her any more worried than she's goin to be."

Al opened her eyes. "That's right, Dad. We can just say Gramps bandaged it up for me."

Raymond's eyes went back and forth from one to the other of them. "Oh sure, sure. As long as you're all right, baby."

"I'm fine, Dad." She started to stand, wobbled a little, caught hold of the table and let herself down again. "I'll be okay in a minute."

Sonny and Raymond got on each side of her and helped her to the couch in the front room. They just about had her settled when she remembered the unwashed pots and tried to get up again.

"Sit still, honey. It ain't even noon yet. You can do 'em later."

"But what if I forget? Ma's goin to be mad enough as it is."

Sonny and Raymond looked at each other. Raymond stood his curls up with both hands. Al was half-sitting and half-lying on the couch. Her eyes were closed, and her face was pale. It was obvious that she didn't feel all right, no matter what she said.

Sonny was about to motion to Raymond that they should sneak away without bothering her when Raymond said, "You just stay right there, Al. I'll do those pots for you, so you don't have to worry about your ma."

Al opened her eyes, but she didn't raise her head. "Gee, Dad, thanks. That would be great." Her eyes closed again, and they left the room.

9

It was warm outside, and the air smelled fresh. The sun was much brighter than it had been when Isabel went in. She followed Leroy down the sidewalk to his car, the huge American car she had seen last night outside Roxy's. When she opened the door, she could smell the leather upholstery. She got in and sank into the softness of the seat.

The car slid noiselessly into motion. Leroy looked over at her and smiled. He had a wonderful smile. "Now isn't this better than staying indoors, Chérie?"

"Yes," she said. "It's much better. Do you mind if I open my window?"

"Are you too hot?" He reached for the knobs that controlled the temperature.

"No. I just feel like being outside....well, the wind...." She took her hand away from the button, but the window went down anyway.

"Chérie, whatever you say. If you want wind, we will have wind."

"Thank you."

"There *is* air conditioning. Some women don't like their hair blown all over the place."

"I don't care about that. And I hate fake air."

He laughed. "The air is the same. It's just the temperature that changes."

"It smells like it came out of a machine."

"It has been filtered."

"Everything real's been taken out of it."

He laughed again. "That's funny. How could that be?"

"I don't know. It just feels like it."

Leroy laughed once more and pushed his hat back on his head so that he looked quite boyish. "Well, La Belle, whatever you say."

"Where are we going?"

"I have to go to a farm up above St. Johnsbury. It's a pretty drive, and I don't have to be at the farm very long. That's all I have to do. We can go anywhere else you would like to go. I'm at your service."

"I don't have anything to do. I had no plans."

"That's perfect, Chérie. We can spend the whole day together, getting to know each other."

"I'd like that."

"So would I." He looked around at her and smiled again.

"You are being awfully nice to me. I should think everyone in town would want to work for you."

"I wouldn't treat just anyone like this. I only give this kind of treatment to special people."

"Am I special then? How do you know? You don't know much about me."

"Tell me about yourself then."

Isabel looked out the window. They were going through North

Severance. She saw the post office and a garage with North Severance Volunteer Fire Department painted over the doors. Then there were some houses close to the road before the fields and woods began again. The car was so smooth that Isabel felt as though she was sitting still while the scenery unspooled before her.

"Well, Chérie?"

"Oh, I'm sorry. I was looking at North Severance."

"Not much to look at. It's pretty depressed. Tell me about yourself, about why you are here. I want to know everything about you."

"There isn't much to tell. I grew up in Shaker Heights. That's a suburb of Cleveland. There are a lot of people with money there, but our family didn't have all that much. I think our parents wanted to live there because the schools were good."

"I grew up without much of anything also. I decided when I grew up, I was going to do something about that." He paused for a minute. "And I have."

"Oh yes, Roxy told me all about you. She's very proud of you."

"Roxy and I grew up on a farm not too far from here. I got out of there as fast as I could."

"Don't you miss the country? I would think living on a farm…"

"Ah Chérie, I know that's your dream, but it can be very hard."

"When I left home, it was to go to Green Mountain College. But you know that already."

"That was a long time ago."

"Yes, it was. Twenty-five years ago last spring when we came to Jeff's reunion. I quit school when I married Jeff. What a painful mistake that was."

"I'm sorry."

"That's okay. The divorce is over now."

"If there was anything I could do to take the pain away, I

would do it." He reached over and patted her shoulder.

"Thank you. You are very kind."

"I mean it, Chérie."

"I know you do. I feel as though I have known you much longer than a day. I guess it's because you understand what it feels like."

"I do understand. I just wish there was something more I could do for you. If Jeff was around...."

"Well, I'm glad he's not. And anyway, it isn't all his fault. A divorce is a painful thing for everyone."

He reached out to pat her shoulder again, and this time he left his hand there on the headrest behind her head.

It felt so comfortable to be with him, gliding through the spring countryside past farmhouses with lilac bushes in bloom and fields turning green. It felt comfortable and right. She looked around at him. He was watching the road. His profile under the brim of his hat was dark and sharp against the bright green behind him. She was struck by his strangeness. "Why did you want me to work for you?" she said. "You don't have a lot of office work, do you?"

He laughed. "Just a hunch you would be good. I always play my hunches."

"Why?"

"If you don't play them, you might stop having them." He was quiet for a minute. "I don't know why. I just do. I guess I don't like to think about it. What do you do about yours?"

"I don't get hunches."

"What are you doing in Severance then?"

"What?"

"Isn't that a hunch—your decision to move here?"

"Would you call it that? I would call it an idea—an idea of the possibility of a different kind of life."

"What difference does it make what you call it—you're playing it out, aren't you?"

"I am?"

"Yes, Chérie. I think so."

"Do you really think so? I have wanted to change my life for a long time, and ever since I saw that farm, I have been determined to live like that, in the country, in harmony with nature."

"What makes you think it's like that in the country?"

"Well, isn't it? I mean, I saw it. I could feel the peace, the serenity. It was in the air—that old man....I mean, that's the way people are meant to live."

"I don't know, Chérie. If it's Carroll Trumbley you're talking about, he's a tough old bird and not all sweetness and light either."

"It isn't just *that* farm. This is something I have thought about for a long time. I've always known I would try it someday. I want...." She stopped.

He looked around. "Go on. What do you want?"

"Oh," she sighed. "I'm afraid I want so much. I want to unclog my brain, to get free of all the trivia our society teaches us to care about, to...." It was hard to make sense of what she wanted. "See, my boys are grown up. They don't need me any more. No one needs me any more, and I feel as though I haven't even started to live my own life."

There was a silence. She didn't look at him. "All right," she said. "I know what you're thinking. You can say it. It's just typical hippie ideas left over from the sixties. That's what you were going to say."

"No, I wasn't."

"That's what Jeff always says. Jeff says I'm still saying what the hippies used to say, and it just shows I never grew up." She was angry now, but it was Jeff she was angry at, not Leroy, who really seemed to understand.

Neither of them said anything after that, and the silence got stiffer and stiffer. Isabel began to be sorry for her outburst. When she looked over at Leroy, he kept his eyes on the road. She could see his cheek moving slightly as he clenched his jaw.

If she had thought about it, she would never have done such a thing, but without knowing she was going to, she reached over and touched the hard place on his cheek which was moving with the clenching of his jaw. "I'm sorry," she said. "I didn't mean you."

He didn't reply. He just shook his head a little, as though a fly was bothering him.

"Don't be mad," she said, but she pulled back her hand, surprised that she had been so forward with a stranger, and a little scared of him too.

There had been more houses along the road for a while now. They drove up a hill and down the other side into the middle of a town.

"Is this St. Johnsbury?"

"That's right, Chérie."

"It's lots bigger than I thought," she said, relieved that the awkward moment had passed.

The traffic light turned green. Leroy eased the big car around the corner onto the main street and slid it smoothly into a parking place that wasn't much longer than the car itself. Then he said, "I thought we would have lunch here."

"That's okay," Isabel said, "I don't...."

Leroy was opening his door. He looked around. "Chérie, we aren't going to have another good chance to stop. At least not for several hours."

"Well," Isabel said, "I mean, I hadn't planned...."

Leroy opened the door the rest of the way. "If that's all it is," he said, "don't worry about it. This is my treat." He got out of the car and shut his door.

Isabel sat there, embarrassed by the possibility that she might have tricked him into saying he would buy her lunch. And then he must have thought she was expecting him to wait on her too, because he came around to her side of the car and opened the door.

"No. I couldn't let you...."

He tilted his hat down over his eyes. "Isabel," he said. "Come on. I'm hungry."

She got out of the car obediently. Standing beside him, she was suddenly aware of how long and lanky he was. She could feel the strength in his thinness—flexible and tense like wire. He put his hand firmly in the small of her back to maneuver her along the sidewalk, and she went where she was guided without saying any more.

Part way down the block, he opened a dark door and stood aside to let her go first into the restaurant, a room with a low ceiling and tables covered with white tablecloths. Only a few of the tables were occupied. The hostess showed them to a table in the corner and left them alone.

Isabel said, "That's strange. Why do you suppose she stuck us way back here?"

Leroy took off his hat and set it carefully down on an empty chair beside him. "Would you like to sit some place else?"

"No. I don't care. I was just curious. There are so many empty tables. It's like she's ashamed of us or something."

"Not at all, Chérie. This is my table. I always sit at this table when I come in here." He hung his jacket over the back of the chair. "Sometimes it's nice to have the privacy." He searched her face with his eyes. "We can move if you want to."

"Oh, no. I'm sorry. I always seem to say the wrong thing."

She picked up her menu, but she couldn't see what she was reading. In spite of his romance with Renée and in spite of the fact that he was a married man, she knew he was attracted to her, and she had to admit to herself that it pleased her. She kept her eyes on the menu even though she didn't see it.

When she finally looked up, there was a waitress standing at their table with her pencil poised over her order book. She and Leroy were smiling at each other in a way that made Isabel feel as though she was the subject of their joke.

"Do you want some more time to make up your mind, Leroy?" the waitress said.

"I'll have what I always have. But maybe...." He looked at

Isabel doubtfully. "Do you want Jackie to come back in a few minutes?"

"No. It wouldn't do any good. I can't decide." She looked at Leroy helplessly.

He turned to the waitress and said, "We'll both have the steaks then. Be sure they're careful not to overcook them." He studied Isabel over the top of the menu. "You want it rare, of course."

"Do I?"

"Yes," he said. "You do."

A minute after she left, the waitress was back with two tall glasses of beer. Isabel started to protest.

Leroy held up his hand. "Don't worry about it. Just drink what you want, and I'll have the rest." He paused, looking into her face. "Unless you would rather I didn't drink out of your glass."

"Oh no, not at all." But she looked down. There seemed to be so many overtones and hidden meanings.

After a few minutes she decided she was being silly. She looked up and said, "You must come to St Johnsbury a lot."

"What makes you say that?"

"Because you have your own table here, and they know you by name and everything."

"Not a lot, but over the years it mounts up."

"Do you come on business?"

"You ask a lot of questions, Chérie. You know that?"

"Oh well, I didn't mean.... I was only trying to make conversation."

"I don't mind. Yes, I have some business in St. J. I also have relatives here." He gave her a significant look. "And from time to time, I have had friends here."

Isabel was saved from having to reply by the arrival of two large platters of steak.

Leroy laughed with pleasure when the waitress set the plate down in front of him. He picked up his knife and fork. "I hope you are as hungry as I am. They really know how to do a steak here." He took a large bite. "It's always good. And the meat is local. How is yours? Is it cooked right?"

Isabel took a bite. "It's delicious," she said. "I didn't know how hungry I was. It's been so long since I've had meat. I thought I didn't like it any more."

"Well, let me know if you want something else, Chérie. I wouldn't be pleased with myself if I didn't get you what you wanted."

"That's nice of you."

"Yes, but it's something more also. I think I know how to treat a woman when she's with me. And that's a matter of pride. It's because I'm French." He smiled. "And what nationality are you?"

"My father's family was Polish."

"So that explains why you have this lovely wide face, like a madonna—you get it from your Polish father."

"And my grandmother was Italian, from the north."

"When I was a boy in North Severance, we had two churches, the Polish church and the French church. The Bishop wanted to combine the two, because there weren't that many people in either one. They wanted to sell our church because the Polish church was nicer."

"What happened?"

"They finally did sell it, but not until after I was grown and had moved to Severance. For a long time the people wouldn't stand for it. The two groups didn't get along. I never told anybody, but I always thought their church had the best statue of the Holy Mother. She had the same sweet smile you have."

"Is there only one church in town now?"

"Just one for Catholics. They sold our church."

"I wonder which statue is in it."

"I can't remember. Maybe they kept both of them. It has been so long. I haven't been out there in quite a while."

"It's an interesting story."

"I haven't thought about it for years. Your smile brought it back."

Isabel leaned forward. "Do you think I'm making a mistake?"

"What kind of mistake, Chérie?"

"Do you think I'm not really doing what I meant to do? I mean I intended to learn to live in the country, and I'm not really doing it, am I?"

"I guess I don't understand, Chérie."

"Oh," she sighed, "it's just that I meant to live in the country....and I'm not. Severance is almost as big as Abingdon. And I meant to get a job working on the land. That was one reason I waited until spring to come here. But I'm not doing that either. I'm going to be working in town and in an office. See what I mean?"

"Chérie. How long have you been in Severance?"

"Almost a week. It'll be a week next Tuesday."

"That's nothing. Give yourself some time."

"But don't you see—I'm going in the wrong direction. I'm starting to make a life that's like the one I had before, and I meant things to be different."

"I think you're doing fine. Don't be impatient. You sound like a twenty-year-old."

"I feel like that. I know it's silly, but I feel as though I'm just starting out, that I haven't done anything yet, that I haven't really had a chance until now, but now I can really *do* something with my life, and I don't want to waste it." She laughed uncomfortably. "The funny thing is, I didn't feel that way when I was twenty. I was too scared when I quit school to marry Jeff. I knew my parents wouldn't approve, and I was afraid I wouldn't have the nerve to go ahead with it if they told me not to. And after that it seemed like getting over one obstacle just lined me up to deal with the next one. I don't remember having time to think about anything but what I would need to deal with next, even before my boys were born." She took a big gulp of air. "But you don't want to hear about all this. I know you don't."

"You can talk to me, Chérie. I'll always understand. You don't need to feel alone while I'm around."

"Oh that's so nice. I really appreciate that." She was leaning toward him across the table until she happened to glance around and see that the waitress was standing by the kitchen door with two others, and they were all watching her and Leroy. She sat back.

Leroy said, "Can I get you something else? Dessert maybe? Coffee?"

"Thank you," she said. "Coffee would be nice."

He raised his hand and snapped his fingers for the waitress.

When the coffee was there and the waitress gone, Isabel said, "That's why I don't want to get side-tracked by things that don't matter. I mean if I was twenty now, I would have time for things like clothes, like what I looked like."

"Chérie, listen to me, it *always* matters what a woman looks like."

"Yes, at least I'm afraid I still care. I look in the mirror and worry about what I'm going to wear, but I'm trying to get over it."

"Oh no, Chérie. Don't say that. Believe me—I'm older than you are, and I know what I'm saying—a woman is never too old...."

"It's not that exactly," Isabel said. She was touched by the concern on his face. "Although of course there's an aspect of it that's related to my age. I mean, it's time for me to go on to something else. See?"

"Remember that I'm here."

"That's comforting. But don't get me wrong. I mean, I have my sons, and I really miss them, both of them, although I think I'm closer to Nicky. He has gotten to be a good friend. I can talk to him about anything...." She hesitated because it suddenly came into her head that she wouldn't tell Nicky about Leroy, wouldn't or couldn't, she wasn't sure which it was, and she didn't want to think about it. "I miss Joey too. He's...."

Leroy said, "Shall we go? We still have to get to the Edmunds farm. We can continue this conversation in the car."

"I would like that."

"So would I."

Isabel went into the bathroom. When she came out, she caught up with Leroy at the cash register near the door. He was just putting his money away. Isabel noticed the thick roll of bills and also how he tried to keep it from being conspicuous.

Neither of them said anything until they were in the car. Then Isabel said, "Thank you. You know, that was a wonderful lunch. I don't know what I expected this morning, but it certainly wasn't anything like this. So much has happened since I got to Severance. It seems like a long time ago, even though it has only been a few days."

Leroy turned toward her with his generous smile.

"And this is how I repay you," she went on, "by talking only about myself. I don't mean to be selfish. You can't think how nice it is to have someone who feels like listening. And I hardly know anything about you, although...." She stopped, suddenly afraid she had said too much.

"Although what, Chérie? You didn't finish."

"It was nothing."

"But please." He looked around at her. "I'd like to know."

"All right. I'll tell you....but don't get mad. Okay?"

"Agreed."

"Okay. I just suddenly thought how you were my new boss and that wasn't the way to talk to your boss." She paused and then hurried on. "You don't mind?"

"Of course not." He reached over to touch her shoulder and then left his arm lying along the back of the seat.

She was so comfortable and full of good food, and it felt so natural to be there with him, that she had to struggle to keep from falling asleep. After a little while she said, "You seem very old-fashioned somehow."

He laughed. "Why?"

"I don't know—maybe all of Vermont belongs in the nineteenth century."

"Oh?"

"And you are so black and white."

"Because I wear a black jacket and a white shirt?"

"Oh maybe, but....okay, listen to this. I bet you were a very strict father. I bet you laid down the law to your children."

Leroy chuckled a little. "Yes, you could say I was old-fashioned. Still, I think it paid off. My kids didn't turn out the way a lot of kids do these days—destroyed by drugs. They had to do what I said, yes, that *is* true." After a while he said, "I didn't let my girls date when they were in high school."

"You didn't?"

"No. That's too young. Girls don't know how to protect themselves. I didn't want my girls....well, you probably remember experiences of your own. I didn't want any daughter of mine ending up like Roxy." He glanced around at her. "You know what I mean."

"Yes, but....well, that's not so bad. Roxy is nice."

"I know. Rox is a good old girl, and she's family, and I wouldn't say this to very many people either, but she's a no-good too, and everyone in town knows it. I couldn't have my girls turning out like that."

"I only had boys, so I didn't have to worry about any of that," Isabel said, feeling sorry for Leroy's daughters. How much they must have missed.

"Your reputation matters. And it wasn't just theirs. It would have reflected on the whole family. You know?"

"Yes. I guess so."

"Good," he said. "I'm glad of that, because it's important. People think it isn't, but it is." After a minute he said, "I suppose that's old-fashioned too."

"That's what I was trying to say before. That's what I have felt about you since I met you." She looked over at his sharp profile under the black brim. "There's a recklessness too, of course. I mean, I wasn't implying I thought you were stodgy." He looked at her. "Because I don't think so....not at all."

He had a way of looking very directly and very hard, as though he were looking right through the surface to something more important underneath. Isabel regretted feeling sorry for his daughters.

He smiled. "Thanks. I'm glad you don't think I'm stodgy, Chérie."

"Oh no, not at all," she said, but suddenly she felt shy. "Did you say we were going to a farm?"

"Yes. Luke Edmunds' place. It's not too far from here."

"A dairy farm?"

"He has cows."

"Oh, that's great. I *knew* this was the right way to get to know....I can't tell you *when* I was on a real dairy farm. What kind of cows?"

"I don't know."

"You don't? I would have thought that was important, the kind of thing everyone would know." She laughed. "That just shows how much *I* know about it, doesn't it?"

She looked over at Leroy, but he wasn't laughing. He was staring straight ahead at the road. Isabel began to think he might be embarrassed to arrive at this farm with her, that he was regretting his generous offer to take her along.

She was wide awake now. "Why don't I wait in the car?" she said quietly.

"What?" He looked startled.

"When you go in to talk to the people at the farm. I was thinking I would probably be in the way if I came with you, but I could wait in the car." She was picturing a neat white farmhouse and a neat farm family. She wished she was dressed like Renée.

Leroy looked around at her for a minute, coldly, appraisingly. Then he turned back to the road and said in a harsh voice, "If you don't want to be involved, why did you agree to work for me?"

"I....I don't know what you mean. I don't want to be in the way."

Leroy didn't say anything. When Isabel looked around at him, she saw that his jaw was clenched. He turned the car off the highway onto a small, town road and soon after that onto an even smaller unpaved road that went steeply uphill. There were trees arching over the road, trees which were still brown and bare, as though the spring weather hadn't really gotten there yet. The road got rougher, full of ruts and potholes, so that Leroy had to pick his way along, driving on whichever side seemed the smoothest at the moment. His mouth was shut in a tight line, and his hat was tilted down to shadow his eyes.

Isabel wondered why they were taking such a lonely road, but she didn't like to ask. They went past several trailers set in temporary-looking clearings. The road was still going up. The lovely mood of sleepy peace had blown away, and it was her fault somehow. She had been feeling so at home with him and so comfortable, that she hadn't been paying enough attention. This was the result.

And then the road came out of the woods. On Isabel's side was a jumbled stone wall and beyond it a scrubby field, which sloped so steeply downhill that sitting in the car on the road, she could see over the tops of the trees growing at the bottom of it to a blue and silver ribbon of river in the valley, and beyond that to ranked rows of slate-blue hills in the distance.

Leroy stopped the car and turned in his seat, looking past her out the window. "That's New Hampshire over there. That river is the Connecticut."

"What an incredible view," she said, thinking that the place was so beautiful that it made everything all right again.

"Something needs to be done about this road. I'd hate to come up it in an ordinary car."

"Wouldn't this field be a wonderful place to build a house?"

"Yes," Leroy said. "The thing about a view is that you can sell it for so much, and it costs you nothing."

"I don't know about selling it. I think it would be a beautiful place to live."

"That's right, Chérie." He started up the car again. "That's what I mean."

At the end of the field the trees closed in again. Then on the high side of the road they came to a dilapidated house, and to Isabel's surprise, Leroy drove in the driveway and stopped.

He got out of the car and nodded to her across the shimmering expanse of the car's hood, and she knew that meant she was to come with him. She got out of the car and followed him across the muddy yard.

The house was old. It looked abandoned. It was covered with cheap siding which was scored to look like bricks, but the thin sheets were pulling away from the walls in a way bricks wouldn't have done. There were flat stepping-stones across the mud. Isabel followed Leroy, wondering what he was doing here.

The porch step was a chunk of wood, a section of tree trunk with the bark still on it. Leroy stepped up easily and then reached out to help her. Steadying herself with his hand, she stepped onto the wobbly stump and from there to the porch, which was large and filled with junk, mostly cardboard boxes stacked on top of old furniture.

Someone had stapled sheets of plastic between the posts of the porch to keep out the weather, but the plastic was torn in so many places that it was useless. The ragged edges flapped together with a brittle sound.

Leroy knocked on the door, rattling the pane of glass. "I don't dare knock any harder," he said. "This glass could pop right out."

"Does anyone live here?"

"They're here." He opened the door a little way and stuck his head inside. "I can hear the television going. Hello? Anybody home?"

"What are we doing anyway?"

Leroy looked around at her. "This is what we came for, Chérie."

"This is the Edmunds farm?"

"That's right." He pointed down the length of the porch. "The barn's over there, across the road."

Isabel went to the edge of the porch and looked out, past the flapping plastic. Beside the road and leaning over it was an old red barn so tall Isabel had to kink her head around, and even then she couldn't see the top. For a second she felt disoriented—it was so big, and she hadn't even noticed it when they drove up.

"How funny," she said. "I pictured this place so differently when you said it was a dairy farm."

"How so, Chérie?"

"Well, I....more open fields maybe, and things not so....not so messy, maybe."

Leroy smiled. "If it was like you said, they might not need to sell out."

Leroy was still standing by the door which he had left open a few inches when he turned around to speak. Isabel saw his smile, and then she looked past him at a pinched and pale face that hung moonlike in the dirty glass of the door. Leroy must have seen her startled look because he whirled around, drawing up his hands. His briefcase fell to the floor. A second later he had recovered himself and was smiling and tipping his hat to the face in the glass. It happened so quickly that Isabel would have thought she had made up the whole thing, except that the briefcase still lay on the floor. She went over and picked it up. Leroy didn't notice. He had pushed the door further open and was facing the teenaged girl inside.

"Is your daddy at home, Chérie?"

"Sondra, not Sherry," the girl said, looking sullen.

"Okay, Sondra, could I talk to your daddy, do you think?" He turned to Isabel and held out his hands for the briefcase, rolling his eyes a bit to let Isabel in on the joke.

"He might be over to the barn."

Leroy tilted his hat and smiled at the girl again, but she closed the door without offering any comment, without noticing the smile.

"So, Isabel, let's see if Edmunds is in his barn."

"All right."

Leroy went first, stepping to the stump and then to the ground. He held out his hand to steady Isabel and then put his arm around her briefly as they walked to the car. "I'm glad you are here with me, Chérie. It makes it so much nicer." He tossed his briefcase in through the window of his car, and started down the driveway toward the road and the barn.

Isabel followed, walking slowly to avoid the muddy ruts and puddles.

There were two large barn doors on the roadside held shut by a rusty chain, but Leroy didn't hesitate. He walked past them and around the side of the barn.

By the time Isabel got to the corner, Leroy had followed the path down a steep bank toward the back. She could see him up ahead, walking under burdock stalks taller than he was.

There was a sound of metal banging on metal. The sun warmed the wall of the barn that rose so high above, and the air was full of the buzzing of flies and the country smell of cow manure. There were rusty pieces of machinery and faded red barn boards lying under the burdocks. Isabel slowed down, trying to notice everything. This was the country, and she was in it. Then her foot slipped and when she jerked her arms out for balance, both sleeves of her sweater got stuck with burdocks. She was looking down, trying to pull them off when she went around the back corner of the barn and walked right into Leroy. She said, "Jesus," before she could stop herself.

Leroy said nothing, but he spun around and grabbed her by the shoulders. For a second he had her in a tight grip, almost lifting her off the ground. Then she could feel his fingers relax, and he smiled down at her and said, "Are you all right, Chérie? What were you doing, anyway?"

Except for the feeling in her shoulders where his fingers had tightened, she would have thought he was perfectly calm. "I guess I wasn't watching...."

He gave her shoulders a little shake and dropped his hands. "That's all right, Chérie. I'm glad to be of service. If I hadn't stopped you, see what you would have walked into." He turned, gesturing.

Isabel wanted to rub her shoulders where she could still feel the grip of his hands, but even though he was looking the other way, she didn't dare. He might notice that she minded. She looked past him. At the corner of the barn, the ground changed abruptly. The hard-packed path sloped down into soft, black muck, pocked by the footprints of cows. Out in the middle of the mud was a tractor and a manure spreader. In the spreader a mud-colored man with a hammer in his hand stood looking at them.

Leroy said, "Hello, Luke. Your girl said I'd find you here."

The man lowered the hammer and squinted at them. "Is that you there, Mr. ....?"

"Leroy," said Leroy.

"Well, Mr. Leroy, I didn't expect to see *you* down here."

"I get around," Leroy said. "You can expect to see me wherever you see me. I've done my share of barn chores."

The man jumped out of the spreader and waded toward them in slow motion. "This is really great," he said. The mud sucked and popped around each foot as he pulled it out. When he reached solid ground, he stopped and began to wipe his hand back and forth on the leg of his trousers, but since his trousers were almost as covered with mud and manure as his hand was, he didn't make it much cleaner. He wiped a few strokes, inspected his hand and wiped again.

Finally he offered his hand to Leroy who took it without hesitation and said, "Nice to see you, Luke. And this is Isabel, who works in my office."

Luke's round face swung slowly in her direction. He grinned and nodded. Isabel was glad he didn't offer her his hand. She couldn't have been as cool as Leroy.

"I see you're having trouble with your spreader," Leroy said.

Luke's mouth tightened. His grin got stiff and uncomfortable. "Aw, the g. d. thing—I can't get it to engage. I been workin on it half the day."

"Sounds to me like you might have a broken chain."

"I hope not. I'd have to unload the s. o. b. by hand. Excuse my French." He looked at Isabel.

"That's okay."

"I've poked around underneath a bit, cause I been worried it might be the chains. I got to move it to higher ground and take another look, but as near as I can tell, they're okay. It's got some other problems too. It's always somethin, ain't it?"

Leroy nodded. He dug at the dirt of the path with the toe of his cowboy boot, but he didn't seem restless or impatient. And he didn't seem to have any particular reason for being there, although Isabel knew that this conversation was the whole purpose of their trip.

"Things is a whole lot better since warm weather got here. Charlene was real bad there last winter." He looked at Leroy and waited, but Leroy said nothing. "Like I say, she's improved so much, that I guess I ain't got nothin to complain about." He stopped and looked at Leroy again.

"That's good news, Luke. I'm glad to hear it."

Luke's eyes rolled white, as though he was trying to look everywhere at once. Then he focused on Leroy again and seemed calmer. Leroy's face was empty of expression, shadowed under the black hat.

"Actually when I looked up and seen you standin there, I thought you might have some good news for us. And, boy, we need it. We're sure in trouble. I know that."

"Well, I didn't mean to get your hopes up."

Luke's eyes looked as though they were going to pull themselves away from Leroy's face and start rolling again. "You mean you don't got good news?"

Leroy smiled stiffly. "You know the old expression: 'no news is good news'? That's the only kind of good news I've got. I just stopped in to say hello."

"Aw, that's real bad. I was hopin...." His eyes went white again.

Leroy said, "I'm sorry, Luke. You know what the economy is these days. Real estate's just not moving like it was. I'm sure it's temporary."

"Yeah, but...."

"I'm sure you don't have to worry. We haven't had any interest yet, but we've been doing all we can for you."

"I'm sure you have, Mr. Leroy. I'm sure you have. It's just that I don't know how long we can hold out. We need the money bad."

Leroy pushed back his cowboy hat and scratched his head. In his concern, he looked boyish and accessible. "Well, Luke, I know things are tough. They're tough all over. Of course I'm doing everything I can." He paused and drew a circle in the dirt with the toe of his boot. He looked troubled. "Listen, if you've got time to come up to my car, I'd like to show you something."

"Sure," Luke said. "I ain't got nothin but time." He looked around for a place to put the hammer, and then laid it carefully in the middle of the path.

Leroy gave Isabel a sweet smile. "You don't mind, do you? I think this will make him feel better."

"Oh no, I'd be glad," said Isabel, wishing she could be as sympathetic as Leroy was able to be.

They went up the path to the road and across it to the car, Leroy first with long strides, and then Isabel. By the time Luke got to the car, Leroy had his briefcase open on the seat and was taking out papers.

"Come over here, Luke, and see what you think of this." He took a handful of brochures over to the hood of his car where he unfolded one and smoothed it out.

Luke stepped up beside him, but instead of looking down at the paper, his eyes wandered over the sleek surface of the car, through the windshield to the plush interior. His mouth was slightly open, but he didn't say anything.

Leroy straightened up, knocked his hat back, and looked around at Luke. "I think you should take a look here at what we've done for you. Here's your house in our 'Century Farms' series."

Luke stared at the bright paper like a solemn child.

"See here, we've done this whole brochure just on your place. Doesn't it look great?"

Luke nodded. "It's amazin," he said.

Isabel leaned over their shoulders trying to see also, but the sun was on the page, and the pictures were small, and she couldn't see much. She hoped Leroy would move over to make room for her, but he didn't, and she didn't like to ask.

"I have some copies of this brochure for you." He folded up the paper, and put the whole stack in Luke's dirty hand.

"Oh no, that's okay. You don't need to...." He was holding them delicately, trying not to touch them any more than he had to, offering them back to Leroy.

Leroy pushed his hand away. "We want you to have them. Show them to anybody you like. We got plenty of them made to distribute. You see, we believe in doing all we can for you."

"Thank you, sir. I really appreciate it."

Leroy held out his hand to Luke, and they shook. "Well, it's good to see you. Hang in there. I know things are tough." He held onto Luke's hand and patted it. "You must be patient. It's all going to be fine. I can promise you that." He turned to Isabel. "Well, Chérie, we have a long drive ahead of us. We'd better get going."

Luke stood watching while they got in the car. Leroy started the engine, and then he opened his window a little more. "Don't hesitate to call about anything, any time." He smiled and touched his hat and backed the car smoothly out into the road.

When they were heading down the hill again and the Edmunds house was out of sight behind them, Isabel said, "You made him feel better."

"He'll feel better soon. I think we can make him an offer almost any time now. But...." He looked at her. After a minute, he said, "Thank you, Chérie. I'm glad you think I was nice to him."

"There was so much poverty. That's not my picture of a farm. It's hard for me to see it. But *you* didn't seem to have that trouble."

"I grew up on a farm like that. My dad used to work like that. He was a good man."

"Like that? All his life?"

"No, not all his life. He's still alive, but he....his mind is gone." Leroy's jaw got tight. "He's out in Sherwood Manor right now. That's one of the best nursing homes around. He's much happier there than he would be any place else." After a pause, he went on. "I pay for everything. He has all the extras. He could even have a single room if he wanted it. But when I go out to see him, he cries. He never used to cry. His mind is truly gone."

"That is too bad."

"It's very sad, but what can I do? I try not to think about it. He used to be a very good man." He sighed.

"I'm so sorry."

"Thank you, Chérie. You don't know how much that means to me."

Neither of them said much on the way home, but the silence was companionable. Isabel was thinking about the poverty of the Edmunds farm and how caring Leroy had been and how he was such a strong person. It felt exciting and a bit dangerous to be with him, and yet she felt that he would take good care of her.

10

IT WAS JUST getting dark outside when Leroy came out after supper. He drew in a deep breath. The clear spring air made him feel better. Of course it wasn't that he wasn't the master in his own house, but there were rubs, sore places that he couldn't say anything about. He got into his car and slammed the door hard, cheered a little by its solid sound. Like the way she cooked a nice meal just for him and sat across the table to watch him eat it. As always, tonight he suggested that she join him, and as always, she said that she had already eaten some and just wasn't hungry. And what could he say to that? How did he know whether she was hungry or not? Still, he couldn't help feeling there was a hidden message, that it was a way of reminding him of how different she was, a way of holding him at a distance. She had so many ways of pushing him away. But she was always careful to do it so that he couldn't say anything about it.

For some time he cruised smoothly through town without thinking where he was going. It was nice to be with the big Lincoln while he let the irritations work themselves out of his head. After a while he thought he would like to see what was going on at the Country Club Bar. May thought Carol Ann was going out tonight, so he hadn't left the packet he made up for her. It would be convenient if he could run into her tonight. He turned on Maple Avenue and headed back downstreet. At the same time he knew running into Carol Ann was just an excuse he told himself, easier than trying to explain his restlessness tonight, his wish to be with lots of people who were restless the way he was.

There weren't any parking places out front, so he drove around to the back. That probably meant there was a pretty good crowd there already. It was better not to have his car out front anyway. It wasn't that he was sneaking around, just that it wasn't anybody's business whether he went to a bar on a Saturday night, and everybody knew his car.

They wouldn't let anyone come in through the back door any more, so he had to walk around to the front. When he opened the door, a blast of music and voices and the clinking of glasses came swirling out into the street on the warm, smoky air. He went inside and ordered himself a Scotch and water at the bar. There were only two or three empty stools. He saw some familiar faces, but nobody he really wanted to talk to, so he stayed where he was, standing at the end of the bar. He nursed his drink and looked around, getting used to the dynamics of the scene, like testing the temperature of the water before jumping in. Every night had its own story line, even though the scene and the people were mostly the same.

By the time he finished his drink, they had shut off the juke-box. He could hear the band tuning up in the back room. He paid for his drink and pushed his way down the narrow hallway. The hall was always crowded because the bathrooms were there, and the waitresses had to go through to serve the customers in the back. It was a terrible set-up. If it was his place, that bottleneck would be the first thing he would change. Not that he would like to run a bar—too many headaches for too small a return. He had to stop to let a tight knot of people decide where they were going, and someone touched him on the shoulder. He turned around. It was Joyce Morrison.

"Hello, Leroy. It's been a long time."

"Too long, Chérie," he said, because he knew what she meant, and he knew what she wanted to hear.

She started in with, "I've been wondering...."

But he cut her off. "You are looking more beautiful than ever." He let his eyes travel over her, touching her, admiring her. She had on tight black pants and a spangled shirt open at the neck. In her clothes she looked so thin, skinny almost, but underneath there was always more flesh, more softness than you expected.

The group of people was moving now toward the front room, and a man said, "Come on, Joyce."

She gave him a long, hungry look. "I'll see you soon, Leroy. Okay?"

He liked the way she always seemed half-starved for everything. He said, "Soon, Chérie," and went on into the back room. He knew he didn't mean it. It had gotten to that stage where it was complicated, where she wanted more from him than just his company, where, no longer satisfied with the way things were, she was beginning to make serious demands.

He stopped just inside the back room to let his eyes get used to the dark. The only light in the room came from the spotlights on the band. Across the empty dance floor a fox-faced man with long hair was tuning his guitar. The other members of the band were arranging chairs and instruments. Leroy stopped by the railing to check out the booths. About half of them were full. The other half of them would fill up fast when the band got going.

He had known he would find Carol Ann here. When he missed her at the Texas, and May said she had gone home early because she had plans for tonight, he had known what those plans would be.

Carol Ann and Raymond were sitting alone. Leroy walked around to their booth. His boots clicked in a satisfying way on the wooden floor.

"You look incredible tonight, Chérie," he said, looking down at Carol Ann. All of her that he could see above the table was covered with large, bright flowers. She probably thought she looked great like that, covered, like a piece of furniture.

On his side of the booth, Raymond moved over to make more room. "Take a load off your feet, Leroy," he said.

"Thanks, Ray." Leroy slid in beside him. "How's the band? Any good?"

"I don't know." Raymond flashed his crazy, crooked grin. "I...." He looked over at Carol Ann. "We never heard 'em before." He reached his hand part way across the table toward hers, but she was busy picking up her drink. Raymond eased his hand back a bit and looked at Leroy to see if he noticed.

Leroy pretended to be concentrating on the band. "I hope they're good," he said.

Carol Ann took a delicate sip of her drink. She acted as though she really didn't like the taste of it at all, but Leroy suspected that was just Carol Ann's idea of refined manners.

The band played a few opening chords, and then the guitar player introduced the others. Leroy looked over at Raymond, and Raymond nudged him with his elbow.

The band swung into their first song, and Leroy turned to Carol Ann to ask her what she thought, but she couldn't hear what he said. Raymond was smiling and nodding his head.

Leroy looked down at his hands, and when he looked up again, both Raymond and Carol Ann were looking intently toward the dance floor. He turned to see, and there was Roxy dancing with Ely Singleton, right out in the middle with no other couple on the floor. They might as well have had a spotlight on them. Leroy hadn't even known she was in the place, although he should have guessed. Roxy, of course, was making a spectacle of herself, a real sideshow that everybody in the booths was enjoying. He turned around to look at Raymond, but Raymond dropped his eyes to the table. Carol Ann wouldn't look at him either. He turned back to watch. They were dancing with their arms around each other, pressed tightly together. Ely kept trying to kiss her, and she coyly avoided his lips, while at the same time she managed to make it clear that she wanted him to keep trying. It was quite a performance. This was just the kind of thing he had been trying to explain to Isabel in the afternoon.

Of course, it was nothing new to have Roxy make a fool of herself in public, but hadn't he warned her about Ely Singleton just last night? Everyone in town knew he was a drunk and a bum. She always had bad taste in men. Reggie Fox was a good example, and she had *married* him. Even so, she seemed to be sinking lower all the time, and after he had told her to stay away from Ely Singleton too. She probably even knew he was here watching. He would have to make her pay for this.

A waitress walked by, so he stopped her and ordered himself another Scotch and water and a round for Carol Ann and Raymond. They both smiled at him. There was no use in words. The music was too loud.

Raymond held up his cigarette pack, and Carol Ann frowned back at him, so he asked Leroy to let him out, and he went off to look for a place to smoke. Leroy felt the folded papers in his jacket pocket. They were ready to hand to her. He could do it without speaking, but he could hear that the song was coming to an end. He couldn't have planned it more conveniently. He looked at Carol Ann. She was watching the dance floor with her mouth slightly open. He turned to see what she saw. He had forgotten about Roxy for a moment, but there she and Ely were, finishing the dance with a passionate 1940's-style kiss. The music stopped, and people clapped and cheered and whistled. Carol Ann looked over at him with sympathy and curiosity.

He just had time to say, "There's no fool like an old fool," before the band started up again. He was grateful that the singer didn't make it worse with some comment, because it had to be good for the band, an extra piece of the show. He would have to make Roxy pay for this embarrassment sooner or later; that was certain.

Carol Ann was sipping her drink delicately and with distaste. He slid the envelope across the table toward her. She looked at it and at him, and then recognition of what it was spread over her face, and she nodded her thanks to him. The new drinks arrived as she was dropping the papers into her purse, and Raymond came back just then.

Leroy paid for the drinks with a twenty that he pulled off his roll of bills. He managed to appear very discreet and still see that Raymond and Carol Ann got a good look at the twenty and the rest of the roll. He left a couple of dollars on the table for a tip, so they could see how generous he was. It never hurt to cover the bases. Advertising money was what he called it, but only to himself.

They sat without trying to talk, sipping their drinks. When the band started into a slow number, Carol Ann and Raymond went out to dance. Leroy only had time for one more swallow of his drink before Joyce was there. When he felt a hand on his shoulder, he almost jumped and came up swinging, but he stopped himself in time. Raymond had offered him the seat, so he took it, but he didn't like to sit with his back to the door. He always wanted to know who was coming before they got there.

Joyce was standing so close that he couldn't see her face. "Will you dance with me, Leroy?" She swayed against him. "Just once. Please."

He felt the old hunger for her, and he stood up beside her. He knocked his hat back with his knuckles and took a sip of his drink, so that she wouldn't think he was eager to hold her. "All right," he said. He took off his jacket and his hat and laid them on the seat. "Let's go."

They walked out onto the dance floor. He had his hand on the small of her back, and he could feel her body moving beneath it. Then they were dancing, and he could feel the whole length of her pressed against him.

"You are good, Joyce, very good," he said in her ear.

"I was standing in the doorway, waiting for them to leave," she said breathlessly. "Stan thinks I'm in the bathroom."

"You want to be careful, Chérie."

"I can't help it, Leroy."

He stepped back a little; he had to be the one to make that kind of decision.

"Maybe I could meet you some place later, Leroy? I've got to see you. I think I could sneak out when Stan gets to sleep or something."

Leroy didn't say anything.

"Please. I could meet you at your room. I need you, Leroy."

She was still pressing close, trying to move against him, talking into his ear, but he was beginning not to like it so much. He didn't ever like to be crowded by anyone.

The song was ending. Joyce pressed even harder against him. "I want you, Leroy. I'm desperate."

The music stopped, and he turned her loose with a small shove because she clung to him. It could be noticeable in that group of couples who were stepping apart from each other. "It's impossible tonight, Chérie," he said firmly, although he began to regret his decision as soon as he heard himself. When she was this hungry, it was always very good. It was only afterward, when she was satisfied, that the nagging started. And he really needed a woman tonight to take away the restlessness that overwhelmed him. He guided her gently into the crowd that was leaving the dance floor. When they got to the door into the hallway, he gave her another little push and said, "Thanks, Chérie. Say hello to Stan for me."

She looked up at him pleading, and he stared back with a harsh expression. All around were people who knew them both, and in the absence of the loud music, they had no privacy to say anything to each other.

He turned and went back to his drink. She had woken up the hunger and discontent, but, by God, he wasn't going to be so indiscreet as to start something here in front of everyone, with her husband right out in the next room. And he wasn't going to sneak around under her bedroom windows waiting for Stan to fall asleep either.

Raymond and Carol Ann were not back at the booth. He looked around the crowd of dancing couples and saw them, a thin dark shape with a bright, upholstered one. Roxy was out there too, bouncing around and looking foolish. He downed the rest of his drink without sitting and put on his jacket and hat.

He had done what he came in to do, and he didn't feel like being here any more. He might as well go home. He figured he would just go out the back door so he didn't have to see Joyce again. If he stayed, she would be back, and everyone would notice. He didn't get where he was by being indiscreet. He'd hardly ever made a fool of himself over a woman, and he wasn't going to start at his age.

He headed toward the back door. He looked down into the last booth and saw Renée and George, remembering then that when he was dancing, he thought he saw her there and meant to look again and forgot. She looked up at him, smiling an unguarded smile which might have been meant for George beside her. The sweetness of it stopped him in his tracks, and he smiled back, nodding curtly at George. He didn't mean to be rude to George, who was an all-right guy, although not nearly good enough to deserve Renée, but he couldn't help it; he was caught off balance by the sweetness of that smile. He stood like a block of wood and watched while she put her lips up close to George's ear and said something to him. They both smiled. She gave George a quick kiss on the temple, and he stood up beside Leroy, so she could slide out of the booth.

Renée didn't look at either of them again. She walked right past Leroy, headed for the back door, and he followed. That happened so often between them. They communicated without words or gestures. They both knew what they were going to do next. If any other woman had whispered to her boyfriend in his presence, Leroy would have fumed. He might have tried to even the score somehow, but not with Renée. They understood each other too well for that.

Outside the parking lot was dark, and the air seemed transparent, it was so clear. The music and laughter swirled behind him with the smoke.

"Get me something to keep the door open, Chérie."

"Let it go, Leroy. I don't care. I'll go around front. I'd rather have the quiet."

He let go of the door, and it slammed shut with an aggressive click. He looked at Renée, and she shrugged.

"Are you cold, Chérie? We could sit in my car."

"No. It's nice out here. It clears my head."

They walked over to his car anyway. Her high heels made a sharper sound on the pavement than his boots did, but even so, he noticed that they walked in step with each other and in time with the music.

"I'm glad you're not mad at me any more."

"I wasn't mad at you."

"What about this morning? At the office?"

"Oh that," she said. She leaned back against the hood of his car and looked up at him. Her arms were folded across her chest. "I saw you dancing with Joyce Morrison."

"One dance only, Chérie."

"But what a way to dance! You never dance with me like that."

His jaw clenched. His first thought was what a night it was turning out to be. He really didn't need the aggravation. But then he stopped himself and thought about it and was able to say, "No, I don't. That doesn't mean I wouldn't like to, but that's the way it is." He shut his mouth with a snap.

"I'm sorry, Leroy," she said, dropping her eyes to the ground.

"You'd better be careful though. A lot of people saw that."

"It doesn't matter, Chérie. It's all over with Joyce. She just doesn't know it yet."

"Well, it's about time. I never could see what you saw in her."

"Chérie, you don't...." He laughed. There was no sense in finishing his thought. "I went up to the Edmunds place today. I left him with that brochure we had printed up. He was impressed. He thinks we're the only ones who can help him. He's just about ready to jump at whatever we offer."

Renée nodded.

He looked her up and down slowly. She liked him to notice her. The dress she was wearing was bright, made of some silky material, and tight, showing a lot of leg as usual. How different she was from the lumpish Carol Ann. But then of course, Renée was French, and that made all the difference in the world.

"You look wonderful tonight. Did you have a good day today? I think you must have."

"No. It was a complete waste of time. Those people from New Jersey wanted to see the old Booth place, but they didn't like it. She had to look into every cupboard, and he tried to put his hands on me every time her back was turned. And it was all for nothing. They just wanted somebody to show them around. I could have dropped them both off a bridge."

"And I suppose they left thinking you were their best friend, eh, Chérie?"

She grinned at him. "Well, I learned from a dear uncle how to put in a good appearance, didn't I, Uncle?"

"You are good, Chérie, very good," he said, and then he hesitated, because he realized when he heard the words that they were the same words he had said to Joyce Morrison, although he meant something else when he said them to her.

"You took that woman up to St. J. with you." It wasn't a question.

"How did you hear that?"

"You aren't the only one who gets around, Uncle Leroy."

"Are you having a good time tonight with George?"

"Leroy." She dragged out the syllables of his name in mock exasperation. "I asked you a question."

"You did, Chérie?" He grinned, making a joke of his pretended ignorance.

"Tell me about it. Tell me about her."

He tilted back his hat and looked into her eyes, cat's eyes, shrewd and yellow-green. "After you left this morning, I left too. But when I was getting into my car, I thought about what a beautiful day it was, so I went back and invited her to ride up there with me."

"You're so sweet," Renée said. It could have been sarcastic, but Leroy chose to think she was sincere.

"I know," he said. "I try to be. It was an uneventful trip. I told you I saw Luke Edmunds. I bought her some lunch. That's about all."

"Come on. You know what I want to hear. I want to know what you think of her."

"I like her. I like her a lot. You know, Chérie," and he reached out to stroke her shoulder, although the way she was standing, leaning back against the car with her arms folded across her chest, made it hard to get too close to her. "It was a brilliant idea to hire her."

She laughed and shrugged. "That was Roxy's doing, not mine."

"Oh God. Roxy. Did you see her tonight?"

"Of course I saw her—just like always. So?"

"With Ely Singleton. I warned her about him yesterday, and then she goes carrying on like that right under my nose."

"Leroy, have you ever seen Roxy when she wasn't making a fool of herself with somebody?"

"I just got through telling her to stay away from Ely."

"Leroy, you'll never make Roxy behave. You might as well not bother." She stood up straight. "I've got to go in. George'll be wondering." She gave him a quick and businesslike kiss on the cheek. "I'm not coming in tomorrow."

"Neither am I. Marie has plans for me."

"I'll see you Monday then." She gave him another kiss and clicked away on her high heels without looking back. He watched the way she walked until she went around the corner, and then he got in his car, planning to go home.

He drove the long way through town with his window down so that the cool spring air poured over him. He even went by his own house. There were not very many lights on, and he couldn't tell whether Marie was still up or not. He didn't stop. It wasn't quite ten o'clock, and he felt too restless to sleep. He crossed the River Street bridge and turned toward Roxy's without any plan. The downstairs was dark except for the dim hall light. Old man Mooney's light was on upstairs. He drove into Roxy's tiny parking lot and stopped beside a beat-up white Volvo with Massachusetts plates that had to belong to Isabel. Up above was an open window with a light on. The shades were up, but he couldn't see anything except a piece of the wall and the ceiling. He got out of the car and shut the door quietly. His boots made a crunching sound on the gravel.

II

ISABEL WAS SITTING on her bed in her bathrobe with only her underclothes on underneath. Her journal was open on her lap. There was nothing on the page except the day and date and the words, "Dear H.D." which she had written in Leroy's office that morning. It seemed a long time ago.

She wrote, "St. Johnsbury, Vermont, is an old railroad town, a place where all the country people come to shop, like Faulkner's Jefferson, Mississippi. The main street lies at the bottom of a steep hill near the _____ River." Then she was at the end of what she had planned to say. She sat there for a few minutes, hearing possible next sentences bounce around inside her head and rejecting them.

It was cold in the room with all the windows open and the shades up, but she loved the night sounds. The spring peepers reminded her of that visit to the magical farm last year when everything changed for her. If she shut the windows and pulled the shades, the night breeze wouldn't come through the room with its smells of secret earthy places. She stuck her legs under the covers and leaned back against the one limp pillow. She had stuffed some of her clothes behind it to make it a little more comfortable. There was nothing else she knew about St. Johnsbury, and she couldn't stop thinking about her mother and their conversation. It was a mistake to have called. She had thought her mother would like to hear about the job, and how nice Leroy was, how he had taken her to lunch and to visit the farm north of St. Johnsbury. But her mother hadn't heard any of it. She'd been totally stuck on the fact that now Isabel had a job, she was going to stay in Severance. Finally, Isabel had to cut the conversation short by saying she was standing out on the street at a pay phone, which was true, and that there was someone waiting to use the phone, which was not true. She had called Jeff next, but that only made things worse. He didn't seem pleased that she had a job, and he hadn't heard from Nicky or Joey. Isabel hung up and went back to her room at Roxy's, feeling that no one she used to know understood what she was doing now.

She couldn't put any of these things into the journal because it was supposed to be a journal of ideas, like Thoreau's, a journal about moving to Vermont, not a diary of personal problems. But what she ought to have said to her mother and to Jeff kept getting in the way and crowding out other ideas.

What she really felt like writing about was Leroy—how nice he had been to her, how comfortable and happy she had been with him, how different this trip to a farm was from the one she had taken a year ago with Jeff. Did Leroy really like her as much as he seemed to? But to write about whether he liked her would turn the journal into a teenager's diary, and she certainly didn't want to do that.

She skipped to a new page and started again. "I am staying at a rooming house in the middle of Seveance, Vermont. It's a creaky old house, beside a little river in a run-down part of town.

It's owned by a nice but eccentric old woman whose cousin is an important real estate dealer named Leroy LaFourniere. He has hired me to work in his office part time, a job which will help me learn about Severance and the country around it." She stopped writing and sat there thinking about what could happen if he wasn't married, or if she hadn't decided to put all ideas of romance behind her as part of her past life that was over and finished. She shook her head to shake out the fantasies and sat with her pen poised, trying to think of what to write next.

There was a knock on her door. It was strange because she hadn't even heard Roxy's shuffling step. "Come in," she called, but apparently not loud enough because the knock came again. Roxy was drunk.

Isabel sighed. She didn't feel like listening to second-hand barroom adventures. She pushed aside the covers and went to the door. She jerked it open and looked right into Leroy's white-shirted chest. Slowly she looked up. He was laughing.

"Whoa. Don't run me down. You said, 'Come in,' you know."

It took a minute to make sense of what she was seeing. She had been so sure. "I thought you were Mrs. Fox. Nothing's wrong, is it?"

"With Roxy? No such luck. She'll have to pay some day, but tonight she's out on the town, having a ball, as usual."

Isabel wrapped her robe a little tighter and retied the sash, conscious that Leroy was watching. She wouldn't have come to the door that way if she had known he was on the other side.

"Well, Chérie, did you mean it when you said I could come in?"

"If you want to....I mean...." She stood back from the door, not sure what she did mean.

Leroy walked in. "I was wrong," he said. "I shouldn't have come. Everthing has been rubbing me the wrong way tonight, and I wanted to be with someone sympathetic. But I can see you don't want me here."

"How did you know this was my room?"

"I saw your light from the parking lot. And your car is there."

"Oh."

"Shall I go, Chérie? Just say yes, and I'll be gone."

"No. Of course not. I don't want you to go."

"Okay," Leroy said, "but when you get sick of me, just say the word."

"Would you like to sit down?" She darted past him and grabbed her clothes from the chair where she had dumped them after her shower. "Here."

Leroy shut the door quietly and went to the chair. He took off his cowboy hat and set it neatly on the floor and sat down and crossed his long legs. He looked around the room. "Typical Roxy décor," he said. "Except for all the books. You have a lot of books. It looks like a library in here."

"These are my favorites. I didn't want to leave them behind in my old life."

"Why don't you ask Roxy for a bookcase?"

"They're okay on the floor. I don't mind." Then there was a silence while Isabel tried hard to think of something to say. Things weren't easy and comfortable the way they had been in the afternoon.

Leroy leaned forward and put his hand down on his hat. "Well, Chérie, I'll go now. It was out of line to come up here. I'm sorry. I saw your light on, and I thought I could take you downstreet for something to eat. We had a nice time together today. I guess I didn't want it to be over. But I shouldn't have come."

Isabel leaned back against her bed, half sitting and half standing. He seemed disappointed. There was something she should do to make him feel more at home. "You are my first visitor, except for Roxy, of course. And I haven't even seen her other tenant. I just hear him in the bathroom sometimes."

"Gene Mooney? You won't see much of him. He keeps to himself. His AA meetings are pretty much his only social life."

"I can't offer you anything to eat or drink. I don't have anything here. I wish I did."

"I shouldn't have come. It's late. You were going to bed. I was driving around, and I didn't want to go home, and I saw your light, but...."

Isabel bent over and picked up her clothes from the floor between them. She was conscious that they were rumpled and not clean, but she didn't feel comfortable enough to get fresh clothes out of the bureau with him sitting right there, and she couldn't ask him to wait in the hall either. "I'll go into the bathroom and get dressed, and we can go get something to eat. I could treat you. I owe you one. You were so nice to me today." She walked to the door.

He was watching her. "No, Chérie. I couldn't let you do that. I had a special time today also. And that was your doing. It has been a long time since I have felt like that. I guess I just didn't want it to be over."

Isabel stopped with her hand on the doorknob. She was surprised and confused, and of course she was pleased. She said, "Oh," but what else was there to say?

"But don't get dressed. It's late. I had better go home now."

"Don't go. I mean if you don't want to go home yet.... I mean." She walked back to the bed and half sat on the end again and dropped her clothes on the floor, but this time around the end of the bed where she hoped they would be out of sight. "I don't know what I mean. It feels a little funny to be here like this. I mean, if Roxy comes home...."

"Oh Roxy. Don't worry about her. She won't be home for hours, and she'll probably be shit-faced when she does get home. Excuse me for swearing."

"I don't mind."

"Roxy is just one of the people who have been getting on my nerves tonight. I warned her yesterday about going out with Ely Singleton. He's a no-good. Everybody knows that. And here she is tonight making a fool of herself as usual, dancing with him and kissing him in public. It's disgusting."

Isabel didn't know what to say. She could certainly picture

Roxy being disgusting in public.

"I should have saved my breath. She didn't hear a word I said."

"I guess she's old enough to make her own mistakes."

"But you don't understand. She's my family. What she does reflects on me. I don't want her to ruin my reputation. *I* am very careful. People don't see *me* making public mistakes like that. You have to be careful in a town like this where everybody knows your business better than you do."

He seemed cross and unhappy, very different from the way he had been in the afternoon, very different from the way he had been with her. He sighed and stood up. He hadn't taken off his jacket. Now he settled his hat on his head and walked to the door. "I'm really sorry I bothered you like this. I don't know what's the matter with me tonight. Everything seems to be wrong." He turned around and looked at her where she sat on the end of the bed. "Everything but you. I guess that's why I came here to see you. I really didn't plan to bother you. I was just driving around when I saw your light." He had his hand on the doorknob, ready to leave.

"Do wait a minute," Isabel said. The reason she said it was that he seemed so defeated, as though someone had let all the air out of him. She was really sorry, and she wanted to help. He had been so kind to her. She had only known him for a little more than twenty-four hours, but she felt tenderly, almost motherly toward him, seeing him so disappointed.

He turned, looking hopeful. "You really want me to stay?"

"Well…. yes," she said. "Please." And then she could feel the blood rising up into her face, because she realized that what she was saying had a whole other set of meanings. Before, she had thought abstractly about what it would look like that Leroy was in her room on a Saturday night and when she wasn't dressed.

But now she was seeing it differently, having to choose about it, and without any time to sort out her feelings either, because he had turned away from the door and was coming toward her, smiling at her and looking into her face. "I won't stay long, but I'm so glad you want me here. I haven't thought about anything but you all day long, Chérie. It has been a wonderful day. I couldn't bear for it to be over."

"Yes," she said. "It was a wonderful day." It was flattering and intoxicating to hear him talk like that, but…. There were lots of buts. She didn't know him at all. She wasn't used to this kind of situation. She was no good at maneuvering in it. The small amount of experience she had had was long ago, out of date, applied to different people. She didn't know what to do.

He was sitting beside her on the bed now, caressing her shoulder and stroking her back, and it felt very nice. "I didn't mean it before when I said everybody was rubbing me the wrong way, Chérie. Because *you* weren't. *You* have been all I have wanted all day."

She shifted a little, and he immediately pulled back his hand, so that she was glad and sorry at the same time. She was glad to see that she was in control of what happened. Still, she didn't want him to stop. It was nice to be wanted. She couldn't remember when Jeff had felt that way. Years ago probably. Sex between them had gotten automatic and sort of impersonal before it dried up altogether. And as it did, she was secretly glad, because it hadn't been any good at the end, and it had never been great, even in the beginning. Whatever reasons she had had for marrying Jeff, they weren't about sex.

"What are you thinking about, Chérie? You seem a million miles away."

"I'm sorry. I'm just confused, I guess. Things seem to be happening so fast."

"Too fast? Just say the word, and I'll go. Only don't tell me it's hopeless. That's all."

All this time, he kept reaching out to touch her and pulling himself back, as though he was almost out of control. It was exciting. He hadn't even kissed her yet, and she wanted him to. She didn't know whether it was because she was curious, or because she wanted him. Everyone else was always talking about the sexual revolution, and it had mostly passed her by. This was her chance to find out what she had been missing. And at the same time, she remembered that she had decided that her life would go in a different direction. Leroy hadn't been part of her plan, and how could he have been, since she hadn't ever met anyone like him before and couldn't have predicted him.

"Say something, Chérie. Anything. So I know what you want."

"But I don't know what I want. I don't know what that is."

"Well then," he said. "Let me show you. You haven't ever had a man like me." And he laughed. "No," he said, putting a finger to her lips. "Don't say a word. I know you haven't had such an experience, because there's no lover like me. I'm the only one. I'm the best there is. I can make your fantasies come true, Chérie. You don't know that yet, but I will show you. Just say the word, and I'll make your dreams come true."

"Why not?" Isabel thought. Everybody else was doing it. Maybe there was something she was missing. She thought, "I'd like to know. I'd like to find out before it's too late, and I'm too old. Or maybe it's like Jeff always said, that I live too much in my head to ever enjoy sex, that it's hopeless. Still, if I really mean it about having a new life, then I need to learn new things. And sex is a simple thing, a natural part of life." That was what she thought. Out loud she said, "I don't know what to say. I don't know what I don't know."

"All right, Chérie. I will show you what you have been missing all your life, and then you will know. You have come to the best teacher. And if you don't like it, you can tell me to stop."

So then she remembered their conversation of—was it really this morning? It seemed years ago—the conversation of how you had to let things happen as they did, and how you had to trust yourself, and more than that, she remembered how he understood what she was saying, what she meant, when no one else had ever understood before, and she turned toward him and put her arms around his neck.

"Oh Chérie. Thank you. You won't be sorry." He reached over and turned out her light, and the pale light from the moon came streaming in the window with the sound of the river outside.

For a while it was in her head, a matter of curiosity, but gradually something else took over, a person inside her that she didn't know was there. He touched new places and made her feel in new ways, and she got hungry for more, so that when he stopped and stood up and said he thought he ought to go, she became wild and clung on to him, begging him not to go, and he laughed and said he told her he could please her and that now she knew he was the best of all.

Some time later Isabel woke up. A car door slammed, and there were voices. "Roxy's home," she said. "What's she going to think when she sees your car out there?"

When he didn't answer, she felt sleepily across the bed. He wasn't there. That woke her up enough to turn on the light and look around the room. There was no sign of him. She could have dreamed the whole thing.

12

FROM WHERE SHE sat at her sewing machine in the dining room window, Carol Ann could see Gramps sitting on a log whittling at a stick. It was all she could do to keep from shouting at him out the window. There he sat, doing nothing, like he had unlimited amounts of time, when in front of him stretched the garden, brown and bare, hardly started yet. She did restrain herself, but only because she knew it was useless. He would just say what he always said, that there was a right time to plant each crop, and there was no sense in struggling to get something in early, because it wouldn't grow until it was supposed to. And it didn't do a bit of good when she told him that she saw lots of other gardens on her way to work that were ahead of his. He just laughed and said that she should wait until later and see if they stayed ahead. She always began to worry about something else later on, and she could never remember which ones she meant to keep track of.

Behind Gramps sat the woodpile, or what was going to be the woodpile—a few logs that he had dragged out of the woods and hadn't cut or split yet. It was a very small start. Of course it was a long time before winter, but Gramps was old and didn't work very fast, and there was no one to help him except Alison. They had to get enough, because there was no way they could buy wood when they had heating oil to pay for.

And it wasn't just the woodpile and the garden anyway; it was everything. No one else took any responsibility for what had to be done around the place. Raymond was hopeless. He had promised absolutely and unconditionally to have the front room cleaned up before she got home. It wasn't the first time he had promised to get that stupid engine out of there either.

And when she came home yesterday, he met her at the kitchen door to tell her he hadn't been able to do it because Alison was in there resting, and he didn't want to bother her. He was acting so strange that she didn't know what to think except that it was obvious he was hiding something. For one horrible second she thought Allie must be dead, and they had laid her corpse out in the front room. She pushed Raymond out of the way and headed down the hall to see for herself. Luckily, she met Allie coming out of the bathroom, obviously able to walk, even though her head was bandaged. God knows if she could have stood it if she had gone into the front room and seen Allie lying there asleep with her head like that. As it was, she had had a plenty bad enough fright.

It was about time Alison grew up, but Gramps and Raymond didn't help her a bit. In fact, they encouraged her to be as foolish as they were themselves. Carol Ann had been so relieved to see Allie on her feet and alive, that she hadn't even pointed out that Allie didn't need to be up there in the woods fooling around with Gramps and his old cows. At the best, she came home smelling like a barn, and of course there was always the danger of getting her head broken. It wasn't something a girl had any business with. If she had any hope of enforcing her order, Carol Ann wouldn't hesitate a minute before she told Allie she was absolutely not allowed to have anything to do with Gramps' oxen. But it was no use, and she knew it. They were all against her. It would end up being a game for them, and three against one besides.

She sighed and looked down at her sewing. She was putting a new hem in a summer skirt she had made for Allie last year. Allie had grown so much taller over the winter. Carol Ann had been trying to get around to this job for more than a month because Allie said she was embarrassed to wear the skirt when it was so short. Carol Ann suspected that was a dodge, and that Allie objected to it because it was pretty, because it made her look like a girl for a change. Carol Ann smoothed out the material with her hand. Great big flowers in shades of pink with green leaves and vines, it looked like a summer garden, not a workaday garden like Gramps had, but a real flower garden, something just for beauty. And Allie looked so sweet and feminine in it, like a young flower herself.

Carol Ann was trying out the special stitch for doing hems. It didn't work all that well, but she knew she wasn't going to get around to doing the skirt by hand, at least not before school let out for summer vacation. She sewed a two-foot section and then turned the cloth over to see what it looked like on the right side. The stitches showed a lot more than hand stitches would have, but it was okay, not too noticeable, what with all the flowers in the pattern. She sewed along, calmed by the whirr of the machine. She and Allie had picked out the cloth together. Carol Ann loved to sew, not that she had much time for it these days. Of course, if she didn't have to do so much work taking care of this hopeless, old house....

She looked out the window, and there was Alison walking over to the woodpile. Carol Ann watched as she sat down on the log beside Gramps and reached down to pick up something, probably a chip of wood, from the ground at her feet. There they sat, Allie breaking off little scraps of wood and throwing them, and Gramps whittling on a stick, not talking, as far as Carol Ann could tell, not even looking at each other, just sitting like two lumps and wasting time.

Carol Ann stood up and raised the window. Cool wind blew in, ruffling the material of the skirt.

"Alison, come in here. I need you."

Allie said, "Okay, Ma," without even turning around.

Carol Ann shut the window, but she didn't sit down. She was watching Allie, who went right on throwing small scraps of wood as though no one had said anything. Carol Ann began to grit her teeth. Gramps just sat there too. She hated it when Gramps seemed to ignore her interests and authority with Allie. And sometimes she hated it more when he told Allie to obey her mother, as though Alison would only be good for her mother if he told her to.

Carol Ann had her hand on the window to raise it and call again, when Allie got wearily to her feet, resting a hand on Gramps' shoulder. Carol Ann didn't watch any more. She sat down at the machine and went back to work.

"What do you want, Ma?"

Carol Ann didn't even slow the machine. "I'm doin this skirt so you can wear it to school, and I want you to try it on and see if it's okay."

"Aw, Ma, I'll have to take off all my clothes."

"Just your blue jeans."

"I'll try it tonight."

"Allie...."

"You ain't even finished with it yet."

"Alison LeStage, I'm goin to all this trouble to get this skirt ready for you, and you are goin to try it on, and that's final."

"Okay, Ma, if you feel that way about it. I mean, if I have to. Call me when it's done."

Carol Ann stopped sewing and looked around. "Allie, you stay right where you are. I'm just about done. Take your pants off."

"Aw, Ma...."

Carol Ann sewed the last bit and cut the thread. She pulled the skirt out of the machine and stood up to shake it out straight. Allie hadn't moved. She was still standing in the doorway, leaning against the frame of the door, looking distressed. Carol Ann threw the skirt to her, and she caught it.

"Put it on," Carol Ann said shortly.

Allie pulled the skirt over her head and arranged it, buttoning it at her waist. She stood in the doorway, looking uncomfortable, saying nothing.

"You can't tell anything about it like that—with your blue jeans stickin out the bottom. How are we goin to know if it's the right length or not?"

Allie didn't answer. She rolled her eyes toward the ceiling in exasperation and then raised the skirt so that she could unfasten her blue jeans. She carefully put down the skirt before she let the blue jeans drop around her ankles, as if she had something to hide from her own mother.

"Alison, are you wearin underwear?"

"Yes, Ma. Of course I am."

"Well, I don't see what the fuss is all about then."

"It's just private. Okay? Leave me alone."

Carol Ann let that comment pass. She tried to tell something about the skirt, but Allie stood in the doorway so awkwardly with her blue jeans around her ankles. It was impossible to see what the skirt was going to look like. It took all the pleasure out of it.

"Alison, take off those blue jeans."

"But Ma, I'll have to take off my sneakers and everything."

"Well, do it then, and stop wastin my time."

Allie sighed. She sat down on the floor in the doorway to untie her shoes. Over her head Carol Ann could see Raymond going down the hall toward the front room again. She hoped he was picking up the last pieces of his engine. It would be nice to get that room straightened around.

Allie stood up. "Okay Ma. Now what?"

Carol Ann looked at her in her awkwardness, her legs and arms as stiff as sticks. "What do you think? How does it feel to you? It looks right, I think. I like it."

"I don't know if I should wear it to school."

"Why not?"

"I would just get it dirty or something."

"Well that wouldn't be the end of the world. And anyhow, you can be careful."

"But the kids would probably make fun of me or something."

"Allie, they won't. And anyhow if they did, it would be just jealousy. You look sweet. Go upstairs and take a look."

"Aw, Ma...."

"No. I mean it. I want you to take a look. Now go."

"If I have to," Allie said and swung around the corner into the hall.

"Uh-oh, Sugar. Look where you're goin, will you?"

"Gee Dad, I'm sorry. I didn't even see you."

"No honey, that's for sure. It's lucky I didn't get you all over engine grease when you're dressed so pretty. Where are you goin, all fixed up like that?"

"No place. Ma's just sewin this skirt for me."

Carol Ann came out into the hall behind Allie. "Tell her how nice she looks, Raymond. She won't listen to me."

"You look so sweet, honey, all the boys are goin to turn around to watch you."

"Aw Dad, I don't want people to look at me. I want them to leave me alone."

"When you get up to the mirror, take that stupid cap of Gramps' off your head, so you can really see what you look like."

Allie looked right straight at Carol Ann, a cold look, as though she didn't believe that Carol Ann had said what she said, although anyone could see how out of place that stupid feedstore hat was with her pretty skirt. She pushed past her father and went down the hall on her bare feet to look in the large, old-fashioned mirror in the spare bedroom upstairs.

Raymond stood there, his arms full of engine, watching her until she went out of sight at the top of the stairs. "She's just shy, that's all. She appreciates it when you do stuff for her. She just don't know how to say so."

"Don't make excuses for her, Raymond. She's terrible! She'd rather wear that old hat and smell like cow manure out behind the barn with Gramps than have something pretty to wear. She's gettin too old for that."

"She's only fourteen, honey. She'll grow up. Did I tell you how great you looked last night?"

"Oh Raymond," and she gave a sigh. "Don't tell me how I looked great just to get my mind off Allie. You don't need to protect her. And I know what I looked like."

"Sweetheart," Raymond said, and he took a step toward her, but his arms were full of greasy metal, and he couldn't do anything but look at her.

"If I just had more time, I think I could lose some weight...."

"Honey, don't you...."

Carol Ann made a flapping motion with her hands. "Get on out of here with that old engine, and don't try to flatter me, cause you can't do it." But she was smiling, and she wasn't so stiff and bitter as she had been with Allie.

Raymond started walking toward the kitchen and the back door.

"Are you goin to get that thing picked up today?" Carol Ann called after him.

"For sure. I only got one more load after this."

"Great. I'll get in there and straighten up when you're done."

"I'll help you with the cleanin," he shouted back from somewhere near the door.

She went into the dining room. "I'll believe *that* when I see it," she said, but she said it quietly and cheerfully and to herself. She turned off the sewing machine and pushed in the chair. Allie hadn't come back downstairs yet, which was a surprise. Her sneakers and jeans lay in a tangled pile just inside the door. Carol

Ann hoped she was taking a long look at herself in the mirror, and not just daydreaming up there. She thought of going upstairs to see, but then she noticed her pocketbook lying on the table where she left it last night, and she remembered the envelope Leroy had given her. She sat down at the table and pulled the pocketbook over.

"It looks fine, Ma. Thank you. Can I take it off now?"

Carol Ann looked up at Allie standing in the doorway. She looked like a flower, so spindly and frail and so very young. "Sure, honey. I'm glad you took a good look at yourself to see how sweet you look."

Allie didn't say anything. She just gave Carol Ann a look. Then she picked up her clothes and went across the hall to the bathroom.

Carol Ann felt the bitterness rising up around her again. For a sweet, few minutes she had forgotten that they lived in a state of war with each other. She had felt like touching Allie on the shoulder, saying something nice to her, and she had hoped, had almost believed, that Allie felt the same. But of course, it wasn't true. She sighed again, heavily, and opened her pocketbook. She hadn't looked in the packet of papers when Leroy handed it to her, and she had forgotten about it when she got home last night. She pulled out the thick white envelope. Across the front of it, where the address should be, Leroy had written a note in his large, sprawling handwriting. It said, "You can see from the enclosed what your house is worth on today's market. L."

Carol Ann read it twice. Then she took everything out of the envelope. There were two or three brochures on shiny paper and a thick wad of white pages folded together. She laid the brochures neatly off to one side and unfolded the white pages, setting them precisely in front of her and smoothing them out with her hands. She let herself look at her hands with pleasure before she moved them to see the words underneath.

There were lots of words and numbers, but the words weren't real; they were all abbreviations, and ones Carol Ann didn't know. It made her feel nervous. She looked at the next page and the next. They were all the same. She laid the pages down carefully in the order she found them in and folded them over again on the same folds. Then she put all the white pages back into the envelope. May would know. May could help her make sense of it. She would show the white pages to May.

She picked up a brochure. 'Century Farms' was written on the outside in curly black letters over a picture of a farmhouse all fixed up, with mountains behind it. Someone with a lot of money owned that house. Carol Ann sat up straighter. When the brochure was unfolded all the way, it was quite large, and there were lots of pictures of houses with fields and woods and mountains in the background. They looked all fixed-up and beautiful, like they already belonged to out-of-staters, not old and run-down like Gramps' place.

Carol Ann read, "We are proud to be able to offer this farm to...." but she stopped. It made her feel kind of uncomfortable, like she was dealing with somebody else's private business. She was sure she couldn't figure it out all by herself. Raymond wouldn't be any help. He always counted on her to do anything that had numbers and words in it. He would just tell her not to mess with it. She couldn't very well ask Gramps. Allie was smart enough, but Allie would take Gramps' side; she always did. Even Ma and Dad would tell her to leave it alone. But May would help, and May was smart, and she already knew about Leroy, so she would know what to look out for.

Carol Ann folded up the shiny paper and put it into the envelope. Then she picked up the other brochures. She almost opened another one, but she knew it wouldn't do any good to look at it by herself. With a feeling of relief, she put the rest of the brochures into the envelope and slid it back into her pocketbook to wait for Monday when she went to work again. She had saved herself some time which she could put to good use by giving the front room a real thorough clean-up. She pushed back her chair and stood up.

13

AFTER A LITTLE while Al came back and sat down on the log beside him again. She picked up a chip of wood and broke pieces off it which she threw out in front of her. Sonny had his pocket-knife out, whittling down the end of a stick to a smooth, sharp point. The air was full of the damp smell of earth and moss. There was a bit of ice in it too from last night's frost, but it was going to warm up and stay warm for a few days. They might have one more cold spell to go in about a week when the moon got full. But before that, these next few days were going to do a lot to get the ground ready. Sonny had a lot to do to get ready himself.

"What did your ma want, darlin?"

Al sighed. "Oh Gramps," Al said, and she sighed an even larger sigh and threw down what was left of the chip of wood, "if I wear that thing to school, everybody will laugh at me."

"Now, darlin, that's surely not your ma's intention." Without turning his head, Sonny took a sideways look at Al. He didn't want to invade her privacy, but he could hear the trouble in her voice. Under the tilted bandage, her face was contorted. He was filled with tenderness for her, amazed that she cared so much. He wanted to comfort and protect her, but he didn't know how, so he took refuge in fairness. "Your ma thinks she's doin somethin nice for you. She wants you to be happy."

"I've *told* her and *told* her that nobody wears skirts like that to school."

"See, darlin, that's what *she* would like to look like, so she thinks...." He stopped. He was making it worse.

"If she wanted me to be happy, she would let me wear what I wanted to. Then the kids wouldn't laugh at me."

"How does your head feel this mornin?"

She looked at him with surprise. "You're just tryin to change the subject."

"Well, darlin, what if I am?" He grinned at her. "What are you goin to do about it?"

"Oh, you old Gramps!" Then they were both laughing, and they were on the same side again, ready to take on the rest of the world if they had to.

"I don't care about those kids anyhow, because they're all stupid. I don't even want to *think* about school. I got a whole day before I have to think about those dumb kids. Is there any more firewood ready to come down?"

"You still haven't told me how your head is. And we were on the last load when you got hurt. Remember?" He paused to give her a sly smile. "Or maybe that branch knocked out your memory. I've heard of such things."

"You old Gramps." She swatted his shoulder. "It don't hurt at all. It wasn't nothin to worry about. I heard you tell Dad that a head wound always bleeds like that."

"A lot of times it does. It still could've been serious. We want to watch out."

She held onto his arm and looked up at him seriously with just the pleading expression she used to have when she was four or five and he was trying to sneak off on his own to get some work done without her tagging along behind. And he would have to give in now just the way he used to then. He never could resist that look on her face.

She saw how things would turn out. "Oh goody. What are we goin to do?"

"We got to get some more of this garden turned over. It's gettin to be time to plant the next piece of it."

"Okay. Let's get goin."

"Wait a minute. I ain't got it all figured out yet. I got to know where we're goin to put the potatoes and onions this year. We want to put them in next week when the moon is right."

"We could put the potatoes right over there by the peas."

"That's where we had 'em last year."

"Well, that's okay, Gramps. It was a good place. We got lots of potatoes."

"But the potato bugs are right there and waitin. We got to try and fool at least some of 'em."

"I forgot about the bugs."

"We can't afford to forget about the bugs. *They* ain't goin to forget. So this is what I thought we'd do. Right there by the peas, where we had potatoes last year, we'll turn that over, but we won't plant it yet. We'll save that piece for tomatoes. Then we'll work down to the other end and get a place turned for potatoes and onions where I didn't put manure down this year."

"Okay, Gramps. That sounds good. Let's go get Buck 'n Ben."

"Yes, darlin." Sonny put his hands on his knees as though he was going to push himself up, but he didn't move yet. "Just one more thing. Do you have a headache?"

Al was already on her feet. She glanced down at him with startled eyes, suspecting a trap. "No, I don't. I mostly don't even remember about it."

She was so afraid he was going to try to leave her behind. It made him smile to himself. Didn't she know that he always liked a job much better when she was beside him sharing it? "I don't want to leave you behind, honey. I just don't want you to be foolhardy and do yourself some damage." He stood up. He tried to look into her eyes to make her know he was serious, but she was still enough shorter so that all he could see under the bill of her cap was her mouth and chin. He said, "It won't be long now until you'll be the tallest, and then I guess you'll have to do the yokin up, and I'll just have to retire altogether."

That made her smile. "Oh you old Gramps. Buck 'n Ben 'n I couldn't do anything without *you*."

"Well, let's go get 'em then. But listen here, honey. You know how they hate the cultivator? I got to get 'em used to it. Okay?"

"Okay, Gramps."

"I'll let you take over as soon as they know they ain't got no choice, that that's what we're goin to do today."

"Okay, Gramps."

"When they get into it, they'll find out they don't hate it as bad as they thought they did. Anyhow, as they get older, they'll get so they don't care so much." And he thought how that would happen to Al too.

"Okay, Gramps," she said over her shoulder. She was already on the way toward the barn.

By the time Sonny got to the oxen's stall, Al had the shovel out, ready to pick up the neat puddles of manure that lay on the sawdust floor behind each ox.

"It's the new grass that's got 'em so loose," he said, as she picked up the manure. "They ain't used to it yet."

He took the halters and lines off both oxen, so they were standing free in their places, before he got the yoke from where he always leaned it up in the corner. It was taller than he was and heavy, awkward to carry, so he always kept it close by. He set it down between the heads of the oxen and took out Ben's bow. He always put Ben in first.

Al had put the shovel away and was watching. "I want to learn how to yoke 'em for you, Gramps."

"All in good time, honey."

"It don't look that hard. I bet I could do it just fine."

Sonny chuckled, remembering how Leroy said he'd like to see him yoke such big cattle, and him so small. And Leroy was country enough to know any job was mostly in the know-how and the practice. He leaned the yoke against Ben's shoulder. Ben held his head still while Sonny put the bow around his neck and through the holes in the yoke and shoved the bow pin into place.

"Don't laugh at me, Gramps. It's not dumb. If I'm goin to drive 'em, I ought to know how to yoke 'em. Suppose you got sick or somethin?"

"I ain't laughin at you, darlin." Ben held his head steady, so Sonny could take out Buck's bow and swing the other end of the yoke up onto Buck's neck. Their horns were getting long, but they weren't in the way.

"Well, what's so funny then?"

"Remember when that tall, skinny, cattle rustler named Leroy was out here the other day?"

"That guy that came out to see Ma?"

"That's the one." Sonny put Buck's bow in place and set the pin. He patted Buck on the shoulder. "I guess we're ready then, boys." He looked over at Al. "Leroy said he didn't see how a little, runty guy like me could yoke such big oxen, but of course that's just because he ain't never worked cattle."

"He said *that* to *you*?"

"Not in exactly those words, but that's what he meant."

"Boy, Gramps, that makes me mad."

"Well, that's okay. You ought to take a little time to think about Leroy. He's not a bad guy, as long as you don't *never* turn your back on him. That's somethin to learn that's as valuable as how to yoke cattle."

He went around behind the team to where Al stood watching.

He put his hands on her shoulders. She looked up at him wondering why he was so serious. He looked into her eyes. It was hard to love her so and to know he didn't have much time left. Would she be able to take care of herself when he wasn't there any more? The only thing he minded was how much of her life he was going to miss.

"It's okay, Gramps. Don't worry."

"Your ma's a good girl, honey, but sometimes she don't worry about the right stuff. I don't think she knows to watch out for Leroy like she should. It could happen that that was left up to you. You might be called on to remember everything I taught you."

He let loose of her shoulders, and she threw herself at him and hugged him. "Don't talk like that. You scare me. You ain't goin to die, old Gramps. You can't. I won't let you."

He patted her back, so frail, so bony, so young. Then he pulled away and picked up his whip. "Well, I guess...." he said, and his voice trailed off.

Both oxen put up their ears and turned their heads to look at him, and Al moved back into the corner, out of the way.

"Git up," he said, and Buck and Ben swayed and shuffled sidewise, creaking into the ninety-degree turn.

He shouted "Haw," and they turned into the passage toward the big doors. Of course, that command was just a formality. They always went the same way, and all of them knew it. But Sonny didn't want to get sloppy so that Buck and Ben thought they were making the decisions. And he especially didn't want Al to see him being sloppy.

They followed the oxen out the open door, and then Sonny told them to whoa. He turned to Al and held out the peeled stick he was using in place of the whip. "Do you want to drive 'em over to the cultivator, honey?"

"Sure, Gramps." She took the whip and stepped up beside Buck. "Come up, boys," she said, and she waved the whip in a small circle. The oxen lumbered into motion. And there was

Sonny again where he loved to be, walking along behind the three of them in the rich cow smell and the creak and clank of their gear.

Al had to shout when they came to the fork in the road, because Buck and Ben believed, or at least pretended to believe, that they were going to the woods. Al wanted them to go the other way, to the woodpile and the garden. They hesitated but then gee-ed smoothly down toward the house.

The cultivator was standing beside the garden where they had left it after they had turned over enough dirt to put in the peas. Al walked the oxen to it, turned them, and backed them over the tongue.

"Good girl," Sonny said. "Neatly done."

Al smiled and patted Buck on the shoulder.

Sonny picked up the tongue and chained it to the yoke the way he always did. "Now, honey, I'll take 'em around so I can break out the first furrow or so and get 'em used to the idea that we ain't goin to get up in the woods today. After I've been around once or twice, you can drive."

"Okay, Gramps."

"Climb up there and ride. I don't think you'll have to fool with the levers. It ought to be set deep enough the way it is, but we'll see about that."

"Okay, Gramps."

She settled herself on the seat, and he started Buck and Ben and walked beside Buck's head. They went around the edge of the garden making a tight reverse circle at the corner to turn the cultivator.

The oxen weren't glad to be pulling the way they sometimes seemed to feel up in the woodlot, but they didn't balk either, and they didn't turn wrong when they knew better, the way they did once in a while when they really wanted to mess up the work. Today they were just unenthusiastic, plodding along without taking any pleasure in anything.

That didn't stop Sonny from loving it as much as he always

did. The damp smell of the turned earth, the way his feet sank almost to his ankles in the loose soil, so that they all had to walk in slow motion, straining against the pull of the ground, the metallic creak and rattle of the machinery, which always complained no matter how recently it had been oiled—it all came together to make Sonny feel just plain satisfied somehow, as though the world was an orderly place, and his life was a smoothly fitting piece of the whole. Everything just seemed right.

When he looked back at Al, she smiled. One more round to mark the path they should take, and then he could let her take over. She was holding onto the seat to steady herself, but before he turned away, he saw her let go long enough to brush the black flies away from her face. They were flying around his head too, but not many yet. They'd be worse in a week or so. And pretty soon the big flies, the deer and horse flies would be getting to work. It was time for him to think about starting at first light in the morning, the way he did every summer, so that he could quit for the day about ten-thirty or eleven o'clock, before the heat and the flies got too bad for him and the boys to work. It was time to make the switch. The only one who didn't like the summer schedule was Al, who had a hard time getting up that early any more.

When they finished the next round, Sonny whoaed them.

"Okay, Al, honey. Are you ready to take over?"

"Sure, Gramps."

"And your head don't hurt?"

She had climbed off the machine and was just reaching for the whip when she heard his question. Her eyes went wide for a second and then dropped away from his.

"Oh no."

"You sure now, honey?"

"Cross my heart, Gramps. It's the truth."

She looked right at him, and her eyes were steady, so then he wasn't sure which way it was, and he didn't want to treat her like a baby.

He handed her the whip, mumbling something about not wanting her ma to take out after him. Then he climbed up into the cultivator seat. He made a few minor adjustments to the way the tines were digging, and after that he just rode. He didn't even bother to swat at the black flies.

Sonny wasn't watching where they were going, so he was surprised when Al stopped the oxen.

"What's the matter, honey?"

"The circle's gettin too tight. We've only got that last little bit there in the middle. See?"

"I see. It's lookin good, darlin."

"What must I do, Gramps?"

"That's easy. There ain't any law that says you can't run over the part you already done. Just go around on the part that you've already been over and then come by and make another pass at the new part, until you've been over all of it."

"Oh, you old Gramps. You always know the answers." She grinned up at him.

"It'd be a surprise if I hadn't figured out somethin, after all the years I been turnin over this piece of ground."

They went around a few more times, and then the job was done. Al drove the oxen over to the place they had picked up the cultivator, and then she stopped them.

"What must we do with the cultivator now, Gramps?"

"We probably won't use it again until fall," Sonny said. He climbed down from the seat. Let's take it over to the machine shed, unless your dad's got the place all filled up with his junk. Just let me hitch up these tines, and you can drive it."

"Okay, Gramps."

Al drove, and the cultivator clattered along behind. The oxen went willingly. Although they had to take the road around the other side of the barn, and although it was only noon, they knew that they were done working for the day. It gave Sonny a comfortable feeling when they sensed his plans.

When they had the cultivator put away, Al drove the oxen into the barn, and Sonny unyoked them and gave them each a couple flakes of hay.

After dinner Raymond helped Sonny, or really, it was more the other way around, Sonny helped Raymond change the brake lines on Sonny's cattle truck, a job they'd been meaning to get to for quite a while. They weren't finished, but they were getting along well when a couple of Raymond's buddies came over to visit. It was Jimmy Trepanier and Charlie somebody who Sonny didn't really know. It was okay with them if Raymond went on working. They were more comfortable outside than they would be in the house around Carol Ann anyway, and the brake work gave them a good excuse not to go in.

It would have worked out fine if it had been anything but brakes. But Raymond had to lie down underneath the truck, and it slowed the work down too much because he kept having to come out to hear what everyone said.

Finally Sonny decided to quit for a while and go see who was at the Texas Café. He told Raymond to tell Carol Ann that he'd be back in a little while, and he took off in his pick-up.

By the turn onto the main road, there was a woman hitchhiking. Sonny would have been too embarrassed to pick her up, too afraid she would get the wrong idea, but he didn't even see her until he stopped to check if the road was clear before he made the turn, and they looked full into each other's eyes quite unexpectedly. He didn't feel right about going past her after that. It was such a personal look that she gave him, and then she stuck her thumb right out. Anyway, he knew her from somewhere, or he thought he did. She wasn't a young woman, but she wasn't old either, and that was another thing, because he had to think of who else might come along to pick her up if he didn't.

So he stopped the truck after he made the turn and watched in the rearview mirror to see what the woman would do. She hesitated for a minute, but then she gave a little skip and hurried up to the passenger-side door. She was smiling.

14

It was mostly a joke. The driver hadn't put his turn signals on, so Isabel didn't even know if he was going her way. It was a surprise when he stopped. She ran up and opened the door to ask him where he was going. He had to think for a minute before he answered.

When he said Severance, she climbed in. The air inside the truck was much warmer than outside. It smelled of pine. There were cans of oil, and tools, and engine parts on the floor. It was hard to find room for her feet. The old man told her to kick things out of the way, but she didn't want to do that. She couldn't get the door to stay closed. He had to do it himself. He leaned across her to shut it. He was very careful not to touch her. She could see it embarrassed him, and it embarrassed her too. She felt like saying, "Don't be so polite. I won't break, and I don't even deserve such gentlemanly treatment, not after last night."

But she didn't say anything. It would have embarrassed both of them even more.

She looked at him while he watched the road. She couldn't figure out why he looked familiar, a generic old country man, in his green work clothes and boots, with a faded red feedstore cap on his head. He was small, with a bulbous nose and white stubble on his chin. His hand on the gear shift lever was wonderful, an ancient tree root, so marked and lined with work that it was like a map.

She could tell that it made him nervous when she looked at him, so she tried to keep her eyes on the road. She didn't want him to think she was coming on to him. But every time she thought of where she could know him from, her eyes would drift around for another look.

All of a sudden he slowed down. They were going past the forlorn diner that Isabel remembered from the trip out. When she looked over to see what he meant by it, he gave her a brief smile and speeded up again.

She said, "You look so familiar. I've been trying to figure out where I've seen you before."

"I have the exact, same feeling."

"It's funny, you know, because I only moved into town last week. I don't know anybody here."

"Maybe it's just a coincidence and don't mean nothin."

"But you had the same feeling."

"This is true."

And then maybe it was the sweetness of his smile that triggered her memory because all of a sudden she was sure that by some amazing coincidence this was the same old man whose ox team had pulled their car out of the mud a year ago, the old man who lived on the magic farm she had been dreaming about all year.

"Oh," she said. "I think I might have figured it out."

He looked at her and then quickly back at the road, shy again.

"Don't you want to know?"

"If you want to tell me."

"You have a team of oxen, don't you?"

"I do."

"Well then, I'm right. I know I am." The wonderful coincidence excited her. "Last year my husband and I got our car stuck in the mud in front of your place, and you pulled us out with your ox team."

When he looked at her this time, she could see he was remembering it too.

She said, "You wouldn't even take any money for it."

"I remember."

"And here you are, doing me another favor."

"It ain't much of a one."

"And you don't even know how much your place has meant to me."

He looked around, surprised by that, but he didn't ask her what she meant.

"See, my husband and I were just about to break up, and I was going back and forth in my mind about what I was going to do if I divorced him. That was exactly when I saw your beautiful farm, and I knew right away that I wanted to live the way you did—a simple, country life. No, I guess I didn't know it right away. But your place was the metaphor I used, the vision that it was possible or something. It's funny because I don't even remember your name."

"It's Trumbley. Sonny Trumbley."

"Mine is Isabel Rawlings." She held out her hand, and he shook it with his own weathered one. Some day she would have hands like that, hands that had worked and lived hard.

It was a bit of luck to meet up with him like this, and just when she was getting confused, when she might have been going off the track because of Leroy. It was an amazing coincidence that Sonny Trumbley of all people would happen along to set her straight again. She wished she could make him see what it meant to her, but she was afraid to say too much. She could feel that it made him nervous.

They were coming into Severance now. "Where shall I leave you?" he asked.

"Any place downtown will do. Where are you going?"

"Well, to tell you the truth," he said, and he looked uncomfortable, "I was goin to the Texas Café back there, outside of town."

"Where you slowed down? I'm sorry. You've gone out of your way. You could have let me out back there. I would have gotten another ride."

"I suppose I could have...." He hesitated and then said it all in a rush. "I don't think it's safe for a woman to be hitchhikin. I don't think you ought to do it."

"I know. I never do, really. I mean, I did today, but that was because I took such a long walk. I had a lot to think about, and I didn't realize how far I was going, and I went a whole lot farther than I meant to. Then when I saw you....well, I just stuck my thumb out to see what you would do."

He wasn't paying attention. "I might just as well take you where you're goin....I would like to, in fact."

"And see, if I hadn't been hitching a ride, I wouldn't have met up with you again. So it's a good thing I did."

"You want I should go down Merchants Row?"

"I live on the other side of the river. You could let me off at the River Street bridge. I can easily walk from there."

When they came to the bridge, he drove across it. "I want to take you all the way. What's next?"

"Turn past that brick warehouse. I live in the house right beyond it."

He pulled into the little parking lot beside the house. "I know this place. Rowena Fox used to live back here."

"She still does. I rent a room from her."

"You do?" He watched while she opened the door and got out. "They used to call her 'Foxy Roxy.'"

She smiled, but she didn't want to talk about Mrs. Fox. She had been trying to figure out how to get him to ask her out to his farm. This was her last chance. She had to come out with it now or never. She took a breath and said, "Do you think I could see you again some time?"

She could see that her question surprised him. He had to take off his hat and rumple up his hair before he could say it would be okay.

She tried again to explain. "You don't have any idea how important you have been to me, you and your oxen and your farm, this last year, kind of a symbol of...." But then she saw how nervous he was getting. There was no way to make anyone understand how she felt about that place, how it meant freedom to her and the possibility of living her life the way she wanted to at long last. Everyone said, "Follow your bliss," and hers had always been this fantasy that she would live close to the earth.

"It's just that I would like to see your oxen again," she said, looking at him across the seat of his truck. "Do you still have them? Could I come out, do you think? Maybe when you were using them to do some work?"

"Wait," he said, holding up his hand. He was smiling. He was less stiff than he had been. "That's too many questions. I do still have my team, and yes, you can come and see 'em."

"Can I call you and see when it would be a good time and get directions and everything?"

"All right."

"Oh, thank you."

"Carroll Trumbley. That's how it is in the phone book."

"Carroll?"

"That's me. That's how I'm listed."

"I won't forget. Thanks for everything." She slammed the door of his truck and went into the house.

She was just starting up the stairs when she heard Mrs. Fox calling to her.

"Come in here a minute, darlin. I want to ask you somethin."

Isabel opened the door and stuck her head in, even though she didn't want to. She could smell dime-store perfume and mentholated cigarette smoke. It was hot and stuffy.

"Come on in and shut the door, honey," Mrs. Fox said. "I won't keep you but a minute." She was sitting in a sagging, over-stuffed chair. Her hair was up in curlers.

"Did anyone leave me a message? I gave your phone number to my mother," Isabel said. Maybe Leroy had called her, or better yet, had stopped in to see her.

"No. No messages, but come sit down here by me, so we can talk." She patted the empty chair beside her.

"I can't stay. I have some laundry I need to do."

"It won't take but a minute. You'll let the heat out with the door open like that." She patted the chair again. "Come on, hon. Relax."

Isabel shut the door and picked her way across the overcrowded room. She sat down stiffly on the edge of the chair.

"Wasn't that Carroll Trumbley's pick-up I seen you climbin out of?" Under her orange scarf, the curlers stood up like tiny ears.

"Who wears curlers these days? Hasn't she heard of blow-dryers?" was what Isabel was thinking. What she said out loud was, "Yes, Sonny Trumbley. That's what he said."

"Well, tell me, hon," Mrs. Fox began, and then she turned toward the little table at her elbow and shook a cigarette out of the pack that lay there.

Isabel tried to keep her impatience from showing in her face.

Mrs. Fox blew a long stream of smoke toward the ceiling which she watched through half-closed eyes. Finally, still looking at the ceiling, she said, "A few days ago you didn't even know Sonny's name, and now I see you goin out with him. I was just wonderin...."

"He gave me a ride home. That's all."

"I always thought Sonny was a real good-lookin man." She looked hard at Isabel with her little, watery eyes.

Isabel didn't say anything.

"Wouldn't you say so?"

"I don't know. I guess so."

"Course he's a lot older than me, but I always thought so, even so. Always, I mean." She sucked on the cigarette and blew another stream toward the ceiling. Her eyes were closed to slits against the smoke.

"It was nice of him to give me a ride."

"I ain't got nothin to say against old Carroll Trumbley. On the contrary, I always had a real high regard for the man." She paused, looking Isabel over thoughtfully. "I could tell you things, honey, that'd make you....but not about him, see, cause he's always had to be so careful. I was just wonderin is all, just curious as to how he came to give you a ride."

"That's simple." Isabel tried to look directly into Roxy's eyes, but they wouldn't meet hers and slipped off sideways. "I was hitchhiking, and he picked me up."

Roxy gave a little gasp and tried to cover it by a noisy suck on her cigarette.

Isabel stood up.

"Don't run off, darlin. I ain't goin to say nothin. You know your own business best." She poked her fingers in between the orange lumps, scratching her head. "We girls have got to stick together. I'm kind of a rebel myself."

Isabel couldn't think of anything to say to that.

"So, tell me, what did he say about me?"

"Who?"

"Well, Sonny, of course."

"Oh."

"That's who we was talkin about, wasn't it?" She stuck her lower lip out in what she probably thought was a cute and girlish pout. "I know what it is. He said somethin bad about me, and you don't want to tell it."

"No. He didn't say anything about you."

"He *must* have said somethin!"

"He said, 'Rowena Fox used to live here.' And I said you still did. That was it."

"He could have said to say hi. He knows me better'n that."

"He probably didn't want to talk about you to a stranger, to a hitchhiker."

"I always thought a lot of Sonny. He's a good-lookin man. He's been alone for a long time, sort of like me." She smiled bravely. "There was plenty around who would've been glad to get a good man like Sonny. I always wondered why he didn't never find himself someone after Ellen....unless that old Carol Ann didn't want anybody around. That's his granddaughter, that Carol Ann. She's kept house for Sonny ever since Ellen got sick. Carol Ann's always had it her own way out there. She probably wouldn't let him find somebody else. She probably was scared someone else would take her place away from her."

Isabel shifted from foot to foot uneasily, wishing she could think of a way to leave.

"I know, darlin. I can hear you. You are thinkin, 'Now what about Roxy? She's been alone for years, and she don't even have a granddaughter to take care of her.'"

"Oh no I wasn't. I wouldn't think anything like that."

"I'll let you in on a little secret, darlin. Just between us, you know."

"That's okay. You don't need to. Really."

"It's very simple. I just liked my fun too much, my freedom, you know. I just never could give it all up and settle down. I mean, I been the marriage route—two times was enough for me. Let the good times roll. You know what I mean?"

Isabel went over to the door and put her hand on the knob. She turned awkwardly. "That's very interesting, and now I have to...."

"I'm older than you are, hon, a little bit anyway. I thought it might help you to hear that. I know you're havin a hard time splittin up with your husband, but you'll get over it. Believe me."

"Thank you." Isabel opened the door.

"Aw, that's okay, darlin. I'm always glad to help out."

Isabel stepped into the cool air of the hall, grateful to be out of that overstuffed room. She was sorry she had been so stiff, when Roxy was trying to be helpful, but Roxy was always blundering in much too close.

"Oh say, hon, I almost forgot what I meant to ask you."

"What was that?" Isabel said through the partly closed door, all sympathy for Roxy, all appreciation of her kindness now absolutely gone from her mind.

"How did it go yesterday? Was it good?"

"What?" Isabel tried to sound as though she didn't understand what Roxy was asking, but inside her head, it was an exclamation. What!!! That's how sure she was that Roxy knew Leroy was in her room last night and was asking her how she liked sleeping with him.

"Did you work for Leroy yesterday like you was goin to?"

"Oh yes....yes....I did, yes." Her relief that Roxy hadn't meant what she thought she meant was short-lived. Roxy was looking at her, trying to figure out why she was acting so strange. She could feel her cheeks getting hot.

"So how was it?"

"All right. I didn't do much."

"I mean how was Leroy?" She peered at Isabel with her greedy, little eyes. "How did you two get along?"

"All right. Fine, just fine, and now I...."

"Sometimes Leroy can be a little stiff. He can seem like he don't like you, but that's just because he's got his responsibilities. He's got a lot on his mind sometimes. It ain't that he's mad or anythin."

"I see."

"What's the matter, hon? Is everything all right?"

"Oh yes. Fine....fine."

"You look a little funny."

"I'm fine. I'm fine. Thank you for telling me about Leroy."

She closed the door firmly and started upstairs. "God, Isabel, it's not going to take her long to figure it out, the way you're go-ing," she said to herself as she walked up the stairs. She didn't even see the man coming down until they were only a few stairs apart. She never saw what he looked like. All she saw were his feet and legs coming toward her down the stairs, as she pushed past without raising her eyes. As soon as Roxy found out, she would remember how Isabel said she certainly wasn't going to have any men in her room, that Roxy didn't have to worry about that.

It was strange that she had actually slept with Leroy. It wasn't the kind of thing she did, or at least, it wasn't a thing she had ever done before. Now, looking back on it, it seemed unreal, like something that had happened to someone else. She would have thought she had dreamed the whole thing, except that she was sore down there, and that made her know that it had really hap-pened.

She went into her room and shut her door and lay down on her bed. The same thoughts had circled round in her head all day. It was why she walked almost to West Severance before she realized how far she had gone. On her bureau, the pictures of Joey and Nicky were looking at her, Nicky with his direct and penetrating gaze. Joey was sitting beside a campfire. He was laughing. Isabel lay on her bed and looked at them for a while. Then she got up and put both pictures in a drawer, closed the drawer and went back to the bed and lay down again.

It was going to be almost impossible to go to Leroy's office tomorrow. She would have to face Renée. But she didn't have a choice because she wanted to see him again. Maybe she was fall-ing in love with him. Maybe that's why it had happened. There was a wildness, an abandon in her that she had never experi-enced before. It must have come from somewhere. But how did he feel? Would he want to see her again? She had no idea what she would do if he thought it was all a mistake.

She got up off the bed. She would take her laundry down to the laundromat, and try to think about something else for a while.

15

WHEN CAROL ANN got out of Raymond's car in the parking lot, she could smell flowers. She stuck her head back in the car. It smelled like motor oil in there.

"Thanks for the ride. I'll see you tonight."

"Okay, hon. See you."

She slammed the door and watched him drive off. Then she turned to go into the Texas, even though she wished she didn't have to. It was six-thirty in the morning, and all the birds in the world were singing in the sweet, spring air. She didn't know what she *did* want. The only thing she was sure of was that she didn't want to cook all day for a bunch of men.

But she had no choice. She could feel May watching her through the window, and if there was a customer in there, she was probably saying, "What do you suppose Carol Ann's up to now? She's standin out there in the parkin lot doin nothin, just standin like a lump, when she ought to be in here already with her jacket off, gettin the griddle scraped down." Carol Ann sighed.

Inside, the air was greasy. There weren't any customers. May was wiping down the counter. For some reason, the big, circular swipes she made with the dishrag irritated Carol Ann.

"Nice mornin, ain't it?"

Carol Ann hung her coat on a hook. She was going to say good morning and something about the weather, but for some reason, she couldn't. She felt restless and sleepy at the same time. She started down the aisle to go around the counter at the far end.

"So what's the matter with you all of a sudden?" May said when Carol Ann walked by her. There was a hard edge to her voice.

"Oh, I don't know, May. Don't be mad. I just feel fat and stupid today." She turned around and went back down the aisle to the end where the coffee urn was. "Maybe I just ain't awake yet." It was like she couldn't quite make herself get over on the proper side of the counter.

May went on wiping, although it was perfectly clean already. "That's the trouble with a day off. It's twice as hard to get to work the next day."

"Oh, May."

"Get yourself some coffee, honey. You'll live."

Carol Ann got out a cup and poured herself some coffee and stood there drinking it black. It was fresh and hot and bitter, and it jolted her awake.

Behind her the door opened, and the three linemen came in and sat in a row in the middle of the counter, like they always did.

"Mornin, boys," May said. "Do you want anythin besides coffee today?" She turned toward Carol Ann and gave a quick shake of her head, but she didn't need to. Carol Ann knew they all took coffee, as well as May did, and she was already reaching for the cups when May gave her that look. Nobody wanted anything else, so May got the cream out of the refrigerator and went back to cleaning the counter.

Carol Ann brought over the three cups of coffee, carrying two cups in one hand. She set them down in front of Rickie, and they all reached for one.

"Hey, Carol, was that you and Raymond I seen slow-dancin at the Country Club Saturday night?"

That made her smile. "I didn't see you there, Ed."

"You was kind of busy talkin to Leroy LaFourniere, it looked like."

May looked up when she heard that.

"He didn't stay very long. I'm surprised I didn't see you." She really said that because she knew May was listening.

Rickie said, "Was that band any good? I almost came in to check 'em out, but we went to Jake's instead."

"I don't know how good they were," Carol Ann said. "*I* liked 'em."

"They were okay," Ed said.

"You had a good time, Carol Ann." It wasn't a question, and the men didn't notice, but Carol Ann knew May was telling her she wasn't being careful enough. She tried not to look in her direction.

For a few minutes no one said anything. Then May looked up. "Well, boys, it's gettin close to seven, and my clock's not fast."

It was Ed's morning to pay. He gave Carol Ann the money, and she brought his change, and they all three hurried out. Ed could have told her to keep the change, but then he was the worst about tipping.

As the door was shutting, May said, "What's goin on here? Where is everybody today?" Carol Ann could tell May was thinking that no one was ever going to come in again, and the Texas would go out of business. But just as she said the words, a car and two pick-ups pulled into the parking area.

Carol Ann said, "That's Monday for you." And from then on they didn't have time to think about anything but breakfast orders, and Carol Ann didn't speak to May, except to put in an order or to apologize for squeezing past her.

Around ten-thirty it got quiet enough for them to take their break. May got them each a cup of tea, and Carol Ann brought the cream and sugar over for hers. She picked up her pocketbook from the shelf under the counter where she always kept it and brought that over too.

"Feelin better now, Carol Ann?"

"Nothin like work to take your mind off your troubles."

"Ain't that the truth."

May took her tea bag by the string. She bounced it up and down in the water a few times and then held it over the cup to drip. Without looking up, she said, "You didn't tell me you and Raymond were goin to go out with Leroy."

"That wasn't the way it was at *all*. You're so *suspicious*, May. We were at the Country Club, and Leroy came and sat with us for about fifteen minutes. He bought us drinks, and then he left. There ain't no harm in that, is there?"

"Honey, I'm just afraid you might get in too deep."

"I can handle it. Actually, I think the reason Leroy sat down with us was to give me this real estate stuff he told me about."

"He probably didn't want to give it to you in front of your grandpa."

"I don't know, May. He *could* have. I ain't keepin it a secret from Gramps. He *told* me to find out what the place was worth."

"Okay, honey. Don't get sore."

"I got the papers he gave me in my pocketbook. I was hopin...." She looked into May's wide, calm face, but she couldn't tell anything from her expression. "It's all in them words that ain't really words. Raymond and Allie wouldn't know what they meant. Besides, if anything's got words or numbers on it, Raymond won't fool with it. And I'd feel funny askin Gramps about it, even if he did know what all those funny, little words meant." She paused. "I thought you'd know. You always know about stuff like that."

"Well, I can't promise nothin, Carol, but I'll be glad to take a look for you."

"Oh thanks, May." She couldn't tell anything from May's face. "Would right now be okay?"

"Sure, honey, if you want me to."

Carol Ann already had the packet out. She handed it to May. May took the envelope and looked at it and then set it down on the table and heaved herself up onto her feet. When she was standing, she looked down at Carol Ann and said, "It ain't goin to do no good to look unless I get my glasses." She went around behind the counter and got them off the shelf. On the way back, she stopped to straighten the salt and pepper shakers on the counter.

Carol Ann tried to look like she was relaxing with her tea and wasn't impatient, but she was all tight inside, waiting for May to get back.

May sat down and sipped her tea before she took her glasses slowly out of their case and put them on. Carol Ann didn't want to watch every move May made, so she couldn't tell whether May was going extra slow to aggravate her, or whether that was just the heavy way she always moved.

Finally May took everything out of the envelope. She laid the glossy brochures to one side and unfolded the Xeroxed pages. Carol Ann watched eagerly. May's eyes worked their way down the first page. She took that page and put it last, and her eyes zigzagged down the second page. She didn't look at Carol Ann, and she didn't say anything. She just looked over each page, moved it to the end, and started on the next one.

Carol Ann couldn't tell how much of the stack she had read because the size of the pile stayed the same. Any minute now someone would come in, and they would have to go back to work, and she might not get a chance to find out what May thought about it. She sat there willing herself not to fidget because she had to give May a chance to figure it out.

Finally May looked at her over the pages. "This ain't nothin to worry about, Carol Ann. Once I show you what these things mean, you'll be able to take it from there."

"I don't know, May...."

"Sure, hon, look." She turned the pages sideways and laid them on the table so they could both read them. "See, 'bdrms,' that's bedrooms, ain't it? And 'kit' is kitchen; 'bath' is bathroom. There ain't nothin hard about it. You just *think* you don't know."

"I don't know if you're right, May. See, look there at that little cross thing. What's that then?"

"Hah," was all May said for a minute. Then she picked up the page and looked closer. After a pause, she set it down on the stack. "Okay. See that means 'more or less' acres. You know, plus or minus, see. It ain't hard, Carol Ann. You just *think* it is."

"Well, what must I do then?"

"Okay. I'll tell you. Leroy sent all this to you so you could compare, so you could see how much different places was worth nowdays. Am I right?" She looked directly into Carol Ann's face.

"Well, of course. That's what he said in the first place."

"So you just read these over and find the one that's most like your place, and then you look at the price tag, and you've got it."

"I don't know. I mean, even if I could figure those little words out, like you say, suppose I don't find one that's just like ours?"

"That's why Leroy sent such a bunch of 'em. So you could figure out between several that was more or less like yours."

"Well, I'll try like you say to." She sighed. She never seemed to get very far with anything.

"Take your time over it, Carol. You ain't in any hurry. You're just tryin to find out in case you want to know later on, ain't you? You could end up bein sorry if you get yourself into anything. Especially foolin around with that Leroy."

Carol Ann felt suddenly annoyed with everyone, including May, although she knew May was trying to be helpful. She said, "You don't *know* what I have to put up with. The other day when I got home, there was Allie with her head all bandaged up because those stupid cows of Gramps' had hurt her. Raymond was actin so funny I thought she might be killed. I'm the only one in the whole house that has any sense at all."

"Men. They don't never grow up. I don't care if they get as old as your grandpa."

"Ain't that the truth. And Allie's as bad as they are. It's three against one in that house, and it always will be. You just don't know."

"Was she all right? How bad was it?"

"I think it was just a cut. I hope she didn't need stitches because they didn't get her any. Gramps tried to fix it with a *egg*, if you can believe it."

"I've heard of that."

"Oh May, you're as bad as he is."

"Now, Carol, you know what a good man Sonny is. He wouldn't do nothin stupid, especially not with Allie. He loves her as much as you do."

Carol Ann sighed again. "I know. It's just they acted so strange, and they already had her head all bandaged up, so I never got to see it—her own mother, and I don't even know how bad it is."

May reached out and patted Carol Ann's hand. That was a lot for her to do, and Carol Ann knew it. "She'll be fine, hon, but you can't help worryin about 'em." She picked up the pile of Xeroxed pages and folded them neatly. She picked up the shiny brochures and added them to the pile. "These ones are probably like those others. You see what you can do." She reached for the envelope and started to put the papers back inside it. Then she stopped and looked at Carol Ann. "You got to do the comparin part yourself. I can't remember the last time I was out at your place, so I wouldn't know....see, are you plannin to sell the land and the house together?"

Carol Ann was stunned. She had never thought about the land. Her only goal had been to get a house that was easy to take care of. She said, "Gramps would never...."

"Carol, you better go slow. See what I mean?"

"The land's okay. It's the *house* I got problems with. Gramps knows that."

"Well, you watch out. You could get in too deep. Oh, and by the way, I seen your grandpa drive by with a woman in his pick-up yesterday." She handed the packet to Carol Ann who put it back in her pocketbook. "He started to turn in here and then thought the better of it. I couldn't see much of course, but I didn't recognize her. You probably know all about it." She gave Carol Ann a sharp look. She was eager to hear more.

Carol Ann was too surprised to be crafty. "No, I don't know anythin about any of it. Gramps asked Raymond to help him fix his brakes, but about midway through the afternoon, he took off. He told Raymond to tell me he was comin down here. That's all I know."

"Um-hmm," May said. She stood up. She looked like she knew a lot more than she was telling.

"What do you mean by that?"

"Nothin, honey. I don't mean a thing."

Carol Ann stood up too and put her pocketbook on the table, so she could wipe off the seats.

"What do you know that you ain't tellin?"

May was looking past her out the window. "Here comes the first of the dinner crowd. That's George Peterson's new truck, I believe." Then she looked at Carol Ann. "Hon, all I know is what I already told you. Don't worry, when there's more to find out, we'll hear about it from somebody. Word always gets around." She patted Carol Ann on the shoulder. "Everthin'll be all right, don't worry."

Carol Ann could feel that May was on her side, and May was strong. "Thanks, May," she said.

"Now let's get to work," May said.

16

AFTER BREAKFAST Leroy walked down the hall from the kitchen and put on his jacket and hat before he went into the office. He wasn't sure what he was going to find in there, and because of that, he wanted to look like he wasn't staying long. It gave him a bit of an edge.

It was easy to imagine Renée and Isabel at each other's throats already first thing in the morning on Isabel's second day of work. He thought, "Why do I always get myself into situations like this? Who needs this kind of aggravation?" And then he had to laugh at himself and admit to himself that he liked it, that it was hot and spicy to have women tearing each other up over him. So he came into the room grinning to himself, not knowing what he was going to find, or what he was going to do about whatever it was, but knowing that he was loose and could handle it, could make it work for him whatever it was.

They must have heard his footsteps coming down the hall, because they were both looking at the door when he opened it. He let his eyes slide across Isabel, who was sitting at his desk facing the door, and focused on Renée first.

"Good morning, Chérie."

Renée smiled at him, and that smile let him know that it would have been a terrible mistake if he had looked at Isabel first. He hoped this moment would show Isabel that they had to be discreet. He had already decided that he wanted to see her again, so he was eager to look at her to see what she was thinking about him. He kept his eyes on Renée for a little longer.

"Busy so early, Chérie? I hoped having help would make it easier for you. Having Isabel for help." He said 'Isabel' deliberately and turned to look at her. She was nervous. He could tell. He had felt her eyes on him, but when he looked at her, her gaze dropped away. "Good morning, Isabel," he said.

"Hello Lee....uh, hello," she said with a quick glance at Renée.

"Please call me Leroy. Everyone does," he said smiling, thinking that she caught on fast. He wouldn't even have to tell her to keep their business to herself. So far, so good. Whether she could be counted on to be discreet was more significant at this point than what she thought of him. He couldn't tell about that since she wouldn't look him in the eye. But she had seemed to want him the other night, and they could all be sweet-talked around—all but Marie anyway, and *she* hadn't always been like that. He put the thought out of his head. It only made him feel sour and off-balance. "Has Renée found enough work for you yet?"

"Well, no....not really." She looked at Renée to see what she would say.

Leroy looked at Renée too. She took a few steps toward him and stopped with her hands on her hips. "I'm not sure what you *want*, Leroy. It's a good idea, but I don't know if I can just turn it over to somebody else, just like that. I mean, I've been doing it a certain way, and...."

"Whoa, Chérie." He held up his hands, laughing. He loved women and the ways they had of doing things, the way a horse trainer might love everything about horses. "Don't be so impatient, and you," he turned to look at Isabel, "don't worry. Let's give it some time. We all agree it's a good idea." He looked at Renée again. "It will give you more time to be out selling. That's what *you* are good at. I've told Isabel to work however many hours she needs to, and we'll pay ten dollars an hour. If she goes over twenty hours, we can talk about something different. Let's wait and see. Have you got anything for her to do today?"

Renée relaxed a little, dropping her arms to her sides. "I guess so. There are some letters I didn't get to last week, and there's always the filing." She looked doubtfully at Isabel and then back at Leroy. "If that's what you mean."

"It's certainly all right with me," Isabel said to no one in particular.

Leroy let his eyes slide across Isabel's face in a noncommittal manner. "Chérie, you know what work there is in this office much better than I do," he said to Renée. He stepped forward and took her hands, looking into her cat's eyes which were even narrower than usual. "I need the file on the Booth place. If it's in your car, I can get it myself when I go out."

"It *is* in my car," she said, and she softened a little. "You always know. I don't know how you do it."

"I pay attention, Chérie. But it's because I care." He was conscious of Isabel looking down at some papers on the desk before her so that she would appear not to be listening. He was conscious of her without turning his head in her direction. He was careful not to do that. "I can get it myself on my way out."

"I'll do it, Leroy. You'd never find it in there."

"Try me."

"No," she said, smiling. She pulled her hands away and went out of the office, her heels clicking sharply on the bare floor.

Leroy went over to the desk and rested his hands on it, leaning down to see into Isabel's eyes. He put all the meaning he could into the look. "Chérie," he said, "excuse my coldness. It's not what I'm feeling. We have to be careful."

When she looked up, he could see fear in her eyes, and at the same time color spread up her face. He liked that—the shyness and the startled-animal look.

"Can I meet you later—for a drink?"

She nodded like a solemn child.

He could hear Renée's heels on the sidewalk outside. "Do you know the Mansfield Inn? Near the old railroad station?"

"I've walked past it."

"The bar then. At seven o'clock. Okay?"

The outside door slammed. Leroy stepped back, Isabel nodded, and Renée came into the room carrying the folder.

"What's going on with the Booth property?" she asked, handing him the folder.

"Thank you, Chérie. I'll fill you in on all of it later, when I have more time. I'm meeting someone in Burlington, and I'm late already."

"Leroy," she said, stretching his name out. Her eyes flicked for a second in Isabel's direction, and then she said, "You're *not* going over to New York State, are you?"

He knew she meant the race track, and he stiffened. She had no right to tell him what to do. Then he relaxed a little. He told himself to keep cool. "No, Chérie," he said. "I'm going to Burlington." He could have told her that the track wasn't even open on Monday, but he didn't. He didn't want her to know he understood her reference. If she wanted to know about the track, she could get herself a schedule. "I've got to get on the road. I'll see you both later," he said, letting his eyes rest on Isabel, so that she would know what he really meant. He tilted his hat down a little and left carrying the folder.

The Lincoln was warm from sitting in the garage. He got in and backed out into the street. It was a good move to have asked for the Booth file. Renée was so busy trying to figure out what he wanted with it that she didn't have time to notice that he had been alone with Isabel for a few minutes. If this thing with Isabel went on for any length of time, trying to keep it a secret, especially from Renée, would be a game of cat and mouse. That was for sure. But he could handle it. Hell, he would even *like* it. That's where a lot of the excitement came from. And it could be over before it went anywhere. There was no way to tell at this point.

He got on I-89 and let the big Lincoln loose. He put the windows part way down so he could hear the wind. That was the only way to tell that he was going fast. This car was so smooth— eighty felt like sitting at a stoplight.

He had thought that when he saw Isabel again, he might decide that it was all a mistake, one of those Saturday-night deals that didn't carry over into next week. Instead, she had seemed sweeter, more gentle than he had remembered. There was something about her that reminded him of Marie, of how Marie used to be.

He was looking forward to seeing her this evening. It could be a good thing for both of them. He wouldn't be interested in pursuing it if it wasn't. It took a really sick guy to force himself on a woman, especially these days when there were so many willing women around. He would *never* do anything like that, thank God.

But this could be good for her too. It wasn't healthy for a woman to go for a long time without sex, any more than it was for a man, and he knew he was a good lover, better for being older, much better than he had been when he was young.

It was early, a little after ten-thirty when he got to the Colchester exit, so he went on by and took Route 2 up through Grand Isle. Even with the light, misty rain, it was still a beautiful morning. It was like a picture out of *Vermont Life* with the trees just putting on their new leaves, and all the grass such a bright green.

There was hardly anybody on the road, except a string of

women on bicycles. He went by close and fast, hoping they would wish they were sitting beside him, instead of puffing along in his exhaust. He got almost all the way to Alburg before he ran out of time and turned around.

He knew that saying, that the mark of a man who was really good wasn't how much he won when he was winning, but how he handled himself when he was losing. Still, it was one thing to know it and another to be able to live up to it. Now was the time to find out if he had it. Now was the time to show what he was made of. You ought to be able to bet all you had left and not care which way it went. That is, if you were really one of the good ones, one of the high rollers, and not a small-time faker who could walk the walk and talk the talk but wasn't the real thing.

He passed the women on their bicycles again, but he was on the other side of the road this time. He could see their faces as he went by, so he didn't even care that none of them looked at him. There wasn't one that was worth the bother.

He didn't want to be early, but he was getting nervous. He didn't want to be late either. Ted Houston could get the idea that he was blowing him off and change his mind. He hated to have to ask a jerk like Ted Houston for anything, but he had no choice. Still, it wasn't as if it was a big deal. Houston hadn't earned all that money. He was just another coupon-clipper living off his old man's work. Ten thousand for three months—why he could raise that practically interest-free with credit cards, if he wasn't so over-extended already. There wasn't any reason for Houston to say no. This was just a formality.

Too bad it wasn't sunny. It was a beautiful drive on a good day. Still, he bet the farmers weren't crying. It was only guys like him, guys that didn't need to get their hands dirty that could afford to wish for sunshine every day. Something made him think of his dad, either the farming or the crying. He wasn't sure which. He should have gone out to see him yesterday, but after spending all that time with Jerome and Tammy and their kids, he thought he'd done enough for one day. Those kids were as bad as his old man for crying, and enough was enough. The old man's mind was so far gone, he probably didn't know how long it had been anyway.

He crossed the bridge and poked around going through Colchester. When he pulled into the parking lot of the Bayview, it was eleven-twenty-five. He walked up the ramp and went inside. It was all glass and built out over the water. He supposed it was pretty nice if you were a rich guy and wanted to sit there and look at your boat all day. It wasn't really his kind of place. The people in here gave themselves too many airs for his taste, and part of it was the way they dressed in ripped-up clothes and thought they were pretty smart to do it.

He walked by the bar, but he didn't see Ted, so he looked in the dining room. He hadn't even had a chance to look over the tables when the hostess was on him, asking him what he wanted. She said 'sir,' but the way she said it, he could tell she didn't mean it. He stayed cool and told her he was looking for somebody.

When he saw Ted wasn't there either, he went back to the bar and ordered himself a Scotch and water. He sat down two stools away from a big fat guy in red shorts and a windbreaker. The guy turned on his stool and looked Leroy up and down, but he didn't say anthing. Leroy gave back a look as cold as the one he got.

He took a sip of his drink. He was wishing he had spent another ten minutes driving around Colchester, when someone slapped him on the back hard enough to slosh his drink over the side of the glass. He tightened the muscles in his arms and shoulders and set his jaw so that he didn't respond.

"Hey Leroy. Good to see you, you old dog, you." It was Ted.

Leroy turned, smiling. "Nice to see you too, Ted. Let me get you a drink. What'll it be?"

"I wish I could," Ted said. He was standing slightly behind, so Leroy had to twist around to see him. "It's too early in the day for me. It's against my rules."

"Rules were made to be broken," Leroy said. He stood up. "I'll buy you some lunch then. We need to go somewhere we can talk anyway." He looked around at the fat man as he spoke, and the fat man turned quickly away.

Ted said, "I haven't got time for that either, but let's get a table in the dining room." He led the way without waiting.

Leroy picked up his drink and followed. He felt the fat guy laughing at him behind his back. He could picture himself turning and with one graceful karate kick of his booted toe, putting the guy's front teeth down his throat. It was just what he deserved.

Ted was talking to the hostess, and she was smiling at him. She said it was fine if they sat at one of the tables. Leroy followed Ted to one by the window. Before they were even sitting down, the hostess was there with a cup of coffee for Ted and a smile of contempt for Leroy.

"Can I get you anything, sir?"

"No," Leroy said and raised his drink an inch off the table to show her he was all set.

Ted was putting sugar in his coffee. The light from the window shone on his glasses, so Leroy couldn't see through them to his eyes. "What's on your mind?"

Leroy was surprised by the crudity of the way Ted went right to the point. Anybody with decent manners knew you had to make small talk for a while before you brought up the real subject. If you were raised in the country, you always had that kind of manners, but if you weren't raised that way, you probably never knew the difference. "Not much. I think my mind's a blank." He gave a short laugh and took a drink of Scotch, trying to collect his thoughts.

Ted didn't help a bit. He just sat there waiting for Leroy to say more.

"Actually, Ted, I've been down on my luck lately. I need a stake for a couple of months."

"I don't know, Leroy. I'd like to help you out...."

"Then do it, you bastard," was what Leroy was thinking, but he didn't say anything.

Ted took a long drink of his coffee, set the cup down, and looked past Leroy, out the window at the pier with all the yachts tied up to it. "See that mast down there, the farthest away in this group of three—the tallest? That's mine. The Sea Skimmer."

Leroy turned in his seat to look. He nodded as though he saw, without trying to figure out which boat Ted was talking about. Just like the jerk to name it the sea something when it had probably never left the lake in its life. He knew Ted was stringing him along and wasn't going to give him the money. And why not? He had so much, and he knew Leroy was good for it. He turned back toward Ted, but all he could see was the mirrored surfaces of his glasses. "Why not?" he said sharply.

"I....uh....I just don't have much capital floating around these days."

"Hey, I'm not talking about anything major. All I need is ten. You could practically do it with credit cards." He hated to beg.

"I'm sorry, Leroy."

"Jesus. I bet your old man wouldn't be such a tight-ass."

Ted stood up. "Well, go ask *him* for it then."

Leroy got a grip on himself. He stood up too and held out his hand. It was how guys acted at a time like this that separated the men from the boys. He needed to remember that. "Hey, no big deal, Ted. It's nice to see you. I'll get the coffee."

Ted shook his hand. "Thanks, but she's already put it on my tab. Come back some time, and I'll take you out on the lake."

"Great. I'll do that," Leroy said, but he was thinking, "Not a chance, you bastard," and Ted knew that's what he was thinking.

He got on 89 going toward Severance before he thought about it. He just wanted to get out of there. He had to do some thinking, and he didn't want to see anybody until he knew what to do next. He didn't have to be in Severance until seven o'clock to meet Isabel. He decided to just head south for a while to sort things out, to let the big Lincoln soothe him and take the kinks out of his mind.

He couldn't ask Roy Houston for the loan, not after the words they'd had last time. He wondered if Ted had been taunting him, or if his old man really hadn't mentioned it. He didn't know how well they got along. Maybe the old man was disappointed in how his son had turned out. Leroy could understand that. He had a lot of respect for Roy and almost none for his son.

And that was another thing—he meant to leave a big tip for the hostess. He wanted to show her how far she was beneath his notice, how he could be generous to her, even though she had done nothing for him, how he was thinking she must need the money more than he did. He meant to show Ted that he could still throw his money around when he didn't have any, how money just wasn't important to him, like it was to Ted and his stuffy yacht-club friends. But he forgot. And now it was too late.

He ended up driving all the way down to the Massachusetts border and back. It took the whole afternoon, but it was just what he needed—to spend some time alone, sorting things out. He took a side trip over to Rutland in the late afternoon and had a big steak dinner in a restaurant there. Then he called Marie and told her he wasn't going to be home until after ten.

Coming up on 89, he saw he was going to be early, so he stopped in Williamstown for a drink. He definitely didn't want a replay of this morning. He wanted Isabel to get there before he did. And he timed it just right. It was seven-twenty when he pulled in.

The great thing about the Mansfield Inn was the big parking lot behind it, which everybody in town used when they went shopping or to the movie theater across the street. No one who recognized his car would be surprised to see it there. No one would speculate about what he was doing. It was where everyone parked for everything. It made the Mansfield Inn the most anonymous place around.

He walked through the lobby and down the hall to the bar and stopped dead in the doorway. For some reason he had pictured Isabel sitting at one of the little tables that stood between the bar and the booths. Even more, in his mind she was facing the door, watching for him. So when he saw the empty tables, it stopped him cold. For a second he thought she had stood him up. Then he walked on in, trying to look casual, glad to see that the bartender was looking the other way and hadn't noticed.

He went up to the bar and asked for a Scotch and water. While he stood there waiting, he was able to look over the booths. They had high, wooden backs—another reason he liked the place— and it was hard to see who was sitting there.

Tonight the booths were all empty except for the last one. All Leroy could see over the top of the back was a little brown hair, but he was sure it was Isabel. She was being almost too discreet. He might have missed her way back there, and she wasn't even watching for him. She had her back to the room.

He got his drink and went over. She was writing something in a book. When he stopped by the table, she looked up at him and smiled. At the same time, she closed the book and slid it onto the seat beside her as though she didn't want him to notice it. She had a glass of red wine sitting on the table in front of her. It was almost full.

"Chérie," he said, putting a lot of emotion into the word. "I'm sorry I'm late."

"That's okay."

He sat down, giving her a look full of meaning.

Her eyes dropped away. She picked up her wine glass and took a sip without looking at him.

He took off his hat and set it on the seat. In a way he hated to do it. He knew he looked better with it on. "I'm glad you're not mad at me for being late."

She put down the glass and looked at him and took a gaspy breath. "On Sunday I was worried about what it was going to be like to go in to your office. I was nervous about seeing you again." She was talking fast. "I thought it was going to be embarrassing. But you were nice about it. It was okay. It wasn't embarrassing at all."

"I was glad to see you again, Chérie, even more than I thought I was going to be." He took a drink of Scotch, watching her over the tilt of the glass.

"But now I'm worried about Renée."

"Why? What about her?" He set down the glass and leaned forward a little. "What happened after I left?"

"Nothing. I don't mean that. She didn't stay very long. She left me some letters to do."

"What do you mean then?"

"You *know* she's in love with you." It wasn't a question.

He laughed.

"It's true. And she doesn't like me a bit." She paused. "Although I don't think she thinks....but what's she going to do if we keep on...." She looked down at the table. "....if we keep on seeing each other....that would be awful for her."

"Chérie, you sound uncertain about it."

She looked up at him. "I am."

"Why, Chérie? Are you sorry I came to see you the other night?"

"Of course not...." But she sounded unsure.

"What then?" Nothing was going the way he planned it today.

"I just feel so sorry for Renée. That's all. I know she's in love with you."

"I *hope* that's all. Because you have it wrong. It's not like you think."

"It's not?"

"Not at all. Renée is my niece."

"She is? But...."

"What kind of a man do you think I am, Chérie? She's my *family*. Even if it was all right with her, which it wouldn't be, it wouldn't be all right with me. Do you see? It's taboo. We work well together, Renée and I. We understand each other. But that has nothing to do with you and me. All right?"

She nodded.

"Good. Because I want you to understand."

She nodded again.

Maybe he had said more than he needed to. He didn't want to put her off. He reached out and took her hand. "Chérie, let's talk about you and me. I've heard what you are feeling about Renée, but what I *want* to hear is what you're feeling about me." He leaned across the table, trying to look into her eyes. "Tell me."

"I'm so glad you told me about Renée. I didn't want to think about you when I thought she was in love with you. It wouldn't have been...."

"You're not answering my question, Chérie."

She took another sip of wine and put down the glass before she looked into his face. "The other night was amazing for me. I didn't know I could feel like that." The pink rose up in her face, and she looked down. "I suppose I'm falling in love with you. I guess that's what people mean when they talk about it like that."

He reached across the table and took her hand. "That's just what I wanted to hear. What I've been waiting for all day long." He was surprised by the strength of his feelings, by how much those few sentences meant to him.

His Scotch was gone, and so was her wine. He stood up. "I'll be right back. I'll get us each another drink."

"Not for me thanks." She smiled up at him. "I only ordered that one so they wouldn't mind my sitting here."

"Okay, Chérie. Don't move. I'll be right back." He felt a lot better now.

When he came back with his Scotch, he sat down and took a drink, and then he said, "I have a room here." He tried to make it sound like he just got it, not like he always kept a room at the Manchester. "It's more private than Roxy's. Shall we go up?" He tried to sound casual.

"Oh," she said. "I wasn't....I didn't expect...."

"What?" It took him by surprise. "You just said…."

"I know. It's that I wasn't planning…."

"What difference does that make?"

"I thought we were going to talk tonight, to spend some time getting to know each other."

"Come on. If you want to talk, we can talk up there. But we already know each other. I feel as though I know you well, even though I've never met anyone like you before. We have plenty of time to talk. We can talk later."

"I can't. I told my mother I'd call her at eight-thirty. She would be worried if I didn't call."

He reached out to take her hand again. "That's nothing. There's a phone in the room. You can call from there."

She looked distressed. "I can't do that. It would feel so—so funny." She blushed again. "I'll come to your room soon. I want to very much. I never knew it could be like that, but…."

"Well then, why not now?" He hoped he didn't sound like he was begging. She looked so pretty with her face all pink.

"See, I threw away my diaphram when I was in the middle of the divorce. I didn't think I would…I need to make an appointment at Planned Parenthood. I meant to do it today."

"You can leave that to me, Chérie. You can trust me. I would never do anything to hurt you. You don't need to worry about the other night either, you know."

"I did wonder a little, but all this is so new to me….and not what I had planned. I need a little time…."

Right then he could see there was no use in saying any more. Her mind was made up. He was more disappointed than he had thought he would be. He wondered why he was surprised. Nothing had gone right for him all day long. He dropped her hand and picked up his drink. The only part of the day that was all right was when he was alone in his car. He sat back, and his hand went down to his hat, ready to pick it up.

"Oh," she said. "I didn't mean to hurt your feelings." She reached out toward him as though asking him to take her hand again.

He pretended not to notice.

"Don't be mad. It's just that it's all happening so fast, and I didn't expect....and I told my mother I'd call." She looked down at the table, and the pink rose up in her cheeks again. "I couldn't talk to her in your room, because I couldn't tell her.... She wouldn't understand. But I want to see you again. I really do."

He downed the rest of his drink.

"Don't be mad. I'll come to your room soon. I really will."

"Okay." He picked up his hat and put it on his head. Why did everything have to get so complicated?

"I just hope you understand why I can't tonight."

"Sure. I understand." He stood up. "Where'd you leave your car? I looked for it in the parking lot."

She slipped the book from the seat beside her into her bag, zipped the bag shut and then stood up beside him. "I walked."

"I better give you a ride home."

"No thanks," she said. "Roxy...."

"Chérie, that's no place to walk at night. Why didn't you bring your car?"

They went down the hall and through the lobby. "It's not even dark yet," she said. "The phone call won't take long. I'll be fine. Good night, and thanks a lot."

"Thanks for nothing," he thought, but he just smiled and didn't say anything.

She waved and walked off.

He decided to go home. There wasn't much else to do. At least the day was almost over. Maybe tomorrow his luck would change.

17

WHEN CAROL ANN stuck her head back in the kitchen to tell
Sonny the telephone call was for him, she couldn't help rolling
her eyes, so he was already nervous before he even picked up
the receiver and heard an unfamiliar woman's voice. It was the
woman he had picked up hitchhiking last Sunday. She seemed
as nervous as he was, so what could he say? When she asked if
she could come out and see his cattle, he didn't feel right about
saying no, even though he regretted it as soon as he hung up the
phone. But it was too late then. They had already agreed that
Thursday would work out, and he had given her directions to
the place.

When he hung up the telephone, he went on down the hall to
the bathroom and stayed there for quite a while. He knew that
was mean of him, but he couldn't help teasing Carol Ann sometimes. By the time he got back to the kitchen, she was about to

jump out of her skin, she was so anxious to know what it was all about. He sat down at the table with her and Raymond.

"Where's Allie?" he asked.

"She went up to her room. She said she had homework."

Nobody said any more for a minute, but Sonny knew that wouldn't last, and it didn't.

Carol Ann stood it as long as she could, and then she said, "What was that woman callin you up about, Gramps?"

"Aw, she just wanted to know could she come out and see Buck 'n Ben."

"Did you tell her no?" Raymond asked. He was interested now too.

"I probably should have, but I didn't. I told her to come out on Thursday at half-past two. That way it can't drag on too long before I have to get over to the Texas to pick up Carol."

"What day's she comin, Gramps? I got to do Janet's shift on Thursday."

"There goes my good excuse then, cause Thursday's the very day."

"Who *is* this woman, anyhow?"

"I don't really know. I don't think she's from around here. She don't look like she is anyhow."

Raymond put his elbows on the table and leaned toward Sonny. "How does she know about your cattle if she ain't from around here? Is she some kind of inspector or somethin?"

At the same time Carol Ann was asking, "What does she look like, Gramps? How old is she?"

They were both looking at him hard. Sonny stood up, laughing. "Hold it," he said. "Too many questions." He walked over to the sink and ran the cold water while he was getting a clean glass out of the cupboard.

When he had filled the glass and shut off the water, he turned around. They were both still waiting, watching his every move.

"So, Carol," he said. "I don't know. She ain't real young, but she's still youngish. Forty, maybe? I ain't good at that kind of guesswork."

"Where did you meet her, Gramps?" This was from Raymond.

"She claims we pulled her out when her car got bogged down in the mudhole out front last year. I don't remember....no, that ain't right. I remember the car and pullin it out. I just wouldn't have remembered her, I guess."

He was sitting down at the table again by the time he finished his sentence. He glanced at Carol Ann who was studying his face. She looked suspicious.

Sonny definitely didn't want to mention how he picked this woman up when she was hitchhiking, but he could see the wheels going around in Carol Ann's brain, and he knew he had to fill in the blanks. He looked her in the eye and said, "I ran into her downstreet the other day, and she reminded me how Buck 'n Ben pulled her car out of the mudhole. She said she wanted to see them again." He looked over at Raymond, and Raymond's eyes dropped down to watch his own fingers drumming on the table.

Sonny stood up. "Well, I guess...." he said. He took off his feedstore cap and hung it up on its nail by the door. He stood there a minute looking out through the glass.

"What's it goin to do tomorrow, Gramps?"

"I guess this rain'll go on most of the day."

"Is that for sure?"

"There ain't nothin for sure, Ray."

"Well, I know, but it seems like it always happens the way you say it's goin to. I'd bet money on you."

"There ain't no reason to do that, Ray." He walked back to the table and stood looking down at both of them. "Well, I guess I'll turn in then. Good night."

They both said, "Night, Gramps," as he left the room.

Upstairs, Al's door was closed, but there was a light shining under it, so he knew she wasn't asleep. "I'll see you in the mornin, darlin," he said as he passed.

She was probably sitting on her bed to do her homework. At least, he heard the springs creak, and then she said, "Good night, you old Gramps."

He went slowly down the hall in case she was coming out to see him, but she didn't say anything else, and her door stayed shut, so he went into his own room and closed his door and got ready for bed.

On Thursday after he cleared away his dishes in the kitchen, Sonny stepped outside. The wind had died a bit, and the sun was out for the moment. He could smell the lilac bush, which was just getting ready to flower. It was half-past one. He had one of those little pieces of time too small to do much with.

He went around the house to the woodpile, thinking he might split up a few chunks of firewood while he waited for the woman to arrive. That way he could hear her when she drove up. But when he got there, he saw that he didn't have anything ready to split. He would have to get out the chainsaw, and it needed to be sharpened. He *ought* to sit on the porch and sharpen it while he watched for her, but he felt too restless for a job like that. He decided to go see Buck and Ben instead. He went around the back way and left the gate open in case he wanted to bring them out later.

When he stepped through the doorway into their stall, both oxen looked hopefully around at him. They didn't like to be stuck in the barn. They wanted to be out on the new spring pasture. They weren't used to grass yet, and their stall was a mess. It was a good thing he had a chance to clean up before she saw them. When he reached for the manure shovel, Buck saw him and looked away, disappointed. Ben wasn't as quick. He was still watching, still hoping.

"You'll get some time outdoors, boys," he said. "It's early yet."

He cleaned up the floor and spread a little fresh sawdust under their feet. Then he gave them each another flake of hay. He guessed it wasn't half-past two yet, so he got the curry comb to work on the matted winter hair that was still left on their haunches. He started with Buck, the way he always did. Buck might take offense if he wasn't first, and Ben never expected anything and was satisfied with whatever he got.

It was pleasant work brushing them. Sonny forgot he was waiting for the woman to come. He was nearly finished with Ben, and his back was to the door, when both oxen looked around in unison. Sonny straightened his stiff back and turned, and there she was, standing in the doorway with her arms hanging at her sides, smiling shyly, and looking smaller and more like a child than he remembered.

"I knocked on the kitchen door, but no one answered. I hope you don't mind my coming in here without being invited."

"No. It's fine." He stood there with the brush in his hand, not sure what to do next.

Buck and Ben went back to eating hay. Sonny stayed where he was, tapping the brush against his leg. The silence was going on too long, but he didn't know how to stop it.

"Which one's Buck, and which one's Ben?"

He looked at her in surprise. He was pretty sure he hadn't said their names when he talked to her on the telephone the other night. Maybe when he picked her up last Sunday she had asked? He couldn't remember.

She answered his question without him asking it. "I know this is weird, but I remembered *their* names, even though I couldn't remember yours."

He smiled, pleased by what she said. He believed her. He didn't think she would make up something like that so he would like her better.

"I *did* remember the Sonny part, but that was all. I have wanted to see your farm again ever since last year, but I wouldn't have found you so quickly if you hadn't given me a ride the other day." She paused and looked at him more directly, as though she was trying to see what he was thinking. Then she went on. "Do you think some things are just *meant* to happen?"

Sonny didn't know what to say to that. He wasn't used to speaking about personal matters, and especially not to a stranger. It made him uncomfortable. "I don't guess I know one way or the other," he said. That was the only way he could think of to get out of it.

She didn't seem to notice. She took a few steps into the stall toward Ben's head. "Is this Buck? Will he mind if I pat him?"

"That there is Ben. He's my off-ox."

She was looking at Sonny with her hand raised near Ben's shoulder.

"Go ahead. Pet him. He likes it."

She stroked the side of Ben's neck. He turned his head to look at her, chewing thoughtfully. "Nice boy, Ben," she said, and then, "He's soft. I don't think I ever actually touched a cow before."

Sonny didn't know what to say to that either. He walked around to Buck's side and scratched his throat so he wouldn't feel left out. Buck stretched his neck as far as it would go, trying to get all the mileage he could out of the scratching.

"He loves it, doesn't he?" She had followed Sonny around the oxen and was standing right behind him.

"Yes sir. Buck's a good boy," Sonny said, scratching hard the whole length of Buck's neck. "Buck's what you call the nigh-ox."

"What's that?"

"That's the ox on the left, the one the teamster walks beside. You put the one that's the boss beside you like that. The other one is farther away, so he's the off-ox. See?"

"Oh, I get it, so you always put them on the same sides."

"If you didn't, they'd get confused, and they might be thinkin when they ought to be pullin. That wouldn't be good."

"They smell wonderful. It reminds me of going to the circus when I was a child." She noticed the ox yoke leaning against the wall in the corner. "When I saw your oxen last year, they were wearing that. It's called the ox yoke, isn't it? Is it hard to put on?"

"Not if you know how."

"It looks heavy."

"It is."

"Oh," she said. She seemed disappointed. She opened her mouth, as though she was going to say more, but she looked away, first at Buck and then down at her own feet. "I was planning to ask you to do it, to put it on them, but since it's so heavy...."

She reminded him of Al. Maybe it was just that he wanted to please her, to give her what she wanted. He often felt that way about Al. "No hon...." He hoped she didn't notice that slip. "I mean, I can put it on so you can see....if you want me to."

"I'd *really* like that a lot. Would you?" She was excited now, and that was like Al too. "You see, I don't know *anything* about living in the country. I have so much to learn, because I want to try it—living in the country, I mean."

"Plenty of people live in the country who ain't seen a team of oxen."

"I know. But that's cheating. I mean, I want to *experience* all of it, to live the life fully—the way you do."

"Well, I don't...." Sonny realized he wasn't sure what he was going to say. He felt uneasy. He turned away from her and unhitched both oxen. He took off their halters and hung them up and went to the corner where the yoke stood. He was conscious of her eyes on his back.

"Oh stop! Wait a minute," she said suddenly, just as he was lifting the yoke.

Sonny rested it on the floor again and turned to look at her. "What now?" he thought, but he didn't say anything.

"Do they hate it? Are they going to mind having to wear it?"

"Women," Sonny was thinking. "What *is* it about 'em that makes you love 'em and drives you crazy both at the same time?"

"I mean because if they don't want to...."

"You don't need to be so tender-hearted. It's their job, after all. But no, they don't mind....mostly. Sometimes I can tell they feel real good about what they done. Of course, they might rather be havin a day off up the pasture, but today they'll be glad of it. At least they'll get outdoors." He didn't tell her it was her fault they had to stay inside all morning. Buck and Ben didn't know whose fault it was either.

He picked up the yoke again and carried it over and set it down on its end between the boys' heads. He was taking out Ben's bow, when he looked up just in time to see her trying to crowd in past Buck's horns. Buck didn't want to let her go by.

"I want to help you put it on," she said. She looked scared, but she kept coming, and that was like Al too.

"I appreciate it, but don't do it. Stand back over there until I get 'em yoked." He thought he had to speak so rough, or she would push right past his words too.

She stopped, but she didn't back up, and she was still in the way. He hoped Buck wouldn't swing his head at her.

"I thought I could help you lift it since it's so heavy."

"Well thank you, but you can't. Besides I do it just about every day. You stand over there out of the way and watch."

"Okay," she said meekly, backing up. She didn't seem hurt by what he'd said, but he didn't want to look at her closely either. He was glad to be busy.

After he got them all yoked up, he stepped back beside her and picked up the stick he had been using for a whip since the other day when Al got hurt. He wished now he had tried harder to find his good whip up in the woods. He was embarrassed to have nothing but a peeled switch when she was watching. It looked like he didn't know what he was doing. He just hoped she wouldn't notice.

"Gee around," he said loudly.

The oxen started into the shuffling turn they had to make to get to the door. When their noses were out in the passage, he shouted, "Haw."

It was tight for them, going through the doorway side by side, but they were used to it. When they were in the hallway, Sonny whoaed them and went out beside Buck before he started them up again. He didn't say anything to her, but he was glad to see that she was sensible enough to stay behind.

When they got to the turn in the road, the oxen hesitated, thinking they would be going up to the woodlot, but they were willing enough when he gee-ed them down the road to the house and told them to whoa near the kitchen door.

She came up to them with bright eyes. When Sonny told her she could pat them, she went to each one telling him he was a good boy and scratching his neck. Both oxen rolled their huge eyes around at Sonny, trying to figure out what was so great about walking from the barn to the house.

"What are you going to make them do now?"

"What would you like to see 'em do?"

"I don't know. I love to watch them walking. It's like being in a movie—no, it's better, because I can touch them and smell them. You can't do that in a movie."

"I'll walk 'em down to the road and back," Sonny said. He didn't look around to see if she was following, so he didn't know until he turned the oxen in a big circle out on the road and headed back toward the house. He only knew then because he didn't see her, so he knew she was behind him.

They stopped near the kitchen door with him wondering what to do next. He kept thinking she would get bored with the cattle. Most people would have, but she just kept on being delighted by all of it. He had to like her for that, even though he was getting bored himself.

The school bus stopped at the end of their road, and Al got off. No one waved to her as the bus pulled away, but she didn't look around to see either. Carol Ann had put her hair in two pony-tails in the morning, and they bounced up and down as she came hurrying up the road, intent on finding out what was happening. She looked shocked that something could be going on at home without her knowing about it.

Sonny was glad to see her, the way he always was, but he felt a little uncomfortable about the way she was looking.

Al slung her bookbag toward the steps. She didn't notice that it missed them altogether and landed in the dirt on the path. She said, "What're you doin, Gramps?" It sounded like she thought she'd caught him in the act of doing something bad. She walked over to him and stood facing him with her back to Isabel, and her hands on her hips. She acted as though Isabel wasn't even there.

Sonny had to chuckle, although he was careful not to let anything show on his face. In her own way, Al could be as fierce as Carol Ann. He said, "We're not doin nothin. I was just showin this lady here how I yoked 'em. She asked me to."

Al looked as though she didn't believe a word of it. For a second he thought she was going to say, "I can't even turn my back on you long enough to go to school."

Sonny was afraid she was going to make a scene right out in front of a stranger. He was trying to remember what Isabel said her last name was so that he could tell Al, so maybe she would act better, when Isabel helped him out by stepping around Al so that she was facing her. She introduced herself as one grown-up to another.

Then she said, "Is he your grandfather? I think he's wonderful."

Al gave him a look of even greater suspicion when she heard that. She said, "Wait for me, Gramps. Don't do *anything* until I get back. I got to change." She ran into the house without even stopping to pick up her bookbag.

Sonny walked the oxen over a few steps until they were standing in the yard. He pushed each big head down a bit to tell them to take a break and that it was okay to eat some grass while they waited.

Isabel was watching him. "Your granddaughter is sweet," she said. "What's her name?"

"Alison, but she likes to be called Al. She's kind of a tomboy."

"How old is she?"

"Fourteen. She's my great-granddaughter. Her mother is my granddaughter."

"Oh." She thought a minute. "When I came here last year—the time you pulled our car out of the mud—there was a young boy with you."

"I don't know who that would have been."

"I looked out the door of your barn and saw you coming out of the woods with your oxen in the golden, evening light. You and the boy were walking in front, and the oxen were following you. It was very beautiful. Was it your great-grandson maybe? I remember it so plainly."

Sonny thought a minute. "I don't have a great-grandson," he said. Then he laughed. "That was Al. I'll have to tell her you took her for a boy. She'll like that."

Al came banging out of the house with her cap in her hand. When she stopped beside Sonny and Isabel, she stood with her back toward Isabel again. "Where's Ma at?" she said. She pulled her cap down over her eyes and stuffed her ponytails up out of sight.

"Your ma has to work late tonight."

"Oh. Okay. So what're we goin to do with Buck 'n Ben?"

"Nothin. I was just showin her....I mean, Isabel here, how I yoked 'em up."

"I asked your great-grandfather if he would show me, and he was so nice about it. Buck 'n Ben pulled our car out of the mud last year. I've wanted to see them again ever since."

Al glanced over her shoulder when Isabel was speaking. Then she looked at Sonny. "I don't remember that. Where was I, Gramps? Why wasn't I there?"

"You were there, darlin. This lady remembers us comin down from the woods together. She thought you were a boy."

"She did?" She turned toward Isabel and gave her a long, thoughtful look. She didn't turn her back on her this time when she spoke to Sonny. "So are you goin up to the woodlot with 'em now?"

"Well no. I mean, I guess I hadn't thought about it. I was about to put 'em in the barn again."

"But you *can't* do that, Gramps. It ain't good for 'em to get 'em out and not work 'em." She glanced at Isabel to see if she was following the conversation, or maybe to see if she was impressed by how much Al knew.

Sonny said, "Al, you got a lot of homework you got to get done tonight?"

"No I don't." She looked at him, pleading. "*Honest*, Gramps. And anyhow it's a perfect chance cause Ma ain't here."

"I don't know, honey. I hadn't planned....see, I don't know what we got that's ready to come down." He looked at Isabel. He didn't know whether to call her by her first name or not. "What about you? Do you want to see how the boys work in the woods?"

"I'd love to," Isabel said. She turned to Al. "Would it be all right with you if I came too?"

Al seemed to smile all over, like a puppy, even though all she said was, "Sure. I don't mind."

But Sonny wasn't sure. "This is goin to take quite a while—to go up and get a load and bring it down—probably a couple of hours anyway, before we're all done." He looked at Isabel.

"That's fine with me. I don't have anywhere I have to be," she said.

"Great," Al said. "Can we go now, Gramps?"

"Hang on a minute. We got to get the tools and the chains. And the saw ain't sharpened."

"Do we need it? How much you got cut up there?"

"I don't know. See, that's the thing. I wasn't plannin on bringin any down today, so I don't know. You'll have to hold on while I sharpen the saw."

"Let's go up and see. Maybe we won't need the saw. We don't want to keep Isabel waitin."

Sonny glanced around to see what Isabel thought about Al acting so familiar. She was smiling, so it must have been all right. She nodded at Sonny, as though she was saying she could see why he was so proud of Al. Sonny liked her for that. "Okay, darlin," he said to Al. "Get the ax and the peavy. I don't even know does the saw need gas. I'll tend to that."

"What can I do?" Isabel asked.

Sonny was just about to say that she didn't need to do anything, that she could wait here with the oxen while he and Al got what they needed, when Al said, "You come with me, and we'll get the chains. Come on."

Sonny opened his mouth to say he would get them, but Al was already marching off with Isabel right behind her, so he went into the old milkroom to get the tools himself. He decided not to take the ax after all. If there was anything to cut, he could do it with the saw. He stuck the files in his back pocket and took the saw outside to fill it with gas and oil. He put the cans back inside the barn and set the saw and the peavy on the edge of the road near the oxen. Buck was looking around curiously. He knew something was up. Ben was just happy to have some grass to eat.

Those chains were heavy. It would have been easier to walk the oxen around to the back door of the barn. Sonny would have suggested it if they hadn't taken off before he had a chance to.

In a little while they came out the milkroom door together, draped with chains. They were both staggering under the weight, and they were giggling to each other about some girl something. It made him smile to see them.

Al told Isabel to drop her chains. With the end of the big chain over her shoulder and dragging the rest of it, she pushed in between the boys and hung it on the yoke, looping it over the ends of their bows so they wouldn't have to drag it. Sonny would have helped, except that she seemed so proud of herself. He didn't want to spoil it for her, and he liked the way Isabel was watching.

When Al had both chains looped up to her satisfaction, she walked around the oxen to stand beside Sonny at their heads.

"Can I drive, Gramps?"

Sonny didn't even say yes. He just smiled at her and handed her the whip. He wanted her to impress Isabel too.

They went around the machine shed, past Raymond's junks, and out across the night pasture. Al walked beside Buck with her back straight and the whip cocked over her shoulder like a rifle. She didn't forget and grab the end of Buck's bow, the way she did when she wasn't paying enough attention. Sonny felt proud of her. He sneaked a few sideways looks at Isabel to see what she thought. She was watching it all with great seriousness, but he couldn't tell if she liked what she saw.

On the far side of the pasture, Sonny set down his tools and went ahead of Al and the oxen to open the gate. When he went back to get the tools, Isabel was holding the peavy. She smiled at him.

"At least I can carry this thing. What is it anyway?"

Sonny picked up the saw. They both went through the barway, and then Sonny turned back to fasten the gate.

"That's a peavy. It's for rollin logs."

"Oh," she said. She looked confused.

Sonny was going to say more, but Al and the oxen were waiting.

"Where we goin, Gramps?"

"Well, let me see. That's the trouble with this trip. I ain't had time to figure it out."

"There must be somethin we could draw down, just so we can show Isabel how we do it."

"I suppose we'll have to get up there before we know. Let's go to where we got that maple the other day. We can take a look and see what we got. Okay?"

"Okay, Gramps." She waved the stick and said, "Git up." The oxen lurched forward up the steep road.

Sonny turned toward Isabel, or where she had been a minute ago. He was going to say something about going on, but she wasn't where he thought she was or anywhere on the road behind.

She was clear over by the sugarhouse. When she realized that he saw her there, she said, "Do you mind if I look inside?"

"Go ahead," he said, wondering whether to wait for her or to follow Al up the road.

Isabel opened the door and looked in. It had been five years since Sonny had sugared, and probably almost that long since he had been inside the sugarhouse, so he had no idea what she would find in there. Al and the oxen were already quite far ahead. They wouldn't be able to do anything until he got up there and figured out what they had to bring down.

He didn't know what to say to Isabel about moving along. When she disappeared inside, he decided not to wait any longer. She could poke around in there all she wanted. They could pick her up on the way down. She had probably seen as much of the oxen as she wanted to anyhow. People always thought they were interested, but they weren't really. What they said sounded good, but it didn't last long, not when it came to doing something, not when it stopped being just talk.

He hurried along after Al, puffing a bit and not really enjoying himself. Al was so pleased to have someone watching how she did with the oxen. She was so proud of the way she could drive them, and she *ought* to be proud of it too. She would be disappointed when she saw that Isabel hadn't bothered to come up the hill, even though they were making this trip for her.

Halfway up the hill ahead of him, he could see Al already turning the oxen onto the side road. That was when he heard Isabel running up. She stopped a few feet behind him, panting, leaning on the peavy, struggling to talk.

"I didn't mean....oh my, that's steep...." She started to walk again, but slowly, dragging her feet, as though they were too heavy to lift.

Sonny slowed down beside her, although he knew Al was waiting for them.

"I hope I didn't hold you up?" She said it as though it was a question, but she didn't wait for an answer. "And I didn't want to miss any of it either."

After that neither of them said any more. They needed their breath to hurry along. They walked up the side road into the clearing where the maple tree had been. Al already had the oxen turned around. She was standing beside them.

"Hey, Gramps," she said. "I found us a tree. See that little one over there." She pointed with the whip. "The one you had to put down so you could get to the maple."

"Oh yes," he said. "Sure. I forgot all about that one."

"We can take the limbs off and bring it down in one load. It ain't that big."

Isabel was looking back and forth at each of them.

"I could've had the branches off already, if I'd just had the ax."

"That's okay, darlin. I'll get 'em with the saw. You can't do everythin all by yourself."

Sonny saw when he said that how Al's eyes flicked over to Isabel to see if she noticed. He looked at her too, but he couldn't tell if she appreciated how grown-up Al was being. She was right—the tree would be no problem to take down in one load, and they wouldn't be long getting it ready. He wouldn't even need to sharpen the saw.

He started it and took off the limbs. Al had already laid out the chains. She had even dug out the butt end of the log and worked the small chain around it. All Sonny had to do was check to see that it was good and tight.

He smiled at her. "Good work," he said. Isabel looked interested, but he couldn't explain it to her. She didn't know enough to understand what a competent worker Al was getting to be.

She backed up Buck and Ben so Sonny could hitch on the load, and the oxen got the log started. When the butt was out on the road, Al whoaed them and backed them up again, so Sonny could shorten the chain. Then they were ready to go.

Buck and Ben walked down to the barway at a steady pace. They were being as good as Al was. Maybe they were trying to impress Isabel too. She and Sonny came along behind carrying the tools. They didn't speak, but every time Sonny sneaked a sideways look at her, she was smiling. He liked that.

At the barway, as he opened the gate, Sonny remembered that he meant to look for that lost whip on the way down. He told himself he would have to make a special trip to find it. It was probably off the road under the trees somewhere.

"Wow!" Isabel said as they went through the gate together. "I had no idea how simple it was. Simple and beautiful. It's incredible."

Sonny said, "Well, it went okay today, but it ain't always like this." He shut the gate, and they started across the night pasture together.

"What do you mean?"

"Accidents happen. Al got hurt last week. It ain't always this easy."

"She got hurt?"

"She's all right. It wasn't bad. She got knocked down by the load and cut her head open."

"Really?"

"That's what that bandage is, on her head there."

"I didn't see a bandage."

"It's under her hair, and she pulls her cap down over it, but it's there."

"I didn't even notice."

"Al's a good girl. She went right back to drivin 'em the next day. I don't think she was even scared. She's quite a girl." He couldn't help bragging. Besides it was all true.

Up ahead Al and the oxen were taking the log around the house to the woodpile. By the time Sonny and Isabel got over there, Al had them unhitched and the chains looped over the yoke.

She said, "I guess we're all done, Gramps." Then she looked at Isabel and smiled. She was too shy to brag on herself.

Isabel said, "That was amazing. Thank you so much for showing me. I can't believe you can do that—make them do what you say. I'm so glad I got to see it. Maybe I could...."

"Maybe you could drive 'em yourself sometime," Al said.

"Do you think so?"

"Sure. Couldn't she, Gramps?"

"Well...."

"They'd let her. They like her. You can tell when they like somebody. Say yes, you old Gramps."

"Well, honey, we could try. That is if Isabel...." He looked around at her doubtfully. She was probably just being polite. It would hurt Al's feelings if she was saying things she didn't mean.

Al said, "They won't let just anybody drive 'em, you know. Nobody but me and Gramps ever does."

Isabel said, "Oh, I would love to, if you think they would let me." Her enthusiasm sounded real enough.

"Well, we'll give it a try then," Sonny said.

Al and Isabel looked at each other grinning. It was good to see Al have someone to be friends with, someone who wanted to be friends with her. He didn't want her to always be alone. Maybe Isabel was someone who would be there when he was gone, someone who was old enough to help her through the hard times, someone with more sympathy than Carol Ann had it in her to give. Sonny hoped so.

"So, here," Al said, handing the peeled stick to Isabel. "You take 'em to the barn." Both of them looked around at Sonny. "Can't she, Gramps?"

Isabel looked scared. Her face was pale and set, but she was reaching for the whip too, so she was all right.

"It's a good way to start," he said, more to her than to Al. "They already know they're goin to go back to the barn, and that's where they want to go. So all you got to do is tell 'em and act like you thought of it first."

"Okay," said Isabel, although she sounded doubtful.

"You say, 'Gee around,' real loud and wave your whip, and

they'll go in a circle here and back out the road. They know to do that, but you want 'em to know that they're doin it because you said to. Then when you get to the fork in the road, not the first one, but the one where you go to the back door of the barn, you got to say, 'Haw,' so they know you don't want 'em to go up to the woodlot again. Then they'll go right into the barn, and you say, 'Gee,' when they get to the stall and 'Whoa' when they're inside. That's it."

"Okay," Isabel said, but her eyes were wide. "Will you and Al stay close in case I do it wrong? I hope I can remember."

"It's easy, Isabel," Al said. "Gee means right and haw means left. See? I always remember gee is Ben's side and haw is Buck's side."

"Oh, I guess so. Okay."

By this time Buck and Ben were both rolling their eyes around, trying to figure out what all the talk was about. Sonny didn't want them to think it was a big deal to have Isabel drive, so he said, "Are you ready? We need to get goin."

"I'll walk beside her, Gramps, in case she needs any help. Stand right there beside Buck's shoulder, Isabel, like I did before."

So Isabel said, "Gee around," in a loud but trembly voice, and they went to the barn with her driving, and Al right beside her looking proud. The boys didn't even notice the difference, or more likely, they did notice, but they knew where they were going, and they wanted to go there, since they were always glad to get back to the barn when they were done working, and they had already forgotten that they spent the whole morning in there and were happy to get outdoors just a few hours ago.

They turned into their stall, and Sonny went on to the milk-room to set down his tools. While he was there, he filled two water buckets and carried them back.

Al was standing by Ben, scratching his neck, and Isabel was around the other side by Buck. Sonny put a bucket of water in front of each one. He stepped in between them and started to take out Buck's bow.

When he happened to glance over at Isabel, he was startled by the look of happiness on her face. She said, "Now it's really happening at last."

He didn't know what she meant. He was glad to be busy swinging down Buck's end of the heavy yoke, so that he couldn't answer.

She said, "That sugarhouse would make a wonderful cabin to live in. It's in such a beautiful spot."

Sonny put the empty bow back in the yoke and turned to Ben. Over his shoulder he said, "It wouldn't work."

She went on as though she hadn't heard. "It even has a chimney already."

Sonny started to explain how the arch took up the whole space, and it was lined with brick, but he didn't get very far before he was interrupted by Raymond shouting from the other end of the barn.

"Hullo. Anybody there?"

"We're down here, Dad."

"What's goin on?" He was shouting as he came down the hall. They didn't have time to answer before he was in the doorway. "Well, there you are, Al. I been lookin for you. Where's Gramps anyhow?" He started around the oxen still talking. "There's some car with out-of-state plates up by the house. What's...." That was when he realized the person standing beside Buck was not Sonny but a woman he had never seen before. "Oh, I...." he said. He started backing up.

Sonny straightened his back and looked down between the oxen. "We'll be all done here in a minute, Ray."

"Oh, there you are, Gramps." He sounded grateful.

"That car belongs to this lady here."

"Okay."

"We've been up back for some firewood."

"I was just wonderin." He was still backing up. "I think I'll go up to the house and see if Carol Ann left us anythin for supper." Then he was out the door and gone.

"See you, Dad," Al called after him.

Sonny said, "That was Raymond, Al's father. I would've introduced you if I'd had time."

"That's okay," Isabel said. "He seemed like he was in a hurry."

"That's just Raymond," Sonny said. He had the yoke off both oxen and had put their halters on.

"Do you want me to give 'em their hay, Gramps?"

"Yes, darlin. We might as well go ahead and get done with 'em."

He hitched them both to their short lines and carried their yoke to the corner where he stood it on end and wiped it over with a rag like he always did. He could feel Isabel watching him.

"Isn't there anything I can do to help?"

"I thank you," Sonny said, "but there ain't a thing. Al's gettin some hay, and we'll take those buckets with us when we go, and that's about it."

They all three walked out through the front of the barn. It was evening now and much cooler. He and Al waited while Isabel thanked them and got in her car and left. Then they started toward the kitchen.

"Your Dad must've picked up your bookbag."

"I guess so."

"You go on in, honey, and wash up. I'm goin to go back and fasten the gate to the night pasture. Then I'll be along."

"Okay, Gramps."

18

THE CLICK OF the bathroom door closing was what woke her just as she was sliding into sleep. She opened her eyes in the shadowy room, Leroy's hotel room. The only light came from the open window, and it was almost night outside.

Isabel lay there, naked under the sheet, feeling at peace with everything. All her muscles were loosened and so relaxed that she couldn't imagine ever moving again. The sheets felt like silk against her skin. She had been afraid to go to Leroy's hotel room with him, afraid that it couldn't happen twice, that the way it had been with Leroy on Saturday night had been some kind of accident that couldn't be repeated, or that she wouldn't know how to make it happen again. But it had. It was mysterious and wonderful, and it was Leroy. She lay there too content to move or even think.

After a minute, she saw that his clothes were gone from the

chair where he had set them neatly. He had slipped away without saying anything. If it wasn't for his cowboy hat lying on the chair, she might think he had gone without even saying goodbye. She lay there dozing, thinking about him leaving, about him sneaking away, and a little irritation crept into her thoughts. She tried to push it aside so she could stay in the lovely place of peace.

When the bathroom door opened, she woke up again and looked at him. He was dressed. "Ah Chérie," he said. "I thought you were asleep."

"Are you sorry?"

"Pardon?"

"I was just wondering if you liked to sneak off after making love—you did last time."

He pulled the chair over, picked up his hat, and sat down. "No, Chérie," he said. "It wasn't like that. You were sound asleep. I tried to wake you up to say goodbye, but you were too tired. It would have been mean to do more. So I kissed you and left."

"That makes it sound different."

"That's the way it was."

"I'm glad you told me." She sat up a little, leaning against the piled pillows and pulled the sheet around her. Her loose hair slid across her shoulders. "Doesn't your wife wonder where you go in the evenings?"

"Chérie," Leroy said. He sat up straight with his hat in his hand, and his voice was cold. "Don't talk about my wife. It's not your business."

That hurt so much that she tried to think of some way to pay him back. And at the same time, she wanted to reach out for his hand, to say, "Please don't go. Stay with me."

She didn't do either. After a pause, she said, "Let's not fight. I want to tell you something that I have been so happy about all day. I think you'll think it's great." She smiled at him, anticipating his surprise. "I went out to that farm yesterday."

"What farm?" He was still sitting stiffly on the edge of the chair, his hat in his hand, poised to leave.

She wanted him to stop being annoyed, to want to hear what she wanted to tell him, but she couldn't say so. Instead, she said, "That farm I told you about. The magical place that made me want to come back to Severance. I meant to tell you the other night, but we were talking about us and Renée, and I didn't get a chance."

"I thought you didn't know where it was."

"I didn't until the other day. It was the day after you....the day after we...."

She stopped, thinking how strange it was to be able to actually make love and still feel too shy to talk about it. "It was last Sunday. I took a walk out into the country, and I hitched a ride back with...."

"You what?"

"I hitched a ride...."

"You shouldn't do that, Chérie."

"What?"

"You were hitchhiking? That isn't safe for a woman."

"I know, but...."

"Why do you need to hitchhike? You have a car."

"It was almost an accident. I was taking a walk and...."

"It hasn't broken down, has it, Chérie?"

"What?"

"Your car. Is it all right?"

"Leroy," Isabel said. She could hear the annoyance in her voice, and she knew he could too. "Will you stop interrupting? Do you want to hear this, or do you want to talk about cars?"

"All right, Chérie," he said. "I just didn't know you would do something like that."

"Well, I do if I want to, but I don't want to very often. Okay?"

"Go on with what you were telling me."

"The man who picked me up was the old man whose oxen pulled us out of the mud last year." She couldn't tell from his face what he thought. His face gave nothing away. "And Roxy was right. Remember? She said she thought his name was Carroll Trumbley."

"How did you find out?"

"I recognized him."

"What luck, Chérie."

She sat up a little and adjusted the sheet. "There's lots more. I asked him if I could come out to his place some time, and he said I could, so I called him up the other day, and he gave me directions. I was dying to see if it was the same place, the place I remembered."

"When are you going to go out there?" He set his hat down on the floor beside the chair and leaned back.

"I told you. I already did. I went out there yesterday."

"Oh yes, Chérie. Go on."

"It *was* the place I remembered. Sonny got out his oxen, and we went up in the woods with them and brought down a load of firewood."

Leroy frowned. "I've known Sonny Trumbley for years," he said. "He's not the kind of man that would take a woman like you up in the woods with him."

"Do you think I made this up, Leroy?"

His eyes dropped away from her face. "No. I'm just surprised. That's all."

"It was his granddaughter. No, I mean his great-granddaughter. She talked him into taking the oxen up in the woods to show me how they worked." She thought about how much she liked Al, how Al reminded her of what Joey and Nicky were like just a few years ago. "She's fourteen. Her name is Al."

"I know the family, Chérie.'

"Oh, of course. I keep forgetting."

He smiled then. "Is there more?"

"Oh, lots. The best part was the oxen. I thought they wouldn't be at all like what I remembered, but they were even better. And you know what?" She sat forward and looked into his face, but she didn't give him a chance to say anything. "You're not going to believe this. I actually got to *drive* them. There. What do you think of that?" She sat back with a smile, waiting to hear his amazement.

But the smile slid off her face. He didn't take it at all the way she expected. He looked shocked and even angry.

"That's damn dangerous," he said. "I'm really surprised at Sonny. He ought to have his head examined, putting someone who doesn't know anything about animals in a position like that. What *was* he thinking of?"

"It wasn't like that. You've got it wrong. It wasn't dangerous." She took a breath and tried again. "It was his great-granddaughter. She was the one who suggested I try it. *She* drives them. He taught her how. She was right beside me the whole time. She and Sonny are the only ones who ever drive them, but they let me do it. I'm really proud of that."

"Chérie, did he say anything to you that...." When he saw her look of surprise, he stopped mid-sentence and turned to look past her at the window.

It was dark in the room now. She could hardly see his face, and she was glad to think he couldn't see hers any better.

"I thought maybe....Chérie, did he say anything to you that was...."

"What?" she asked impatiently.

"Anything he shouldn't have said. That's what I mean. You might not have...."

Suddenly the ridiculousness of the whole thing broke over her, and she began to laugh.

Leroy was indignant. "There's nothing funny about this at all."

"Oh, but there is. You thought Sonny Trumbley was coming on to me? Don't you think that's ridiculous? And *you* of all people."

"I thought you might not know what he was...."

"Leroy," she said slowly. If it wasn't so funny, it would have been exasperating. "His fourteen-year-old great-granddaughter was there the whole time. And anyway, *you* are the one I have to watch out for, not Sonny. I mean, you have already...."

"That's an entirely different thing, Chérie, and you know it."

"Some people might not see it that way."

"There are always people around who distort things."

"Well, suppose he *did* come on to me. I mean, it's ridiculous, but suppose he did. We're both consenting adults, and neither one of us is married. What would be wrong with it? *You* are the one who is married. *You* are the one who isn't supposed to do that kind of thing."

"Chérie," he sighed. "I have told you before. That is not your business. I hope I don't have to tell you again."

Isabel was thinking that it was time to leave before things got even worse. So maybe it was laziness, not wanting to deal with getting out of that room and away from him, that made her say, "There was the most wonderful cabin up in his woods. I'm going to see if he'll rent it to me."

"I had no idea there was another house on Sonny's property."

"Well, there is. Maybe you've never been back there." She was surprised at how interested he was. "It's just inside the woods, where the road starts to go uphill. It's an old sugarhouse, actually. That's what Sonny said."

"Oh, a sugarhouse. I see."

"That's what I said."

"Sonny thought you could *live* in a sugarhouse?"

"No he didn't. He said it wouldn't work. But I don't see why not. I thought he didn't know that I wouldn't care if it was rough. I could live like Thoreau. I wouldn't mind."

"Did you look inside, Chérie?"

"Yes, but I couldn't see much. There was a lot of stuff piled up in there, and it was dark."

"There's not much room in a sugarhouse. The arch takes up all the space."

"What's an arch?"

"Haven't you ever seen anyone making maple syrup?"

"I guess I must have when I was in school here, but I don't remember it."

"The arch is the firebox that the big pans sit on. You must have seen pictures of the sap boiling in big, flat pans. That's what fills up the inside of a sugarhouse. There wouldn't even be enough room for a bed."

"I could take the arch out."

"He wouldn't want you to do that."

"If I bought it? And a little land around it, maybe?"

"Chérie—impossible. Cut a chunk out of the middle of Sonny's land?" He stood up and began to pace back and forth between the window and the door, walking past the foot of the bed. The little light that came through the window was from the street-lights now. "You're an outsider. You can't understand how a man like Sonny feels about his home place. And changes in the deed, rights of way, where would you get water? What a mess! No Chérie, you'd better forget it. When you are ready to buy a house, come to me. I'm the one who can find you something suitable." He stood at the end of the bed for a long, silent moment. "And there is another reason why this would be a mistake—the most important reason of all—I would never get to see you if you lived out in the woods."

"You could come visit me in my cabin, couldn't you?"

"Oh yes, and everyone would see my car and know where I was."

She pulled the sheet up around her shoulders and hunched down against the pillows, feeling too small to say anything.

"Could I walk up and down through the woods in the middle of the night, Chérie?"

"There's a road all the way to the sugarhouse," she said. But she spoke without conviction. It's true that she couldn't picture either Leroy or his car on that road, and certainly not in the middle of the night.

"You can't have any idea what a Vermonter's land means to him, Chérie. Sonny was born in that house, and he is going to die there, and then the next generation—in this case his grand-daughter and her husband—will take over the place and keep it going." He gave Isabel a stern look. "You have no way of understanding the significance of that. No, Chérie." He shook his head solemnly. "I hope you didn't suggest it."

"No. I didn't get a chance."

"Good. You haven't insulted him then."

Isabel felt relieved. It could have been worse. She was an ignorant outsider, but at least only Leroy knew the full extent of her ignorance.

After a minute, she said, "I know you're right, and I'm not disagreeing with you, but it's funny, you know. Right behind their house—I'm sure they must be able to see it from all the windows in the back—is a huge junkyard. I mean, if they love their land so much, you would think...."

He was standing at the foot of the bed looking at her. In the dim light from the streetlights, one side of his face was white and the other in dark shadow. "Chérie," he sighed. "Don't talk about what you don't know about. A man has a right to do what he wants on his own land, wouldn't you say?"

"Of course. I didn't...."

"Well then, don't talk about whether or not Raymond should put his cars behind his own barn."

"I wasn't. I was just surprised that...."

"People come in here from some place else, and right away they want to change everything to make it just like the place they came from."

"No, Leroy. I wasn't thinking they ought to change. I was just...."

"Everybody always thinks they know what's right for somebody else."

"Don't say any more," she said. She threw back the sheet and stood up, hoping she could find her clothes, or at least some of them, and get into the bathroom in the dark before she started to cry. This whole thing was a horrible mistake. Maybe even coming to Severance was a mistake, a crazy idea that she didn't even want to think about now.

She bent down beside the bed and felt underneath it. Leroy hadn't moved or said a word. She found her bra and her underpants under the bed. She remembered dropping her shirt on the floor near the head of the bed. She found it with her foot. That was enough. She headed into the bathroom without saying anything. The solid slam of the door said all she meant to say.

Now that she was safely on the other side of the door, she found she no longer wanted to cry. She was angry instead. She stood there in the dark, holding her clothes. He was an outrageous asshole. She was so furious at him that she had no idea what she was doing there. How could she have gone to his room with him? How could she have slept with him? How could it have been any good at all?

She thought about Sonny and Al and how they loved each other, and she thought about her own boys and how far away from them she was. Even if they could sympathize with her move to Severance, neither of them would understand what possessed her to get involved with Leroy. How could they when she didn't understand it herself?

She turned on the bathroom light and put on her clothes. She looked awful. Her hair was a mess, and her eyes were bloodshot. She splashed some water on her face and rubbed it hard with a towel, but even with some color in her cheeks, she didn't look much better.

She had no idea what she was going to say to him, but she opened the door and went out anyway. The light was on, and Leroy was gone. She had to look around the corner of the room by the windows before she believed it. He must have opened the door very quietly because she hadn't heard a thing.

She put on her blue jeans and sandals and grabbed her sweater and her bag. She already had the door open before she remembered what a mess her hair was and had to go back to comb it.

She turned out the light, closed the door and hurried downstairs. She thought he might be waiting for her in the lobby. Maybe he wanted to apologize.

But he wasn't there, and that was a good thing because what would she have said to him?

19

AFTER LEROY HUNG up the telephone, he sat there for a minute, trying to get calm. Marie was in the kitchen doing the breakfast dishes, but the door was open between the two rooms. He couldn't be sure how much she had heard. He had tried to keep his answers noncommittal in case she was nearby clearing off the table, but he lost track in the middle of the conversation when Donny started putting a lot of pressure on. He felt like a pack of wolves was closing in around him. It made him want to strike out, but he couldn't. He had to keep it to himself. It wouldn't do to have Marie find out, and she was already suspicious.

He walked into the kitchen and stopped by the table, pushing in the chairs while he thought of what to say to her.

Marie shut off the water and turned to look at him. "Who was that?"

"Just some guy I know in Albany."

"What did he want?"

"Not too much."

"You sounded upset." Her eyes were traveling back and forth across his face, looking for clues.

Leroy didn't worry too much about that. He was good at keeping his feelings off his face. "He wants me to meet him tomorrow at Saratoga."

"Oh Leroy."

"I know. I wasn't planning on it, but I think I'll have to go. He says he really needs to see me." Leroy liked the way he put that. It sounded like he was the one doing Donny a favor. "Do you mind?"

"No, of course not. It's your business. You didn't sound too happy about it though."

"I'm not, but I don't think I have any choice. I'm afraid I'll be late getting home. You didn't have any plans for me, did you?"

"No, I didn't, and I haven't talked to any of the kids." She turned back to the dishes, and he knew he had gotten past the tricky place.

He walked up behind her and kissed her on top of the head. Her hair was soft and smelled of shampoo. He could feel her stiffen a little, waiting to see if anything else was coming, waiting to see if he was going to put his arms around her. He had been going to, but that stopped him. "See you later, Chérie," he said. He crossed to the door and opened it. "Have a nice day."

He started down the hall, feeling angry. What the hell was Donny Patarka doing, calling him so early in the morning? He wouldn't have thought Donny would even be out of bed at ten in the morning.

He stopped at the coatrack to get his jacket and hat. The office door was open. Isabel was sitting at his desk. She was looking at him. Her brown hair was spread across her shoulders, and her cheeks were pink. She looked pretty, even prettier than he remembered. He had managed to avoid her all week, hoping to teach her a lesson, hoping she would figure out that she couldn't treat him the way she did the last time they were together—stomping into the bathroom and slamming the door. She would be sorry when he didn't come around any more. But this morning he had been so busy thinking about Donny Patarka that he had forgotten to stay out of her way.

Renée said, "Hey Leroy, what are you doing out there? Aren't you coming in? There are some things I want to ask you about. I've been missing you all week."

He looked into the room, conscious that he had been thinking about Isabel and hadn't even noticed that Renée was there too. "I've had a lot of things going on, Chérie."

He hung his jacket back up and walked into the office. As he went past Isabel, he nodded to her without really looking. "I'm in a hurry," he said, mostly for Isabel's benefit. She should know how unimportant she was in his life. "But if there's something you really need me to look at before I go...."

Renée was shuffling through a pile of papers. "Well, no.... let me just look. It seems like there was something....I was noticing that you hadn't opened any of the mail, but I don't see anything...." She looked up at him, smiling. "I guess I was just wondering what was going on."

He walked up close to her and laid his hand on her shoulder. She leaned toward him a little. "I'll be back later to fill you in. I'm running late. I have a meeting with Joe Rosen and Emory Collins." He massaged her shoulder, and she moved under his hand. "I don't know what time I'll get back. Are you going to be around this afternoon?"

She nodded.

"Great. We can talk then." He could feel Isabel watching. He started for the door, being careful not to look in her direction. "I'm going to take them out to eat, although I don't know why I bother. They want to talk about that land in West Severance, the land on the flats, and they don't have the money to do anything. I should have told them to leave me alone a long time ago. Still...." He turned to smile at Renée. "That's not the way we operate. Is it, Chérie?"

He went into the hall and put on his jacket and hat. Then he stuck his head back in the room to say, "I'll see you later," to Renée. Without looking directly at Isabel, he said, "You too, Chérie."

Outside it was bright with sunlight, even though it was quite cool. The clock on the dashboard of his car said ten-forty, so he had almost an hour before he was supposed to meet them. That was good. He needed some time to think. He felt as though he could be getting onto some really thin ice. Marie already had her suspicions. If he didn't look out, Renée was going to get suspicious too.

He hadn't heard from Donny Patarka since late last fall, and he hadn't heard anything about him either. In that way, it was a nasty surprise to get his phone call. Still, Leroy had to admit that it had been on his mind all winter, because he knew he was going to hear about it sooner or later. Someone like Angelo didn't just loan $20,000 to some guy he didn't even know very well and then forget about it. So Leroy knew he was going to hear, and he didn't know what he was supposed to do, what they expected of him. Of course if he could have gotten the money together, he could have handed it all back without figuring out the deal, but no such luck. He didn't even have half of it yet, and he had skimmed off every place he could think of.

He took his car through the car wash, got it filled with gas, and went to the bank and took out $500 in cash so he wouldn't look like somebody's poor relation tomorrow. Then he headed to Stefani's to meet Rosen and Collins for lunch. On the way he had a great idea. If he took Isabel with him to Saratoga, it would be hard for the conversation with Donny to get too heavy. Besides she looked pretty; she might bring him a change of luck, and it would be nice to have some company on the drive. He ought to get a chance to ask her this afternoon. He was sure she would say yes.

He was fifteen minutes later than he said he would be when

he pulled into Stefani's parking lot. He drove in the front and then around to the side before he found a place to park. They would be watching out the window, and his lateness would put them both a little off balance. Anyone in there who knew them would see that they were waiting nervously for the big man to arrive, and almost everyone who went to Stefani's went to see or to be seen.

Just as he had expected, they were sitting by the front window. Emory Collins was watching the door and saw him as soon as he came in, but Joe pretended he was too absorbed in what he was saying to notice. He didn't look up until Leroy was standing beside him. Then he said, "Oh here you are, Leroy. I didn't see you drive in."

"How are you, Joe?"

"Never better. Have a seat."

"Thanks," Leroy said, sitting down. "How're you doin, Emory?"

"Fine, Leroy, just fine," Emory said, grinning and nodding. He always looked a little furtive, like a rat, but he probably wasn't hiding as much as he thought he was.

Leroy sat down in the empty place at the end of the table facing the window. He was looking right into the sun. Both Emory and Joe's faces were dark against the bright window. They could see him much better than he could see either of them. He stood up.

"Hey, what's the matter?" Joe said, a little too loud, a little too quickly.

"The sun's in my eyes. Help me pull the table out so I can sit on the other side, will you?"

Emory and Joe both stood up then and lifted the table about a foot away from the window. Leroy carried his chair around to the other side of the table, and they all three sat down again.

"That's better. Now I can see your faces." What he didn't say was that they couldn't see his as well. Besides that, now he could keep an eye on what was happening in the rest of the room.

A waitress came over to see what they were doing, and Leroy ordered a Scotch and water. The others were drinking coffee. When she came back with his drink, she brought menus. Leroy didn't open his. Instead he looked up at her, smiling. He hadn't seen her before. She was young and thin, but too pinched-looking to be pretty.

"Thank you, Chérie. Tell me what you have that's good today."

Staring past him out the window, she began to recite the menu in a flat, automatic voice. When she got to the special of the day, which was lasagne, he stopped her.

"Wait a minute, Chérie. What about this special? Is it good? Would *you* have it?"

She looked at him then. "It's very good, sir. They use...."

He smiled and handed her his menu. "That's what I'll have, if *you* recommend it."

She looked at Emory, but he had just opened his mouth when Joe asked her what they put in the chicken caccatore. She began to list the ingredients while Joe whistled softly through his teeth, looking at the menu and tapping on it with the tips of his fingers, as though she wasn't saying anything. Before she finished speaking, he interrupted her to ask about the spaghetti. She had just begun to tell him about that when he decided to order the lasagne also.

Leroy could see the waitress stiffen, trying to hide her irritation. She turned to Emory who had been watching the whole thing nervously. As soon as she looked in his direction, he handed her his menu, smiling sheepishly. He said to bring him lasagne too.

"Great," Leroy thought. "This isn't going to cost much."

After the waitress left, no one said anything for a few minutes. Joe tapped a rhythm on his water glass, and Emory's eyes flicked back and forth from Leroy to Joe.

Leroy smiled to see how nervous they both were, a little surprised that they didn't know it had already been decided. If he had wanted to be in, he would have moved long before this.

"What do you think of the weather we've been having, Leroy?" Emory said.

"Oh, I can't complain."

"Pretty nice, huh?"

Finally their food came, and for a while they all concentrated on eating.

Then Joe began to look at him more directly than before, and Leroy thought, "Okay, here we go. Here's the pitch."

"Emory and I think we have stumbled onto quite an opportunity. Haven't we, Emory?" He smiled at Emory who was leaning forward, nodding eagerly. "We may have mentioned it to you?"

Leroy said, "Yes, you have." He leaned back in his chair, relaxed, smiling at them both. "But don't let that stop you. I'd like to hear about it."

"It's an incredible deal. You know that field on the right side of the road as you go along the flats in West Severance?"

Leroy nodded. Maybe nothing he said would have changed the spiel.

"Well, it isn't on the market yet, but it looks like we can get it for under a thousand an acre if we play our cards right, and we're all set to move. We can't miss. It's actually amazing that it wasn't developed years ago—water, sewer—it's all right there. Oh, it's an amazing deal." He smiled at Emory. "So, we're feeling pretty good these days. I don't know where people get this shit about a slump in real estate, do you?"

"Things have been slow for me lately," Leroy said.

Emory looked worried. "I guess it looks different to us because of this deal. Maybe if we didn't have it...."

"I'm glad you boys are doing so well. It's nice to hear good news. I'm going to get myself some coffee. I'll be right back."

He wanted to give them a chance to confer with each other. He took his cup across the room to the coffee pot and filled it up. As soon as he left, they leaned toward each other, planning a strategy to hook him. He went slowly back to the table, giving them plenty of time to see him coming. "Did either of you want some coffee?" he asked before he sat down. "I'm sorry I didn't think to ask you before."

They both shook their heads impatiently, and Leroy sat down again, smiling to himself. He was having fun.

As soon as Leroy was in his seat, Joe said, "We were just saying—maybe you saw us talking when you went to get your coffee?"

Leroy tried to look thoughtful. "No, I can't say that I noticed."

"Well, we were, and what we were saying was what a nice guy we thought you were."

"That's right, Leroy. That's exactly what we were saying."

"And because we like you so much, we thought we really ought to move over and make room for you. I told Emory that friendship was a lot more important than money...."

"That's right. That's exactly what he was saying, Leroy." Emory was leaning forward across the table nodding eagerly.

"And if you can't move over to help a friend...."

Leroy held up his hand. "Whoa, hold on here. It's nice of you guys to want to give me a chance like this. I wish I could take advantage of such a kind offer, but I can't right now."

"We could wait for you," Emory said quickly.

"I couldn't ask you to. That would be a mistake. Somebody else might jump in front of you."

"We don't know of anyone who's looking at it right now...."

"I really appreciate it, Joe, but I'm afraid I'm just going to have to pass on this opportunity. I'm glad you guys are onto such a sweet deal. You deserve it." Leroy was smiling at them in a friendly way while inside he was chuckling to himself because he was making them squirm. They were such small-time guys that they still thought they were trying to trick him. They didn't even know he was on to them. Maybe Joe looked uncomfortable, but that jerk of an Emory wasn't even suspicious.

Joe leaned across the table. "Look, Leroy, we really need to have you in on this with us. It could be big. We both feel that your expertise could make all the difference here. Right, Emory?"

Emory shook his head like crazy in agreement.

"Thanks for the vote of confidence, Joe."

"Oh, but we mean it. You are the best around. Everyone agrees on that. Why, just to put your name on something like this would open doors."

"Yeah, but you know how that is—you put my name on it, even though I'm not active in it and haven't put in any money, and pretty soon everyone finds out, and then they get to wondering why I'm not more involved. It could end up hurting you more than it helped." He was watching their faces so he saw how hard it hit them when he said he wasn't putting up any money. Did they both think he was being cute before?

Emory was the first to speak. "Actually, Leroy, we were thinking you would feel like putting up some money too."

There. He made them say it. Leroy looked past them and waved to the waitress. When she came over, he asked her for the check. Then he let himself look directly at each of them in turn while he said, "You boys have been so nice, I want this lunch to be on me."

"Thanks a lot," Joe said. Emory just nodded.

The waitress handed Leroy the bill. He took his money roll out of his pocket, and peeled off two twenties and handed them to the waitress. As soon as she left, both Joe and Emory leaned forward.

"I'm sorry to disappoint you," Leroy said, knowing that by putting it so bluntly, he was disappointing them even more. He didn't want to leave any ambiguity for them to hold on to. "It wouldn't fit into my plans. But it sounds like a pretty sweet deal. I expect I'll be kicking myself one of these days, while you guys are riding around in Mercedes. But that's the way it goes."

The waitress came back with his change, two fives, two ones, and some change on a little plastic tray. Leroy picked up one of the fives and stood up. He looked at them both. Neither one of them was able to hide his disappointment any longer. "It's been good to see you guys. I'll be interested in how your project comes along. Next time you'll be buying the lunch, I guess."

They were mumbling thanks and goodbye as he left. It made him feel a lot better about the whole Donny Patarka thing to jerk Joe and Emory around a bit. It was a hierarchy. The big fish ate the little ones.

He had made up his mind about something else too. He would definitely ask Isabel to go with him to Saratoga tomorrow.

20

IT WAS A LITTLE before four in the afternoon and a Saturday, and the parking lot was full. Isabel felt lucky to find a place in the back. It would be empty when they returned. Leroy said they would be very late. She was sitting in her car, wondering if she ought to walk up to the front where he could see her, when she saw the big black car. She put up her window and got out.

When Leroy's car glided to a stop beside her, she opened the passenger-side door quickly, before he had a chance to do it. She felt glad to see him, to be sitting beside him again. All week she had been wishing to see him and picturing how different it would be this time. She looked around at him, but she couldn't see much of his face under the tilted-down brim of his hat. She had no way of knowing if he was glad to see her.

"Have you been waiting long, Chérie?"

"No. Only a few minutes, and I think I was early."

"You look wonderful."

"I'm so glad you think so," she said. She suspected he thought she was too sloppy and that she ought to take more trouble to look well-dressed the way Renée always did. Today she had spent a long time on her hair, arranging it to hang loose down her back. She could feel it moving softly on her shoulders. And she was wearing her favorite green and white striped dress. She put her shoulder bag on the floor and fastened her seat belt.

"Tell me again where we're going. I know it's in New York State, but...."

"The racetrack in Saratoga Springs. I guess you've never been there?"

"No. I don't even....it's horses, isn't it?"

"Yes, harness racing. The other track doesn't open until July."

"I've never been to a horse race. Do you go there a lot? Are you going to bet money?"

"I've got to meet a man I know. He asked me to meet him there," he said, glancing around at her and then back at the road. "And, yes, I might bet."

"What fun! Will you show me how?"

"If you like."

"I've never bet on a horse race before. It was nice of you to invite me to come along. I haven't seen much of you lately. I've missed you."

She waited for him to say something in reply, and when he didn't, she looked around at him to see what he thought of what she said. His face was still shadowed by his hat. He was watching the road. Maybe he hadn't heard her.

After that they were both quiet. Isabel regretted that she had been so glad to see him. She was sorry she had admitted that she missed him. He didn't act as though he had missed her much.

Outside the window everything was bright and green. The air was full of sunshine and birds. Almost every house had a lilac bush flowering in front of it. With delight Isabel saw that she was connected to all this rebirth. Her new life was beginning too. It was right that she had moved to Severance in the spring.

After a while she said, "I talked to my son Nicky this morning. I've been trying to get him on the phone for weeks. We had a great conversation. He's the one who really understands what I'm doing here, why I want to be in Severance."

Leroy's profile was dark, sharp against the bright spring landscape outside his window. He didn't say anything.

"Nicky just moved out to LA with some of his friends. They think they want to get jobs in the movies. Nicky's father thinks he's being irresponsible, but I think a person ought to try to do what he wants to do, especially when he's young. Don't you?"

"It depends," Leroy said without looking around. "I didn't even know you had a son named Nicky. You never told me."

"I thought I had. Actually, I have two sons. You didn't know that?"

"No."

She waited, but he didn't say any more. Finally she said, "Do you want to hear about him? Nicky, I mean."

"If you want to tell me."

"He's my oldest. He just graduated from Hampshire College. I'm very proud of him."

"I'm sure you are."

His voice had an edge to it, but she ignored it and hurried on. "Nicky and I can really talk. Our conversations are about the truly important stuff, you know. We really understand each other. It's so rare...."

She looked at Leroy then, and it stopped her mid-sentence. She had been feeling so happy about her conversation with Nicky, so warmed by their closeness, so proud of it. On top of that, she felt like being with Leroy. The day was full of sunshine. She knew she looked pretty. But when she looked around at him, she was silenced by doubt. She hadn't said anything to Nicky about Leroy, even though she thought they had had an open and personal and significant conversation. Could she ever tell Nicky about Leroy? Probably not. Could she ever talk to Leroy the way she talked to Nicky? Probably not. Would either of them like the other? Probably not.

Leroy turned toward her, frowning. "Go on, Chérie. What were you saying?'

"I don't know. I guess I just lost my train of thought. How queer."

"You were telling me about your son. Go on."

"This road is getting very steep and winding. I guess it made me feel dizzy. What mountain is this?"

"It's called Lincoln Gap. It's between two mountains."

"Oh."

"We'll be at the top in a minute, and then you'll see."

There were trees on both sides of the road. Then just before the top, there was an opening. Out Leroy's window, beyond the mountain they were on, there were rows of other mountains, each one a deeper slate-blue than the one behind it. The lines were horizontal, softly rounded, full of peace and harmony.

"Oh how beautiful Vermont is! Aren't you glad you live here?"

Leroy looked at her with a frown. He said, "Of course, Chérie," and turned back to concentrate on the steep descent.

After they got to the bottom of the mountain, the land was flat, farmland with cows in bright fields. There wasn't any place as wonderful as Sonny Trumbley's farm, but it was still fun to watch out the window as the old-fashioned Vermont country-side rolled by. When they drove across the bridge into New York State, everything was different in some subtle way. After a while they got on a big highway, and there wasn't much to see. Neither one of them had said anything for a long time. Silence filled the car. Isabel thought about turning on the radio, but she didn't like to do it without asking. It was a relief when they turned off the highway into Saratoga Springs.

As they went through town, Leroy pointed out the other race-track. Then he was silent again until he stopped the car. It was evening, and long shadows from the trees lay across the rows of cars in the parking lot.

Leroy said, "We have to hurry. The first race is just about to start. Lock your door, please." He got out of the car and walked off fast without even looking at her.

Isabel sat where she was without moving. He was so mean. She thought about staying in the car, but it wasn't much use as a protest if he didn't notice. If he had looked back to see where she was, it might have strengthened her resolve, but he didn't. She watched his back getting farther and farther away in the evening light.

She got out of the car and followed him. The gravel crunched under her feet and worked its way into her open-toed shoes when she tried to hurry. When she finally caught up to him at the ticket window, he had bought her a ticket. "Here," she said, holding out a ten dollar bill. "You don't need to pay my way."

Leroy put his hand on her arm. "It's nothing. Only a couple of dollars. Put your money away, Chérie." He smiled at her, and she felt better in spite of herself.

They walked along a covered walkway. Leroy put his hand on her back to guide her through the crowd. He seemed to want her there for the first time since they left home. She didn't understand the way he was acting, and she tried not to think about it. Maybe it would be better from now on.

Just as Leroy opened the door for her, a loud bell rang. "Oh damn," he said. "I knew we were going to be late."

"Is it all over?"

"We've missed the first race, that's all. It's nothing."

They walked through a large room, bare but elegant, like the lobby of a fancy hotel. Isabel wanted to stop for a better look around, but Leroy's hand was still on her back, pushing her forward. They went out through glass doors on the far side of the room. There were tables outside with people sitting at them. They sat down at an empty table, and right away Leroy jumped up again. "I'll be back, Chérie," he said.

It was a while before Isabel realized that there was a race going on. The horses were on the other side of the track, so far away that they looked like brightly colored toys. The people at the other tables didn't act interested. Only the announcer seemed excited.

Then the horses swept past the grandstand, close enough for Isabel to see the foam on their mouths and the intent look on the drivers' faces. Leroy sat down again. He laid a program on the table and took a black pen out of his pocket.

"Oh, can I look at that?" Isabel said.

Leroy pushed the program toward her. "You won't like it."

"I might. How do you know?" She picked up the program and opened it. But after flipping through a few pages, she handed it back to him. There were no photos of horses or men, nothing to make anyone want to read farther, only columns of tiny numbers and mysterious statistics. "I see," she said.

Leroy smiled. "I told you, Chérie." He took the program back and began to study it, even though the horses were coming around for the end of the race, and the announcer was excited. There was a little cheering from the crowd when the horses crossed the finish line, but Leroy was making notes, and he didn't look up.

Isabel got out her journal. It was a good chance to try to record the scene. Leroy was making notes, and so were lots of other people. No one would notice her. She could write in her journal all she wanted, without feeling self-conscious.

"Saturday, May 25 Harness Racing at the Saratoga Springs Racetrack. A beautiful warm, spring night. The sky is like black velvet out where the grandstand lights don't reach. In the center of the track are two fountains with colored lights shining on them—right now the lights are blue and green, but a little while ago they were red and pink. Now the race has ended, the winner has come back to the front of the grandstand, and a man in a suit is handing something to him. He sits half off his cart, with his leg sticking out to the side."

By the time she finished writing that much, the horses and drivers were gone. Isabel was watching the empty track, trying to decide what else she could describe, when a trumpet sounded. A procession of horses and carts came out onto the track and circled around in front of the grandstand while the announcer called the names of the horses and the numbers and names of the drivers. Leroy stopped making notes. He watched intently.

Some of the horses looked happy, as they circled back and forth, but some of them seemed nervous and scared. The one with an eight on its head was a beautiful shade of reddish brown. Isabel wanted to see what that horse was named, but just then Leroy left and took the program with him. He didn't come back until the race had started. When he sat down, he smiled at Isabel and said, "Now we'll see if I made a smart move bringing you here."

"Let's bet on number eight. He's such a wonderful color."

Leroy waved his hand. "Be quiet and watch the race, Chérie." He picked up the program and went back to studying it.

Isabel tried to see where number eight was when the horses ran past, but the only thing she could see was that he wasn't out front. When they came around again for the finish, number eight was lagging way behind.

Isabel looked around. She was going to make a joke to Leroy about how she wasn't going to be much help to him, but he was walking away through the crowd. He hadn't even said he was leaving.

She opened her journal again, and this time she wrote:

"So far in this journal I have tried to describe people and places, keeping my personal feelings out of it. But I really need to say something here about the uncomfortable circumstances I am in at the moment. I am being treated badly. I need to stop hoping it will change. I need to stop picturing to myself how different it could be. I need to stand up for myself and say...."

But when Leroy came back, he was smiling. He called her 'Chérie' and asked her if she was hungry.

"Yes, I am," she said. She decided not to say anything for a while.

"Good," he said. "Let's go upstairs. My friend will know that's where we are."

At the top of the wide staircase was a restaurant built into the grandstand. The tables were in tiers. A waiter showed them to a table near the top. Isabel looked around. The front wall of the restaurant was made of glass. Everyone could look out at the track. A race was beginning. Leroy turned on the television that sat on the table, and the race was there too.

Leroy left her sitting at the table alone several times before they even got their dinner. Soon after their food arrived, a small man in dark glasses slid into the empty seat beside her. He was wearing a bright blue jacket with the sleeves pushed up. He leaned on his elbows, looking across the table.

"How you doin, Leroy?"

"I can't complain."

"Me either." He looked at Isabel and then at Leroy again. "So, who's your friend?"

"This is Isabel Rawlings," Leroy said. "Isabel, Donny Patarka, the man I was telling you about."

"Isabel, huh?" He turned in his seat so he was facing her. "Pleased to meet ya." He held out his hand.

Isabel set down her fork slowly and shook his hand. Her mouth was full of chicken. She couldn't say anything.

He squeezed her hand hard before he let it go. "So what bad stuff has Leroy been sayin about me?"

"He didn't say anything, just that you wanted to meet him here." She smiled at Leroy, but he looked past her as though she wasn't there. "Is there something he should have told me?"

Donny made a face. "I better not answer that." He looked at Leroy again. "Hey, what you're eatin looks real good." He stood up and waved at a waiter, who hurried upstairs.

"I want to order what he's got."

"Sirloin, sir?"

"Whatever. Do it just like you did his. Okay?"

"Of course."

Another race was beginning. Both Leroy and Donny were watching, although Isabel could see that neither of them wanted the other to notice.

She said, "Leroy, tell me what...."

But the horses were coming in to the finish line, and he waved his hand, motioning her to be quiet.

At the end of the race, Donny said, "Damn." When the bell rang, Leroy got up and left the table. Donny watched him walk away. "He's goin to collect, I suppose," he said. Then he turned to Isabel.

She didn't know whether to eat or not. Donny's dinner wasn't there yet, but hers was getting cold. She picked up her fork and pushed the food around.

"So, tell me about yourself, Isabel."

"There's not much to tell," she said, not looking directly at him. "Can you explain about these races to me?"

"That's easy. The first one across the finish line is the winner."

They both laughed.

"I know *that*," Isabel said. "What I meant was...." She looked up.

Leroy was sitting down. He took off his hat and put it on the empty seat beside him. He looked at Isabel, then at Donny, and back at Isabel again. His eyes were narrow. "What's so funny, Chérie?"

"Oh nothing," Isabel said. "I can't explain. It would sound too dumb." She looked at Donny, and they both started to laugh again.

Leroy looked grim. His hair was flattened by his hat. He was opening his mouth to say something when the waiter arrived with Donny's dinner. He shut his mouth with a snap. But while Donny was talking to the waiter, Leroy gave Isabel a look that plainly said he was furious at her.

Isabel reached out across the table, thinking to touch his hand to show him she wasn't laughing at him and that she was glad to be with him, but he pulled his hand back, away from hers.

Donny looked around in time to see the whole thing. Nobody spoke. They all began to eat, pretending nothing was wrong.

Donny's left hand lay on the table between his plate and Isabel's. There was a ring with a blue stone on his last finger. The stone was so bright that it looked like blue glass. His fingers kept up a nervous rhythm, tapping on the table. Suddenly he looked up at Leroy. "How long have you two lovebirds known each other anyways?"

"Not very long," Leroy said.

"About two and a half weeks actually," Isabel said.

Donny turned to her. "Two and a half weeks? And already you're...." He laughed. "Hey, don't mind me. It's not my business, is it?"

"That's okay," Isabel said. "It's not a secret." But after she said it, she wasn't so sure. She tried to catch Leroy's eye, but he was cutting his steak and didn't look up

"So where'd you meet? Not in that little one-horse town Leroy comes from."

"Severance," Isabel said. "I just moved there. I'm renting a room from Leroy's cousin. She introduced us."

Donny grinned. "Well, that's a sweet deal, Leroy."

Leroy looked up, letting his eyes travel back and forth from one to the other of them. His face was set into a hard mask. "Is your steak rare enough, Donny?" he said, before he took another bite of his own.

Isabel looked down at her own plate, and nobody spoke. Donny didn't even bother to answer the question. The chink of their knives and forks on the plates was the only sound at their table. Leroy left again.

After a few minutes Leroy came back. Nothing was said as he sat down again. All around them other diners were laughing and talking. Isabel looked at the other tables, wishing she was at one of them, having a good time. But then she and Donny happened to look at each other, and they both began to laugh again, like children conspiring against a cross parent. That was fun, even though Isabel felt guilty, knowing it was at Leroy's expense.

Donny's eyes flicked across Leroy's face. "So, Isabel," he said, ignoring Leroy. "There must be an interestin story here. How did you end up in a place like —what is it?—Severance?"

"I went to college in West Severance."

"West Severance?"

"Of course that was a long time ago."

"It couldn't have been very long ago, not judging by your looks anyhow. Am I right, Leroy?"

"When a woman is beautiful, what difference does age make?" Leroy said, without looking up.

Isabel waited for him to say something more specifically about her, or to smile at least, but he didn't do either.

"Maybe I'm not hearing so good. I thought you said you just moved to Severance." Behind his dark glasses, Donny's face was pinched. Everything about him was stingy, except for his confident manner, and that seemed all for show. "I'm confused."

Isabel said, "Both things are true, but you don't want me to go into all the details."

Donny said, "Yes, I do." He looked at Leroy. "It isn't as if we were talkin about anything else right now."

Leroy looked tired. "Don't mind me, Chérie. Tell him whatever you feel like."

Isabel didn't answer. A minute ago she was angry at him. Now she just felt sad and empty and alone.

"So, don't tell me anything," Donny said. "You look like you're about to cry."

"No I'm not."

"Maybe we *should* talk about something else." Donny turned to Leroy. "So, what do *you* think we should talk about?"

But Isabel didn't give him a chance to suggest anything. "It isn't actually that interesting, but it's not a secret. Last year my husband and I went to his class reunion at the college. It was his twenty-fifth. We were out driving around the back roads, and we got stuck in the mud."

"I didn't know you were married," Donny said with a quick glance at Leroy.

"I'm divorced."

"That's too bad."

"No it's not," Isabel said quickly. "That's why we were driving around. We were having a fight. That's why Jeff wasn't paying attention to his driving, but it made him even madder when I said so. And if we hadn't gotten stuck, we never would have found that place. We were too busy fighting to be looking at the scenery."

"I would have been too busy worrying about my car," Donny said.

"We had to walk all over the place—into the barn and all around—looking for someone to help us get the car out. Finally, a team of oxen pulled us out, if you can believe it."

"What happened to the car?"

"Not a thing. They were very gentle, actually."

"I guess your husband must be kind of a trusting guy. I don't know if I...."

"No. He didn't like it a bit. He was really worried, but it was getting late, and he wanted to get out of there. I was the one who talked him into letting the oxen pull the car out. I wanted to see what would happen. The whole thing seemed like a fairy tale— the place was so magical. There are mountains all around it in a circle, but it's flat there where the house and barn and fields are. I never saw any other place that was anything like it."

"So you bought it."

"Oh no. It wasn't for sale. When I came back to Severance, I didn't know where it was. I didn't even know where to look, just that it was out in West Severance somewhere near the college." Leroy was looking down at his plate, but Donny was watching her with real interest. "After I moved to Severance, I took a walk out that way, and when I was hitchhiking back...."

"You were hitchhiking?"

"Yes, and I got picked up by this old man, and he...."

"You shouldn't do that."

"Do what?"

"Hitchhike."

"That's what Leroy says."

"Leroy," Donny said, smiling. "What kind of a crazy woman have you got ahold of here?"

Leroy shrugged.

"If I hadn't been hitching, I might never have found that place again." She decided not to explain how she had stuck out her thumb on impulse because she and Sonny had looked into each other's faces as he was waiting to turn onto the road to Severance. "The old man who picked me up was the same one who pulled our car out of the mud with his ox team." Isabel looked from one to the other of them. "I don't believe things like that are accidents. Do you?"

"I don't know."

"I thought when I went out there again, I would find that it wasn't nearly as wonderful as I remembered, but you know what?"

"What?"

"It was even better."

"It must be quite a place."

"Oh, it is. It's the most beautiful place I ever saw in my life."

"I'd like to see it some time."

"You would agree with me. I'm sure you would. There's definitely something magic about it."

"I know what. Here's a deal for you."

"What?"

"I'll come over there, and you can show me around."

"Okay."

"You can give me a good time." He was watching her face.

She said, "Okay," but she looked away and said it in a flat, quiet voice. She felt they had crossed a line she didn't want to cross.

Both of them seemed to remember Leroy at the same moment. Isabel looked up at him just as Donny was saying, "It sounds like quite a place, don't it, Leroy?"

Leroy's eyes were cold and flat as pebbles. Isabel shivered and stood up. "I'll be back in a few minutes," she said. She went downstairs. The only bathroom she knew about was in the lobby. It was a long way to go, but she was glad to be away from both of them for a while.

When she got back to the table, Leroy was leaning forward, looking angrily at Donny. She sat down. Neither of them paid any attention to her.

Later, in the car going home, Isabel said, "If you wanted to talk to Donny privately, I would have been glad to get out of the way."

"I didn't."

"When I came back from the bathroom, it seemed like you were having a private conversation."

"I wasn't."

On impulse Isabel said, "It wasn't about me, was it?"

"Of course not."

"It seemed like...."

"I don't discuss my women with anyone."

"That's nice to know," Isabel said, feeling sour. "Except I would have preferred it if you had said woman, instead of women."

Leroy didn't reply, but his glance was cold. When he looked back at the road, he knocked his hat down low over his eyes and disappeared behind the brim.

Isabel stared straight ahead.

"Besides, Chérie, you were the one who wanted to be alone with him."

"What do you mean by that?" she asked, trying to keep the tremor out of her voice.

"You were certainly coming on to him."

"I was not!"

"What was all that talk about how he'd like to see this 'magical place'?" His lips curled in a sneer.

"That was nothing," she said. "I was just making conversation. It was nice to have someone who wanted to talk to me. It was the only good part of the whole trip."

"You invited him to come visit you, Chérie."

"Oh, God. He's not going to drive all that way just to see a farmhouse that isn't even for sale."

"No. I don't think that's what he'd be coming for either."

"I don't know what you mean by *that*."

"You embarrassed me in front of him."

"I'm sorry, but I don't see why."

"You were with *me*, Chérie. And you were coming on to *him*."

"I was not." She was indignant. "But so what if I was? You don't own me."

"When a woman is with me, she's with me, Chérie. She doesn't act like she wants to go off with someone else."

"Leroy, I'm sorry you were embarrassed, even though I don't think I did anything to embarrass you. I don't know what I'm doing here. Sometimes, like tonight, I think this whole thing with you has been a mistake, a wrong turn. It happened so fast, and in such a backwards kind of way." She looked at him then, and he looked back at her, just a quick look. He didn't say anything. "But then I remember the day we drove to St. Johnsbury together….and the lovemaking….I never knew it could be like that with anyone. That must mean something….but I can't be anybody's property, not even for great sex. And if that's all it is…. well, I don't know. I wish it made sense to me, but it doesn't."

Leroy didn't respond. He tilted his hat down over his eyes and stared ahead at the road.

Isabel felt that what she had said was a jumbled confusion, but she was too tired to sort it out, so she said nothing more, and after a little while she fell asleep and didn't wake up until they were driving into Severance.

21

THE SCREEN DOOR opened, and Gramps came into the Texas. He sat down on one of the stools. Carol Ann wiped off the counter in front of him and asked him if he wanted a cup of tea.

He looked up at the clock before he answered. It was five of three. "No thank you, honey. I want to get on home as quick as we can."

"Okay, but I can't leave just yet."

"Ed Briggs already started to bale before I left. They were goin to start to pick up without us."

"I'll hurry, Gramps," she said, trying to keep the annoyance out of her voice. She had already done a day's work, and she didn't feel at all like hurrying just to get out in a hot hay field.

She walked down to the end of the counter where May was filling coffee cups for the group of men in the second booth.

"I'm goin to go on, if that's all right, and not wait for Janet to get here. Gramps is in a big rush. We got hay to pick up."

May nodded.

Carol Ann got her pocketbook and started for the door, and Gramps got up and followed her out. She looked up. The sky was a high, blue dome with only a few feathery, white clouds sailing overhead. It wasn't the kind of sky you had to hurry for.

Gramps went past her and got into his pick-up. When she opened the passenger-side door, he said, "Yes, I know. We might have tomorrow too. But Ed's goin to have it all baled, barrin breakdowns, and you know how I hate to leave bales out on the damp ground."

"I didn't say nothin, Gramps."

"Yes, honey, but I know you're tired and don't feel like gettin it in right away."

"Well, *that's* the truth."

"I hope it won't take too long."

"Where's Raymond? Did he get home already?"

"He's out there, and so's Al. I hope they're pickin up. Oh, and that woman that's been out a couple of times, that Isabel?"

He looked around at Carol Ann when he said the woman's name, and Carol Ann could feel her face getting stiff. She nodded, but she didn't say a word.

"She's out there too. She's goin to help us pick up."

Carol Ann sniffed. She couldn't help herself. "What does *she* know about pickin up hay?"

"Nothin, I suppose. At least, I don't know if she does, but she seems ready enough. I guess she can pick up bales and throw 'em on the truck."

"We'll see."

"Well, it don't matter. It won't slow us down any, even if it don't help."

"I know."

"She's okay, Carol. Al likes her quite good."

"Oh, Al.... Don't talk to me about Al."

After that neither of them said anything, until they could see the field. There was a ring of finished bales around it. They could hear the thumping sound of Ed's baler, and then they could even see Raymond throwing a bale up to Allie in the back of the cattle truck.

Gramps said, "So far, so good."

"Drive me over to the house first. I got to change my clothes."

"Okay, honey."

When Carol Ann came downstairs in her jeans and an old shirt of Raymond's, Gramps was filling two of her half-gallon Mason jars with ice water.

"You made sure you got the chipped ones, didn't you?"

"Yes, I did."

"Because I got some new ones out there on that shelf, and I don't want you to take those and get 'em messed up so I can't get a good seal on 'em."

"I know, honey."

"Well, I'm ready whenever you are."

"Good. Let's go."

Gramps picked up a jar in each hand and went out to the pick-up. The ice cubes clinked and tinkled against the glass with each step he took. He slid the jars carefully into the space behind his seat.

They drove into the field and along the edge where the hay had been baled and the bales picked up. They went around to the far side. The cattle truck was halfway loaded. It was sitting with the driver's door open and no one behind the wheel.

Carol Ann walked toward it. Raymond smiled and waved when he saw her, but Allie didn't even look in her direction. The Isabel woman looked at her, but she didn't say hello or wave or anything, so Carol Ann didn't either. She looked red in the face from lugging bales in the hot sun when she didn't know she ought to have a hat on.

Carol Ann climbed up into the driver's seat. The truck was

running, and the cab smelled of exhaust. She would have to say something to Raymond about how stupid it was to leave the engine running without a driver when Alison was up there stacking bales. Suppose it slipped into gear and started to move? She sat there with her hands on the steering wheel, feeling irritated because she was the only one who ever noticed things like that. Sometimes it felt as though she was the only grown-up. Just then she heard a rapping on the roof of the truck, and Allie shouted, "Okay, Ma. We're all set."

Carol Ann put it in the lowest gear and drove between two rows of bales, going as close to each bale as she could, so they wouldn't have to carry them very far. In the side mirrors she could see them picking up bales and throwing them up to Allie. She went as slowly as she could, but she still had to stop sometimes.

Raymond was running everywhere. He threw three bales to every one that Gramps got up there. Once he raced past the truck after a bale up ahead. He said, "Hi, baby," and grinned at her as he went by. Crazy Raymond. No hat, of course. He always said his hair was so thick he didn't need one. He'd be lucky if sunstroke was all he got. It was stupid, but she couldn't help smiling at him too. He looked like a little kid, dashing around the field like that.

Just after she made the turn to the side of the field that was beside the road, Gramps came up to her window.

"You can stop here, Carol. We've got a load, as soon as Al gets done stackin."

Carol Ann put it in neutral and opened her door for some air. She swung her feet around, but she couldn't very well get out, unless she turned off the engine, and that was risky since you never could be sure Gramps' old truck would start again when it was hot. Even Raymond couldn't figure out what was wrong with it.

From where she sat, she could see Gramps and Isabel standing at the back corner of the truck watching Alison work. Isabel said something, and Gramps smiled at her. Carol Ann felt left out. She wondered what Alison was doing up there. She jumped down from the seat and walked a few steps away from the truck so she could see. If she stayed close, she would be able to run for it if the truck jumped into gear or something.

The load was like a wedding cake, each tier set in a little from the one beneath it. It looked neat. Alison could do good work when she wanted to, and she always wanted to do the jobs that Gramps taught her. She looked over the edge of the load.

"Hi, Ma. I'm just about to come down." Her hair was straggling out every which way from under her cap. Her face was red and sweaty and stuck all over with hay chaff and dirt. She put her feet over and started to slide down the load from row to row, holding on behind herself.

It made Carol Ann's stomach flip over to watch. She said, "You be...." before she caught herself and changed it to, "That looks like a good load."

Allie was pleased with her work and concentrating on coming down without messing up her stack, and she didn't hear anything.

When she got to the ground, Gramps patted her on the shoulder and said, "Good girl." Then he turned to Carol Ann. "Why don't you take it over, honey? We'll meet you there."

Carol Ann got behind the wheel again and put it in the lowest gear. She drove very slowly to the corner and over the hump of ground on the edge of the road, trying to make it as smooth as possible. That was the trickiest place. She looked in the mirror as she left the field. Behind her, Isabel and Allie were standing together and watching the truck. They were too far away for Carol Ann to see their faces, but she knew the relaxed way they were standing meant she had made it without losing any of the load. She drove up the road between the house and barn and then backed slowly around the corner of the barn until she was as close as she could get to the end of the hay elevator. She had to open the door and look out because she couldn't do it with the mirrors.

Just as she stepped on the brakes, Raymond came running up out of breath. He looked behind the truck and held up his hand. "That's good. You can stop right there."

"I already am," she said.

He came up to the door as she was opening it. "Can I turn this thing off so I can get out?"

"Go ahead," he said. "We can roll it from here if we have to. It hasn't been actin up lately anyway."

Carol Ann got out and stretched. They stood side by side and watched the others come up the road. They were all three walking together with Isabel in the middle.

"It's nice of Isabel to come out and help," Raymond said.

Carol Ann gave him a look, but he didn't notice. He was watching the others come up. They were right beside Raymond before Carol Ann had time to say anything.

"I bet there's a hundred and twenty on this load," Gramps said. "What do you say, Raymond? You think we got a hundred and twenty bales on there?"

"I don't know, Gramps."

Isabel said, "How many do you usually get on a load?"

"A hundred and twenty's pretty much the most we get."

Allie said, "One time last summer we did a hundred and thirty-five. Remember that?"

"We were tryin to see how many we could do that time. We were goin for the record."

"I know, Dad, but that's how come we got so many on."

"Well," Gramps said, "there ain't no help for it. There's only one way to find out what we got on here now, and that's to take it off again. Come on, Raymond. Are you goin upstairs with me?"

"All right, Gramps."

"Let's go then."

Gramps climbed up the hay elevator as though it was a ladder. Raymond went up behind him. Their feet clattered on the metal, and the frame jiggled and swayed. As soon as they were both safely up in the hay loft, Carol Ann plugged in the motor, and the sharp teeth of the conveyor belt started traveling toward the black opening of the loft. Allie was already up on the load of hay.

"Here they come, Ma. Are you ready?"

Carol Ann nodded, and Allie landed a bale right in front of Isabel.

She looked at the bale and then looked at Carol Ann and smiled. "Is there a special way to do this?"

"No, just so they're flat and hooked on those teeth. You'll see." Carol Ann was putting on her gloves. She knew she ought to offer them to Isabel, but she really didn't want to mess up her own hands working without them. "I'll get you some gloves before we go back in the field again," she said.

"It's okay. I'm fine. It's kind of hot for gloves anyway."

"Hey! What are you ladies doin? We need some action up here."

Carol Ann gave a final pull to her glove and sighed and picked up the bale by Isabel's feet. "All right, Raymond. We're comin." She set the bale solidly onto the prongs of the conveyor belt. The rickety apparatus gave a shudder, and the bale started moving up toward Raymond, who was waiting in the opening of the loft. "Are you and Gramps goin to count?"

"Okay."

Isabel was standing at the end of the elevator, holding a bale by one string. "Do I need to wait until that one gets up there?"

"No. Put them on as fast as you can. It can usually handle it."

Isabel swung the bale on. The string pulled off, and the bale split open. The conveyor belt picked up loose packages of hay and carried them part way before they rained down on the ground. Isabel looked like she didn't believe what she saw. "Oh, I'm sorry," she said. "It's trickier than it looks. What did I....?"

"Look," said Carol Ann. She was sorry to lose the bale, but she couldn't help being pleased that Isabel did it wrong. She acted like what they did was so simple-minded that she could come along and instantly know how to do something they had all been doing for years. This was a good chance to have her see there was more to it than she thought.

Allie had been landing bales all around them. Carol Ann picked one up and plunked it down on the conveyor. "You have to hold onto both strings, so you don't break them open. And you have to put them down flat. Some of 'em ain't as tight as they should be."

"Hey, come on," Raymond said. "Do you want me to come down there and help you?"

"You'd like that, wouldn't you?" thought Carol Ann. "Then you could show off in front of Isabel." But she didn't say it out loud. She plunked another bale on the belt and looked up and said, as sweetly as she could, "Thanks, honey, but we're goin now. We'll keep up."

And then for a while she got busy, not thinking, not noticing anything, except whether Isabel was putting on a bale at that very moment so that she would have to wait. She became a machine, picking up a bale and putting it on and then turning to pick up another and another and another. The whole world narrowed down to the sound of the motor and the clatter of the conveyor chain, the heat and the dust, the feeling of the bales' strings across her fingers, and the ache in her back from picking them up.

"Hold on a minute, Carol Ann."

She looked up. Gramps was leaning out the opening of the loft. "Don't send any more until we catch up."

"Okay."

Isabel smiled and said, "I guess we women can keep up all right."

Allie threw another two bales and then said, "I better wait too. Hadn't I, Ma?" The truck was more than half empty. Allie was standing on the floorboards.

"Sure, honey. Take a rest," Carol Ann said. She wiped her face with the tail of Raymond's shirt. It felt wonderful to be still.

Allie sat down on the truckbed with her legs dangling over the edge, and Isabel jumped up beside her. Carol Ann would have liked to sit there too, but she was afraid of the awkward struggle it would take to get there. She couldn't just jump up nimbly the way Isabel did. So she stood beside them, leaning on the truck.

Allie said, "It's fun, ain't it, Isabel? I told you you'd like it."

"It's hard. I'm tired out already. But you're right. It *is* fun."

They were quiet then, while Allie swung her legs back and forth. They could hear Ed's baler and the thump of bales on the floor of the loft as Raymond and Gramps tried to make a neat stack.

Much too soon Raymond stuck his head out the opening. "All right. We can take some more."

Carol Ann plugged the conveyor motor back in, and they began again. Carol Ann was slow at first, as though all the muscles in her body had built up a resistance to moving. But slowly she got back into it, and then she didn't notice anything until there wasn't another bale to pick up, and she looked around and saw Isabel putting the last one on the conveyor.

Allie jumped off the truck. "I'm goin up to the house, Ma. I'll be right back."

"Bring a pair of my work gloves for Isabel."

"No. It's okay. I don't need any."

"Bring 'em anyway, Allie. She might change her mind later."

"Okay. Ma."

"They're on the shelf behind the woodstove."

"I know."

Carol Ann unplugged the motor again. She and Isabel stood there in the new quiet. Isabel started to say something, or at least Carol Ann thought she was going to, but she just took a deep breath and shook the front of her shirt, trying to shake the hay and dust out of it. Her shirt was pretty, made of some light-colored cloth with little flowers on it. "If I had a shirt like that," Carol Ann thought, "I wouldn't wear it to do work like this."

Isabel had her sleeves rolled up. Carol Ann could see the red scratches all up and down the insides of her forearms from the cut ends of the hay. Her arms were going to burn tomorrow.

"Where's Al?" This was from Raymond who came out of the barn with Gramps. They had come down the stairs from the loft instead of trying to climb down the hay elevator.

"She just went up to the house. She'll be right back."

"I guess we should wait for her, so she don't have to walk over."

"It's okay by me if she don't take too long," Gramps said.

"How many more trips we got to make, Gramps?"

"I was figurin about three hundred bales all told, so that'd be one more good load and then a little one, a half load."

"How many bales were on the truck?" Isabel asked.

"Raymond was countin. What'd you get for a total, Ray?"

"A hundred and fourteen, but there were a couple, three broken ones."

"That's not bad."

Allie came running from the house, her sneakers slapping on the road. She pulled up breathless beside Gramps. He put his arm around her shoulders.

"No need to hurry, darlin. We were goin to wait for you."

Allie held out the gloves so Isabel could see them. "I'm goin to put 'em on the dashboard of the truck, in case you want 'em later. Okay?"

Isabel smiled at her as though the whole thing was Allie's idea. "Thanks very much," she said to Allie, without including Carol Ann in her gratitude.

"Well," Gramps said, "I guess...."

Carol Ann got into the driver's seat. Everyone else climbed in back. The truck started up just fine. As she was driving into the field, she heard rapping on the roof of the cab, and Gramps shouted in to her to take it over to his pick-up. When she got there, she stayed in the truck with the motor running while everyone but Allie got off.

Raymond came up to the window of the truck carrying one of the bottles of ice water.

"Want a drink, baby?"

Carol Ann took the open bottle. The ice cubes were melted down to tiny scraps. She drank. The opening of the jar was wide. Some of the cold water ran around the sides of her mouth, down her chin, and onto her chest.

"Oooo," she said, wiping her face. "It's just water. Why does it taste so good?"

"Because you're real thirsty, that's why." He took the jar from her and drank. Then he poured some on top of his head and grinned one of his crazy, crooked grins, while the water ran down his face, making trails through the hay dust on his cheeks.

"I'll see you later," he said. He sounded like it was something he was looking forward to.

Carol Ann put the truck in gear and started slowly around the field, feeling contented with the idea of seeing Raymond later when all the work was done.

By the time the truck was loaded, Ed had finished baling the field and had driven off down the road with the baler clattering behind him.

Carol Ann was sitting in the truck with the door open when Gramps came over. It was cooler in the field now with evening coming on, but inside the cab of the truck it was still as hot as ever.

"Why don't you take it over and leave it by the barn, ready to unload, Carol? We're goin to put the last of these on the pick-up. Then we'll be over."

"Okay, Gramps. I'll turn it off when I get it there, shall I?"

"Sure, darlin."

"And I'll go up to the house and lay out a cold supper. I think there's enough ham left over from Sunday."

Gramps nodded, but he didn't say anything.

Carol Ann looked at him a little harder, but his face was expressionless and still. "Unless you and Allie got into it at noon."

"No, darlin. We knew better." He patted her on the shoulder. "Go on now. We'll be along in a little while."

"Okay. When I get done up at the house, I'll be back to help you finish gettin it in the barn."

"Okay, honey."

Later on when both trucks were unloaded, and they were all walking up to the house together, tired and hungry, Gramps asked Isabel if she would like to stay for supper.

"I would like that very much."

"Oh goody," Allie said.

Carol Ann was just thinking how no one asked her what *she* thought about it, when Isabel turned to look back at her, since she and Raymond were walking behind the other three. "Would it be all right with you if I stayed, Carol Ann?"

"I guess so," she said. "We'll have to put another place at the table...."

"If it's too much trouble...."

"Oh no, Allie can do it."

"Come on, Isabel," Allie said, running up the steps. "We'll get it done before they even get inside." They both disappeared into the kitchen, and the light came on.

Raymond took Carol Ann's hand and squeezed it.

Gramps said, "Ain't it nice to see Al with a friend."

"You'd think they were the same age, but they ain't," Carol Ann said. "She's older than I am."

"Hush, Carol. That don't matter. It's still nice to see."

Carol Ann pulled her hand loose from Raymond's as they went into the kitchen. Isabel and Alison were washing their hands in the kitchen sink and giggling. They certainly seemed like two teenagers. And Alison knew better than to wash up in the kitchen. She was counting on her mother not being able to say anything in front of company.

Carol Ann clenched her teeth together and pretended not to notice. She went to the refrigerator and got the plate of ham and the cole slaw that she had made on Sunday. She put them on the table. She had already laid out the bread and butter. The bread was sitting there in its plastic bag. She picked it up, hoping no one noticed, and carried it over to the sink where she took it out of the bag and put it on a plate.

Allie was proudly shepherding Isabel around, showing her where they kept the dishes and the silverware out in the dining room.

"Bring a chair from in there, Alison."

Gramps and Raymond had both gone to wash up in the bathroom, so Carol Ann washed her hands in the kitchen sink, hoping no one would see her doing what she always got after them for doing, and counting that no one would see that she had laid out the food with dirty hands.

Raymond met Isabel at the kitchen door and took the chair from her and carried it the last few steps to the table.

"Put it on my side, Dad. We can both fit over there."

Carol Ann stood with her hands on the back of her chair and looked at the table, trying to think if there was anything else she could get out. "Well," she said, "I hope there's enough for everybody."

"Come around this side and sit by me, Isabel. Your dishes are over here," Allie said, sliding into her chair without pulling it out.

Gramps didn't wait for Isabel before he sat down in his seat. "Don't worry, Carol. It's fine."

"I really appreciate this, Carol Ann," Isabel said, and she smiled a nice smile. "I think it's amazing that you could be working out in the hay field and still get dinner for everybody like this, and work a job too. How do you do it?"

"Thank you, but a cold supper ain't much."

"It looks delicious to me."

"It's nice to have somebody take notice. I will say that. They all think the food just flies over to the table without any help."

Raymond said, "Aw honey, that ain't so. You're makin it up."

"When I used to come home from the bookstore with Jeff, when our boys were still at home, I would be so tired. All I wanted to do was sit down and put my feet up."

"I know," Carol Ann said. "That's exactly how I feel too. Pass the ham to Isabel, Alison."

"Thank you. And Jeff would sit down to read the paper, and the boys would do their homework, and I would have to start cooking."

Raymond got up. "Isabel, you want a beer?"

"Yes, please. That would be nice."

"What about you, Gramps?"

"No thank you, Ray. Is there any iced tea in there, Carol Ann?"

"Get the iced tea and some glasses while you're up, will you, Raymond?"

Isabel said, "Now I wonder why I did all the cooking. If I had it to do over again, we would take turns."

"That wouldn't work in my house," Carol Ann said. "These men can't do anything like that."

"Aw Ma, that ain't fair. Gramps can cook quite good. Can't you, old Gramps?"

"I don't know about good...."

Carol Ann tried to give Raymond a look, so he would put the beer in glasses, but he didn't see her. He set Isabel's bottle down in front of her with a thump and took a long, gurgling drink of his own before he even sat down.

"This ham is delicious."

Gramps said, "We haven't got pigs this year. We raised them two last summer."

"This is your own meat? How wonderful. That's just the kind of thing I want to learn about."

"It costs a lot. You have to put a lot of grain through 'em."

"It don't cost anything like as much as it would to go out and buy all that meat."

Gramps said, "Well, *that's* the truth. You got that right, Ray."

"And you cured this ham yourselves?"

"Gramps does it. He always cures our hams." Carol Ann had to admit to herself that Isabel's enthusiasm made things seem special.

Isabel looked at Gramps. "Do you think you could teach me how some day?"

"It'll be a while before...."

"I always help Gramps with all of it," Allie said. "I keep the smokehouse fire goin. You can help me next time."

"I'd like that. It was fun working out here today. Is that enough hay for the winter?"

"No, it ain't. We'll get a second cuttin off that field late in August."

"How many was there today, Gramps?"

"Two hundred and ninety-two, countin broken ones. We might get two hundred next time if we're lucky. With five hundred we'd be all set."

"Well, we got a good start on it," Raymond said.

"That's the truth," Gramps said, and everyone was quiet for a minute, feeling satisfied about the good start.

After supper Gramps went out to see his oxen, and Raymond asked Carol Ann to go for a walk down the road. Outside, it was just dark. The stars were all pricked out, but the sky still had a greenish tint to it over in the west. Behind them in the kitchen they could hear the clink of the dishes as Allie and Isabel washed up.

"I feel guilty leavin a guest to do the work."

Raymond took her hand and pulled her along. "Well don't. She offered."

"Can you believe Alison volunteered to clean up?"

"She's growin up. She's a good girl."

"I know. But sometimes it seems too slow." Carol Ann shivered.

"Are you cold, honey? We could go back for your jacket."

"No. I don't want to. It's nice and quiet out here. Let's just go to the corner, and then we can go back and help 'em finish up."

"Okay."

The moon was a thin sliver just above the mountains in the west. Their feet made patting sounds in the dirt of the road, and behind them, behind the barn, they could hear a few deep croaks from the first frogs. By the time they got to the corner, the mosquitoes were beginning to notice them, and it was less peaceful.

22

Leroy sat in his car while the buffing machine slapped long strips of cloth all around him, drying the big Lincoln after its bath. The conveyor moved the car to the door. He put it in gear and drove out. The sun threw dazzling lights off the polished, black hood.

It was a beautiful morning, still cool and clean. Later it would be too hot, and everything would get limp and sweaty, but for now it was fresh. It would have been better if he could have avoided bringing Renée into it, but he didn't see how. It was okay. He could trust her, and he might be able to keep from telling her much.

As he pulled into Stefani's parking lot, he looked over the cars for her little red Miata. He was so busy checking out the parked cars that he didn't look in his rearview mirror. She was right behind him. When he saw her, he put on the brakes for a joke, and she honked her horn, pretending she was going to rearend him. He could see her smiling in the mirror.

He parked at the end of a row, and she pulled in beside him. They both got out at the same time.

"You've been to the carwash already, I see."

"I told you I was going."

"It looks nice."

"Thanks."

"I've got a phone number for you. Don't let me forget to give it to you."

"What's it about?"

They were walking across the pavement toward Stefani's door. "Mmm," she said. "I love the smell of tar. You know it's really summer when you smell that."

"Me too," he said. "But what's this phone number about?"

"I don't know. Some guy named Donny something I never heard of. I think it started with a B or a P."

Leroy held open the door, and Renée ducked under his arm and clicked inside on her high heels. She did it gracefully, as though she was doing the steps of a peasant dance.

Inside, the air conditioner made a cool breeze. It was hard to see after the bright sunlight. They stood in the lobby waiting for the hostess.

"Was it Patarka?"

Renée turned to look at him. "That was it. Who is he anyway?"

"He's a guy I know, an out-of-stater." He started to say, "He's the person I wanted to talk to you about," but at the last minute he changed his mind and decided not to say it. "I wonder what *he* wants," was what he said instead.

"I don't know. I asked him, but he didn't want to talk about it. All he would say was that he needed to speak to you right away, and for you to call as soon as possible." She was searching his face for more information as she spoke.

"Come on," he said, putting his hand in the small of her

back—he loved the way she felt under his hand—and pushing her gently into the dining room. "Let's find our own table. We can have that corner booth over there. It'll be good to have the privacy."

As they walked to the booth, he kept his hand lightly on her back for the pleasure of feeling her move. She slid in on one side, and he sat down facing her. He took off his hat and put it on the seat beside him.

"I'm hungry," she said. "Will you buy me some breakfast, Uncle Leroy?"

"Of course, Chérie. But isn't it a little late for breakfast? Why don't you have lunch instead?"

"No. First things first. I haven't had any breakfast today. And that's what I feel like, anyway."

"All right, Chérie. Whatever you like."

Later on, after they had ordered, Renée leaned toward him across the table. "I've missed you," she said. "It hasn't been the same in the office since Isabel got there."

"I know, Chérie," he said, reaching across the table to touch her hand. "I feel the same way."

"It seems as though she's listening to everything we say. I don't suppose she is, but still....so....how are you two getting along anyway?"

That startled him. He said, "Chérie," and then didn't say anything else while he thought about the situation. For some time he had suspected that she knew, but neither of them had said anything. "How long have you known?"

"Oh, for a while," she said airily. "But what I can't tell is how it's going. Sometimes I think one thing and sometimes another."

"It's up and down." He made a quick calculation. If she already knew, he might as well at least get the benefit of being open. "I guess it's not so good right now."

Renée sat back so forcefully that her seat made a smacking sound. "Oh, I told you so!"

"Chérie...."

"No, but I mean it. I told you way back in the beginning that she wasn't your type. Why won't you *ever* listen to me?"

"Chérie, you can't...." Just then the waitress arrived with their food. Leroy looked at Renée's pancakes. "I don't know how you can go on looking so wonderful, when you eat the way you do."

Renée was already buttering the stack of pancakes. She looked up just long enough to give an exaggerated shrug.

For a few minutes they were both busy with their food. Then Renée gave him a searching look. "Leroy," she said. "Look at me."

"What, Chérie?"

"Give me a straight answer. Okay?"

"If I can, Chérie."

"What's *really* going on between you and Isabel?"

"Damn it, Renée. I hate that kind of question, and you know it."

"I don't mean to pry into...."

"Well, don't then. If you don't mean to do it, then don't do it."

"But I want to know...."

"Then you *do* mean to pry."

She seemed to sag. All her bright self-assurance fizzled, like a balloon when the air is let out. "Don't get mad at me, Leroy. I just worry about you, that's all."

"Chérie...."

"We've been so out of touch, and you haven't looked happy, and I knew you were seeing her, and...."

He started to ask her how she knew, what they had done that gave it away, but he figured she would say it was woman's intuition, or some other vague thing like that. Even in her crumpled state, she would play it close to her chest. She was so much like him. And he hadn't meant to snap at her.

"Chérie, if I knew what was going on, I would tell you."

"What does *that* mean?" She was already more like herself

again.

"Just that I don't know what to say about it. It's not that I'm holding out on you. I'd tell you if I knew myself." He looked into her cat's eyes, holding her look with his own. "You know that, don't you?"

"Well, no....yes." Her eyes fluttered away from his, down to her plate of pancakes and then back to his face again. "I *don't* know. Would you?"

"Of course, Chérie." They were both leaning toward each other.

"Well, tell me then."

"Chérie," he said in exasperation. He sat back. "I just got through telling you that I *don't know* what's going on." He thought for a minute, letting his eyes go over her short, dark blonde hair, the looks he loved so much. "All right, Chérie. I'll tell you as much as I can."

"Oh good," she said leaning forward a little more.

"But it isn't much, because I really don't know. She's a strange person, and she's got funny ideas about things. She went to that Green Mountain College back in the sixties when it was full of hippies. You probably don't remember."

"I do too remember. It was that way when I was in high school. We used to drive out there, and...."

"I think Isabel was one of those anti-war, hippie types back then, so, I mean, she's really different from us."

"I told you, Leroy. I knew she wasn't your type before you even saw her." She started to eat again.

"Well, you were right." He paused. "But that's not all of it. She's not like you, Chérie, but she's somebody to be with."

"But, Leroy...."

"It isn't a serious thing, but then I didn't expect it would be."

"What does *she* think about that? Is it casual for her too?"

"She's just getting over a divorce. She's too confused to have anything serious right now."

"I don't think you're right, Leroy. I've seen the way she looks at you when you come in the office."

"You have too many romantic ideas, Chérie. You see what you expect to see, that's all."

"Do you tell her you are in love with her?"

"Okay," he said, picking up his fork. "That's enough. I told you I would tell you as much as I know about what's going on. I told you because of how close we are. I wouldn't have told any of this to anyone else in the world. But that's different. That's in a whole different category."

"I'm sorry, Leroy. You're right. It was out of line. But you haven't really told me anything. I mean I can't really picture how it is. I guess that's why I asked that dumb question."

"Chérie, I've told you what I could. If it doesn't make sense to you, it's because it doesn't make sense to me either. It's hot, and it's cold. A couple of times it has been good. We've talked and made love." He cut himself a piece of steak and ate it.

Renée didn't say anything. She watched him eat, waiting to hear more, waiting to hear how it was when it wasn't good.

"Still, we don't have that much in common."

Renée nodded. Her mouth was full of pancake.

"I think she doesn't know how to have a good time. She's too serious. She hasn't got much savoir faire. You know what I mean, Chérie?" He wanted Renée to know it was nothing.

"Yes, I guess so."

"Or maybe she's just moody. Anyway, I don't understand her." He sighed. "But sometimes it's okay. You know what?"

"What?"

"It's great being with a woman who doesn't know anyone in town. I mean, she's not going to talk about me to anyone."

"What about Roxy?"

"Oh well, Roxy. I don't think she likes Roxy too much. I don't think she would tell Roxy anything." He paused long enough to eat another bite of his steak. It was starting to get cold and was less good than it had been. "Besides, no one pays attention to Roxy. Suppose she went around talking about me and Isabel.

People wouldn't necessarily believe her."

Renée smiled at that. She had a way of narrowing her eyes, squeezing them shut when she laughed. It was something he loved to watch.

He smiled back at her, and then he said, "Now I have something serious to talk to you about."

"Oh no, what's wrong?" Her eyes opened wide as she looked at him.

"Nothing's wrong. Well, I mean, it's just something I have to straighten out, but you don't have to worry."

"Oh, I thought I'd done something you didn't like. I thought you were going to fire me or something."

"Chérie, I don't believe it." He was amazed. "How could you think that? Don't you know...." Her hand was lying beside her plate. He reached out and picked it up and pulled it toward him, putting his other hand on top, so that he held hers as though it was a little animal, or a bird. "I would never, never do that."

She shrugged, but she didn't pull her hand away. After a minute of thoughtful silence, she said, "Well, what is it then?"

"You remember that man that called you this morning?"

"Of course."

He paused, thinking of what to say, hating to tell any of it. "I owe some money to his boss."

"Oh, Leroy." Her eyes were flitting back and forth, studying his face. Her hand twitched in his.

"It's okay, Chérie."

"How much do you owe?"

"Twenty thousand." He tried to keep his eyes from dropping away from hers.

"Oh, Leroy. How...."

"It's a long story, Chérie."

"I want to hear it."

"It's really nothing. I've been going over to Saratoga too much, and I got on a bad run of luck last year—and maybe it started the year before. Anyhow, this guy made a killing one day last summer when I was with him, and he loaned me the twenty thousand, no strings attached, to clean up all my debts. Now I have to start paying it back."

"Oh, Leroy. I didn't like that man when he called up. Is he with the mob?"

"No, Chérie. Don't worry about that."

"He sounded like a gangster."

"That's just his New York accent."

"Are you sure?"

"Trust me."

She pulled her hand away and sat back. She picked up her fork and pushed the leftover pieces of pancake around on her plate. She didn't say anything.

"Chérie, look at me." She looked up at him then, her eyes wide. "This isn't about Donny Patarka or his boss. This is about me. I have to break this jinx. That's why I can't stop now. I have to turn this losing streak around. I even took Isabel with me a while ago to see if that would change things."

"I remember that."

"You do? You knew about it back then? That was about a month ago."

"Sure. I know more than you think." She smiled at him, pleased with herself. "Actually," she said, "I think that was the first time I suspected. But tell me this—what did Isabel think about it when you took her to the track to try to change your luck?"

"She didn't know that's why I brought her." He paused. "And I had other reasons too."

"Did it change anything?"

"No. I won a little one. I think it paid a hundred or so. I can't remember. And then I went right back to losing. Sometimes I'm scared I've jinxed my luck forever. But that can't be true, and I don't even like to think about it. Thinking could make it worse."

"I don't think you should go to Saratoga any more. I always knew you would get in trouble over there."

"Renée," he said, exasperated. "Don't talk like my mother. I didn't spill my guts to you so you could lecture me."

"I'm sorry, Leroy, but...."

"No buts. You make me sorry I told you. I wouldn't have told anyone else."

"But, Leroy...." She looked distressed.

He reached across the table to stroke her hand. It was important that he not get annoyed now. "I want you to help me, Chérie. Okay? I need you."

"Well," she said slowly. "If you think...."

"Renée," he said. He could hear the warning in his own voice. "Don't go back on me now. We understand each other. What about that?"

"It's the gambling, Leroy. I'm not sure I understand about the gambling."

"Yes, you do. I've seen you. You take chances the way I do."

"Do I?"

"That's what makes us different from all those other people in their safe, little lives. You and I know how to live with excitement."

Her face brightened when she heard that. She smiled a little and nodded. She was on his side now.

"Chérie, it's not the gambling you don't understand, it's the losing. But let me tell you—that's a necessary part of it. If you didn't lose, it wouldn't mean anything."

"But twenty thousand dollars...."

"I know. I've hit a real bad patch, but I'll get through it. It's how a man handles his losses. That's what counts. That's what shows what you're made of."

"No one would doubt *you*, Leroy."

"Well, right now I'm up against it. I need to start paying that money back. Are you with me?"

"Sure, Leroy. I'm always with you. Where else would I be?"

"That's my girl."

"What do you want me to do?"

"You're one in a million, Chérie. I knew I could count on you. Don't worry. I don't need much. Just a leg up over this bad place."

"Okay."

"Let's get out of here, and then I'll tell you."

"Okay."

He paid the check, while Renée went into the bathroom. When she came back, they left together.

On the other side of the door, the air was heavy with heat. The light was so bright, it hurt his eyes even under the brim of his cowboy hat. Renée stopped several steps out the door and began digging in her shoulder bag.

"I'll be right there....as soon as I find my sunglasses."

Leroy said, "All right," and kept walking toward their cars. When he heard Renée's footsteps hurrying to catch up, he stopped to wait for her.

"Okay. What were you saying in there?" she asked, a little out of breath.

He took her arm, and they walked slowly. "That Donny Patarka has called a couple of times in the last couple of weeks. I've managed to avoid him so far, but I'm going to have to call him back sooner or later."

"I almost forgot to give you the number."

"That's okay. I have it. I've been avoiding him because I wanted to be able to tell him what I was going to do, and I didn't have it figured out. But I do now."

They stopped between their cars. Renée was searching his face, but she didn't say anything. She was waiting for him to go on.

"I want to offer him ten thousand now. I figure they'll be willing to wait a while for the other half if I do that."

Renée nodded. Her face was serious.

"If I take those two commissions, that's seven. Then you know the money we have in escrow on that Chapman deal?" He didn't wait for her to say anything before he hurried on. "I thought I could take three out of that, just until we sell something else."

"But, Leroy, when it's in escrow...."

"Chérie, who's going to know? It'll just be for a few days or weeks, just until we sell something. Don't go back on me now."

"I won't, Leroy."

"Good girl. You're probably going to be what turns my luck around. You've always been good for me, Chérie."

He could see how much it pleased her to hear that. She stood on tiptoe and brushed his cheek with hers, and then she got into her little car and drove off.

He watched until she was out of sight before he got into his own car. He decided he might as well get the call to Donny Patarka over with, so he went to the bus station, smiling to himself because he was the only one who knew what a great place the bus station was to make phone calls. The telephone booths were down at the end of a short, dark corridor. They had old-fashioned, wood-framed, glass doors and little wooden seats. Leroy never saw anyone he knew in the bus station, so the telephones were very private.

Donny answered the phone himself. "Hey, man, it's good to hear from you."

"I'm sorry I haven't had a chance to get back to you," Leroy said, wondering why Donny sounded so friendly. "I've been right out straight. Business always goes crazy in the spring."

"How's that nice, little girlfriend of yours?"

"She's okay."

"Glad to hear it."

"I've been wanting to talk to you about that loan."

"I've been wantin to talk to you about the same thing."

"I'm sending ten thousand now, and I was...."

"Hold on, Leroy."

"I thought if I gave him half now, but if that's not...."

"Angelo's decided he wants to do it a different way. That's what I've been callin you about. He wants you to move on that farm your girlfriend was talkin about."

"That place isn't for sale. But...."

"Why was she talkin about it like that then?"

"I guess you'd have to ask her that. But...."

"Well, man, that's your department. All I know is that I told Angelo what she said, and now he's all fired up about the place."

"I guess I could ask around, although I don't think...."

"I didn't call up to tell you how to do your job. That part's up to you. I'm just tellin you how you can solve your money problems. If Angelo could do some good with this property, it would be pretty simple to figure something out about your debt."

"So he's looking for some property to develop, is he?" Leroy asked. He was thinking how maybe his jinx was starting to break up.

"He wasn't lookin for property until this came along."

"Because I know of an incredible spot up near St. Johnsbury. Over a hundred acres, a lot of road frontage, views. I've even got the guy all softened up. He's desperate to sell. I was planning to buy it myself when I could get the cash together. That's how good a deal it is."

"You didn't hear me right. Angelo's interested in the place your girlfriend was talkin about. He knows a guy in New York who wants to do a chalet village type of thing."

"This other place I was telling you about would really work much better if that was what...."

"No, I don't think so. It was what your girlfriend said. It just kind of like took his fancy. I don't think any other place would do."

"You'll have to give me a little time to see what...."

"All right. We'll back off and give you some room, and you let us know when you've got something started."

After Leroy hung up the phone, he opened the glass door and sat there in the dark for a minute, thinking it over. He'd never get Sonny's farm while Sonny was alive, even though he'd have to try. But maybe in time he could get Angelo interested in something else. He'd have to be careful how he handled it, but still, this could be the beginning of something good.

23

SONNY WAS JUST dozing off when suddenly he was awake again. He shifted in his chair and opened his eyes. Buck and Ben had stopped chewing. Both of them raised their heads. They were looking at the door of their stall. Their ears were pointed that way too, listening for sounds in the passage.

Even while he was thinking that it was probably Al, he knew that it wasn't. The boys didn't act like it was Al. It couldn't be Raymond or Carol Ann either. It was too early in the afternoon for them.

While he waited to see who was coming, Sonny thought with satisfaction about his morning. He and the oxen had been in the woods at first light, and Al had come to help as soon as she got out of bed. They were all tired now, but that was because they'd put in a good day's work by dinnertime.

It was Leroy LaFourniere who stepped out past Ben's backend.

He said, "Hello there, Sonny. You look like a man who knows how to spend the day."

"How're you, Leroy?"

"I can't complain."

"Hot enough for you?"

"I guess so. Yesterday was something. Did you get those thunderstorms late in the day?"

"We did."

"Did they do any damage?"

"I don't think so. The plants ain't big enough yet. Now if we get storms like that in August....but right now I guess it's still pretty good growin weather."

Leroy didn't say anything to that. He dug at the sawdust with the toe of his boot. Sonny didn't say anything either. What they'd said so far was just for politeness. Now he was waiting to hear what Leroy was out here for.

After a while, Leroy looked around at Buck and Ben. He said, "These oxen of yours ain't gettin any smaller, Sonny. I hope you've made up your mind to take 'em to some fairs this year. I still want to see you work 'em."

Sonny smiled. He picked up his cap and scratched his head, thinking, "Could this be the reason he came out here?" And then he thought, "No, he just lost his nerve. He hasn't brought it up yet." He settled his cap back on his head and said, "Well, I haven't made up my mind. I might take 'em to Tunbridge. That's a good one."

"I'll be lookin for 'em," Leroy said, still trying to talk country.

Then there was another silence. Sonny made up his mind to wait it out, to give Leroy a chance to sort out what he had to say.

Finally, Leroy said, "I have an interesting idea for you, Sonny." He was patting Ben's rump, and he didn't look around. He was watching his hand stroke the tufty line of hair at the top of Ben's tail. "I'd like to know what you think of it."

"I'll be glad to tell you if I know myself," Sonny said. "What is it?"

There was a pause, and then Leroy said, "Some guy from New York saw your place and asked me to ask you if you would sell."

"I thought that might be what it was about," Sonny said.

"It isn't very often that you can sell a whole place like this without splitting it up."

Sonny thought about how many of the old places had been split up, how there were almost always a couple of little new houses on each side of the farmhouses, where there had been open fields in the old days. The old places didn't look so proud now, squatting like mother hens surrounded by chicks.

"I know this is a surprise, Sonny," Leroy said. His eyes were shadowed by the brim of his black hat, but Sonny could feel him watching, sizing him up, calculating his advantage.

"No problem, Leroy."

"I think I could get you a very good price from this guy." He swung around a little too quickly to look at the doorway. Then he laughed. "You startled me," he said.

Sonny couldn't see past the oxen and Leroy, but he didn't need to see to know it was Al. She often came in so quietly that Buck and Ben didn't look up. "Come here, darlin'," he said, knowing that she would be wondering what was going on, and that she would remember what he had said to her about Leroy.

Al slipped around Leroy, staying as far away from him as she could. She stopped behind Sonny's lawn chair. He could feel her hand on his shoulder. He reached up and patted it with his own. "This here is Mr. LaFourniere, honey."

"Your grandfather is quite a man," Leroy said, smiling at Al.

"I know."

"Why don't you convince him he needs to put his oxen in the pulls this summer so we can all watch him work?"

Sonny could feel her other hand come gently down onto his other shoulder. Neither of them said anything.

"I'm counting on you to convince him, Chérie," Leroy said, still smiling at her.

"Gramps knows what to do," she said quietly, and her hands tightened a little on his shoulders.

And of course she was right. He did know. "Leroy," he said, "I appreciate your offer, but I guess I ain't got any plans to go anywhere."

Leroy bumped his hat with his hand, tilting it back a little. His eyes were visible. He looked younger, more honest. "It's a standing offer, Sonny. Keep it in mind. Sometimes circumstances change."

"I appreciate it, Leroy, but I guess there ain't any circumstances that could change my mind."

"Okay, then. I just thought I'd ask. I better let you get back to your nap," Leroy said. "It's been good to see you." He tilted his head at Al. "And your granddaughter too."

"Great-granddaughter," Al said distinctly.

"Excuse me, Chérie." He bowed very slightly. "I'll see you soon." He left the stall, stepping carefully to avoid the little pile of manure behind Ben's back feet.

As soon as Leroy was out in the hall, Sonny could hear Al taking a deep breath, getting ready to say something indignant. He said softly, "Hush, darlin. It won't do no good to make a enemy of the man. He can't bother us anyhow."

"But Gramps...."

"Pick up that little bit of manure for me, honey."

"Okay, Gramps." She got the manure shovel and carried each pat of manure separately to the barn door where she flung it out onto the manure pile.

Sonny thought about how he ought to start piling manure in one of the empty stalls. There was plenty of room in the barn these days. But somehow he couldn't quite make up his mind to it. It seemed like bad farming not to get the manure out of the barn, even though he knew some of the good leached out of it, sitting outside like it did.

When Al came back, he said, "Why don't you get your chair and come sit with me for a while?"

"No, Gramps. You're goin to go to sleep. I'll be back later. I just came over to see who was here. I guess he's gone by this time, don't you?"

"If he's still here, it wouldn't hurt to know what he's up to."

"Oh," she said. "I didn't think of that. I'll be back in a while, old Gramps."

Later, Sonny went to the Texas to pick up Carol Ann.

As she got in the truck, she said, "Look at that sky, will you. Think we'll get another storm like we had yesterday?"

"We could."

"I hope it holds off for a while. I got wash out on the line."

Sonny didn't say anything. He was thinking about Leroy's visit.

"It's no use hopin Alison'll take it in."

They rode along in silence for a while, and then Sonny said abruptly, "Leroy LaFourniere came out to see me today."

"What did he want?" she asked, turning quickly to look at him.

"He wants to buy the whole place. He knows someone who's real interested, some rich guy from New York. Leroy thinks he could get us a good price." He took a deep breath, and then he said, "I told him no."

They both faced forward, watching the road. Sonny snuck a quick sideways glance at Carol Ann, but he couldn't tell anything from her impassive face.

"You got a problem with that, Carol?"

She turned to look at him then. "No, Gramps, I honestly don't. I never meant you should sell the whole place. Where would we live? I only meant us to get a house that wasn't so much trouble to keep up. That's all."

"All right, darlin. I understand."

"Did Leroy say anything about all that other?"

"He didn't say anything else, except that he wants to see me at Tunbridge, at the ox pull."

"Remember when he came out here before?"

"Last spring?"

"That's when it was. Well, he gave me some real estate papers. I was supposed to compare the houses in there to ours to get an idea what ours....what yours was worth." She sighed.

Sonny waited, but she didn't say any more. Finally he said, "Go on, Carol. What did you find out? I told you to do that. Remember? You don't have to be afraid I ain't goin to want to hear it."

"Oh Gramps, I know that, and I appreciate it."

"So what do you think it's worth?"

"Well, that's just it, Gramps. I ain't got it figured out yet. I took it in and showed it to May, and she told me what all those funny, little words meant, and then she told me I could figure it out from there, and I just haven't had a chance to get at it yet, so I don't know. I've been *meaning* to do it." She took a deep breath. "Leroy didn't tell you anything about how much the house would bring, did he?"

"Leroy didn't talk money at all, but then I didn't give him much opportunity."

Carol Ann looked at him for a minute and then turned away. "Gramps, I never intended you should sell the land and all. I know you couldn't do that. But...." She looked at him then and sighed again. "A while back Allie said that Isabel woman wanted to buy the old sugarhouse. Remember?"

"I do."

"We could sell that. A little piece like that wouldn't matter. We could get enough to make taxes for a couple of years if she bought a few acres at a thousand dollars a acre."

"You can't get that much for woodland. That's robbery."

"She probably don't know that. After all, where *she* comes from...."

"That don't stop it from bein robbery, Carol Ann."

"Why, Gramps, you know it's worth whatever someone's willin to pay for it."

Sonny sighed. "It ain't just the price, anyhow. We'd have to put a right-of-way through the middle of everythin. Why she'd have to drive right past the house to get in and out. We'd have people around all the time. *She's* nice enough, but suppose she sold it to someone else?" He thought a minute and then went on. "And if I spent the money on taxes, it would be gone in a few years, and we'd have nothin to show for any of it. No, Carol, it would be a mistake, and anyway, we don't need to do it. The price they're payin at the mill is up, and it's easy enough to make taxes with a little loggin."

"Well okay, Gramps. I don't want to fight about it. I see what you mean about havin people drivin through our dooryard at all hours."

"Good, Carol. I'm glad you do. And go ahead and figure out what the house is worth. You'll need that information some day when I ain't around any more."

Carol Ann reached across the seat to pat him on the shoulder, something she didn't often do. "You got to stay with us a lot more years yet. We couldn't make it without *you*, Gramps."

"Thanks, honey," he said. "I appreciate it."

By the time they were through eating supper, the thunderstorm was over. Sonny got up from the kitchen table. "Thank you, darlin," he said to Carol Ann. "That was real good." He carried his dishes to the sink and then went over to the screen door. With his face up close to it, he could smell the coolness and the water outside, even while he was standing in the stuffy kitchen.

It was still daylight out, but the shadows were long. The sky was luminous and bright, washed clean by the storm. In the east it was darker with the incoming night that hadn't got to the west yet.

"I'll be out back workin on the woodpile," he said, as he opened the screen door.

He went around the side of the house. He could hear the birds chattering as they got ready to roost. It made him laugh to hear them all talking at once. They were even noisier than usual. They were probably talking about the storm and the narrow escapes they had.

He stood looking down at the tangle of logs and partly cut up wood that was going to be their winter supply. What he ought to do was get out the chainsaw and buck up the logs that he and the oxen had brought down today, but it was such a peaceful evening. He hated to make all that smell and racket. He decided he would split a few first. When he got tired of that, he could get out the saw, if there was any daylight left.

He stood a chunk of wood up on the chopping block. The maul was leaning against the house. He shook his head over that. Raymond must have left it out last night.

He carried the maul back to the chopping block and stood there for a minute, getting ready. Behind him, inside the house, he could hear the clink of dishes, as Al washed up.

He raised the maul, held it suspended between going and coming, and then brought it down with everything he had. There was a satisfying pop, as the chunk of wood split, and the maul kept going down into the chopping block.

"I came out here to help, but it looks like you're doin okay by yourself," Raymond said, as he came around the corner of the house.

"I still got a few chops in me before I have to rest," Sonny said. "But it ain't like it used to be. It don't take long to tire me out."

Raymond sat down on the woodpile and took out his cigarettes. "There ain't many guys your age that can split anythin." He lit a cigarette and blew out a stream of smoke. "Ah, that's good."

Sonny picked up one of the halves, arranged it on the block and split it in one stroke. Then he did the same with the other half.

"Way to go, Gramps," Raymond said.

Sonny set up another chunk. There was nothing like having them split clean. He was full of energy. He brought the maul down hard, and it bounced off to the side.

Raymond watched with interest. "Give it a good one, Gramps."

It took three whacks before he got through it, and even then the maul didn't go all the way. The chunk was one of those stringy ones. Sonny had to pull the pieces apart. He managed to finish that one and another, but whether he was getting tired, or picked difficult chunks of wood, he didn't have the luck he'd had at first.

After Raymond finished smoking, he offered to take a turn, and Sonny was glad to give up the maul. Raymond worked fast. There was plenty for Sonny to do stacking what Raymond split.

Al joined them. She slid right into helping Sonny stack. The light drained slowly out of the sky while they worked without talking.

After a time Raymond brought the maul down so hard it stuck in the block while the two pieces popped off, one on each side. "That's it for me," he said. He sat down on a log and watched them finish stacking while he smoked another cigarette. "Where's your ma at, anyways?" he asked Al.

"I don't know. Indoors, I guess."

Sonny sat down beside Raymond, and Al came over and stood in front of them. She broke up a stick and threw the pieces at their feet while they talked. It was almost dark. The night air smelled of cedar. They were talking about Sonny's social security check which was late again.

"It'll probably get here tomorrow, Gramps."

"I expect you're right, Ray."

Al threw a little chunk of wood that landed on the toe of Sonny's workboot. "Tomorrow you'll have lots of money, old Gramps."

Sonny shook his foot, and the piece of wood slid off. "I know," he said. "Here I am worryin about when it's goin to get here, when I don't feel right about takin it in the first place."

"It's yours, Gramps," Raymond said. "If you didn't take it, they'd just give it to somebody else."

"If I could see my way clear to doin without it, I'd tell 'em to go ahead. But that would be a hardship for Carol Ann. I'd probably have to ask her for gas money for the trucks and the saws, and she wouldn't want to have to fork out money for Buck 'n Ben's grain. So I'm caught in the middle. It wouldn't be right not to take that check when it comes, and yet it don't seem right that they should pay me when I ain't done nothin for 'em. You see my problem, Ray?"

"Not really. I mean, everybody else gets it too." He dropped his cigarette on the ground and mashed out the fire with his foot.

Sonny stood up and stretched. He patted Raymond's shoulder. "I know. You always say that. Well, it don't matter. I got to take it, because we need it."

Raymond stood up too, and they all three started around the side of the house. "Wait a minute," Sonny said. "I forgot the maul. Somebody left it out last night too."

"Don't look at me," Raymond said. "I didn't do it."

"It don't matter who did it," Sonny said, "as long as I get some oil on it." He went back for the maul and followed the others around the house in the dark. On the kitchen side, the windows were yellow with light, and a rectangle of it lay across the porch and down the steps.

Sonny said, "Still, I can't help feelin kind of uncomfortable to have 'em pay me when I ain't done nothin to earn it. It don't seem right at all."

Al ran up the steps and opened the screen. "I know, Gramps. It makes you feel like a baby." She disappeared into the house.

Sonny and Raymond looked at each other and smiled. "She's somethin, ain't she?" Sonny said. "We'll always agree on that."

Raymond nodded. He laid his hand on Sonny's shoulder as they went up the steps.

24

A THIN MOON, yellow and old-looking, was traveling with her. Isabel was afraid she wouldn't recognize the turn. The road looked so different late at night. She sat forward, hunched around the wheel. She couldn't make herself lean back, even though she knew sitting like that didn't help her see the road.

She had been to the Trumbley farm quite a few times in the last month, and sometimes, when she left to go back to her room at Roxy's, it had been dark outside. But that was going the other direction. She had never driven to their place in the dark. That was why everything seemed strange.

Even though it was almost the end of July, the night was cold. It was clear too, except for shreds of fog caught in the low places between Severance and West Severance. When Isabel got to the turn, she did know where she was, and she relaxed a little.

There was a time, back before her divorce, when she wouldn't have dared to go all the way out to the Trumbley farm by herself in the middle of the night. She was a lot braver than she used to be. She wished she could tell that to her mother, but if she tried, her mother would only pay attention to the chances she had taken, to the new things she had tried and the risks of trying them. Maybe someday she could bring her mother to the Trumbley farm and introduce her to Sonny, and Sonny would work his oxen for her. She would love to tell her mother that Sonny had let her actually drive them, but she knew she couldn't make her mother understand.

Being out late at night made her think of Leroy. He was probably at home in bed, although with Leroy you couldn't ever be sure. She had learned that much in the last few months. Tonight she and Leroy were going to drive to Burlington and have dinner beside the lake. The weather was supposed to be good, and Isabel was looking forward to the evening, even though sometimes she had a hard time believing that she still wanted to be involved with him. The truth was that she still believed it *could* be good. She couldn't quite make up her mind to stop seeing him altogether. She was ambivalent.

But she could think about Leroy later. For right now, she wanted to concentrate on going up in the woods with Sonny to help him with his logging. It was something she had been planning to do for a long time. Today they were going to bring down some logs for firewood. Al would be there too.

Isabel drove up the road and parked between the house and the barn. Over the sheds, behind the barn, she could see the wooded hillside. Just above the ridge, the sky had a greenish glow from the coming sunrise. She was filled to bursting with the beauty of it. She sat and watched the sky for a minute. It was four thirty-five. She was only five minutes later than she meant to be.

She took off her watch and put it in the glove compartment of the car. There were lights on in the barn, but the house was dark. She got out of the car into the icy air and shut the door carefully so that it made only a small clicking sound.

As soon as she stepped into the barn, she could hear Sonny's voice, low and murmuring, talking to his oxen. She walked down the passage. Suppose he didn't want her there so early? Her feet made no noise on the sawdust-covered floor. He would be surprised. Maybe he would be disappointed, and it would show on his face. She walked slowly, wishing to put off the moment when he saw her.

She could hear Sonny talking. "Eat a good breakfast, boys. We got a lot of...." That was when he stepped out into the hall, carrying a pat of manure on his shovel. He almost bumped into Isabel by the door. "Oh," he said. "Good mornin. I thought you might come along later. Al usually does."

In his shy way, he seemed pleased to see her, and Isabel felt relieved. "I didn't want to miss anything," she said. "It's okay to come so early, isn't it?"

"It's fine, darlin." He walked to the big double doors at the end of the passage, and with a neat snapping motion, he threw the manure out the opening into the blackness.

It looked darker out there than it had a minute ago when she came into the barn. "Did I get here too early?" she asked.

"Oh no, darlin. We'll be leavin as soon as Buck 'n Ben get done with their hay." He went into an empty stall and came out with a shovelful of sawdust. "I like to be up there by first light. We have to quit before it gets too hot."

Isabel followed him into the stall with the oxen. When she got close to him, she noticed again, as she always did, the way he smelled of pine. "I hope I can help today. I think I'm beginning to know what I'm doing." She wanted to ask if he had noticed how much she had changed, but she didn't know how to say it. In some ways he was such a formal old man; anything personal made him uncomfortable.

He began to brush the ox who stood farthest from the door without answering her.

After a silence, Isabel said, "You'll tell me if you see anything I ought to do, won't you?"

"If I don't, Al probably will." His old face lit up with pleasure at the thought of Al. "Course she might get after me for workin you too hard."

"Are we going to wait for her?"

He looked around the great brown flank that he was brushing. "We don't need to wait. Sometimes she has a hard time gettin up."

"That's fine with me. Is that Buck you're brushing?"

"That's him," Sonny said. He stroked with the brush, raising a little cloud of dead hair and dust.

"That was just a guess on my part," Isabel said. "I don't really know how you tell them apart."

"They ain't all that much alike when you get to know 'em. If you keep on comin out here to spend time with 'em, you'll get so you can tell. You'll get to know how different they are."

"I hope so. I want to. And Al won't mind if we go without her?"

"Naw. She'll be along as quick as she wakes up. She's growin so fast. She needs her sleep." He took a few short strokes with the brush. Both of the oxen had their heads turned, watching him while they chewed. "Look at that," he said, laughing and pointing at them with the brush. "They wonder why we're standin around talkin, when we ought to be yoked up and on the way. They're sayin it just as plain as words. They always know what we're supposed to be doin."

He put the brush back on the beam where he kept it and went around Buck to the corner where the ox yoke stood propped against the wall. He was smiling. "They don't let me get away with nothin."

Isabel followed him. "Shall I take out the ox bows for you? I think I'm ready to learn how to put the yoke on."

Sonny set the yoke down on its end between the two big heads. "Thank you, darlin, but I don't need help. Besides, Al would skin me alive, if I taught you how to yoke 'em before I taught her. No, you just stand over there. I'll have 'em ready to go in a minute here."

Isabel's cheeks got red with embarrassment. She hated to have him think she wanted to push in front of Al. She watched while he lifted the heavy yoke and laid it across Ben's neck. Ben held his head almost to the floor to make it easier. When Sonny raised the other end of the yoke up onto Buck's neck, Ben held his head up. It was amazing how they could maneuver their heads so close together and never poke each other with their horns.

Isabel said, "At least, let me carry your tools for you then. I want to do something, and I've gotten a lot stronger in the past month." Again, he didn't answer, and she couldn't tell whether he'd heard her or not.

When the yoke was on, Sonny drove the oxen out into the hall and whoaed them in the doorway. They stood patiently while he took down the heavy chains that hung near the door. He draped them over the ox yoke, so the oxen could carry them without dragging. Isabel watched silently.

Sonny straightened up and looked at her. "Now," he said, "I appreciate your offer, but the only thing I got to take up is the chainsaw, and it might could be too heavy."

"No," she said. "It won't be. I'll carry it. I want to."

"All right, then." He pointed with his stick. "There it sits, in that corner."

Isabel picked up the saw. It was awkward and unbalanced, and heavier than she thought, but she was determined.

"Okay, boys," Sonny said. "Git up."

They went out of the barn. Sonny walked beside Buck's shoulder, and Isabel followed the oxen, holding the saw in front of her and carrying it with both hands.

The light outside was soft and gray now. It was still cold, and the air was sharp and spicy with night smells. The oxen lumbered across the field, past the huge rock that sat like a monument behind the barn. There was a creaking sound from the yoke and once in a while the chink of a chain. Isabel thought of Al, warm under her covers, and how, if her window was open, she might wake up enough to hear the clinking and know that her great-grandfather was already on his way to the woods.

Everything was wet with dew. Cobwebs strung with beads of water hung from the grass stems like little jeweled cloths. Isabel stayed on the path, but even so, her tennis shoes and the bottoms of her blue jeans were wet before she had gone very far. Ahead of her, she could see that the bottoms of Sonny's workpants were wet also.

"What's the weather going to do? Is it really going to be hot and sunny like they say? It doesn't seem like it. It's so cold now."

"It'll get up there. That's for sure. But the northwest breeze'll keep it from bein too bad."

"How *can* you tell? I'd give anything to be able to predict the weather like that."

They were at the gate. The oxen stood still while Sonny opened it. They walked through the opening and stopped when Sonny told them to.

When Isabel went past him, Sonny said, "All you got to do is look. There's signs everywhere of what's to come." He shut the gate and picked up the stick he used for a whip.

Isabel watched him slowly bend over and even more slowly straighten up, as though he had to rearrange his old bones, restack the vertebrae of his back. She was thinking, "But how do you know which things are signs and what they are signs of? How is a person supposed to choose right?" She didn't say any of this out loud because Sonny and the oxen were already starting up the hill into the woods.

There was enough daylight now so that Isabel could see their shapes dimly even under the trees. She shifted the chainsaw to her left hand and followed them.

"You want me to take that saw for a while?" Sonny said over his shoulder, as though he knew she was having trouble without even looking.

"No thanks. I'm fine. I've never been in the woods early in the morning like this."

"The birds make a racket, don't they?"

"It's lovely."

The woods smelled of damp earth and moss. Water dripped from the trees with a ticking sound, and all the birds in the world seemed to be trying to sing at the same time.

Sonny said, "They're sayin, 'Hey, I made it through the night. I'm still here. Look at me.' I guess they got to give all the neighbors the good news, don't they?"

Isabel laughed.

After that the road got steeper, and they didn't talk any more. The oxen rolled along, and the light got stronger, and the chainsaw got heavier, so that Isabel had to keep shifting it from one side to the other. Halfway up, they went by the road where they had been working last week.

Isabel had been encouraging herself to go on by telling herself they were almost to the turn. She was dismayed when she saw Sonny and the oxen go past it. She stopped in the middle of the road and stood there watching them walk away up the hill.

Without looking around, Sonny said, "We moved to a new place a couple days ago. I'll be glad to take that saw the rest of the way."

Isabel shifted her grip and started walking again. "No. I'm fine, really. I just didn't know."

Sonny looked over his shoulder. "It's up at the top—a long haul, but there's some good wood up there."

Isabel didn't answer. She was concentrating on not stopping, not putting down the saw. She didn't want to think about the top of the hill and how far away it might be. She wanted to keep going. How did he do it without getting tired?

She hadn't had to give up when at last, he said, "All right. Here we are. Haw, boys."

The oxen turned into an open place not far from the road. Sonny didn't tell them to whoa until they had walked into an evergreen tree on the far side of the clearing and had buried their faces in the branches. First he patted Buck and scratched his neck, and then he walked around to do the same for Ben. He didn't even notice what an uncomfortable place he had left them in.

Isabel stood behind them, watching and thinking how unusual it was that Sonny, who was always so considerate of everyone, and even more particular about his oxen's comfort than he was about that of the people he was with, how odd it was that Sonny didn't notice this. He should have told them to back up a few steps, so their faces wouldn't be bumping into the branches.

She watched while he dropped a chain onto the ground and dragged it out of the way, so the oxen wouldn't step on it. When he went past her, he said, "Set that saw down, darlin. You don't have to lug it any more."

"Oh," Isabel said, realizing again how heavy the saw was. She looked around to see what would be the right thing to do with it.

"Put it any place, honey. It don't matter. I'm goin to be usin it in about a minute here." He dropped the second chain with the first. "And get comfortable yourself. It'll be a while before we have a load. I haven't even got the tree down yet."

"Okay," Isabel said. She was thinking about Abingdon and how surprised everyone would be if they could see her here in the forest at dawn with this gnome-like old man and his huge, gentle beasts. It was a scene from a fairy tale, and she stood in the middle of it, holding a chainsaw as though she knew what she was doing. She wished her friends could see her.

"I've learned so much since I have been here, working with you and Al," she said smiling at him. "I really appreciate how much you have taught me. I want to be able to help you more. I think maybe I'm ready to learn how to run your chainsaw."

"Oh no...." his voice was full of distress. He looked past her without saying any more. After a minute he picked up his red feedstore cap and began to scratch his head. The cap flapped back and forth in his hand.

In spite of his reaction, Isabel went on doggedly with what

she had planned to say. "Perhaps you could show me how to run it?"

Sonny settled his cap back onto his head. He looked at her, and then his eyes slid away again to some point behind her. "I appreciate it that you want to help...." he said.

"I could be a lot more useful if I knew how to work a chainsaw." She looked directly at him, waiting for an answer. "Couldn't I?"

Sonny opened his mouth and shut it again without saying anything. He kicked at the dirt with the toe of his boot, pushing away the leaf litter and digging a depression in the soft earth. With the side of his foot, he carefully smoothed out the place he had dug. Both of them watched his foot at work.

Isabel was surprised and disappointed. Sonny had been so generous about showing her how to get firewood out of the woods. She didn't see what was different about operating a chainsaw. And anyway, it was something she would definitely have to know how to do. She wasn't going to give it up.

After a silence, and without looking up at her, Sonny said, "It's too dangerous....and heavy. That's what it is. It's too heavy."

"I guess you haven't noticed—and, of course, there's no reason why you should have—but I've gotten a whole lot stronger."

"I don't think a woman....leastways, I never *heard* of a woman operatin a chainsaw." He paused. His eyes flicked across her face and away again. "And anyhow, I hope Al never gets such a idea."

"So," Isabel thought. "I'm going to have to find some other way to learn, someone else to teach me. Maybe I can learn on a small saw and work up to a bigger one." She pictured how she would do that, how she wouldn't say anything about it until she got good at it. She pictured how she would ask Sonny to hand her his saw and deftly finish a cut that he was having trouble with. He would be surprised, but he would see right away that it had nothing to do with being a woman.

Finally, after an awkward silence, Sonny said, "Well, I guess...."

He kicked at the ground a few more times. "If you would hand me that saw...."

She held it out to him.

"Thank you, darlin," he said gratefully. Without either of them saying so directly, they both knew the incident was closed, at least temporarily.

"Now," Sonny said. "I got to take down this old maple here. You might want to sit over by Buck 'n Ben. You'll be all right there." He pointed down the hill. "I mean it to fall that way, between those two maples."

"Really? You know where it's going to fall? How can you know that?"

"Well, naturally, there ain't nothin sure, but that's the way I'm goin to cut it. So you can stay over here by Buck 'n Ben."

Isabel looked at the oxen who were standing patiently where Sonny left them. "Don't you want to turn them around so those branches aren't hitting them in the face?"

"No, darlin, they're fine. They like it like that."

"It can't be comfortable."

"You wait til later. You'll see. I always try to fix 'em a place so the spruce branches can keep the flies off their faces. The flies drive 'em crazy, especially when they've got the yoke on."

"Oh," said Isabel, laughing at herself. "I was wondering why you didn't make them comfortable the way you usually do. I thought you hadn't noticed."

"They didn't have a spot like this in the other place because there wasn't any softwoods where we was cuttin before. I always try to fix 'em up this way in fly season."

"I should have known you wouldn't neglect them."

"Now, darlin, you go over there and let me get this tree down. We're not gettin any work done this way."

Isabel did what he said. She liked him so much, in spite of his conservative ideas. Maybe she would be able to teach him that these days women were able to do what men did.

In the moments before Sonny started the saw, she could hear

the oxen chewing, and dew dripping from the trees, like tiny feet pattering over the dead leaves. Far away a bird made a liquid call so clear and beautiful that it brought tears to her eyes. Then the saw filled the whole clearing with its scream which changed to a whine as it bit into the tree.

Isabel would have liked to have watched what Sonny did with the saw, but he was on the other side of the tree. How different her evening was going to be—two separate worlds, although Leroy and Sonny certainly knew each other. Leroy had even said so several times. She hadn't heard Sonny mention Leroy, but then, he'd had no reason to. She wondered what he would think if he knew she was dating Leroy, if he knew she was sleeping with him. She was pretty sure he would disapprove, and that made her feel like a hypocrite.

Something landed on her shoulder, and she jumped. She had a sudden vision of the tree falling on her.

Al was standing behind her. "You sure jumped," she said, laughing. "What did you think I was goin to do?"

"I don't know. I guess I didn't think."

"I'm sorry. I didn't mean to scare you *that* bad."

"That's okay. I don't know why it did. I guess I was thinking about the tree he's cutting down."

They both looked at Sonny. He finished the cut he was making and straightened up. Still holding the running saw, he kicked at the tree and knocked out the wedge-shaped chunk he had cut. He looked up at the top of the tree and then walked around to the other side. He didn't look at them.

"I didn't know you were comin so early," Al said to Isabel.

"I probably said I was going to try. I was afraid I wouldn't be able to get up in time."

"I don't remember. Maybe you told Gramps."

Sonny was sawing on their side of the tree now. The saw made a lot of noise. It was hard to talk. Before he had cut very far, he stopped and pulled the saw out of the cut. He stood looking up at the tree, while the saw puttered quietly in his hands.

"What's he doing?'
"I don't know."
He shut off the saw and set it down on the ground.
"What are you doin, Gramps?"
He was walking toward them. "I didn't know you was up here, darlin. I'm glad to see you."
"What'd you stop cuttin for?"
"I don't know. It feels funny. I don't like it." He stood beside them looking at the tree. "I thought I'd put a wedge in it. We brought 'em up the other day, didn't we?"
"I think so."
"Good."
He was turning away to get the wedge when the tree made a loud crack and shivered where it stood on the stump.
Isabel was thinking how interesting it was to watch the tree's death throes. Al dashed toward the tree. She stopped when it began to tilt over in a slow-motion plunge that seemed to go on forever.
When the crash was over, and there was silence again, Isabel said, "What were you doing when you ran over there?"
"I thought it was goin to twist around and come down wrong. I wanted to get Gramps' saw out of the way."
Isabel looked at Sonny, but she couldn't tell what he was thinking. "You moved so fast," she said to Al. "I would *never* have dared to go close to that tree like that. I guess I won't ever get used to this kind of work the way you are. It's amazing. You always know just what to do."
Al's cheeks got pink with pleasure. "You've learned a lot, you know," she said to Isabel. "And we'll teach you everything! Won't we, Gramps?"
"I hope so, darlin," he said, but he seemed distracted.
"I have a long way to go," Isabel said. "I shouldn't delude my-self."
Sonny sighed and walked over to pick up his saw. He didn't say anything or look at either of them. He started the saw, but then

he just stood there, looking at the tree and revving the engine in a series of short, loud bursts.

"Is something wrong with his saw?"

"No, it sounds okay. He worries too much, that's all. That's just the way he is, but I love him anyway."

"He does look worried," Isabel said.

25

SONNY STOOD THERE revving his saw while he tried to decide whether or not to say something to Al. She shouldn't have charged in to grab his saw when she thought the tree was going to twist around. Suppose it *had* fallen that way. And the tree coming down when he didn't expect it—that scared him badly. At least neither of the girls realized how bad it could have been.

He didn't need to look in Al's direction to know she knew what was bothering him. He hated to scold her in front of Isabel, especially since Isabel didn't know enough to know that Al had done wrong. It would be better to talk to Al about it later when they were alone. Then she would be more likely to listen to what he said. She was having such a good time letting Isabel think she knew everything there was to know. He didn't want to spoil that for her.

When he had settled things in his mind, he stepped closer to the tree and started to cut. At first it went fine, but then suddenly, halfway through the log, there was nothing there, no resistance. The saw was biting on air. He expected something solid, but he found nothing. It gave him a bad feeling. He pulled the saw out and turned it off and set it on the ground. This tree wasn't acting right. It made him feel off balance and shaky.

"Gramps, are you okay?" Al and Isabel were watching him with big eyes.

"What, darlin?"

"I've asked you three times what was goin on, and you haven't even answered me."

"I'm sorry, darlin. I didn't hear you." He went over to the end of the log by the stump.

"Well, what *is* it?"

"I cut into a hollow place on that log. I should've known." He looked at the cut end. To his surprise it looked solid. He straightened up. "It ain't hollow down here. That's why I didn't know. This tree has fooled me from the start."

"Is it okay, Gramps? Can we still use it?"

"Let me cut the rest of the way, and then we'll see." He started the saw and cut into the same cut, down past the empty place and through to the other side. He turned the saw off and set it down and put his hands on the log and rolled it just enough to see how heavy it was.

"It feels like there's some good wood here, even with the hollow part. Let's take it down."

"Great," Al said. She was already heading for the chains.

"What shall *I* do?" Isabel asked, standing still in the same place.

Al went by her, dragging the choker chain. "Come on over here with me, Isabel. I'll show you how to put this chain on." She dropped the chain at the end of the log. "Stay there just a minute. I got to go get the peavy."

Sonny loved to see Al bustle around, in charge of everything and pleased with herself. In some ways she was so much like

Carol Ann, although Carol Ann was always angry about something. He couldn't remember if she had been happier when she was Al's age. He was working too hard in those days to have seen much of her, or of anyone else.

Al came back with the peavy and stuck it in the ground by the end of the log. "There," she said. "We'll need that in a minute. We've got to dig it out first. Come here, and I'll show you."

Isabel was paying attention to everything Al said. Sonny was glad he hadn't scolded her. There would be plenty of time for that later. Not very many people knew what Al was capable of. It was good for her to get some appreciation.

He stood there watching the two of them on their knees, digging under the log with their hands. He felt a little funny letting women do the work while he did nothing. He was glad there was no one around to see him. They were having a good time together. They didn't need him to get in the middle of it and make it more like work.

Al got on the peavy to rock the log back and forth, so Isabel could fish the choker chain under it. Isabel was nearly lying down in the dirt. She had her hair in a long pigtail down her back, and when it flipped over her shoulder, she threw it back again out of her way. Sonny liked the way she got right into the job and didn't even notice how dirty she was getting. "I got it," she shouted. "It's through!" She sat back and smiled up at Al.

Al said, "Great job." She pulled the chain the rest of the way around the log. "Now watch. I'll show you how to hook it up." She had to hitch the chain several times before Isabel saw how it was stronger to put the hook over the link instead of through it, the way people who'd never used a chain always wanted to do. Then Al smiled at him. "We're ready, Gramps. Can I take this one down, please?"

Sonny couldn't resist that smile, even though everything about this log had been unpredictable so far. He checked the chain, pulling on it to see if it was tight enough. "This looks good."

"Thanks, Gramps."

"As good as I could've got it."

"You still haven't said I could drive it down, you old Gramps you."

"Aw, honey. Okay."

"Oh, goody."

"But wait a minute. I mistrust this log a little." He saw her face cloud over. He reached out and put his hand on her bony, little shoulder. "I want to start it out. I want to see if it's goin to go all right."

"Okay," she said. "Listen to this. How about if you drive til you get it to the road, and I take it from there. Is that a fair deal?"

"All right, honey," he said laughing. "I guess that'll give me a chance to see how it's goin to act."

"Great," she said, and then when he didn't move, "Well, Gramps, what are we waitin for?"

His hand was still on her shoulder. He pressed down a little for emphasis, as he said, "Okay, let's go. But don't forget, if I don't like the way it's goin, I'm not goin to let you take it."

"I know, Gramps."

He put the long chain on the yoke and walked Buck and Ben over to the log. They'd had a slow morning and were glad to get to work, or maybe they were showing off a little to impress Isabel the way Al was. Whatever the reason, they backed up smoothly and were patient while he made the hitch.

"You could get 'em a lot closer, Gramps. You got a long chain there."

"I want it like that, darlin. Just in case. It'll give it room to roll if it wants to. Like I said, I mistrust it some."

The boys pulled willingly. He took them around the turn onto the road with the log trailing like it was trained. There wasn't any reason to be so uneasy.

When he whoaed the boys, Al was right by his side, looking eager and already reaching for the whip. "You worry too much, you old Gramps."

"Okay, darlin. But take it slow now. Buck 'n Ben haven't done anythin yet this mornin. They might be in a hurry. Keep 'em down."

"Sure," she said. "It'll be fine." She waved the whip, and Sonny stepped aside, out of the way. "Git up, boys. Let's go."

They started off fast, and maybe it caught her by surprise because she didn't do anything to slow them like she should have done.

Sonny followed with Isabel. He was trying to decide if he ought to shout to Al to slow down, when Isabel started to talk.

"It's hard for me to remember how young she is. She knows so much."

Sonny said, "I wish she'd be more careful. She could use some caution."

Al and the oxen were almost to the bend in the road, and Al was behind where she ought to be. It looked like she might be having trouble keeping up.

Sonny turned to Isabel to say that young people always need to learn more caution. He wanted Isabel to know that was the only fault he had to find with Al's work. After he said that, he was planning to shout to Al to slow the oxen down and walk up beside Buck like she should.

But when he turned toward Isabel, he saw her mouth drop open. He looked around. The log was rolling over as it started into the turn. It swept out wide as it went over. Before Sonny could even shout a warning, something, either the log or the chain, caught Al too, and she went down. Her arms went up, and the whip flew out of her hand, and then he couldn't see her any more. It seemed as though he stood there forever looking at the place she had been, and then he shouted her name and started to run. But it was over before he moved. He heard the log dragging and the thud of the oxen's hooves as they dug into their work and then the terrible crack as the log smacked hard against a tree. Leaves rained down. The oxen kept going, and the log swept on around the bend after them.

There was an enormous stillness, and in it Al lay crumpled on the ground by the side of the road. Sonny ran toward her. He was telling himself not to worry, to remember that time she got hurt last spring and how scared he had been then, and she was fine. At the same time, he was telling himself to get ready, because this time it was all over—as if anyone could get ready for something like that. The noise of that terrible smack was in his ears, sounding again and again in between all his thoughts.

He knelt down beside her. He could feel Isabel standing right behind him, but neither of them said anything. Al was lying on her side, almost peacefully. Her face was pale. There were lots of cuts on the side of her face he could see, but none of them looked deep. There was a little trickle of blood at the corner of her mouth. She might have bitten her lip. And her nose was bleeding. That was all. He reached out to turn her over so he could see the other side.

"I don't think you should move her," Isabel said.

"I have to find out how bad she's hurt." He laid his rough hand as gently as he could on Al's cheek. "And I might have to get her down to the house. Maybe she's in shock or somethin....if she doesn't come to...."

"They always say you aren't supposed to move an injured person."

"I might have to carry her."

"You couldn't."

"She's not very heavy. She's all bone," he said tenderly, looking at Al's white face.

"Is she breathing?"

"What?" He looked around at Isabel. Surely she didn't think.... He felt unable to understand.

Isabel knelt down beside Al. Sonny moved aside to give her room. He was glad she was there. She leaned over Al gently, putting her ear to Al's mouth. After a minute she sat back. "Yes," she said. "Thank God. She's breathing. But it doesn't sound strong." She stood up, and then she laid her hand on his shoulder. "Listen. I'm going to go down to your house and call the rescue squad. They'll know what to do."

Sonny nodded. He wondered if Isabel knew something more than she was saying, knew how bad it was, but he didn't ask.

"Maybe they can get all the way up here. I'll see if I can get them to try. I'll wait for them and show them the way."

Sonny meant to say, "All right," but the noise he made came out sounding more like a groan.

Maybe she didn't notice. She was already heading down the road.

Then he and Al were alone. She still lay crumpled on her side. He longed to turn her over, to make her more comfortable, but he knew he shouldn't move her. He wanted to do something. Isabel was a good girl. It was lucky she was here to go for help. He knew she was right.

He didn't know how long it would be. He had dropped through a trapdoor into a dark cellar, into a place he had never been before. His thoughts were waterbugs skittering across a dark surface. There was no time or sunlight or ordinary life. Nothing was real. He felt that this couldn't be, wasn't really happening, and at the same time that he'd always known it would. There was a deep ravine between now and before. He felt as though he might be able to leap over it, back into the then, if he didn't feel so weak and tired.

He looked down at Allie. She was so pale. Her face was as white as it had been that time when she was four and got stuck at the top of the ladder to the hay loft. She was scared, but she wouldn't let anyone help her. Every time he started to climb up to her, she screamed until he got off the ladder. Finally, she managed to climb down by herself. They never talked about it, but he always thought she had to get out of it by herself to punish herself for doing something she had been told not to do.

She always wanted to come with him to do the chores, even when she was only two. Thinking of her round and dimpled arms and legs made his heart ache. Of course, she slowed him down a lot. It took the two of them together to get her dressed for the cold. She, with her baby-fat fingers, and he, with his thick, work-hardened ones—it was an awkward job of work, but it got to be something he looked forward to because they did it together.

And that Christmas morning when she was eight, and no one could find her. She had slipped out extra early to see if the cow had calved. When she saw the calf, she forgot that no one knew where she was. She even forgot that it was Christmas. That calf was the heifer he traded for Buck and Ben.

When he realized he was thinking about Al as though she was gone, Sonny was horrified. After that, he didn't dare let himself think about her at all.

Then he had no idea how long he sat on the ground beside her, waiting for the rescue squad. There were long stretches of time where he didn't think about anything. He just sat. The wheels of his mind were clogged and wouldn't turn.

When he first heard it, he thought he was hearing things. There was no siren, only the sound of an engine so faint it could have been nothing at all. He had to listen for what seemed like a long time before he dared to hope. Finally, he was sure it was the rescue vehicle, and it was coming up the logging road.

He leaned over Allie and kissed her forehead. "It's goin to be all right now, darlin. These people will help us. They'll be here any minute to fix you up. There's nothin to worry about now." He patted her thin shoulder and stood up so they would know where to stop. He felt self-conscious, as though he had been caught talking to himself. But he wasn't talking to himself. He was talking to Al. She was still here. He had to believe that.

When he looked down the hill, he could see the front of the van coming around the curve in the road. The chrome flashed in the patches of sunlight that came through the leaves. The red paint was as dark as blood against the green.

The van pulled up beside him. Before it stopped, a young blonde man jumped out. He nodded to Sonny and ran around the back. The driver came around the front holding out his hand.

He touched Sonny's hand with his own and said, "Jack." Then he went past Sonny to bend over Al. It took Sonny a long, slow minute to realize the man had been introducing himself.

Isabel smiled at him as she got out of the truck. They stood together watching Jack. First he knelt down beside Al and put his face close to hers. Then he sat back and picked up her wrist, feeling for her pulse. Sonny held his breath, all of him suspended, waiting for hope. Jack dropped Al's wrist and lifted her eyelid. Then he looked up and said, "Does she have any allergies?" Sonny shook his head. It didn't make sense. He couldn't ask the only thing in the world he wanted to know.

Jack stood up and looked around. "Where the hell's that stretcher, Terry?" he shouted. "I want to get her in the van and start the oxygen in there."

"Coming right now."

Jack looked angrily at Sonny and Isabel. "Are we going to have to back down to that side road to get turned around?"

Sonny couldn't grasp what he was being asked. All he could think was, why didn't the man say how she was, but as though he was in a nightmare, he couldn't make any noise. He looked at Isabel, hoping she would know what to do.

"There's a road just up the hill," she said. "I'm sure you can turn around there." Sonny hoped she knew he was grateful, even though he couldn't say anything.

Terry laid the stretcher on the ground beside Al. Jack took her head, and Terry took her feet. Almost without moving her, they slid the stretcher underneath.

Sonny stood there staring at the place on the ground where Al had been. There was some blood, a pressed-down place in the dead leaves beside the road and Al's red feedstore cap.

Sonny picked up the cap and followed Al's stretcher like a sleepwalker. He listened to Jack telling the other man that he would have to drive uphill until he found a place to turn around.

When Sonny got to the back of the van, Jack was in the doorway, and Al was already inside. Sonny started to climb in. Jack put a hand on his chest and pushed him back.

"No. I'm sorry," he said. "You'll have to ride up front." He stuck his head out the door to call after the blonde man. "And, Terry, that woman knows where the road is. Okay?" Then he noticed that Sonny was still standing in the same place with one foot on the step. He frowned. "Go get in the cab now," he said.

Isabel came around the corner just in time to hear what he said. She put her arm around Sonny. "Come on. We both need to get in, so they can go. We want them to hurry."

The one named Terry was already starting the engine when Sonny got into the cab beside him. "I hope I can do this," he said. "Jack's going to have a fit if I bounce him around too much."

"The road's on your left," Isabel said. "And you come to it almost right away."

The truck started slowly up the hill. "Is that it?" Terry's voice was tight. "You think I can turn around in there?'

"I think you've got to," Isabel said quietly. "Pull in a little way and back out. You can do it."

"I hope you're right," Terry said, as though he was sure she wasn't. "Jack won't like it if we get stuck up here."

Sonny sat in the middle. He was numb. Would the bumps in the road hurt her or jostle her on the stretcher? Suppose she woke up? She wouldn't know where she was. Would she be afraid?

Terry got the truck turned around and headed down the hill. Neither he nor Isabel paid any attention to Sonny. He felt unable to comprehend what they were concerned about, but he didn't want them to notice his confusion.

After a silence, Isabel sat forward looking past Sonny at Terry. "How bad do you think she is? I mean, do you think she's very seriously hurt?"

"Yes," he said, frowning a little. "It's serious, all right. But I don't know anything definite, because I didn't examine her." He glanced at them both and then back at the road. "You'll have to wait until we get to the hospital."

After that no one said any more until they were driving across the night pasture. They didn't stop to open the gate. Isabel must have guessed that Sonny wondered about it, because she said, "I opened both gates when I came down to call. Your oxen went through to the woodpile behind the house."

Sonny nodded. He didn't try to say anything because his eyes unexpectedly filled with tears. He was afraid they would overflow down his face if he tried to speak. The possibility embarrassed him.

"Will you stop by the house and let me out?" Isabel leaned around Sonny to look at Terry. "I think I'll follow you in my car, so we'll have a way home later on."

"That's better anyway. We're not supposed to carry any passengers, except the accident victim." He stopped the van by the kitchen door. He leaned on the steering wheel watching them get out. "Sometimes we bend the rules, but it's better if we don't have to—something about the insurance. You both take care now."

"We ought to put your oxen in the barn before we go."

"What?" It wasn't that he didn't hear, but that it took him so long to comprehend anything. "No," he said. "They can wait."

"Will they be all right? We might be gone a long time."

"I think so," he said, although even while he was speaking, he knew he wasn't able to think about his oxen. He made an effort. "It's shady back there. They'll be all right."

"Let's go then," Isabel said. She walked over to her car and opened the door. Sonny opened the passenger-side door. "Wait a minute," she said.

He looked at her across the roof of the car, and the worry on her face made a lump of fear twist in his stomach.

"I think," she said slowly, "I'm sorry to say this, but I think you ought to call Al's parents." She was looking at something behind him. "Just in case, I mean. But I don't like to say. You should do what you think."

"Yes, I guess you're right. I should call them." Now it was his turn not to look at her. "What do you mean 'just in case'?"

"I don't know. Probably nothing. I was just talking. Do you want me to....I mean, I could wait for you...."

"Yes, I will, yes. I'll be back." He could feel her watching him as he walked toward the kitchen door, but in his numb state, he couldn't go faster.

He stood in the hall, trying to look up the telephone number of Raymond's garage. The light was dim, and he spent a long time looking for Garneau's Gulf under the C's before he realized he was on the wrong page. His hands were shaking.

Finally, Raymond's boss answered the telephone. He said Raymond couldn't come to the phone but he would give him a message. Sonny told him to tell Raymond that the rescue squad was taking Al to the hospital and that he would call Carol Ann. Sonny was glad he didn't have to hear Raymond's voice when he was told.

Of course, Carol Ann would be the hard one. But there again, he was lucky. May answered the telephone. He told her what he told Raymond's boss.

There was a silence on the other end of the line. Sonny thought May must have gone to get Carol Ann. Then she spoke. "How bad is it?"

"We don't know. We're goin to the hospital right now. We'll call from there."

"Who's we? Is Raymond home?"

"No, he's not, but I called him. It's Isabel. She's goin to...."

"Sonny, where are you at right now?"

"I'm home, but I'm just about to go. Isabel is...."

"Sonny, you stop by the Texas and pick up Carol Ann. You hear me?"

"It might not be all that bad, May. We don't know how bad it is."

"Well, please God, it ain't. But that don't make no difference. You stop for her anyhow. She's goin to want to be there."

"All right."

"Is Raymond goin?"

"I don't know."

"Well, I'll go tell her. A woman can do that better anyways. And, Sonny, you come on and pick her up." She hung up without giving him a chance to say anything.

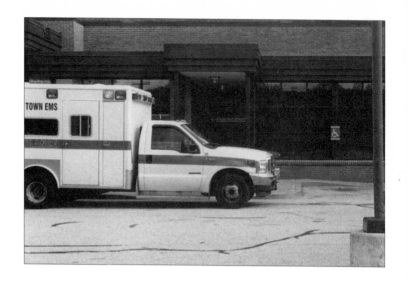

26

Carol Ann was standing at the end of the counter listening to Ralph Merrill complain about his taxes, so she didn't pay any attention to May's phone call, except to notice that May seemed put out by it. That meant it was probably Janet trying to change her hours again. It was the quiet part of the morning. The only other people in the place were an elderly couple who had New Hampshire plates on their car.

May got off the phone and started to clean the counter, even though Carol Ann had wiped down the whole thing not five minutes before. May worked her way along, wiping in big circles, picking up each sugar cannister and all the salt and pepper shakers to clean their bottoms. Carol Ann couldn't stop watching as May worked her way toward them. It got so she didn't hear anything Ralph was saying. And the longer she watched, the more annoyed she felt.

When May got as far as the coffee urn, Carol Ann shocked everybody in the place, including herself, by screaming at May to stop it. The couple in the booth, and Ralph, and May, all stared at her in silence. She was silent too, so they didn't know that she was as surprised as they were. She had no idea what made her lose it like that.

And then there was another surprise. May didn't even get mad. She came right up to Carol Ann and put her arm around her and said, "Carol, honey, I want you to come with me. Excuse us, Ralph." She walked Carol Ann around the end of the counter to a booth, and not the back one that they always sat in, but the closest one, just like she was a paying customer. "You sit right here, honey," she said, and she gave Carol Ann a little push into the booth. To Carol Ann it seemed as though they were all crazy, herself included.

There were three coffee cups on the table. She must have missed that booth when she was cleaning up. May sat down across from her and reached out and took her hand. Carol Ann felt herself getting irritated all over again. She pulled her hand away.

Ralph started out the door. "I'll see you, Carol Ann. You too, May," he said as he left.

Carol Ann was wondering what was the matter with her and why she was acting so bad, when she realized that May was talking about Alison and an accident. May said the ambulance went by a little while ago. None of it made any sense. May just kept on saying more and more words.

All of a sudden Carol Ann felt the air going out of her like a pillow that has been punched. She said, "Ooaaff," and sank lower on the seat. Then she reached out and pushed the coffee cups away. She laid her head down in the space she had made for it and slid into unconsciousness.

The next thing she knew, May was shaking her by the arm. "Hon, they're here to take you to the hospital. Wake up now."

"Is something wrong with me?"

"No, hon, you're fine. You just get up now, so they don't have to wait."

"It's Allie, ain't it?" The queer way she had screamed at May came back to her. Just then she hated May. "I know Allie's been hurt, but you wouldn't tell me."

When she stood up, she felt dizzy. She thought about how easy it would be to sit down and be unconscious again. She wouldn't have to think about any of it—why she was acting strange, or whether Allie was hurt, or what May was up to. She wobbled and grabbed the table for support. She had to find out if Allie was all right.

"Sit down again, Carol. I believe you got up too fast."

"Leave me alone, May. I don't understand any of this. What's goin on, anyhow?"

"I was tellin you, hon, and then you passed out. Allie had a accident."

Carol Ann could feel herself starting to get angry at May again. "How do you know?"

"Your Gramps called up to tell you."

"I didn't know that. Why didn't he talk to me?"

May's face didn't change, but her eyes slipped away from Carol Ann's. "He said he thought a woman could do a better job of tellin you."

Something grabbed deep inside Carol Ann's stomach. "It's bad then, ain't it?"

"I don't know. It might be." She put her big hand down on Carol Ann's shoulder. "But look here. They won't know til they get to the hospital."

Carol Ann resisted the urge to shake off May's heavy hand. "Is Raymond there?"

"That's the very question I asked." She took her hand away. "No, he ain't. Your Gramps has that woman with him. That Isabel?"

"Oh, her."

"What's goin on there anyhow, Carol Ann? Do you know? Is

he goin out with her?"

"No, I don't think so." But even as she spoke, she began to have her doubts. "She's just some hippie woman who wants to learn about drivin cattle. I don't think Gramps...."

Just then Gramps himself walked through the door. He looked awful. He didn't speak to May at all, and he didn't look at Carol Ann or say hello. All he said was, "Are you ready to go, Carol?"

"I got to get my pocketbook is all."

"I'll get it, hon." May bustled off before Carol Ann could say a word. She and Gramps just stood there until May got back. Neither of them spoke. Carol Ann wanted to know about Allie, but her stomach turned over when she thought about what she might hear. She told herself it would be a good idea to wait a few minutes before she asked. She didn't want to pass out again.

May came back and handed her the pocketbook. She followed Gramps out the door and down the two steps. She still felt unsteady on her feet. She was glad Gramps waited for her at the bottom of the steps. He didn't reach out to her, but they walked so close together that their shoulders touched, and that was a help. She appreciated it, even though it felt strange.

The parking lot was almost empty. "Where's your pick-up at, Gramps?"

"We came in Isabel's car, honey. That's okay, ain't it?"

"I suppose so," Carol Ann said, feeling so wobbly and confused that she didn't have the energy to ask why. Suddenly she remembered seeing Isabel's car parked at their house this morning when she left for work. It made her feel uncomfortable when she saw it, as though Isabel was trying to take something away that was hers. She told herself that was silly and that Isabel must be up in the woods with Gramps, and then she forgot all about it, but now she wondered. Maybe there was something to May's suspicions after all.

When Carol Ann and Gramps got to Isabel's old, white stationwagon, Isabel was kneeling on the back seat moving her stuff around. While Carol Ann was watching, she took a couple of books and a jacket and a pair of sandals and dropped them behind the back seat. Then she looked around and saw them standing by the open door. "Oh," she said to Carol Ann, "I hope I've made enough room for you." She climbed out of the car. "I'm sorry it's such a mess."

"You get in front, Carol," Gramps said. He got in back and shut the door. Carol Ann got in front. She wondered if they thought she was too big to fit back there, but she couldn't think clearly enough even to care.

Isabel smiled at her while she was putting on her seat belt. Carol Ann didn't smile back. She knew she ought to put her seat belt on too, but she didn't have the energy. She was sure she would have to adjust it so it was bigger. There was too much of her, and little Allie might not be all right. The contrast was awful. She couldn't think about it. She didn't even know what happened. She wanted to ask, but she didn't.

They drove in silence, all of them staring straight ahead. Carol Ann felt as though her brains wouldn't work at all. She wondered what Gramps was thinking. If Isabel hadn't been there, Carol Ann would have asked him about a lot of things.

When they got to the edge of town, Isabel slowed down a lot. Carol Ann said, "What's the matter?"

"I'm not sure I know the way. It doesn't look familiar."

Carol Ann waited to see what Gramps would say, but he didn't say anything. Maybe he hadn't even heard. So Carol Ann told her the turns to make to go up to the hospital by the back way. She was surprised that she was able to do it. Since she didn't drive herself, she was afraid she might not have paid enough attention to the roads. It made her feel a little better to realize that she knew the way.

When they got to the hospital, Isabel started to turn in to the emergency room parking lot. Carol Ann said, "You're not supposed to park in here. This is for emergencies, not for people like us who are visiting." She knew it didn't matter, but the sight of those emergency room doors really threw her, and she couldn't stop herself. "You're supposed to park on the other side where it says, 'Visitor Parking'. Tell her, Gramps."

But Isabel kept right on. She pulled into the emergency parking lot and stopped the car, and Gramps didn't say a word. They both started to get out of the car, acting as though Carol Ann hadn't made a sound. Maybe she hadn't. Maybe she was only thinking that Isabel shouldn't park here. Maybe she hadn't said anything out loud. How would she even know?

When Isabel got out of the car, she said, "Look, you can see mountains almost all around in a circle. It's beautiful. It must help people get better to have such a beautiful view."

Carol Ann didn't say anything. She was thinking about Allie getting better. And Gramps walked off without waiting for either of them. They didn't catch up with him until they got to the big glass doors, which opened automatically. They all went in together.

The first thing Carol Ann saw was Raymond standing by the nurses' counter, running his hands through his hair so it all stood up. He looked terrible. His face was yellow, and he was filthy from working on cars.

When he saw her, Raymond came straight over holding his hands out to her. He took both of hers and said, "Oh, baby, she's dead."

"No, Raymond," she said. "You don't know that. Don't get upset." His hands were covered with grease. He was getting her all dirty.

Gramps was standing right behind her. "Who told you that, Raymond?"

Isabel said, "Oh no," in a kind of a wail. Carol Ann wanted to tell her to shut up. She didn't belong here. She wasn't even related.

Raymond said, "I asked a nurse where Allie was, and she said to wait a minute and she would find out for me, and then this doctor came out and told me she was dead from a head injury. What happened, Gramps?" He looked like he was going to cry.

Carol Ann pulled her hands away from Raymond's. She started talking before Gramps had a chance to. "Did you see her, Raymond? How do you know that doctor didn't make a mistake?"

"No, baby. I didn't see her. I thought maybe it was against their rules or somethin."

Carol Ann turned to Gramps, "It ain't true, is it, Gramps? Do you think it's true? You thought she was hurt bad, but she was goin to be all right, didn't you?"

Gramps opened his mouth to say something, and then his face twisted up and no words came out.

Carol Ann turned back to Raymond. "Well, *I* don't believe it," she said firmly. "It don't make any sense. It can't be true."

"I hope you're right, baby," Raymond said with a loud sniff.

"I *know* I am. I *have* to be." Right then she felt shaky, but stronger than before. She couldn't let it be true.

After that nobody said anything. They stood in a clump by the door. Everyone who came in and out had to go around them. Usually Carol Ann would have been embarrassed by that and would have gotten them all to move somewhere out of the way, but just then it didn't seem to matter. Nothing seemed to matter. She didn't know what to do next.

Raymond said, "Hey, there he is. That's the guy."

Carol Ann looked where Raymond was looking and saw a youngish man standing behind the nurses' counter. He had a white jacket and glasses on. He was reading something from a clipboard. A nurse was standing beside him, waiting to see what he would say. When he looked up and saw them all staring at him, he handed the clipboard to the nurse and said a few words to her. Then he came around the end of the counter and walked right up to Carol Ann holding out his hand.

"You must be Mrs. LeStage."

Carol Ann nodded. She felt numb. He wasn't smiling at all. The others stood a little behind her. She didn't know what to do. She was embarrassed to shake hands with him, because hers were so dirty from Raymond's grease, but she didn't know how to get out of it.

The doctor didn't seem to notice. He was looking at her face. "I examined your daughter this morning, and I had to pronounce her dead. I'm terribly sorry."

Carol Ann just stood there. She was thinking how she still couldn't believe it, even though the doctor said so, and at the same time she was wondering why she didn't pass out now, so she didn't have to think about any of this.

27

WHEN THE DOCTOR said that Al was dead, they all looked at Carol Ann, waiting to hear what she would say, as though she would speak for all of them. But she didn't say a word. She just stood there, holding the doctor's hand and swaying back and forth. She got so pale that Isabel thought she was going to faint.

An elderly man and woman walked past. They had to squeeze between Raymond and the wall. The woman looked around at them, cross because they blocked the way out. She said something to the man as they went through the door, but she spoke too low to be heard. Isabel looked at the others, usually so polite, so careful not to get in the way, but none of them had noticed.

The doctor held Carol Ann's hand in one of his and laid his other hand on her shoulder. He said, "You and your husband will need to come to the office. There are papers that have to be filled out. I'm awfully sorry. And, Mrs. LeStage, we need to know the name of a funeral home. Who do you want us to call?"

Carol Ann hadn't said anything, but when she heard that, she moaned and pulled her hand away. She said, "Oh, Gramps, what are we goin to do?" and she stretched the do out into a cry of pain.

They all looked at Sonny. He cleared his throat slowly several times. He was staring at his feet, and he didn't look up. He said, "Car...." in a stiff, raspy voice and had to stop to clear his throat again before he could get out the whole sentence. "Carmoli Chapel in West Severance."

Carol Ann's mouth dropped open. Raymond ran his greasy hands over and over through his black curls until they were all standing straight up. Sonny didn't look up from the floor, and no one said anything.

The tension was too much. Isabel told herself that they probably would like to make their funeral arrangements without her around. She slipped quietly away, hoping they wouldn't notice, or would be glad if they did. But when she was around the corner, she began to wonder if *she* was the one who needed to get away from *them*.

She didn't know where she was going, just away. She walked down the long, windowless corridor, bright with florescent lights. All kinds of people passed her, going both ways. Everyone else seemed to know where they were and where they were going.

Then she remembered that she had a date to go out with Leroy. It was impossible to think that she could get dressed up and go for a moonlight dinner on Lake Champlain. It was impossible to think that life could go on as it had before.

At the end of the corridor near the lobby, there was a pay phone set into the wall. No one was nearby. On impulse Isabel dialed the number of Leroy's office. She planned to hang up if Renée answered, but it was Leroy.

"Oh....um....I didn't think I'd get you....um....this is Isabel."

"Yes, I know, Chérie."

"Ah, I have something to tell you."

"Yes?"

"It's so awful...." She paused and then hurried on before he had a chance to speak. "I don't think I can go out to dinner with you tonight."

"That's too bad. But it's not awful. Why can't you?"

"Well, something has happened....oh dear, I don't know how to say it....something that makes it impossible."

"Tell me what it is, Chérie," he said, but his voice suddenly had a hard edge to it.

"I'm trying to, but it isn't easy." She began to cry.

"If you've made some other plan, it's fine. No problem," he said stiffly.

"Oh no, of course I haven't done that. I wouldn't. Is *that* what you thought?"

"That's what it sounded like, Chérie."

"I wish it was." She took a deep breath and went on, still crying. "It's much worse. No. I was out at the Trumbley farm this morning, and....oh God, his granddaughter, no, I mean, his great-granddaughter, the one who is fourteen, you know...."

"Yes, I know," he said impatiently.

"She got killed this morning."

"How terrible," he said, but his voice was flat, as though he hadn't really taken it in.

"I was there when it happened." She waited, but he didn't say anything. "You do see why I can't go tonight, don't you?"

"Of course, Chérie. Whatever you say."

"Thank you for understanding," she said doubtfully.

"Now, if you'll excuse me, I have some people here."

"Oh."

"We can talk more later."

"But...."

"Talk to you soon, Chérie."

Isabel kept listening into the phone, but he was gone. And that was when she realized that what she really wanted from him was some comfort. Why hadn't he said how sorry he was, how he knew she must be feeling awful? Why hadn't he asked her what he could do to help, to make her feel better? She stood by the telephone with tears running down her face.

Then she walked slowly back to the emergency room. When she came around the corner, she saw Sonny standing in the middle of the room with his hat in his hand. He looked right at her, but she knew he didn't see her or anything else. He was so alone. Carol Ann and Raymond must still be filling out papers for the hospital. Isabel thought she would go to Sonny and comfort him, but when he looked at her, blinded by his pain, she couldn't bear it. She turned around and hurried back to the telephone and called Jeff at the bookstore.

"What is it, Isabel? You sound funny. It's not something wrong with one of the boys, is it?"

"Oh no, Jeff. I don't know. I mean I haven't heard, but something awful happened."

"What?"

"This teenaged girl here....she lives on that farm, you remember, the one you and I...."

"Isabel, are you all right?"

"Yes, Jeff, but I'm trying to tell you...."

"Nothing happened to you, did it?"

"No, but she got killed, and I was there, and...."

"Killed? Who killed her?"

"Oh, Jeff, it was an accident. I was there. She was driving that team of oxen. They were pulling a log, and...."

"Isabel, for God's sakes. I don't know how you get yourself into these situations. Yes, I do too. If you...."

"Jeff, don't say any more. I called up looking for some comfort. I thought you might be sorry because I'm feeling so awful about this."

"Listen, Isabel, how can I feel sorry for you when you bring the whole thing on yourself?"

"Okay, that's it. You just reminded me why I'm not married to you any more. Thank you. I'll call in a few days. Goodbye."

And she hung up without giving him a chance to say anything else. She stood by the telephone feeling wrung out with misery and hopelessness and anger. A man asked her if she was going to use the phone, and when she said no, he began to make his own call, standing as far away from her as he could. She walked away down the corridor, looking for a bathroom.

When she looked in the mirror, she realized for the first time what a mess she was. There were tracks down her cheeks where her tears had rolled through the dirt. She washed her hands and face and tried to tidy up her hair, but she didn't have the energy to do a good job. It would have taken a long time to do her braid over, and there was nothing she could do about her clothes. She looked again. She had made some improvement. She hoped they wouldn't notice that she had been crying. Carol Ann hadn't cried at all.

When she got back to them, the doctor was gone. The three of them were standing by the door. They weren't speaking to each other or touching. They were staring in different directions. They all looked as though they didn't know where they were. When Isabel got close to them, they all three turned and went out the door without a word. Isabel followed.

Sonny stopped near Isabel's car, and Raymond went on toward his. Carol Ann followed him.

When Raymond saw her, he stopped. "No, baby," he said gently. "You better go with them. I got to go back to work."

"But, Raymond...." she said, looking anguished.

Raymond started to put his hands on her shoulders. He looked at the light pink of her waitress uniform and at his grimy hands and put his hands in his pockets instead. "I'm goin to ask Ron to let me go home, but it might take a while."

"I don't care, Raymond."

"You'll have to wait."

"I don't mind. There ain't nothin else to do."

"Okay, then. Come on." He looked back at Sonny and Isabel. "We'll see you at home, Gramps, if that's okay." He didn't say anything to Isabel. She and Sonny got into her car.

They drove all the way to the turn in West Severance in silence. Then in a cracked voice, Sonny said, "I ought to have known better. I mistrusted that log right along."

Isabel didn't know what to say. She glanced over to see if he had noticed that she jumped when she heard his voice.

Sonny was looking down at his hands. Without raising his head, he went on. "I never allowed for the fact that they were goin uphill when I tried that log out." Then he was silent again.

For the rest of the trip, Isabel tried to think of how to comfort him. There wasn't any way to do so. It seemed to take forever to get to Sonny's place. At last, she parked her car beside the house.

Sonny said, "And I never should have forgot to shorten the chain." He got out of the car slowly, as if it took more strength than he had. When he turned to close his door, he seemed surprised to see that Isabel was out of the car also. He opened his mouth, but shut it again without saying anything.

"I'm going to stay and help you put your oxen away in the barn," Isabel said, sounding, even to her own ears, more sure of herself than she felt. How did she know that he needed help? How did she know what was right for his oxen?

Sonny nodded as though he understood why she had to treat him like an invalid. "All right," he said. "Let's go."

He walked around the side of the house, and Isabel followed him. She had never noticed how stooped over he was, how his shoulders hunched, and his head thrust forward between them. She longed to say something to help him, or since there was really nothing to say, to put her arms around those bent shoulders to comfort him. But that would have embarrassed both of them. It was better to ignore those feelings. Isabel had lived in New England long enough to understand that.

The oxen were still hitched to the log. They had pulled it partway across the woodpile, so that they could get into the shade behind the house.

"Oh my God," Isabel said. "Look at their faces. I've never seen so many flies. It's horrible." Right away she realized what a rude thing that was to say. She hoped he hadn't noticed. He hadn't noticed much since Al's accident.

He was standing beside Ben's head, and he turned and smiled, not a real smile, only a ghostly flicker, but more than had come from him before. He waved his hand in front of the oxen's faces, sending the flies up in a buzzing swarm. Even before the last ones took off, the first ones were settling down again. "That's why I always make 'em a place under a softwood, like I showed you this mornin," he said. Then his face filled with pain, and he turned away from her again.

"Okay, boys," he said. "Back."

The oxen shuffled from foot to foot without moving. They didn't want to leave the shade.

Sonny stepped in front of Buck and said, "Back," again. This time his voice was louder and sterner.

The oxen moved backward until their hind feet were against the logs of the woodpile and their faces were in the sun. The flies began to land once more.

Sonny said, "If you would kindly stand in front of 'em, so they don't go forward and take out my slack...."

Isabel nodded, glad to be able to do something to prove that she was right to stay to help him.

Sonny climbed up the woodpile and undid the long chain. He tossed the grab hook neatly off to the side so that it wouldn't catch on a chunk of wood. Then he pulled the short chain out from under the end of the log and scrambled down the woodpile. When he had the chains neatly looped over the yoke, he looked up from where he stood between the oxen to Isabel in front of them. "Would you like to drive 'em to the barn, darlin?"

Isabel couldn't meet his eyes. Just then she was too conscious of why she was saying no. "I'd rather you did it," was all she could manage to say.

For a minute Sonny didn't speak, and the only sounds were the buzzing of the flies and the swish and slap of the oxen's tails. But when he walked around his ox team, he stopped beside Isabel and patted her on the shoulder. "Stand over there by the house now," he said gently.

Isabel felt a rush of love and gratitude as she watched him turn the oxen around. She wanted to say something, to thank him some way, but she didn't know how. There was nothing that could make it better.

Sonny started the oxen, and Isabel followed behind them as they went up the road past Raymond's junks and down again toward the back door of the barn. Tears filled her eyes. They walked so slowly, so peacefully. They looked as they always did, as though they lived in some fairy-tale kingdom where nothing bad ever happened. Everything looked just the same, and it was all changed forever.

The oxen walked into their stall, and Sonny stepped in front of them and began to take off their yoke. Isabel stood in the doorway, remembering how Sonny wouldn't teach her to yoke them because he wanted to teach Al first. And now he never would. It was awful to think of what must be going through his mind.

"Shall I get them some water?" Isabel asked, hoping to escape for a few, useful minutes.

"Yes, darlin, if you don't mind."

She picked up Ben's bucket. Sonny handed her Buck's bucket from where he stood between the huge heads. "There's still some water in there. Throw it out the door and get him some fresh, and I thank you."

Isabel walked to the open door and gave the tilted bucket a quick, sharp swing, the way she had seen Sonny and Al do. All the water sailed out in one shining plate that landed with a splat at the bottom of the manure pile. Feeling satisfied, Isabel picked up an empty bucket in each hand and went down the hall to fill them.

The water trough was an old, chipped, enamel bathtub with a wooden box built around it. Isabel raised the hinged cover and dipped each bucket in. Then she carefully closed the lid, thinking how much she had learned about farm life in the two months that she had known Sonny and his family. She already knew to leave lids and gates just as she found them.

She walked back down the hall with the full buckets pulling on her arms and bumping into her legs. Splashes of water fell onto the sawdust and her feet, but the simple, peasant task made her feel right with the world again.

She set Ben's bucket near his head and carried Buck's around to his side. Sonny came through the doorway with a bale of hay. "Thank you, darlin," he said. "I appreciate all you've done."

Isabel nodded. It was time for her to go, but there was so much she wished she could say. Would he be all right? Could he be? Was there anything she could do to made things easier to bear? She knew there was nothing anyone could do. Finally, she said, "I guess I'll go, unless there's something else you'd like me to do for you?"

He nodded, as though he could hear what she was thinking. Then he said, "There's nothin else to do, but I thank you." Isabel could see that he wanted her to leave.

"Take care," she said. She reached her hand toward him before she realized what she was doing and changed the gesture into a wave, an awkward, flapping motion that ended nowhere.

"Thank you," he said again without looking at her, walking around Buck to give him some hay. Isabel wondered if he would break down when he was alone.

She walked along the hall, looking down at the floor. She could see the flattened, damp, flower-shapes where the water from her buckets had splashed onto the sawdust. She couldn't remember when she had ever felt so helpless and awful about anything. And on top of it all, she felt guilty for hoping that when she got away from the place, she would feel a little better.

Driving into Severance, Isabel suddenly realized how hungry she was. It was almost three-thirty. She hadn't even thought about food all day. She drove past a small, cheap-looking lunchroom next to the auto parts store at the poor end of Merchants Row. She could see that it was open, so she turned around and parked her car in front, thinking that she really didn't want an interesting place or good food, not today.

She got her journal out of the pocket behind the passenger seat where she had been keeping it ever since the day she came home and noticed it had been moved. Before that she had wondered if Roxy was snooping around. After that, she knew. It was lucky it happened before she had written anything about Leroy in it.

In the restaurant she ordered a ham sandwich and began to write while she waited.

"July 30, Tuesday

Alison LeStage was killed this morning in a logging accident. I was there when it happened. The rescue squad came and took her to the hospital. We thought she was badly hurt, but we didn't think she was dead, or at least, I didn't.

When we got to the emergency room, they said she was—from a head injury. I didn't know a person could be dead and look so all right. I didn't realize it would be so hard to tell. I thought you would know for sure right away. I feel numb about it still, as though I haven't realized it even now. Either that, or I'm a person who has no feelings, or at least, less than other people. Maybe I will...."

She stopped writing when the waitress brought her sandwich. It was delicious, a skimpy sandwich on white bread. She hated herself for being alive and for being hungry. It was ghoulish to think she felt more alive because someone she knew had just died.

Out in the kitchen there was a crash of dropped dishes, and suddenly Isabel was crying so hard that she was coughing and choking on her food. Luckily, the waitress was out in the kitchen, and there was no one at the counter to see how she had to struggle to get control of herself.

28

Isabel was upset, and Leroy could see she was taking it out on him. That much was clear. Of course, it was a terrible thing. A person would be upset just hearing about it, and Isabel was right there when it happened, which was much worse. It was understandable that she would feel the way she did. Still, she had no reason to take it out on him.

And here was something else. If she really cared for him, she would have wanted to be with him. She would have wanted him to comfort her, instead of telling him to get lost, instead of expecting him to understand why she couldn't, why she didn't want to see him.

All she wanted him for was sex, although she never would admit it. It was crude. That was probably why women always pretended it wasn't so. Even Renée would believe he had it wrong somehow if he told her that it was all sex. But he had known right along that that's all it was. Isabel had broken up with her husband too recently to get serious about anyone. And that was all right with him. *He* wasn't looking for romance, just someone to have a good time with, because it was sex with him too.

Anyway, he was glad she canceled their date. It left him free to make this trip out to the Trumbley farm to tell them how sorry he was. He wouldn't say anything to Sonny about selling. It was too soon. But if this tragedy made Sonny think differently about the future of his farm—and that was a real possibility— then seeing him would remind Sonny of his offer. And in time, maybe....

He drove through the flats, past the fields that Joe and Emory wanted to develop. Nothing happening there yet. It was a little after eight o'clock, and it would be dark soon. The days were already getting shorter. He sighed. Now he could look back down at the flats and see the mist collecting in the valley. It was going to be a cool, clear night with a moon very late.

That old saying, that it's an ill wind that blows nobody any good, was running through his head. He'd always had a funny feeling that Sonny's farm was in his future. He shouldn't think like that though, because it was a long way off. And you never know. Leroy could remember his mother and the neighbor lady, old Mrs. Boudreaux, saying that to each other. It seemed silly then, but now he often thought it, even if he didn't say it out loud.

When he got to Sonny's and looked up the road to the house, he almost turned around and went back to town. There was a solid row of cars and pick-ups parked all the way along, and the whole house was lit up. Leroy could see lights in the barn too. Friends and neighbors come to comfort the family. A lot of them were the same people who were unfairly suspicious of him. He could feel the silence that would settle over the room when he walked in. He stopped the car, trying to decide what to do. It was tempting to think of going back to town. He could stop in at the Country Club for a drink.

A car came up behind him. He had to decide. He parked on the side of the road, telling himself he wanted more time to think it over, but knowing that the decision had really been made when he saw the lights on in the barn. That was where he would find Sonny, and Sonny was the one he wanted to see.

He got out of the car and slammed the door, a loud, solid sound in the stillness. It was just dark, and everything was gray and indistinct. Up ahead on the pale road, the house was lit like a beacon. His boots made little scrunching sounds on the loose dirt. It was eerie. It looked like a party, but it was too quiet, no music and laughing, no loud voices.

He opened the barn door. He was probably going to find a whole bunch of old guys out here with Sonny, hiding out from their women, like they always did. Still, he didn't hear any voices as he walked down the passage toward the stall where Sonny kept his oxen.

He stopped in the doorway. He couldn't see anyone. He said, "Hello Sonny," and walked around the rumps of Sonny's cattle, and there was Sonny, sitting in his lawn chair with his whip in his hand. He was alone.

Leroy said, "Hello, Sonny," again.

Sonny was sitting forward, hunched over, looking at the floor in front of his feet and tapping the sawdust with the tip of his whip. He didn't say anything for a long time. Then he raised his eyes without raising his head. He stared for a while, and then he said, "Leroy," as though it took him that long to take in who was there. After he spoke, he looked back down at the floor again.

Right then Leroy felt really sorry for Sonny. He seemed stunned by his grief. He reminded Leroy of a steer hit on the head with a hammer. After a silence, Leroy said, "I was really sorry to hear about your granddaughter."

Sonny nodded. He didn't look up.

There was another long silence. Leroy couldn't tell whether Sonny knew he was still there. Finally, he said, "I was hoping there was something I could do for you."

Sonny shook his head no.

Silence again. Leroy began to get impatient. Of course he understood how Sonny was feeling, and he sympathized, but there wasn't any sense in standing around like this. It didn't help matters. He said, "I guess I'll go up to the house and tell Carol Ann and Raymond how sorry I am. Let me know if there's anything I can do to help."

Just as Leroy stepped out the door, Sonny said, "Thank you, Leroy, but there won't be." Leroy stopped and stood still, waiting. After a while, in a choked voice, Sonny said, "Nothin matters now. Not one bit."

Leroy turned around and came back a few steps, feeling that he ought to answer that some way. The ox nearest the door turned his big head slowly to watch. In the quiet room Leroy could hear the oxen chewing and the grating sound of their teeth sliding across each other. The ox moved his big jaws sideways, while his eyes stayed fixed on Leroy's face.

Leroy stepped farther into the room, out of the ox's line of sight and back to where he could see Sonny in his chair. Sonny was sitting forward, jabbing at the sawdust floor with his whip. "I was goin to do some loggin this fall to make my taxes, but it don't matter now. The place can go to hell. I wouldn't give a god-damn if it did. "

Leroy had never heard Sonny swear. Even those mild words were shocking. He said, "How'd it happen, Sonny? Maybe it would help to talk about it."

Sonny looked up at him then. "Leroy," he said, "there ain't nothin that can help, cause there ain't nothin that'll bring her back."

"I'm sorry, Sonny. I truly am." And he really meant it too. People thought he was cold-hearted, but that was just because he kept his feelings to himself.

"I wasn't payin attention like I should've been. I was shootin off my big mouth, sayin that young people didn't use enough caution, when that was the very mistake I was makin."

Leroy couldn't make any sense of it. A person didn't get a head injury because someone talked too much, even if sometimes it felt like it. Inside, he smiled at his own joke, but he didn't say anything, and he didn't let it show on his face.

"That damned log was hollow and off-balance. It had already given me a fright by comin down before I thought it would. So why in the hell did I let her drive the team?"

Leroy remembered the argument he had with Isabel about almost the same subject.

"I'll tell you why," Sonny went on, "because there was an out-of-state woman there with us, and Al was showin off a little bit in front of her. I didn't want to embarrass her before that woman. That's what it was. And I knew the log wasn't reliable. I knew it all the time."

"Hind sight's twenty-twenty, Sonny. You know that. You couldn't have predicted...."

"Leroy," Sonny said, looking right at him, "what happened was my fault, and I know it."

"You can't know that."

"Well, I do." He poked at the floor with his whip. "I appreciate you tryin to make me feel better and all, but like I said before—don't none of it matter, because there ain't *nothin* that'll bring her back."

"Sonny, I'm really sorry. If there's anything I can do...."

"Well, all right...." He took a deep breath—Leroy could hear him sucking in air—and then he went on. "I guess there is."

"Good. I'm glad to hear it. You know I'm at your service, whatever it is."

"I appreciate it," Sonny said, but he was jabbing at the floor again, and he didn't look up. The light came from one fly-specked lightbulb in the ceiling. Sonny's shadow on the wall behind him looked like an evil gnome with a poker. Finally, he said, "I always hoped it would be hers someday. I have other kids and grandkids." He looked up at Leroy and then back at the floor. "You know that. But somehow, I always hoped it might work out. And now there ain't nothin to hold on for."

"That's not true, man. You need to think of the others. What about Carol Ann?"

"Leroy," jab, "don't tell me my business." Jab, jab. "You wanted to buy the place once. Do you still?"

"Whew," Leroy said in spite of himself. "The house or the land? Both?" It didn't come out sounding like he meant it to. The whole thing took him by surprise, even though he'd been thinking of it on the drive.

"The whole place. Everythin. I want out."

"Well, yes, sure. I guess that guy I told you about is still interested. Yes, of course, yes."

"You mean that?"

"Yes, I do."

"Good. Carol Ann will be pleased."

"What about Raymond?"

"Who knows about Raymond? I guess he'll do whatever Carol Ann wants him to do."

"Where will you go?"

"I ain't thought about it."

"You could keep out a parcel by the road to put a double-wide on."

"Carol Ann would like that. She's always wanted a new house that was easy to take care of."

"I'm sure we can work it out."

Sonny dropped his whip and got slowly and stiffly to his feet. He held out his hand. "All right," he said. "You've got yourself a deal. Shake on it."

"Okay," Leroy said. "It's settled then." But he was thinking that he had better wait a few days before he said anything to anybody, since it was probably grief and anger talking, and Sonny would change his mind before morning. "We'll do this any way you say, Sonny. That's the least I can do for you."

"I appreciate it," Sonny said. He sat down in his chair and reached slowly for his whip.

"You can almost hear him creak," Leroy thought. "It's time he quit anyway. He's much too old to be working in the woods." Out loud he said, "I'm glad you told me, Sonny. I'm glad there is something I can do for you in your time of need." He took a few steps backward toward the door. "You just let me know how you want it to be. All right?"

Sonny nodded. He looked as though he hadn't understood a word Leroy said, but he didn't speak.

"I suppose I'd better get going. Tell Carol Ann and Raymond how sorry I am about what happened," Leroy said. He patted an ox on the rump, stalling, to give Sonny a chance to get his thoughts together. Then he backed a few more steps toward the door. He couldn't tell if Sonny wanted him to stay or not.

The ox didn't notice Leroy at all. He was looking past him out the door. Then Leroy could hear footsteps in the passage. He stepped back into the room and leaned against the wall, waiting to see who was going to come through the door. Sonny was out of it again, jabbing away with his whip.

Eldon Whitfield and his brother-in-law, Herbert Smith came around the corner. They were old buddies of Sonny's. Eldon was first. He started through the door and then saw Leroy and stopped so short that Herbert almost walked up his back. He stood there, filling the doorway, leaning on the doorframe while he got his breath and got over his surprise.

Herbert was peeping over Eldon's shoulder. He was the first to recover. "We didn't expect to see *you*, Leroy. We was lookin for Sonny Trumbley. You ain't seen him, have you?"

"Sure, boys," Leroy said. "He's right here. Where else would he be?"

Eldon shuffled a few steps into the room with Herbert right on his heels. He nodded to Leroy, but neither of them said hello to him.

"Hey Sonny," Leroy said. "Here are some of your friends come out to see you."

"How you doin, Sonny?" Eldon said. He stepped around the

backend of the closest ox, so that he could see.

Sonny raised his head and nodded, but he looked like hell, like he couldn't hold his head up high enough to really get a good look.

"We was real sorry to hear the news," Herbert said. He turned around to give Leroy a dirty look, as though he thought it was his fault somehow.

Sonny didn't answer. He didn't even nod.

"We was wonderin was there anythin we could do for you."

"No," Sonny said. He paused for a long time before he went on. "There ain't nothin, boys. I thank you for the thought."

"That's what friends are for, Sonny," Eldon said. He gave Leroy a hard look, like he knew *he* wasn't a friend.

Nobody said anything else for a while. The oxen began to chew rhythmically again, and Sonny went back to stabbing the floor. Then suddenly in the silence, Sonny said, "I'm all done, boys. Leroy's goin to buy me out." He looked up then. Leroy thought Sonny took some pleasure in his friends' confusion.

They both said, "What?" in unison, and they both turned horrified stares toward Leroy.

Eldon said, "You can't take advantage of...."

"Wait a minute," Sonny said. "You don't know how it came about. Don't jump to conclusions here."

Herbert said, "It don't matter *how* it came about. You can't make a decision like that when you're...."

"Don't tell me what I can do with my own place, Herbert. It's mine, ain't it?" Sonny was sitting up straighter and looking at them more directly than he had before.

Leroy leaned against the wall with his arms folded across his chest and watched. He was pleased to see poor, old Sonny looking more like himself.

Eldon was distressed. "Well, of course it's yours, Sonny. We just....I mean, I guess you ought to wait until you get over...."

"*Get over?*" The words exploded out of the quiet and gentle Sonny. "It ain't somethin I'm goin to *get over.*"

"I'm sorry, Sonny. I meant until you are more calm...."

"That won't change nothin. I know what I think. It ain't goin to change. There ain't no way it *can* change."

Herbert stepped out from behind Eldon. He had on bright red suspenders, and his gray workpants and shirt were stiffly creased. He must have changed into clean clothes to come out to see Sonny. He said, "We understand how you're feelin right now, and we wouldn't *never* try to tell you what to do with your own place, it's just that...." His voice trailed off as he turned to look at Leroy. "I mean, maybe when you're feelin a little better, you won't want...."

Leroy grinned and pushed himself away from the wall. He took a step toward Herbert while he fixed him with his eyes. And Herbert crumbled right there. It was comical. He started to stammer, and he backed up. He almost hid behind his big, fat brother-in-law.

Leroy kept right on smiling. "Well, guys," he said. "I better get out of your way, so you'll feel free to say what's on your minds. I've been taking up enough of Sonny's time as it is." He looked at Sonny, who was watching the whole thing but hadn't seen any of it. "I'll be in touch, Sonny. You think it over." He deliberately stepped a little too close to Herbert just to make him back up some more. "You boys take care now. Don't do anything I wouldn't do."

He chuckled to himself all the way down the road to his car. It was bright, even though there was no moon. The dirt road was light gray under his feet, and the starlight gleamed on the cars and trucks, as he walked past them. The Trumbley place was a beautiful piece of property. There was no mistake about that.

He turned his car around and headed back to town. When Sonny first mentioned the deal, Leroy had planned not to say anything about it for a while, since Sonny would probably want to change his mind. It took him by surprise when Sonny told Eldon and Herbert. Sonny locked himself into the deal in a way Leroy wouldn't have done. People always thought he was so cold and grasping. They didn't see the other side of it—the way he was willing to be understanding. They only saw how he could be shrewd, how he could get a good deal for himself. It never occurred to them that he wouldn't have stayed in business very long if he hadn't been able to do that.

He would tell Isabel, anyway. He wanted her to know that he was buying the Trumbley place because Sonny asked him to. It was a way to help Sonny, even though in the long run, he was going to benefit from it too. He wanted Isabel to hear it from him first. He didn't want her to get the wrong idea.

29

Sᴏɴɴʏ ᴡᴀʟᴋᴇᴅ ᴀʟᴏɴɢ the hall and into the kitchen. Carol Ann was standing there looking down at the table like she had forgotten something and couldn't remember what it was. She had on her dark blue dress with the pink flowers on it. When she looked up at him, the hurt in her eyes made him think of a deer that had been shot.

His heart ached to see her like that. "You look real nice, Carol," he said softly, to cover his confusion.

She stood a little straighter. "Are you ready to leave, Gramps?"

"Yes, darlin, except that this suit smells awful strong. Is there anythin we can do to get rid of the moth balls?"

"Not now. It's too late. Let's just go. I should've aired it out. I wasn't thinkin...."

"I know, darlin. It ain't important."

He followed her out to the car. She walked slowly and stiffly in her high-heeled shoes. As soon as he stepped into the sunlight, he began to sweat and itch. He only had the one suit, so he had no choice, even though it was made for winter out of heavy black wool, and the arms and legs had gotten too short.

Raymond was already behind the wheel of the car. When he saw them come out, he started the engine.

Sonny stopped by the driver's door. "That sounds kind of rough there, Ray. You want to take the pick-up?"

Carol Ann was already around on the other side, opening the door. "We can't, Gramps," she said. "We got to drive out to the cemetery. Remember? It wouldn't look right."

Raymond looked up at him, smiling one of his crazy, crooked smiles. "Don't worry, Gramps. She'll settle down, when she warms up."

"Okay," Sonny said. "It's all right with me." He went around to Carol Ann's side and got in the back seat. "It'll be a lot cooler this way."

"Besides," Carol Ann said over her shoulder. "I told May we'd stop for her. We wouldn't have room in the pick-up."

The car started down the road. "See," Raymond said. "She's straightened out already."

Carol Ann looked over at Raymond. From where he sat behind her, Sonny couldn't see the look on her face. "It still sounds awful loud. I thought you was goin to fix that muffler."

"I ain't had a chance, baby. I meant to do it yesterday, but...."

"Oh, Raymond," she said impatiently.

"I'm sorry, honey."

Sonny said, "Don't worry, Carol. When we drive in that procession, we'll be goin real slow. It won't sound so bad."

"I know, Gramps." She sighed. "And I know it don't really matter anyhow, not when...." She didn't finish.

Sonny was glad she didn't, even though all three of them knew what she was going to say. After that, they were all quiet.

When they pulled into the parking lot of the Texas, it was

empty except for a little, white Toyota.

"Where's May's car at?" Raymond said.

"Her nephew's got it. He's goin to work on the transmission. That's why she had to have a ride."

"Not that Dick Summers?"

"I guess so."

"Uh-oh."

"What's *that* supposed to mean?"

"I don't know. I hope he knows what he's doin. He don't have...."

"Well, it ain't *our* problem. May can take care of it."

"I guess so. Do you want me to go in and get her, Carol Ann?"

"No. She knows. She'll be out."

Just then the door opened, and a young man came out. Sonny didn't recognize him. He waved at them as he walked to the white Toyota.

Carol Ann said, "See. I told you. There goes Randy Hubbell. She must've kicked him out, and he's the last."

A few minutes later, May opened the screen and stood there in the doorway. She had on a black dress and was clamping her pocketbook to her side with her meaty arm. She didn't wave or look at them. She stood in the open doorway while she flipped the sign over, so that it said 'Closed.' Then she shut the door and tested it to make sure it was locked, before she walked heavily down the steps and over to the car.

"Sonny," she said, looking in the back window. "Carol, honey, and you too, Raymond." Then she opened the door and got in. Sonny felt himself bounced up by the seat as she sat down beside him.

Raymond started the engine and headed the car back toward West Severance.

"God, it seems hot for August, don't it?" May said, wiping her forehead with her handkerchief.

No one else answered her, so Sonny said, "Well, I guess...."

just to be polite.

When they got to the Carmoli Chapel, Carol Ann said, "Oh look, Ma and Dad are here already."

Sonny looked out the window. There was Junior about to start up the steps to the side door. Sue Ann was right behind him. Junior was looking in their direction—he probably heard their car before he saw it. Then Sue Ann looked around too, and they both stopped and waited side by side at the bottom of the steps.

Sonny had a brief, unfair wish that they were not there, barring his path with their sorrow, which *he* had caused. He hated himself for the unfairness of that wish. Junior was his own son. And wishes were useless. There was no sense in ever wishing for anything again.

Raymond parked the car, and they all got out. Carol Ann was the first one to get over to her parents. She and her mother hugged as though they hadn't seen each other for a long time, even though Sue Ann had been over at the house last night helping straighten up for the funeral.

Sonny walked over to them slowly, afraid to look Junior in the face, afraid of what he might see there. But before he could even say hello, he felt Junior's big arms go around him.

"Dad," Junior said. "Oh, Dad."

It was so heartfelt and so unexpected that Sonny couldn't move. The slightest response would have brought on the tears he was fighting to suppress. At least Junior didn't blame him, he thought with relief. God knows whether he could stand it if he lost Junior, and Junior was getting near sixty and not in the best health.

Carol Ann and her mother went up the steps to the glassed-in side porch. They walked together with their arms around each other, and the others followed them.

By the time they all got on the porch, Frank Carmoli's son was there, at the inside door, waiting to shake hands with them and show them the way. Sonny couldn't remember his first name, but he knew he had taken over the business when his father retired.

Sonny, who was sweating hard from those few minutes in the sun, looked at young Carmoli's black suit with envy. It was made of thin, slippery material. It must have felt light and cool.

Carmoli put his hand on Carol Ann's shoulder. He guided her through the kitchen and down a dark hall that smelled of flowers. They all followed. The floor creaked, and the women's heels made sharp sounds on the bare boards. In the distance a church organ was playing.

When Carol Ann got to the door of the front room and looked in, her whole body jerked and then went forward, as though she was being pulled on a string. Sonny knew she was looking at Al's body, so he had that second to prepare himself, before he got to the doorway and saw Al lying in her casket with banks of flowers around her. She was dressed in a long, pink satin dress like a prom dress, and her dark hair was curled in long ringlets around her face and down onto her shoulders. Her face looked made of wax. It was smooth and still.

"Oh honey," Carol Ann said in a whisper, and she pushed past Sonny, reaching out toward Raymond. She acted as though she was blinded by tears, but her eyes were dry. "Come quick and see her, Raymond. Our baby looks just like a princess." She led him back to the casket. They stood there, holding hands and looking down at Al.

Sonny hung back, feeling miserably conscious that Al wasn't there, and that if she had been, she would have been embarrassed. She wasn't a princess, and she had never wanted to be one. At the same time, even in his misery, Sonny could see that the way Al looked was a comfort to Carol Ann and Raymond, and he wanted that comfort for them.

Young Carmoli had been standing in the doorway, looking like he meant to be invisible and available at the same time. Now he came over to where everyone but Sonny was standing in front of the casket. He put his hand on May's shoulder and whispered something to her. She looked around at the others, and then she nodded and followed him as he tiptoed out of the room.

In a few minutes he was back to tell them that whenever they were ready, they should sit down in the front row since they were all immediate family. Then he tiptoed away again.

Junior and Sue Ann sat down first. After a while Raymond and Carol Ann went over and sat down beside them. Finally, Sonny was able to move from his place in the corner.

When Sonny looked up from his seat beside Carol Ann, he could just see Al's face over the side of the casket. He couldn't see all the curls or the party dress. She looked so much more like herself that for one heart-stopping second, he thought she was really there, that she was about to sit up, giggling, that she was about to say, "Boy, I sure fooled you, you old Gramps!" She would be about to vault over the side of the box, wearing her blue jeans and sneakers, and she would stand there, stuffing her dark hair up into her red cap, while she laughed about how she had tricked him.

Then Carol Ann shifted in her seat and bumped him with her large, round shoulder, and he was instantly back in the terrible present where such things were no longer possible.

Behind him, Sonny could hear hushed voices as other family members sat down. Carol Ann was looking around, and Sonny knew he should get a hold of himself and stop acting as though he was all alone with his sorrow. He knew he should turn around and acknowledge the people behind him, and yet he couldn't move. He sat rigid and stiff, until finally Pastor Duggins came in and began to speak, and then it was too late.

30

Isabel stopped the car in front of the Carmoli Funeral Chapel. "I'm not going to try the parking lot," she said to Roxy. "I can see it's full. I'll have to find a place on the street. You'd better get out now."

"Okay, darlin," Roxy said cheerfully. She got out of the car and bent down to look in the open door. "I'll wait for you right here."

"Oh, please don't. We're already late. It's after eleven."

"I could save you a seat."

"Don't bother. I'll find one when I get there."

"Okay then." Roxy slammed the door and wobbled away on her spike heels.

For a second Isabel wondered if Roxy knew that she was glad to get away from her, but then she dismissed it. Roxy never seemed to notice things like that. Isabel felt guilty, conscious that it was her own fault anyway. She could have made up some excuse when Roxy asked for a ride. How often had she agreed to do something she didn't want to do and then felt sorry for herself for being trapped and angry at the other person for trapping her, when she should have stuck up for herself in the first place? It was one of the things she meant to change by coming to Severance.

She drove down the street looking for a place to park. Even with all the windows open, the car smelled of Roxy's cheap perfume. Isabel was embarrassed to be so late. She had meant to get there early. The first trouble she had was finding something suitable to wear. She had been counting on her black dress, but when she put it on and looked in the mirror, she could see that it wouldn't do. There was too much skin showing. Finally, she settled on a black silk shirt and her blue jeans skirt. At that point, she still could have been on time if she had been alone. But Roxy wasn't ready, of course. Isabel had to wait quite a while for her, and that was annoying.

She found a place to park on the street and walked back to the funeral home. The sun was already hot. When she turned up the walk to the front door, the light on the white clapboards made it hard to see.

It was a relief to step into the shade of the front porch. There was a sign on the door. It said, 'Please use the side entrance for the LeStage funeral.' Isabel had to read it over several times to take it in. It made Al's death terribly real and official.

The steps up to the side porch were covered in green carpet. There were two big vases of red and yellow gladiolus at the top. They looked bright and cheerful, more like a party than a funeral. A man in a dark suit was standing in the doorway between the festive flowers. He was watching her.

Isabel smiled at him, conscious of how late she was.

The man nodded. "Friend or family," he whispered.

"What?"

"Are you a member of the family?" he asked in a low, irritated voice.

"Oh. I'm not. I mean, I'm a friend." She paused. "I guess."

He nodded again and motioned to her to follow him. He led her into a room full of people sitting in rows on straight-backed chairs. They faced double doors which were standing open. Beyond the doors was another room full of people. At the front of that room was Al's open casket with Al lying in it, surrounded by flowers. The minister was standing beside her, talking to the people. One of his hands was resting on the side of the coffin, as though he was asking Al to listen to what he was saying.

The man in the black suit pointed to an empty seat on the aisle in the back, and Isabel slid into it. She tried to pay attention. The minister was saying what a good girl Al was—quiet and studious, never in trouble. There was a teenaged girl sitting beside Isabel. She sat up very straight with her hands folded in her lap while tears rolled down her face. Once in a while she dabbed at her eyes with her handkerchief, but mostly she let the tears slide down her cheeks without trying to stop them. Was she a friend of Al's? In the two months that Isabel had known Al, she had never heard her talk about any friends. She never had friends over to her house or went visiting at anyone else's house. She spent her time alone or with Sonny or her parents.

The minister was talking about the family now, what hardworking people they were, people who minded their own business and kept to themselves. The family had farmed that piece of land for a hundred and fifty years. They were real Vermonters.

Isabel could see them in the front row. Even the little bit of Sonny's shoulders and the back of his head that she could see through the crowd looked stiff, and uncomfortable, and self-conscious. Beside him, Isabel could see Carol Ann's large, soft shoulders in a dark dress. A little blonde hair stuck out from under her navy blue hat. The hat had a big pink flower on it.

The minister told everyone to bow their heads. At the end of the prayer, he left the room, and organ music began to play. The man in the dark suit appeared at the end of Isabel's row, and all the people in the row stood up and followed him out a side door.

Isabel wasn't going to go with them, but the teen-aged girl turned around and saw her sitting there and said, "You're supposed to go out this way. Come on."

"All right," Isabel said meekly. She followed the girl down a dark hallway that smelled of flowers. The floor creaked, and people talked quietly to each other. Other people got in line behind Isabel.

A fat woman tapped her on the shoulder. "I seen her already," she whispered to Isabel. "They got her fixed up real pretty. They say she wasn't too disfigured or nothin."

"I'm glad," Isabel whispered back.

The line moved forward, and Isabel was in the room with Al's casket. The people in line ahead of her were moving past the family, stopping to hug each person who sat in the front row. Isabel felt more and more uncomfortable the closer she got to the heavy man and woman who sat beside Raymond. She guessed they must be Carol Ann's parents, although she had never seen them before. They sat solidly in their seats, looking straight at her, but without curiosity. She nodded to each of them and said, "I'm so sorry," almost in a whisper, and then she moved on, hoping she hadn't been rude, afraid she hadn't done what she was supposed to do.

Raymond was wearing a bright blue suit too small for him. Isabel shook his hand. She started to say something, but he looked down at his feet, nodding his head. She was afraid if she spoke, he would lose it and begin to cry, so she moved on to Carol Ann, who stared as though she couldn't remember who Isabel was, or why she was there. Isabel said, "I'm so sorry," again. She knew Carol Ann didn't want to be hugged. She felt out of place in front of Carol Ann's suffering. She was an outsider. Why would Sonny or any of them care how she felt about it? She longed for the funeral to be over so that she could get away from them all.

She wanted to be somewhere else, some place that was home. She was tired of being an outsider, different from everyone around her, always forced to learn other people's customs, always the beginner, never at home. She and Sonny nodded to each other without speaking.

The line of people moved past Al's casket. Each person stopped and stood still, looking down at Al's body. When it was Isabel's turn, she tried to appear reverent and respectful like the others, even though she was standing there thinking how Al didn't look at all like herself. Al would have hated to be seen dressed in pink satin. "If she was my daughter," Isabel thought, "I would have made sure she was put in her grave looking the way she wanted to look." She was careful not to think about her own children.

Then the line moved on, past the rows of people who were still sitting in their chairs, past the empty rows at the back, out onto the porch and down the green-carpeted stairs.

There were already a few people outside, standing in small groups in the hot sunlight. Isabel stopped at the bottom of the steps and looked around. There was no one she knew. She hadn't seen Roxy inside, and she wasn't out here either.

As Isabel stood there, two old women walked past her. One of them had her handkerchief up to her face. As she passed, she spoke to her friend through the handkerchief. "I don't know why he didn't take 'em right out and shoot 'em. It's criminal, that's what." They were out of Isabel's hearing before the other woman replied. Maybe the oxen wouldn't care if they were falsely accused, but Isabel minded on their behalf. She walked through the groups of people crossly, thinking how unfair everything was.

After a few aimless minutes, she decided to go to her car and put some money in the parking meter. She started walking toward the front of the building, glad to have something to do. There were more people outside now. She threaded her way through small groups.

As she passed by a tall, old man in a green shirt, he said,

"That's what I heard. Leroy's goin to buy the whole place." Isabel kept walking toward her car, thinking how odd it was that Leroy had closed a big deal without her knowing anything about it. Then she thought it just showed how out of it she had been since Al died. She hadn't been able to pay attention to anything in the last few days.

The mention of Leroy reminded her that he said he would see her at the funeral. She hadn't seen him, and he wasn't in any of the groups of people standing around the parking lot. She decided to go back inside to find him. Besides, she wanted to hear more of what the man in the green shirt was saying.

She turned around and walked back the way she had come. This time she heard the man say, "He's keepin out a few acres for a double-wide for him and Raymond and Carol Ann."

"What?" Isabel said to herself. "That doesn't make any sense." She told herself that the old man was talking about something different this time. She told herself that she couldn't find out anything by overhearing fragments of other people's conversation, and she kept on walking toward the porch steps. But she knew all along what she had heard, and she knew it was true, even while she was telling herself that it wasn't.

She walked up the steps in a daze, pushing against the flow of people. In the doorway, she nearly bumped into the dark-suited official who had met her there before.

"What can I help you with?" he asked her politely, while at the same time, he managed to let her know that the real question was, "What are you doing in here again, when you are supposed to be outside with the ones we've already managed to get done with?"

"I'm looking for someone," Isabel said apologetically. "I won't be long."

She pushed past the man without waiting for a reply. She told herself that she might not have noticed Leroy in the crowd, but she already knew he hadn't come. She needed to talk to him to find out if it was true. It couldn't be. Leroy wouldn't take advantage of someone's suffering like that. Sonny Trumbley was someone he knew, someone he respected. She walked through the rooms, hardly looking around, feeling as though she might burst into tears at any minute and embarrassed to think that if she did, everyone would think she was crying for Al.

Leroy wasn't there, and neither was Roxy. Isabel turned around and went outside again with the flow of people.

Roxy was waiting for her at the bottom of the steps. "Here you are, darlin. I don't know how I missed you in there. I thought you must have come out already."

"Yes....well, I...."

"Didn't the poor, little thing look beautiful? Ain't it terrible to think they have to put her in the ground?"

Isabel began to cry.

"Yes, it's real sad, ain't it? I was cryin in there. I don't know how them Trumbleys stand it."

"I'm not going to the cemetery," Isabel said, as surprised to hear her words as Roxy must have been. "Do you think you could you get another ride?"

"Well sure, but...."

"I'm not feeling very well all of a sudden."

"It must be the heat. I'll go with you, hon. We'll go back home, and I'll help you get to bed." She looked intently at Isabel. "You don't look too good."

"Well, thanks, but I couldn't ask you to do that," Isabel said, wiping her eyes with her hand and not looking at Roxy. "Anyway, I think I need to be alone."

"Where's your handkerchief, darlin?"

"I think I forgot it."

"I might have a spare one to give you," Roxy said, opening her purse and looking inside, oblivious of the people trying to get down the steps past her.

"It's all right, really. But do you think you could find another ride?"

Roxy looked up. "Oh sure, darlin. No problem, but...."

"Thanks, Roxy. I'll be all right in a little while, probably by the time you get home. I just need to be by myself, maybe."

"Okay, darlin. Now don't you worry about me. Just take care of yourself."

"Thanks, Roxy," Isabel said. She walked off toward the car without looking back. She wasn't sure what she was going to do next, where she was going, or even why she was so upset. She only knew that she needed to get out of there right away.

31

CAROL ANN FOLLOWED the others out the door into the hot sunlight. She had to hold on tight to the handrail to keep from toppling down the steps right onto Gramps. So many people had hugged her, shook her hand, and told her how sorry they were, that she felt confused, like she was waking up from a dream and couldn't remember where she was.

She stopped at the bottom of the steps. Ma and Dad came over, and Ma put her arm around her and patted her shoulder.

"You want to ride out there with us, honey?"

"I don't know. Maybe." It was nice to have Ma hug her. It felt safe. She thought about how often they had fought with each other, and that made her think of Al. She just didn't want to think about how often Al had fought with her.

She watched Raymond and Gramps walk to the car. Gramps was walking in a jerky, stiff way, pinched by his old black suit-coat, which was too tight across the shoulders and too tight in the sleeves. He looked even smaller beside Raymond, who was so tall and thin. The bright blue of Raymond's Sunday suit made his hair look even blacker. Just by the way they walked, Carol Ann knew how much they were hurting, and her heart filled up with love and worry for both of them.

She wanted to be with them, but they were far away across the hot pavement, and her legs felt so weak.

She was standing there, unable to decide who to go with, when May came up beside her. "I been waitin on you, Carol. You feel all right?"

Carol Ann nodded.

"You look kind of pale, honey."

Carol Ann turned to her mother. "Thanks, Ma, but I think I'll go with them. I need to be with Raymond."

Her mother squeezed her shoulder, and her father patted her arm with his heavy hand. She started across the parking lot beside May. She felt light-headed, and her knees were shaking. May took hold of her arm to steady her.

"Thanks, May. I'm all right."

"Take a little help where you can get it, hon. This ain't a easy thing to do."

Carol Ann could feel her knees giving out beneath her. She pulled her arm out of May's, so that she could grab onto May's shoulder. She didn't dare think about what she was doing, not right then. Right then she couldn't think about anything but steadying her legs so she could get to the car without falling. Because if she fell, everybody would see what a mess she was, how weak she was, how she couldn't take it.

"Don't worry. You're goin to make it just fine," May said.

Carol Ann couldn't answer her, but she squeezed May's big arm a little tighter, hoping May would know that she was grateful.

It took forever to get to the car. When they finally got there, Raymond had the engine running. It was real loud, but Carol

Ann was so glad to be there that she didn't even care if everybody was noticing.

May opened the car door for her and helped her ease down into the seat. She said, "Thanks, May," but she didn't have much breath left to say it with, and May probably didn't hear it over the engine noise.

Carol Ann laid her head against the back of the seat and closed her eyes. It felt so wonderful to be there that she didn't care if she never moved again.

She heard the car door slam and knew that May had gotten in back with Gramps.

Raymond patted her on the arm. "Are you okay, baby? Are you ready to go?"

"I guess so," she said without opening her eyes. At that moment she didn't care about anything as long as she didn't have to move.

The car started slowly across the parking lot. They had to stop every few yards to wait for people to get out of the way. After a few minutes Carol Ann opened her eyes. They were in back of the funeral home. The hearse was there and a long, black Cadillac filled with people. She closed her eyes again, afraid she might see them putting the coffin into the hearse. She knew she couldn't stand to see that.

After a little while, the car began to move. It stopped again, and when it started, Carol Ann could feel it turning. She knew that meant they had left the funeral home and were driving down the street. She felt weak. She knew if she opened her eyes, she would see people going about their business like it was a perfectly ordinary summer Saturday, like everything was all right, when in fact, nothing could ever be all right again.

No one spoke until the car turned in at the cemetery, and Raymond said, "I wonder where I'm supposed to park."

Carol Ann opened her eyes. The big Cadillac was in front of them, going slowly uphill. Shadows from tree branches moved in stripes across its shiny, black roof. On both sides of the road were rows of white gravestones in the green grass.

May leaned forward, pulling herself up by holding onto the back of the front seat. "You go right on behind 'em," she said. "And when they stop, you stop."

"Okay," Raymond said. "Thanks for tellin me."

The car crept along the grassy track between the graves. "I can't believe I'm actually doin this," Carol Ann thought to herself. "How could it be true? How could I stand it?" Everyone else in their car and the people in all the cars behind theirs were keeping the whole thing moving. They wouldn't let it stop. There was no sense in pinching herself to see if she was in a nightmare. She knew it was true. She knew it would keep right on happening, even though she couldn't believe it.

Raymond pulled the car up behind the black Cadillac. He turned the engine off, and suddenly it was very quiet. Carol Ann watched the pall bearers getting out of the car. She had to keep looking straight ahead because if she turned even a little bit in Raymond's direction, she would be able to see the open grave with its pile of fresh dirt, and she just wasn't ready for that yet. She knew she would have to look at it, but she wanted to wait a little longer, to give herself a little more time to prepare.

The others sat there with her. No one said anything. It was hot in the car with the noontime sun bearing down on the roof and no breeze coming in the open windows. Carol Ann sighed.

When all the pall bearers were gathered behind the hearse waiting to carry the coffin, Raymond said, "Come on. We need to get over there. A lot of people are there already."

Carol Ann didn't answer. She was busy wishing she could stay just a little longer, thinking she had to have more time before she could get through it.

May and Gramps got out of the car. As Carol Ann sat there watching, the pall bearers picked up the coffin. Someone set bunches of white flowers on top of it, and the men started to carry it toward the grave. Everything happened very slowly, but it wouldn't stop, even though Carol Ann was silently praying that it would.

Raymond was already out of the car and around on her side, opening her door. He reached in and took her arm. "Come on, honey. You can lean on me."

Carol Ann held onto his hand and pulled herself up to stand beside him. She felt weak and dizzy. The hot sun pushed down on top of her head even through her hat, and her heels sank into the ground at every step. She was too miserable to try to walk on her toes so her heels wouldn't dig in so far. It was easier just to hang onto Raymond's arm and to struggle along, pulling each shoe out of the dirt with each awful step, wishing the ground would open up and swallow her down where it was cool and dark and quiet.

By the time they got to the grave, the coffin was there, sitting beside the hole, ready to be lowered into it. May and Gramps were in front of them. They moved over so that Carol Ann and Raymond could stand up close.

The faces of the people around the grave blurred together, but Carol Ann did see a little group of girls from Allie's class and that awful old Roxy Fox who used to call Gramps up all the time. Ma and Dad were standing nearby, which was a comfort. She needed to keep a hold on Raymond's arm to steady herself, even standing still.

They lowered the coffin into the hole, and the minister began to speak. Carol Ann tried to pay attention, but she couldn't seem to get what he was talking about. She had to concentrate on not falling, or getting sick, or fainting when she thought how she was standing there like it was the most normal thing in the world to be looking down into Alison's grave.

Then it was over. People came up to them. People patted Carol Ann or hugged her. Everyone said they would see her back at the house. Carol Ann just stood there, holding on to Raymond. She was numb.

Then Raymond pulled her gently. "Come on, baby. Let's go. Gramps and May are already in the car. They're waitin on us.

Can you make it okay?"

And that was when it hit her and jolted her right out of her stupor. "We can't leave," she said, speaking slowly and distinctly, as though Raymond was a child. "We can't *just go away* and *leave* her." She let go of his arm. She noticed with interest that her voice was getting louder and louder. It wasn't like it was something in her control.

"Don't, baby," Raymond said. "Don't get upset." He reached out to put his arm around her, but she jerked away from him.

"You're not goin to do that, are you, Raymond? You're not goin to go away and leave her in the dirt! You ain't goin to do *that*, are you? She's our baby! We *can't* just leave her here." Her voice had been getting louder and louder until she was screaming. Even in her hysteria, she noticed that people were turning around to look at her. "I don't believe it," she screamed. "I just don't believe it."

Then May was there, holding onto her, making her walk to the car. May was on one side of her, and Raymond was on the other. Carol Ann stopped screaming and let herself be half pushed, half carried to the car. When she got there, she was sobbing, but even through her tears, she saw Gramps sitting in the back seat, as stiff and straight and unmoving as a statue, as though he hadn't seen or heard a thing.

32

Isabel got in her car and drove away before she thought about where she was going. She had left Roxy with the idea that she was going home to bed, but she wasn't sick. She just needed to get away from there.

When she got to the River Street bridge, she realized that what she needed to do was find Leroy. She drove by his office. Renée's little red Miata was out front. The garage door was open, and Leroy's car was gone, so she didn't stop. She drove around the downtown and went slowly through the parking lot behind the Mansfield Inn. She even criused past the car wash Leroy always went to. She was just about to give up when she thought of Stefani's. It wasn't quite one-thirty. He might be having lunch.

There wasn't any place else to look. She really had to find him, had to hear him say that he wasn't going to take Sonny Trumbley's farm away from him. She pictured how he would understand why she felt so awful. He would comfort her. It would be safe in his arms. She wouldn't mind if he said she was a fool to believe everything she heard.

She was so busy thinking about it that she almost went by Stefani's without slowing down. If Leroy's car hadn't been parked near the road, she might have missed it altogether. As it was, she slowed down so abruptly that the person in the car behind her was furious and gave her a long blast with his horn. She didn't care. She drove in and parked, laughing at herself for her foolishness.

The sun poured down on top of her head as she walked across the parking lot, and the heat from the pavement came up, making her feel weak and shaky, unable to breathe.

But on the other side of Stefani's heavy, wooden door, it was cool and dark. She didn't wait for the hostess. She went straight into the dining room, and there he was, sitting at a table in the middle of the room with his back to the door. When she saw him, she wished she had taken the time to fix her face and comb her hair, but now that she had found him, she didn't want to wait.

She walked over to the table and stopped behind him, looking at the man and woman he was sitting with. They were wearing matching green blazers. Isabel knew right away that she didn't like either of them.

"Leroy," she said, putting her hand down on his shoulder. "I need to talk to you,"

Leroy had been leaning forward, saying something to the woman across from him. When he felt Isabel's hand on his shoulder, he jumped and stopped talking and turned around.

When he saw who it was, a little frown passed over his face. For a second, Isabel was sorry that she had interrupted him. But it was too late to leave, and she wanted to talk to him right away.

Leroy smiled, but he wasn't glad to see her. It was a smile with teeth in it. He said, "Not now, Chérie. I'm busy with something important. I'll phone you later." He turned back toward the people at his table. "Now, where was I?"

"No, Leroy," Isabel said. "That won't do." She was thinking that he always said he would phone her when he wanted her to leave him alone. Both of them knew he couldn't call her, not at Roxy's house. Her hand was still on his shoulder. She jiggled him very slightly for emphasis. "I need to talk to you right now."

"Chérie...."

"It can't wait." Her heart was beating fast. She knew she was making him angry. "I'm learning how to stick up for myself," she thought.

"Isabel, *not now*."

The man and woman were watching them intently, and the woman had a mean, little sneer on her lips. She was eager to see him put Isabel down.

Isabel stood there with her hand on Leroy's shoulder, waiting to see what he would do and hating the smug looks on the faces of the horrible people he was with. She knew she had embarrassed him in front of them, and she knew he was angry about it. He ought not to care about appearances so much. There were other things that were more important. She needed to talk to him. Surely, he owed her that much.

Then she felt his weight shift. He reached into his pocket and pulled out his car keys and turned toward her, dangling them in front of her face. He shook them, and they jingled. "Wait for me in my car, Chérie. Turn on the air conditioning, so you are comfortable." His voice was quiet, almost a hiss. "I'm busy now. I'll listen to your little problem later."

Isabel didn't move.

Leroy pushed the keys at her and said, "Go now."

She took the keys and walked away. She was in such a rage that she was unable to speak. She sure as hell wasn't going to sit in Leroy's car. He *knew* she hated air conditioning. He only said that to be mean. She tried the driver's door. It wasn't locked. She opened the door and threw the car keys onto the dashboard and went to sit in her own car.

She could leave. She was so mad that she didn't care if she never saw him again. He probably wouldn't care. He didn't care about her. She sat there thinking about driving away, but she didn't do it. After a while, she sat there thinking about how she hated herself for *not* driving away.

Then she began to think about how she needed to calm down and stop being angry so that she could clarify for herself what she wanted to find out from Leroy. She kept trying to sort it out calmly, but the longer she waited in the hot sun, the angrier she got, and the more tangled and confused her thoughts became.

She was almost sure it couldn't be true that Leroy was buying Sonny's farm. He wouldn't like it if he thought she believed someone she didn't even know who was gossiping about him. She would have to be very careful how she phrased her questions.

The trouble was that she couldn't think at all. She was boiling hot. Every time the door to Stefani's opened, she sat up straighter, but it was never Leroy. It was unfair to keep her waiting so long. He was probably hoping she would leave.

Finally, she saw him come out with the man and woman. They stood talking for a minute, and then the other two got in a car together. Isabel watched Leroy walk to his car. He bent to look in the window and then straightened up and looked around. Even from a distance, she could see that he was puzzled.

She honked her horn and was instantly sorry she had done it. With a catch in her breath and a quick beat of her heart, she knew it was a mistake. Too late now. She could tell that he saw her, even though he gave no obvious sign of it. He stood beside his car until the man and woman drove away. Then he started toward her. She could see how furious he was by the stiff way he walked.

He bent down to look in the window at her. "Chérie," he said. "Follow me to the Mansfield. We can talk in my room."

"No. That's not the kind of conversation I want to have. I need to talk to you seriously about something."

"All right." He sighed. "What do you suggest then, since it has to be your way."

"We could go somewhere else. A restaurant? Oh no, I forgot—you just had lunch. Well, let me think. We could just drive. Do you want to get in here?"

"No," he said, looking into her car with clear distaste. "I'll follow you into town, and you can park behind the Mansfield and then get in with me."

"Why don't I just leave my car here?"

"What is this? Are you doing this on purpose?" He glared in at her. "All of a sudden, for no reason, you want to do everything you can to embarrass me. Why?"

"I don't care where I leave my car. I don't care whether I embarrass you or not. I don't care about that kind of thing. You are ridiculous!" Isabel had thought she was calm, that she had gotten her anger under control, but what he said made her rage come back in a great wave, so that she was boiling over with it again. "And it's ridiculous the way you worry so much about what people think of you. Just don't blame any of it on me. Okay?"

She thought about turning on her engine and peeling out of there without giving him a chance to say another word. Her fingers itched to reach for the key. But she didn't move, because if she did, she wouldn't find out what she wanted to know. In a stiff and tightly controlled voice, she said, "What do you want me to do?"

Leroy was controlling himself too. He said, "I'll follow you into town. You can park at the Mansfield, or anywhere else you like, and I'll pick you up."

"Okay."

He turned and walked away.

Isabel started her car and headed toward town without looking back. She was trying to think of how to ask him about Sonny Trumbley's farm, but her mind was so muddled. Her thoughts kept going back to how she wished she hadn't honked the horn at him in front of his awful friends.

She wanted to park somewhere else besides the Mansfield parking lot, but she didn't see a single place as she went through town, so she ended up doing what he said, in spite of herself. She parked at the back of the lot, shut her car off and got out, thinking that Leroy's car was right behind her. She turned around slowly, as though she didn't care how much time went by before she was with him.

He wasn't there. She wished now that she had watched him in the rearview mirror. Maybe he hadn't followed her at all. He probably set the whole thing up so he could get away. He probably turned the other direction when he left Stefani's. And she hadn't even noticed. She was so busy speculating on how he never meant to pick her up, that she didn't see the big Lincoln until it glided to a stop right beside her. Leroy reached across the seat to open the door. She got in, and the car began to move before she closed the door.

Leroy didn't say a word. He stared straight ahead with his hat low over his eyes. It wasn't until they were out on the highway going south, that he said, "What is it you were in such a hurry to talk to me about?" His voice was hard, and he didn't look at her.

Isabel wasn't ready, even though she had been waiting for a long time to ask her question. She felt confused and afraid. "I thought you were going to Alison LeStage's funeral. You said you would be there." Saying it made Isabel realize how completely she had forgotten about Al in the last hour.

Leroy looked at her coldly. He waited, but she didn't say any more. "Is *that* what you wanted to ask me about?" His hands tightened on the steering wheel. It looked as though he was going to shake it.

Suddenly Isabel remembered Jeff and the fight they had when they got stuck in the mud at Sonny's farm. She couldn't think what it was that Leroy had just asked her. "I don't know," she said. "I can't remember." He looked at her as if he thought she was crazy. "No, I mean, going to the funeral isn't what I wanted to talk to you about. This is what it is," she said, wishing she didn't feel so muddled. "While I was walking around after the funeral, looking for you, I overheard some people talking about how you were going to buy Sonny Trumbley's farm, and I...."

"God damn it!"

The bitterness in his voice made Isabel feel sorry she had accused him so bluntly. "I know what you're going to say—that I shouldn't believe everything I hear. Well, you see, that's why I had to come and talk to you. I didn't want to go around believing something like that."

"Isabel, will you stop it."

"What?"

"Be quiet."

Isabel hunched down on the seat, hoping she wasn't going to cry.

"I wanted to tell you myself, so you wouldn't get the wrong idea." He reached into her lap to take her hand. "Listen, Chérie...."

She pulled her hand back and huddled against the door. "It's true? I really didn't believe it, you know. I never thought you'd do something like that."

"You don't even know how it came about."

"So it *is* true then. I can't believe it."

"Oh, what do you know about any of it." Leroy was suddenly angrier than ever. "You god-damned out-of-staters, you come in here and tell us how to do everything. You think you know it all, and you don't know anything. *You* don't know how it happened, and you won't even listen."

Isabel folded her arms across her chest. She was scared, but determined not to back off. "Well, tell me then," she said. She could feel a tremble in her voice. She hoped he didn't hear it.

"Look," he said. "There's a rest area coming up. I'm going to stop there. We don't have to get out of the car or anything."

"All right," Isabel said, feeling bleak.

Neither of them said any more until Leroy stopped the car under some trees at the end of the parking lot. There was nothing at the rest area but a tourist information booth and some picnic tables. The few other cars were parked close to the building.

Leroy left the motor running for the air conditioning. Isabel put down her window. She heard him take a deep breath, as though he was going to say something. She didn't look around. She stared straight ahead, thinking that she didn't need to justify wanting some fresh air on a beautiful, summer day.

Finally, Leroy sighed. "I don't understand you," he said. "You were in such a hurry to talk to me about something, and now you just sit there. I've done everything your way, and still it doesn't suit you."

"That's not fair."

Leroy sighed again. "Look, Chérie, I'm sorry about what I said before, about out-of-staters. I didn't mean you." He turned toward her. "I wanted to tell you about this deal myself, so you would understand. I'm really sorry you heard it the way you did."

"If you wanted to tell me, why didn't you?" It wasn't really a question. It was proof that she couldn't get a straight answer from him.

"I didn't get a chance. It only came up the other day. And I haven't seen you. You haven't been at work for days."

She looked at him then. "Leroy, there was a terrible, fatal accident, or have you already forgotten? I needed some time to deal with it."

He knocked his hat back so he could see her better, and she looked away again. "I didn't want to say anything too soon," he said. "I thought Sonny would change his mind. I thought it was the grief and anger talking when he said he wanted to get out. I was sure he was going to change his mind."

"I can't believe you would really do something like that—just take that land away from a family who have had it for hundreds of years."

"God damn it! I don't know anybody who can make me as mad as you can. You *never* pay any attention to what I say. Sonny Trumbley *asked me* if I wanted to buy his place. He said he was all done. He said I would be helping him out."

"God," Isabel said softly. "When I heard it, I really didn't believe it. People say bad things about you, Leroy, but I always thought they were exaggerating, that they were jealous and...."

"What kind of things?"

"I don't know. And anyhow I haven't been here long, and it doesn't matter anyway. It's just that I never paid any attention before, and now I see...."

"You haven't even listened to me, so you don't know anything about it."

She turned to face him then. "I know all I *need* to know. You're going to use this tragedy to take away a farm that has belonged to the Trumbley family for two hundred years."

She thought she wasn't mad any more. She thought she had hit a place of calmness and clarity, but as she went on speaking, as she heard what she was saying, she could feel the rage and hate building again. "That poor old man is so broken by Al's death that he hardly knows where he is, and that's just what you were waiting for. That was your chance."

"It wasn't like that at all."

"I can't imagine what I ever saw in you. I hate you." She began to cry. "What was I doing? How could I....?"

"If that's the way you feel, Chérie, there's no reason.... It's not like you were any special prize."

"You said it was Sonny's idea, but I notice you haven't said I should go and talk to him about it." Her voice was full of bitterness.

"Go ahead. It's fine with me. Why haven't you done it already? You could have asked him, instead of disrupting my lunch meeting."

"So it's all right with you if I tell him he doesn't have to go through with this horrible sale?"

"Sure. You can say whatever you like. I don't care what you do."

"And you'll let him out of the deal if he has changed his mind?"

"Of course. I already told you that."

"I don't think I believe you." She tried to read his face, but nothing showed there. It never did. She looked away. "Well, I'll find out. I'm going straight to his place to tell him you said you'd let him off. Then we'll see." She snapped on her seatbelt and leaned back.

"What's that supposed to mean, Chérie? Are we leaving?"

"Aren't we? I've found out what I wanted to know."

"All right then."

"We don't have to leave if you want to stay." She looked at him and hated what she saw, a skinny, old man with tight lips. "I thought you were so busy," she said sourly.

"I was busy at lunch." He started the car. "With something more important than this."

Isabel didn't say anything out loud, but she thought hard about how hateful he was. When they drove into the Mansfield parking lot, she said, "Thanks. I'll let you know what happens." She got out of the car quickly, conscious of the fact that neither of them had said anything about seeing each other later. She slammed the door. It might be over, and she wouldn't be sorry if it was. After she talked to Sonny and showed him how to get out of this mess, she would see how Leroy acted. That would decide it for her.

Leroy put up the window she had put down and drove away without looking at her.

Isabel got into her own car. The seat was hot. It burned the backs of her thighs through her skirt. The air was so thick with heat that it was hard to breathe even with all the windows open. "It's still better than air conditioning," she said to herself defiantly. "I like it better anyway." By the time she left the parking lot, her shirt was sticking to her back.

It was cooler out of town where she could go faster and more wind could blow through the open windows. She thought about talking to Sonny. She didn't need to plan how to say it. She was comfortable talking to him, and he would be glad to hear what she was going to tell him. Leroy tricked him somehow. Now, with a few days to think about it, he would be eager for a way out.

But when she got to the Trumbley farm, she found the road to the house and the main road in front of it lined with cars and pick-ups, and she remembered that this was part of the funeral. She didn't want to talk to Sonny with a lot of people around. She decided to go home and come back later. Maybe she could catch him alone while he was doing his evening chores.

She drove back to town feeling lonely and scared. She thought she had been honest, but she could see that she had been lying to herself right along, refusing to see what Leroy was really like, pretending he was what she wanted him to be. She *hadn't* listened to him. He was right about that. She hadn't listened to anyone. She saw that she had been trying to live someone else's life so that she wouldn't have to look at her own. She didn't belong in Severance, but she didn't belong in Abingdon any more either. She didn't know if there was anywhere she did belong. Nothing felt right.

33

SONNY AND BEN heard the footsteps at exactly the same moment. Ben stopped chewing and swung his head around to look out the door. Sonny sighed. He had only been sitting with the oxen for a few minutes, and now he was going to be interrupted. He felt drained by all the people and all the sadness at the funeral. He didn't know if he could take any more conversation.

He didn't get to the barn to do chores until everyone had left, even Junior and Sue Ann, who stayed to help Carol Ann clean up. Someone must have come back. Maybe he didn't think about Allie quite as much when people were around, but still he didn't feel like talking. He'd had enough company for one day.

He stood up, so he could see past the oxen. Isabel was standing in the doorway. He looked at her without saying anything, thinking that part of him was glad to see her, even though he was sick of people. But she had been there with him and Al when it happened, and that made her special to him in some strange way, as though she was all that was left to connect him to Al.

She stayed in the doorway, leaning on the frame of the door. Ben went back to eating hay. Sonny had only given two flakes to each ox, just enough to keep them from getting too loose on the summer grass. He was planning to put them out in the night pasture later.

"Am I interrupting you?" Isabel said.

"No. Come in. It's all right."

She walked into the room and stopped by Ben's rump. "I have something I want to talk to you about," she said, watching her hand pat the little ridge of hair at the top of Ben's tail.

Sonny nodded. He didn't ask her what it was. He didn't feel curious.

"How are you?" she asked.

He shrugged. He didn't know whether he was all right or not, and he didn't want to know. All he knew was that he was tired, but he couldn't sit down and leave her standing. He went to the corner and took down the folded lawn chair that hung on the wall. He kept it there for Al, who used to sit with him once in a while. "Don't think about that," he told himself. "Here," he said to Isabel. "You have that seat. This one's kind of dusty."

"That's okay," Isabel said. "I don't mind standing."

Sonny took out his handkerchief and swatted at the sawdust and cobwebs. The dust flew all around. He cleared his throat and tried to supress the cough.

"There," he said. "That's good enough." He set the chair down beside the other one and stood there clearing his throat. He felt weak and tired.

After a little while Isabel sat down, and he could too. He picked up his whip and poked at the floor with it, making lines of dents in the sawdust. Neither one of them spoke.

Finally, Isabel sat forward in her chair and looked at him. "The reason I came out here is that I wanted to talk to you about something. I hope you don't mind."

She was watching him, so he shook his head, but he was wondering how he was supposed to know whether he minded when he didn't know what it was about.

"It's this. I heard that you were going to sell your farm to Leroy LaFourniere. Did you know....have I ever told you, that I work in his office a few days a week?"

Sonny shook his head. He didn't think she had ever told him that. Maybe she had, and he had forgotten it.

"I didn't hear it at work though. I overheard someone talking about it at the funeral. So I went and asked Leroy about it, and he said it was so."

Sonny nodded. "He's right."

She sat farther forward and looked intently into his face. "You *must not* do that," she said.

Sonny was embarrassed and had to look away. She didn't know how many times he had said that to himself. She didn't have to tell him. He knew that to end it like that would be to give up on everything. How could he do that? And at the same time, there was another part of him that wanted to smash everything, that wanted to take his arm and push all the dishes off the table, so that he could hear the crashes, one after another, so that he could look down and see it all in ruins—a remembrance for Allie. What else could he do for her now?

"Sonny, listen to me."

"What?"

"I got Leroy to say that if you wanted to back out of the deal, he would let you do it."

"Back out? Is that what he thinks I'm goin to do? *Back out?*" Suddenly he was very angry at Leroy.

"It's not like that," Isabel said. "You make it sound awful."

"I wouldn't back out."

"You haven't signed anything. It's not a deal until it's signed."

"We shook on it. I gave my word."

"But...."

"I've never gone back on my word. Leroy ought to know that."

"But you can't...."

"I can't believe Leroy thinks I would go back on my word. Leroy's got his faults, and I won't say he don't, but he ain't dumb, and he knows me. I can't believe he thinks I would go back on my word."

"But you've got to."

"No, I don't."

"Because how can you sell your....think of your family." She was pleading. Her eyes were full of tears. "Think of Carol Ann and Raymond. Think of your grandchildren."

Sonny didn't want to think about any of it. What did *she* know anyway. She wasn't even from here. He stood up and got the brush off the beam where he kept it and started to brush Buck on the haunch. He didn't say anything, and he kept his back turned to her. He needed a few minutes to calm down. If she was crying, he didn't want to know it.

After a little while, he stepped around to Buck's other side, as though it was just time to work there for a change. It felt good to stand there between the two of them, with Ben's warm flank pressed against his back.

When he finally dared to look, he saw that her eyes were wet and her face streaked. "Look," he said to her. "I know you don't mean no harm, but this ain't a matter you know anythin about. This ain't your business. You come here from away, and you don't know...."

"But this farm has been in your family for hundreds of years. How *can* it be right to sell it? I mean, I just don't understand."

Sonny tried not to notice that she was getting upset again. "Well, you don't need to understand," he said, concentrating on where the brush was going, "cause it ain't your business."

"But...."

"My mind's made up. I gave my word."

That silenced her. He went on brushing Buck for a minute, but he had stopped enjoying it. His legs felt weak, and he thought he had been too hard on her. He went over to his chair and sat down without looking at her. He set the brush on the sawdust beside his chair leg with the bristle side up, so it wouldn't get dirty.

After a while, she said quietly, "What are you going to do?"

"I don't know."

"Where will you go?"

"I ain't goin nowhere."

"I mean, after you sell the place."

"Oh, we ain't goin to leave our land. We'll keep a piece down along the road for a double-wide."

"You mean one of those tra....those pre-fab, ranch houses? The kind you see driving down the highway?"

"Yup." He wished she'd stop asking questions.

"What do Carol Ann and Raymond think about it?"

Sonny picked up the brush and tapped it on his knee. "They don't think anythin about it, cause I ain't had time to tell 'em yet."

"But...."

"Carol Ann's been wantin a new house for years." He stood up and went back to his spot between the two oxen. "I been thinkin we could build a garage where Raymond could work on his cars in the warm. He don't have a place like that now. He even had part of a engine behind the couch in the front room last winter." He watched the brush as it moved across Buck's gray-brown fur. Every little hair snapped back into place as the brush went by.

Isabel jumped up from her seat and began to pace back and forth behind the oxen. She stopped and looked at him. He kept on brushing. "I know it's none of my business," she said, "but I think you might be talking yourself into this because you already gave your word." She took a big gulp of air. "And you just don't *need* to. Leroy already said he wouldn't hold you to it."

Right then Sonny was feeling peaceful, and he didn't want to think about the future or the past. To think would be to let in the pain. He was sandwiched between Buck and Ben, stroking Buck's soft fur. Both of them were lulled by it. All three of them were, because Ben was enjoying leaning on him. Ben knew his turn would come soon. He was content also.

Isabel walked around Buck to where she could look at him across Buck's back. Both she and Sonny were so short that all he could see of her was the top of her head and her eyes, looking at him over Buck. "I promise he will let you off. He told me so. He won't hold you to it. I know he won't."

He watched her from his place of contentment. Her eyes were swollen and puffy from crying. "I'm sure that's true, if you say so. But that ain't it."

"Well, what then?" she said impatiently.

"I got to hold myself to it. I already gave my word. I ain't *never* gone back on that in my life."

"Oh," she said. She stood there patting Buck absently.

"That's all I got now." Sonny hoped that settled it. It certainly should have. He thought how he would put the boys out in the night pasture after she left.

"Sonny," she said, and then she paused, watching her fingers pick at the fur along Buck's backbone. "What do you think Al would say about you selling the family farm?"

That hit him, stabbing a hole right through his comfortable feelings to let in the cold pain. "Don't nobody know that," he said in a voice so gruff he wasn't sure she could understand the words. He coughed and cleared his throat and then tried again. "Al ain't here no more. There ain't no use thinkin about what Al would say." He brushed a few more strokes on Buck and then turned his back on her to work on Ben.

"I'm sorry," Isabel said. "I just...."

Sonny waited, but she didn't say any more. He concentrated on the brushing and tried not to think about Al, tried to get back into that comfortable place where he was content with his oxen, and nothing else was in his mind. He tried to forget that Isabel was standing behind him.

After a while, she said, "What will you do with Buck 'n Ben?"

"I don't know," he said crossly. "I ain't had a chance to think about it."

"Oh dear," she said, "I can't believe this is happening. I don't know what to do."

Sonny didn't say anything. Behind him he heard a snuffling noise. He hoped she wasn't starting to cry again. He had no idea what to say to her.

"I better go, I guess." Her voice was shaky.

Sonny wondered why she was the one who was crying. It wasn't her problem. He didn't feel like comforting her.

"Sonny," she said. "I wish you'd think about this." She walked around Ben so that Sonny had to look at her. "Please remember what I said and don't rush into anything. I know you would be making a mistake if you sold your place."

Sonny sighed. "You mean well, darlin. I'm sorry it upsets you."

She pulled out a handkerchief and blew her nose. "Thank you," she said.

"And I thank you for comin out to tell me what you thought about it." He didn't want her to leave in an upset state, but he didn't want to make her too comfortable either, because he did want her to leave. "I'll think about it," he said, "but it won't do any good to talk about it any more."

"Okay," she said. "I'll come back in a day or two when I'm feeling calmer about things, but please don't...."

Sonny held up his hand to silence her. "I'll think about what you said. I told you I would."

She nodded and went to the door. He thought she was going to walk out just like that, but in the doorway she turned back and said, "It has been an honor to know you." Then she left.

"Now what did she mean by that?" Sonny said to himself, but he really didn't want to think about that either.

He stayed with the oxen for a long time. He gave them more

hay and brushed both of them all over. Every time his legs got weak and tired, he would take a little catnap in his chair. It was better that way. He was afraid if he really went to sleep, he might dream about Al, and he wasn't sure his old heart could stand the pain. It frightened him to think of it.

Sometime late in the night, he unhitched the boys, and they all three walked out the back door into the night pasture. Sonny didn't try to herd them along. They walked together like three old friends.

Sonny stayed with them for a while. He didn't know what time it was, but the house was dark. He could tell by the stars that it was well on into the middle of the night. There was no moon, but it was a clear night, bright with starlight. The Milky Way was a luminous trail across the sky. The air was cold and clean, transparent with other-worldly beauty. The first thing he thought was how he was filled up inside with the beauty of it, and how it made him feel like giving thanks for the great gift of life. But then right away he thought of Al and felt awful.

Then he wondered why he thought he knew. Maybe Al was there somewhere. Maybe she was even up in that beautiful night sky, looking down at him, although as soon as he thought that thought, he felt embarrassed, glad that no one was around to know how silly he was being, and confused too, because he felt closer to her than he had since the rescue squad took her away, so that part of him was sure she *was* somewhere nearby waiting for him, and maybe in a better place than he was.

He sat on the big rock and kept her company for a long time. When he stood up to go to the house, his clothes were cool and damp from dew, and he was so stiff it took him a while to straighten up, but he felt glad for the first time since the accident.

34

Whenever Renée looked at the watch George gave her, she got a special little smile on her face because she was so proud of it. "That's strange," she said. "It's already twenty past ten, and Isabel isn't here. She's usually early."

Renée was sitting at her desk, and Leroy was standing in front of it. She looked up at him. Her eyes went back and forth across his face, as though she was looking for clues. "She said she was coming in this morning. Did she tell you something different?"

Leroy raised his hands, pretending to surrender. "Don't shoot, Senorita. I'm innocent."

"Leeeeroy...." she said, stretching out his name. He could see she was trying not to smile.

"Well...." he said, as though he was thinking it over carefully. "Maybe not innocent...."

They both laughed.

He put his hands down on her desk and leaned toward her, looking into her clear eyes. "But seriously, I had nothing to do with this. I saw her yesterday in the middle of the day. She was okay then. I haven't seen her since."

"Well, it doesn't matter," Renée said. "I guess she'll be in later, unless she changed her mind about working on a Sunday."

"And you, Chérie?" he asked, still leaning toward her. "What are *you* doing here? Aren't you going to take a day off either?"

"I'm not staying. I had some papers to pick up, and I thought I would come in when Isabel did, so I could tell her what needs doing. I can leave a note on the desk in case she shows up later. I'm going out to the lake with George. We're going fishing."

"That sounds nice. You've got a beautiful day for it."

She smiled sweetly at him. "Come with us, Uncle Leroy."

He loved the way her smile went all the way across her face. "I wish I could, Chérie. I'd love to. But tell me, why do you need Isabel on a Sunday? Is something wrong that I don't know about?"

"No, not at all. This was her idea. I suppose it's because she missed days last week. I really couldn't say. All I know is that she called me yesterday and said she didn't care if it was Sunday, that she wanted to work, unless I didn't want her to." Renée shrugged. "But I don't care."

"I hope it won't get in the way of your fishing trip."

"Oh no. I wouldn't let it." She smiled, pleased with herself. "I know what's important."

"Good."

"So why don't you come with us? There's room in George's boat."

"Thank you, Chérie. Some other time. It's nice of you to invite me."

"You know I'd like it if you came. And George wouldn't mind."

"I know, Chérie. I appreciate it, but I think Marie has plans for me."

"Someday you'll have to come, Uncle Leroy. It can be...."

Just then the door in the hall slammed violently open and shut again. Renée's eyes widened with surprise. Leroy looked around. Isabel was standing in the doorway.

Leroy said, "Hello, Chérie."

Renée said, "Hi."

But Isabel acted as though she hadn't heard either of them. She said, "God damn it, Leroy! You set me up." She was very angry.

"What *are* you talking about?"

"You knew Sonny Trumbley wouldn't change his mind."

"I haven't a clue what you're talking about, Chérie. Please explain." He looked over at Renée, hoping to catch her eye, but she was suddenly very busy writing, and she didn't see him.

"You knew I was going to go out to Sonny Trumbley's farm to talk to him about not selling his place."

'I told you it wouldn't work, Chérie," he said patiently.

"Yes, but you didn't....oh, God damn it, I know you set me up."

Leroy began to be annoyed. She was talking so loud. She had forgotten all about being discreet. "Listen to me," he said, giving her a hard look to command her attention. "If I had told you not to bother, that he wouldn't change his mind, you wouldn't have believed me. You would have thought I was trying to keep you from influencing him."

Isabel opened her mouth and shut it again without saying anything. It was too much to hope she was thinking about what he said. He looked at Renée again. Her head was bent over the papers on her desk. Her pen was moving across the page. Even so, he knew she was listening. He always knew what Renée was thinking.

"I don't care what you say, Leroy. It doesn't make any difference. You tricked me. You knew somehow that if I went out there and talked to him, it would make him even more determined to go through with it. It was all a trap."

"No, Chérie. I just didn't stop you. Sonny didn't change his mind because he didn't want to."

"I don't believe you. I *know* he doesn't want to sell his place. Somehow you convinced him." She shook her head, as though she was trying to shake his words out of it. "Oh, you make me so mad, I...."

"Chérie, calm down."

"I know you tricked him."

"How then? Tell me how."

"All I know is that I told him he could back out if he wanted to...."

"Oh Chérie, Chérie, that explains it," Leroy said, trying to keep a straight face. "Did you hear that, Renée?"

Renée looked up and nodded. She gazed solemnly at Isabel without a hint of a smile.

"You tricked yourself, Chérie. That's what happened." He was pleased that it was so clear.

"Leroy, don't play word games with me."

"Listen to what you said. Then you'll see what I mean."

Isabel frowned.

"Why it's like a red flag to a bull to tell him he could back out. That's the best way I know to make him stay in. I should thank you, Chérie."

Isabel's face was flushed with her distress. She looked pretty. Leroy felt sorry for her. He stepped toward her and reached out to put his hands on her shoulders to comfort her.

She backed up as though he was a poisonous snake. "Don't touch me," she said in a voice full of hate.

Renée's head came up again when she heard that. She looked silently from one to the other of them. Her eyes had mischief in them. She was enjoying the scene.

"You people from away," Leroy said. "You come up here, and you think you know our business better than we do. You think we're hicks. You think we don't know anything. And then you walk in there and say something like that to Sonny. You don't understand him, and you never will."

Isabel began to cry. "I stayed up almost all night thinking about this. I couldn't get to sleep I was so furious." She looked past Leroy at Renée. "I'm sorry I was late. I overslept."

"That's okay," Renée said quietly. "It doesn't matter."

Isabel jerked her handkerchief out of her pocket and wiped her eyes roughly. She didn't pay any attention to Renée. "You're trying to put the blame on me, Leroy," she said. "I know it's your fault, and I hate you." She looked down, watching her hands as they folded her handkerchief and put it back in her pocket.

"Calm down, Chérie. Don't say any more. You'll regret it later."

"When I woke up this morning, I thought I would feel different, but I didn't. I'm never going to feel any different. I hate you. I really do. I can't imagine how you could treat that poor old man like that." She clenched her fists. "The more I think about it, the madder I get."

She looked so pretty with her hair lying loose on her shoulders and all around her face. Her cheeks were bright pink. Renée wasn't watching. Leroy reached out again. He wasn't sure whether he meant to pat Isabel on the shoulder or touch her cheek. He only knew that he felt a sudden tenderness for her. Right then, he didn't want it to be over.

As soon as she saw his hand stretching out to her, she stepped up close to him and began to hit him on the chest with her fists.

"Whoa, Chérie, whoa," he said, laughing. He grabbed her wrists to stop her from pounding on him and turned her gently around, so that her back was to Renée. He didn't want her to see the smirk on Renée's face.

"Let me go, Leroy. I don't want to have anything to do with you. I can't believe I ever did."

"Hush, Chérie. Wait til you calm down."

"No, I won't. I know how I feel, and it's not going to change."

"All right," he said. "Whatever you say." He pushed her away from him without letting go of her wrists. "Enough is enough. I have more important things to do."

Renée's eyes were sparkling. Leroy knew that as soon as she got a chance, she would remind him how she had told him all along that this with Isabel was a mistake.

"You do whatever you wish, Chérie," he said to Isabel. "It's not that important to me either way." He looked over her head at Renée to see if she got his meaning. He didn't want her to think Isabel could tell him how it was going to be.

Renée had an innocent smile, as though all this was over her head, but she knew it must be a good joke.

He looked down at Isabel. He was still holding her wrists. "It's not my fault if you got it all wrong," he said softly.

Isabel twisted out of his grasp and stepped back into the doorway. "I haven't got anything wrong," she said, loudly. "You're a crook, just like everybody says. I don't want to have anything to do with you any more. I can't stand you. I quit."

Leroy shrugged. He wanted to smile at Renée, but he was afraid Isabel would catch him at it, so he struggled to keep a solemn look.

"Don't shrug your shoulders like I'm not saying anything that matters. I'm telling you that I don't ever want to see you again, and I'm not going to work here even for five more minutes, and if you owe me any salary, you can just shove it, because I don't even want to touch it." She turned and walked out of the office without looking at either of them, and she slammed the outside door so hard that it flew open again.

Leroy went out into the hall and closed it quietly. He watched Isabel go down the walk, her shoulders hunched with fury.

He stepped back into the office. Renée was looking at him with a mischievous smile which was mostly in her eyes. She ran her fingers through her hair, fluffing it up.

"Don't say a word, Chérie. I don't want to hear it."

"But, Leroy, I hate you too. Surely, I get to say, 'I told you so,' after all I've had to put up with."

Leroy didn't answer. He was thinking how the whole thing was turning out just the way he wanted it to.

Renée was studying his face. "You aren't feeling bad about it, are you?"

He looked down at her. She was wearing one of his favorite dresses—navy blue with dark red flowers, silky and short, of course. He couldn't see her legs under the desk, but he was looking forward to seeing them when she stood up. He wondered when she was going to change into her fishing clothes. "You look beautiful today," he said. "Lucky George."

"You haven't answered my question, Uncle dear."

"No, Chérie, I don't feel bad. To tell you the truth, I've been wondering how to end it. I knew it was time. I was trying to figure out how to let her down easy."

"Oh Leroy, you're such a sweetheart."

"Don't make fun, Chérie."

"I'm not....well, I was a little, but I meant it too. You *are* a sweet guy. The trouble is, you know it."

Leroy grinned and made a little bow.

Renée went on, "I told you she wasn't right for you. You should have listened to me in the first place. You could have saved yourself a lot of bother."

Leroy walked around the desk. He stopped behind her and put his hands on her shoulders, massaging her neck, the way she liked him to do. "I'm not sorry. I had some good times with her. She changed my luck. That's why I wanted to take her to Saratoga in the first place. And it worked. I just couldn't see it at the time." He got interested in what he was saying and forgot about his hands.

"Don't stop, Leroy. It feels so good."

"Sorry, Chérie," he said, but he was thinking too hard to pay much attention. "I got mad when she told Donny Patarka about Sonny's farm. I thought she was coming on to him....and maybe she was. But I was trying to control things. I wasn't giving Lady Luck any room to operate. I'm only just now beginning to see that. You can't tell Lady Luck what to do, or she'll leave you and go to someone else."

"Who's leaving? Isabel?" Renée said sleepily.

"Oh nothing....nobody. I was just thinking....talking out loud." He stopped massaging her neck.

Renée sat forward in her chair. "Well, I guess I don't have to leave Isabel a note telling her what to do."

"No, she's not coming back. That much is obvious."

"So what happens now, Leroy?"

"You mean about Isabel?"

"That too. Both. Everything."

"We wait and see. I think it's all going to come out for me. They've already said if we go in together to develop this farm, that we can work out the payments without any problems."

"And you're not going to see Isabel any more?"

"Chérie, didn't you believe me?" He looked down at the top of her head. Women were all a puzzle, even Renée, even though he thought he knew exactly how her mind worked. "I told you I was looking for a way out, and she handed it to me. No, of course I'm not going to see her any more. She did me a great favor, and I don't even owe her, because she doesn't even know it."

"I'm glad, Leroy. You know how I worry about you."

"I know, Chérie."

"But you do make me feel better. I think you're finally learning to be more sensible."

Leroy stepped around to where she could see him and took another little bow.

She smiled. "I'm so proud of you, Leroy. I mean, you've finally realized that you have to stay away from the horses, and...."

"Renée...." Leroy said in warning. "Honest to God," he was thinking. "You manage to sidestep a trap one of them lays for you, and you walk right into a trap laid by another of them."

The smile slid off Renée's face. He hadn't said anything out loud but her name, but she knew he was mad. She sighed.

"Don't mother me, Chérie. Don't box me in." He went up close to her and kissed the top of her head, smelling her shampoo. "I hope you catch a lot of fish today. I'll see you tomorrow."

He walked out of the room without looking back. He went down the hall to the kitchen to find Marie and see what she had lined up for him to do. He hoped she hadn't heard Isabel's loud voice in the hall.

35

WHEN CAROL ANN stepped out onto the porch, she thought Raymond wasn't there. Then he took a drag on his cigarette, and the little red eye of fire glowed in the blackness. After that, she could make out the darker hunch of his shoulders where he sat in the dark on the middle step.

She held onto the railing and lowered herself down to the top step. She tried to do it silently, but she couldn't help saying, "Oooff," in a small voice as she landed.

Raymond leaned back and bumped against her knees to say hello. "You all done with the dishes, baby?"

"Uh-huh," she said. She hoped he wouldn't say anything about Allie. She didn't want to think about how she and Allie used to fight about Allie cleaning up the kitchen.

"I'm glad you came out to sit with me, baby. I was hopin you would."

Raymond didn't usually say things like that, and Carol Ann felt a little embarrassed. She said, "Gramps still in the barn, is he?"

"Probably." Raymond took another puff of his cigarette. The red light brightened as he breathed in the smoke.

It made her suddenly remember the summer they first started going out together, and all the time they spent at night out on Ma and Dad's porch, so they could be alone, and how Raymond's cigarette smoke would keep the mosquitoes away, or at least she would always say it did, when she came inside and Ma would wonder if the mosquitoes had been eating her alive. How happy they had been then.

They sat there in the dark without speaking. Raymond flicked his cigarette in a long arc out into the road. After a while, he started another one.

Carol Ann couldn't remember when she had felt so tired. May told her to take a few days off, but she didn't want to. If she wasn't working, she might not get tired enough, and if she wasn't tired enough, she might dream about Allie. She was really scared of that. She didn't think she could take it if she did. She wondered if Raymond worried about dreaming about Allie. She couldn't ask him. He might get the wrong idea. There wasn't anybody she could talk to, and she had to sleep sometimes. The only thing she could think of was to get really tired before she let herself go to bed.

"Did Gramps want to talk to you, Raymond?"

"I don't know."

"Did he *say* he did?"

"Want to talk to me, baby? I don't think so. Did he tell you he did?" Raymond looked around at her.

Carol Ann couldn't see his expression, only the pale circle of his face in the little bit of light that came from the kitchen. "Gramps said he had somethin he wanted to talk to me about. I thought he told you too."

"He didn't say nothin to me."

"Well, I wish he'd hurry up before I fall asleep out here."

"Go on out in the barn and find him, baby."

"No. I don't want to. I can't even look at those oxen and think what...."

"It wasn't their fault. They just...."

Carol Ann put her hands over her ears. "Don't tell me, Raymond. I don't want to hear it. I ain't said nothin to Gramps, and I ain't goin to, but I don't see how he can...."

"Quiet now, baby. Here he comes."

The thin strip of light widened into a rectangle, as Gramps opened the barn door, and then disappeared suddenly, as he turned out the light. In the darkness they could hear the creak of the closing door and Gramps' shuffling footsteps.

After a minute he got to the steps. "Hello there, Raymond. I almost stepped on you. What are you doin out here?"

"We been waitin on you, Gramps. Carol Ann said you had somethin to say."

"I told him you said that to me, Gramps. I didn't say you meant both of us."

"It's okay, honey. That's what I did mean. Let's go inside so we can all have a seat."

"Oh, it must be somethin bad the way you're talkin," Carol Ann said, with a sinking feeling in her stomach, although even before Gramps had a chance to answer, she was telling herself that what had happened to Allie was so bad, that nothing could ever seem bad again. After all, what did they have left to lose?

Gramps said, "No, honey, it ain't bad. You'll think it's good."

Raymond stood up and held out his hand to Carol Ann. She grabbed it with one of hers and took a good grip on the railing with her other hand. Between the two of them, they raised her to her feet. "Ooooff," she said. "Thanks, Raymond."

They all three went into the kitchen, blinking in the harsh light from the ceiling fixture.

"We ought to put a different light in here," Raymond said. "One of them kind that hangs over the table. Did you ever see those ones they make out of a wagon wheel?"

Carol Ann and Raymond sat down. Gramps went to the sink and got a glass of water which he carried over to the table. "A light like that would cost a whole lot of money," he said as he sat down.

Carol Ann could tell that they were all three pretending not to notice the empty, fourth chair. She wondered which would feel worse, to take the chair away, or to leave it there and see it every day. It was the same thing with Allie's room. Ma wanted her to clean out all Allie's things, but she couldn't, not yet. She just couldn't. She knew it was wrong of her, but she shut Allie's door, and sometimes when she walked by there, she would let herself believe Allie was inside, doing her homework.

"I might be able to make us one of them lights, if I could find the right wheel. They look real nice and dressy, and they put out a lot of light too."

"That's all we need, Raymond, more light in here to show up the mess."

"Don't get mad, baby. It was just a idea."

"I know. I'm sorry."

After that none of them spoke. Gramps sat looking down at his hands, like he was a million miles away. Carol Ann knew there was no way to hurry him up, even though she wanted to go to bed. Gramps always had to do things at his own speed.

After a little while, he looked up at her and said, "I'm sellin out, Carol. We'll need all that real estate stuff you was collectin last spring."

"Oh," was all Carol Ann could say. It was such a surprise that she could feel a cold ball of fear down in her stomach, like a big gulp of ice water on a really hot day.

She looked around at Raymond. His mouth was open. When he felt her eyes on him, he said, "Well, if that's...."

Carol Ann knew he was trying to make peace, even before he knew whether there was any trouble to make peace about. "The house and how many acres?" she asked Gramps without waiting for Raymond to finish his sentence.

"The whole place, honey," Gramps said to her gently. "I'm all done. I ain't got the heart for it no more."

"But you can't just...."

"Yes I can, honey. It's mine, and I can. You and Raymond don't want all that land. It ain't no good to you. It's just a burden."

"But...." Carol Ann was so confused. Nothing made sense any more. First Allie, and now this.

"Once I thought Allie might....but that was an old man's crazy dream. People can't keep their old home place like they used to. It's too expensive. Even if Allie....but there ain't no sense in talkin about what might have been."

"What will we do? Where will we go?" Carol Ann was very close to tears.

Raymond slid his hand across the table until it was touching hers. "Don't worry, baby," he said softly. "We'll make out."

Gramps said, "Well, Carol, I can't see why you're takin on like this. You've been wantin to get out of this old house for years. Here's your chance, and you act like I'm tryin to turn you out in the cold."

"Oh don't, Gramps," Carol Ann said. She couldn't hold the crying back any longer. She pulled a handkerchief of Raymond's out of the pocket of her blue jeans and wiped her eyes. "Everythin's changin so fast," she gasped. "I can't deal with it. Don't sell the place, Gramps. Let's stay in this house. I won't complain no more."

"It's too late. It's all done. I gave my word."

That stopped Carol Ann's crying. She couldn't understand how things could have gone so far. "Why didn't you tell us you was thinkin about it? We didn't even know...."

"Honey," Gramps said, reaching out to touch her shoulder, "I thought....I mean, there was the funeral, and I....I don't know. I thought you wanted a new house. I thought it would be good for you, for all of us to get away from....I don't even know. It just kind of happened."

Then they all three sat there. Raymond hadn't said a word since Carol Ann cut him off, but his hand still lay on the table where hers had been. Anybody looking in the window would have thought they were comforting each other, but Carol Ann had never felt so alone in her life.

Finally she was able to look at Gramps. He smiled a thin smile. There were tears in his eyes. Until that very minute, Carol Ann hadn't realized how old he was. She always thought he was strong, but suddenly he looked very small and shaky.

"Oh Gramps," she said. "I'm so sorry. Don't do it. This is your place. You always meant to die here."

"It's too late, honey. I gave my word," he said softly, but so firmly that there was no arguing with him.

"What are we goin to do?" She was close to tears again.

"Listen to me," Gramps said. Carol Ann could tell he wanted to keep her from crying. "We'll keep some land on the road— maybe that piece on the far side of the barn where the cedars come right up to the road. We could clear that and make it real pretty. We'll put in a new house that's easy to take care of, one with a modrun kitchen just big enough for...." He had been looking down at his hands while he talked, fidgeting with his empty water glass and making the hole in the tablecloth worse by picking at it. When he stopped talking, he looked at her with a little, quivery smile, trying to keep her from noticing how hard it was for him to say the words. "Just big enough for the three of us. And, Raymond, I ain't forgot you either. I think we can build a heated garage where you can work on cars even in the wintertime."

"Thanks, Gramps," Raymond said, like Gramps was handing him a Christmas present. "I really appreciate it."

Sometimes Carol Ann had to wonder about Raymond. Didn't he notice that this new house and all these fine things, like a heated garage, were going to come to them because their baby had been taken away? How could something good come out of Allie's death?

She was just about to say something, and then she took another look at Gramps and saw that it was impossible to blame him. And she saw that it didn't matter whether he sold his land and his home place or not, because he was already dead. There was nothing left of him but a little dried-up shell, like an old snakeskin, waiting for the first good wind to blow it away.

She reached out then and put her hand over his. For a second she noticed how pretty her hand looked, small and smooth and dimpled. Then Gramps put his other hand down on top of it and patted it, and her hand was entirely covered by Gramps' knobby, rough one. "I'm goin to be glad to have a new kitchen, Gramps," she said, trying not to cry for all of them and how lost they were. "I've wanted one for a long time."

Gramps didn't say anything, but he sighed and squeezed her hand, and she knew he was grateful.

36

WHEN ISABEL STEPPED out of her room with the last armful of books, she almost bumped into Roxy who was coming out of the bathroom.

"Hey, hon, watch it."

"Excuse me," Isabel said, on her way toward the stairs.

"Hold on a minute, darlin. Where are you takin that stuff?"

Isabel stopped one step down. "I was going to load up and then come and tell you. I didn't know you were up."

Roxy opened her arms wide. "Well I am. What's wrong with tellin me right now?"

"Okay," Isabel said. "Just let me put these books in my car. I'll be right back."

The front door was hard to open with her arms full, but she didn't want to wait for Roxy who was clumping heavily and slowly down the steps behind her.

Outside, the sky was overcast, and the air was warm and heavy. Even the birds were quiet. Isabel packed the books into the backend of the stationwagon along with the rest of her stuff. She liked the way she had arranged everything. She could get to what she needed, even if she had to leave most of her things in the car until she got settled some place.

The clock in the car said ten-thirty. She might be able to get away before noon. She ran up the steps and into the house. Roxy's door was partly open. She pushed it and went in.

Roxy was leaning back in her armchair, blowing cigarette smoke at the ceiling. "So tell me, darlin, what's goin on?"

"It's this," Isabel said. "I have to leave Severance."

"Huh," Roxy said, surprised into silence.

"I'm sorry. I would have told you sooner if I could have. I just decided yesterday."

"That's okay. But ain't you goin to stay til your rent's used up?"

"No. I'm not. I'm going to leave today."

Roxy blew another stream of smoke at the ceiling. "That's too bad, seein as how you just paid for the month and all."

Isabel watched the swirls of smoke. "I know," she said. "But that was before....before it happened. That changed things for me. Or maybe...." She wasn't sure about this. "Maybe, it made me see things that I didn't really see before. Anyway, I need to leave, and...."

"It was pretty bad that poor little thing gettin killed like that."

"I know."

"When somethin like that happens, I thank my lucky stars that I never had no kids. I always was too tender-hearted. I never could've took it if I'd lost a kid."

Isabel nodded. "But, Roxy, I was wondering what would be fair to do about the rent. I was hoping...."

"Now look here, hon. We had a arrangement." Roxy stabbed out her half-finished cigarette for emphasis. "I gave you a good deal cause you paid by the month. You can't just...."

"I've thought about it. I mean I know I'm not giving you any notice. But then none of us could have known...it's just that I don't have much money right now...."

Roxy sighed. "I don't know who's in the right here, but I guess it don't make no difference." She sighed again. "Look here. I can't give you your money back, cause I ain't got it."

"You don't have any of what I paid you?"

"Not really." Roxy looked at Isabel shrewdly. "I'm waitin for my social security." Her eyes fluttered away. "But it won't come until tomorrow....or the day after. Maybe even Wednesday or Thursday. It might not come before Friday."

"It doesn't matter," Isabel said, and she sighed. "I really have to leave today."

Roxy looked down at the floor, and neither of them said anything for a minute. Then Roxy looked up. She was smiling. "Hey, I know what we can do. This here is a good idea. You come back any time for a two-week vacation, and I won't charge you a cent, even if my prices have gone up. How about it?"

"Well, that's nice," Isabel said. "But I'm not coming back."

"You never can tell about somethin like that, hon. You didn't know you were goin to leave, did you?" She looked triumphantly at Isabel. "You can't argue with that, can you?"

Isabel shook her head.

"How come you're leavin, anyhow?"

Isabel sighed. "I don't know. I just know I have to." She thought about how hard she had cried yesterday in her room. Her face still felt puffy and bruised from it. She was crying and packing boxes before she even knew that she meant to leave. She was surprised when she noticed what she was doing. It wasn't possible to explain that that was how she had decided.

Roxy lit another cigarette. "Paid for with my money," Isabel thought and hated her own bitterness.

"Where're you goin then?" Roxy asked without much interest.

"I'm going to visit my mother and sister, and I'm not sure

where after that."

"Maybe you'll come back after all. You can have your room back when you do."

"It just didn't turn out the way I thought it would. That's the trouble. It all turned out different than I thought it would." She sighed. "You know what?"

"What?"

"You can't be something different than you are. That's all."

"I wouldn't know."

"I guess that's because you know who you are."

"I wouldn't say that. I never tried to be nothin but a good-time girl, so how would I know?"

"All *I* know is that I don't belong here."

But Roxy wasn't listening any more. She picked up a crochet hook and stuck it between her curlers to scratch her head. "Well, look here, hon. You put all that furniture back the way it was before you go. Okay?"

"If that's what you want me to do. And I'll come say goodbye before I leave. I've still got some packing to do."

"Okay, then," Roxy said. "See you later."

It was a little after twelve when Isabel knocked on Roxy's door. There was no answer. She walked down the dark hall and into the kitchen.

Roxy was standing by the stove with one hand on her hip, jabbing a fork at what she was frying.

"I just came in to say goodbye," Isabel said. She had to say it a second time before Roxy heard her over the spit and hiss of her cooking.

She turned around. "Come in, darlin. You want me to make you some breakfast?"

"I have to go," Isabel said.

"You come back, hon, and have a vacation and use up that rent money any time you want to."

"Well, maybe," Isabel said. "Thank you."

She drove to a convenience store at the end of Merchants Row, where she filled the car with gas and bought a ready-made sandwich and a cup of coffee for lunch.

There was a telephone on the outside wall. She couldn't put the phone call off any longer. She laid her sandwich on the seat of the car and took her coffee with her to the phone.

"Hi, Mom. Are you feeling okay? You sound tired."

"Isabel? Is this Isabel?"

"Yes, it is."

"Is everything all right? Nothing's wrong, is it?"

"No. Everything's fine, Mom. I mean I told you about the accident. Nothing else is wrong. I was thinking of coming to visit you."

"That would be nice."

"Are you sure?"

"Of course I'm sure. When were you thinking about coming?"

"I was planning to leave today."

"Oh Isabel, *honestly*. Why didn't you tell me sooner?"

"If it's not all right, I can...."

"No, it's fine. It's fine. I don't know why you couldn't tell me sooner, that's all."

"I couldn't, Mom. I didn't know myself. I just decided yesterday. I'm leaving Severance for good."

"Well, *that's* something anyhow. I have *no idea* what you are doing there. When are you coming?"

"I'm going to start today, but I probably won't get very far before I stop for the night."

"At least you're not going to try to drive straight through or something crazy like that."

"Oh, Mom. Don't. How's Dianne?"

"She's all right."

"I can't wait to see her. Tell her for me, will you?"

"You call me, Isabel. I'm going to be worried. And remember, if your car breaks down, you just lock all your doors and stay in there until the police come to help you. Do you still have that old car?"

"Yes, but...."

"Do the doors lock?"

"Sure. Of course."

"Well, you lock yourself in. You hear me?"

"Yes, Mom. I will."

"And call me."

"I'll call when I know more about when I'll get there."

"What day do you think? Just so I have an idea."

"It might be Wednesday. I'm going to take it slow. Maybe I'll take back roads through the Adirondacks. I have some things I want to think about."

"Isabel, I wish you'd go back to Abingdon, to the bookstore. At least I didn't have to worry about you all the time."

Isabel sighed. "I'm sorry, Mom. I'll call you soon. Okay?"

"You be careful."

Isabel hung up the phone. She had forgotten all about her coffee. It was still hot, but it was bitter. She sighed again. She wondered if it was a mistake to go home, but she knew she would do it anyway, even if it was a mistake, because she couldn't think of anything else to do.

She told herself she should be excited. She had no responsibilities. She could go anywhere and do anything. But she didn't feel excited, just rootless and lonely and sad.

She unwrapped her sandwich and set it on her lap and began to drive to West Severance while she ate. When she went by the Texas Café, she realized that it would have been a good idea to buy lunch there. She could have said goodbye to Carol Ann at the same time. She considered stopping in, just to tell Carol Ann she was leaving, but she decided not to. Carol Ann always made her feel uncomfortable.

She turned down the road to Sonny's place, thinking how often she had made that turn since she found Sonny's farm. It had only been a few months, but so much had happened that it felt like a lifetime.

There was a large truck with New Hampshire plates parked at the end of Sonny's barn where they had unloaded hay that time when Isabel helped them in the hayfield. The hay elevator was still there, leaning against the wall of the barn.

Isabel remembered Al up on top of the loaded truck, catching bales, and later on throwing them down again so they could be put on the hay elevator. She would never help with the hay again. If that was hard for Isabel to think about, she couldn't imagine what it was like for Sonny, or Carol Ann, or Raymond.

She left her car between the house and the barn and knocked on the kitchen door. No one answered, so she walked down to the front of the barn where the New Hampshire truck was parked.

The truck was old and beaten-up. It had tall sides made of plywood, held together with rusty chains. When Isabel walked around the backend of it, she was surprised by a large man in striped overalls and a torn T-shirt. He must have been just as surprised, because he gave a little jump and turned his head aside to spit on the ground. Then he raised his dirty hat and tilted his head in a mock bow.

"I was looking for Sonny Trumbley," Isabel said, feeling uncomfortable. "Do you know where he is?"

"He'll be along." The man waved his hand toward the road that went around the back of the barn. "He's gone after his cattle."

"I'll wait for him then."

The man shrugged. "Suit yourself," he said. After that, he stood silently looking at his feet, kicking the dirt with the toe of his workboot.

Isabel tried not to show how uncomfortable she felt. After a while she said, "It's not a very nice day, is it?"

"Nope."

"Do you think it'll rain later?"

"Maybe. Maybe not."

There was silence again. When Sonny came around the corner of the barn with Buck and Ben, she was so glad to see him that she called, "Hey, Sonny," and smiled at him.

But Sonny acted as though she wasn't there. He didn't answer her. He didn't even look at her. The big man smiled smugly, as though he was thinking she wasn't as smart as she thought she was.

Isabel would have left right then, except that she wanted to tell Sonny she was leaving She wanted to say goodbye.

Sonny told his oxen to whoa and stood beside them, while the man unfastened the chains on the sides of his truck and took the boards from the back wall and made them into a ramp.

He turned around. "Okay, Sonny. Walk 'em on up."

"Git up, boys," Sonny said, and he waved his stick over their heads. But he acted slow and uncertain. The oxen took a few steps and then stopped at the foot of the ramp. Both their heads swung toward Sonny. Isabel saw that they didn't have their ox yoke on.

"Here," the man said suddenly. "Give me that thing you use for a whip. *I'll* get 'em in there."

Sonny held the whip out to him and stepped aside. He still hadn't looked at Isabel, although she tried to catch his eye.

The man shouted and lashed at the oxen with the stick. They winced and ducked their heads, but neither ox took a step toward the ramp. The man swore, and the oxen swung their heads back and forth, trying to avoid the stick. Sonny stood still, not looking up from the ground.

Finally, after what seemed an unbearably long time, Sonny walked up to the man and grabbed his raised arm. When the man looked down, Sonny said, "Okay, George. I'll load 'em myself." His voice was firm.

The man handed Sonny his stick. "Just so we get 'em in. *I* don't give a damn."

Sonny stepped up in front of the oxen again. He scratched each one under the chin, murmuring softly as he scratched.

"Buck, you be a good boy now. It's got to be this way, honey. And you too, Ben. You've always been a sweetie." He took a step back, and his voice got louder. "Come on now, boys." He stepped around to Buck's side and raised the stick straight up in the air and said, "Git up."

The oxen started together. They walked slowly up the steep ramp and into the truck. The ramp was too narrow for Sonny to walk beside them, so he stayed outside. When he saw that the oxen were near the front of the truck, he said, "Whoa, boys," and they stopped and stood still, side by side.

The big man scrambled up the ramp behind them. "Why couldn't you bastards do that in the first place?" he said crossly.

The oxen were wearing rope halters tied together with a piece of baling twine. The man pulled out a pocket knife and cut the twine. Then with short ropes, he tied each ox by the halter into a front corner of the truck. Sonny and Isabel, standing outside and looking in, saw them standing steady and patient on their heavy legs.

The big man pushed past them on his way out of the truck. When went by Ben, he slapped him on the rump as hard as he could. Ben jumped, but he couldn't turn his head to look.

The man scrambled down the ramp and then began to take it apart, putting the boards up as a tailgate. He looked around at Sonny, who was standing a few steps away watching him work. "Get over here, Sonny, and give me a hand with this god-damn thing."

Sonny stepped up without much energy and helped the man shut the oxen in. The man didn't ask Isabel to help, and she didn't volunteer. When all the boards were in place, Sonny steadied them while the man put up the chains.

After that, they all three stood together in an unfriendly silence, until the man sighed and said, "Well, there ain't no help for it." He put his hand through his overalls to a pocket in the trousers underneath and pulled out a wad of bills. He counted out $80 in twenties and tens and held the messy handful out to

Sonny. Sonny stuffed the wad of bills into his pocket without even looking at it. He didn't say a word.

"That's the price these days," the man said, "since the economy's gone to hell in a handbasket. Pathetic, ain't it?"

"It don't matter," Sonny said quietly.

"The hell it don't! Gas is so high, I can't keep my truck on the road, and them god-damn I-raquis, burnin up all that oil...." He looked at Isabel suspiciously. "Them liberals," he said with disgust. "We should've bombed I-raq off the map while we had a chance."

Isabel opened her mouth to say something, but when she saw the pain in Sonny's face, she closed her mouth again.

"Well, I'd best get on," the man said, looking at Sonny and then at Isabel. "You folks don't have too much to say today." He went around the truck to the cab and pulled himself up by the steering wheel. He started the engine and drove off, leaving them standing in a smell of exhaust.

"He better adjust his carburetor," Sonny said. Then without looking at Isabel, he began to walk up the road to the back door of the barn.

He was walking away, and Isabel still hadn't had a chance to tell him she was leaving. She followed him around the barn and into the empty ox stall. He didn't look back. Isabel stopped in the doorway. She wasn't sure he knew she was there. She watched him pick up the ox yoke from the corner where it always stood. He carried it to the other corner and stood it up behind his lawn chair. He looked at it for a minute and then picked it up again and carried it back to the original place.

"I don't understand," Isabel said. "Where are Buck 'n Ben going?"

Sonny turned to face her then. "I sold 'em."

"That man's going to work them?"

Sonny sighed. "I wouldn't do that to 'em. I sold 'em for slaughter. George is the knacker man."

"He's going to kill them? Why couldn't you...."

"I ain't goin to have no land or a barn."

"But couldn't you have found them another home, sold them to someone who...."

"If I had, I wouldn't never have known if they fell into bad hands. I didn't want 'em abused."

"But...."

"Don't say no more. I guess you mean well, but you don't know what can happen to a animal. I couldn't keep 'em. They ain't never known nobody else. That's just all there is to it."

'But...."

"I really can't talk about it now."

"Oh, I'm so sorry," Isabel said, trying to hold back her tears. "And I came to say goodbye. I'm leaving Severance."

Sonny smiled a weak smile, as though he was far away with his sadness and loneliness. "Good luck, then."

"Thank you," Isabel said, choking a little. "And you too. I wish you luck too." She turned and left quickly without waiting to hear if he had any more to say, because perhaps the only luck possible to him now was to be alone with his grief.

She made it to the car before she actually started sobbing. She cried all the way back to Severance and for a long while after she left town, so that whenever she thought about it later, she always had an image of herself leaving in the middle of a rainstorm, and she would have to remind herself that it was really a cloudy, dry day, and she was crying hard.

37

It was snowing when Isabel turned off the highway at the Severance exit. The ground was bare, but the snowflakes were small and businesslike. Everything was gray and brown. Severance was smaller and shabbier than she remembered.

She didn't know why she wanted to make this trip into the past. She planned to sort out her reasons on the long drive, but she found herself thinking instead about what it would be like when she got back to Ohio and started her new job. The timing was wrong too. She had pictured herself returning to Severance in the spring when everything was getting green, the way it had been when she began her life there a year ago. She hadn't pictured herself arriving in the tired end of winter.

She drove along Merchants Row. Everything was the same. She didn't even slow down when she passed the River Street bridge. She didn't want to see Roxy. And there was always the danger of running into Leroy.

Everything was the same along the road to West Severance too, even the Texas Café. Isabel was lulled into a false sense of how little had changed, and she was unprepared for what she found at Sonny's place. Someone had cut down all the bushes around the house and had painted it dark gray with yellow trim. It looked new and bare. The sheds where Raymond kept his old machines were gone and so were the machines. From her car parked on the road, Isabel could see right into what Sonny used to call the night pasture. The huge rock in the middle was gone. Where it used to be, there was a pile of dirt and two bulldozers. The whole field was in ruins.

Sadly, Isabel drove on, past the barn and the low, swampy place on the other side of it. Before she had a chance to wonder where to find Sonny, she came to a new house under the cedars, a little white ranch house, with red shutters and a pick-up truck in the driveway, and she knew she had found him.

She parked on the road at the end of the drive and walked up to the front door. The ground under the trees was covered with a thin layer of new snow. The red shutters had cut-out hearts on them.

Isabel went up the steps slowly and knocked on the door. She was shaking from the cold. The wind went right through her sweater. Her blue jeans were stiff and hard against her legs. When she left Ohio, it had been spring with everything starting to get green. She had forgotten that March was still a winter month in Vermont.

She stood before the door. She could hear a television going inside. She knocked again louder, and at the same time, she wondered if it was a mistake to be here at all. The wind whistled and sighed as it moved through the trees. Then there was a scrabbling sound on the other side of the door. It opened, and Sonny stood there, blinking and nodding and looking at her. He was smaller and thinner, more shriveled up than she remembered. He looked confused.

"Hullo, Sonny," she said shyly, embarrassed that he didn't recognize her, sorry to be here, now when it was too late to leave. "It's Isabel....Isabel Rawlings....from last summer...."

"Oh," he said. "I thought you was sellin somethin." He paused, and a little frown passed over his face. "Oh yes. Now I know. Come in. It's cold out, ain't it?"

Isabel stepped inside, and Sonny closed the door. "It's warm in here," she said.

"This place's a whole lot easier to heat than the old one. But it don't make no difference. I can't get warm no matter what I do. I guess I can't get used to not havin a woodstove to cozy up to." He was wearing a heavy sweater like a jacket over his green work clothes. He buttoned the buttons while he talked. "I'm always cold. I drive Carol Ann crazy, turnin up the heat." He paused. "And I might as well not bother. It don't do no good."

They were still standing beside the door. Isabel looked around the small room, cluttered with dark furniture. "Can I sit down?" she asked.

"Okay," Sonny said, but he looked doubtful.

Isabel sat down anyway, telling herself she would stay just long enough to find out if Raymond and Carol Ann were all right, and, if she could bring the conversation around to it, what was going on with the development next door. It was obvious how Sonny himself was doing, and she hated to see it.

Sonny adjusted his red, vinyl recliner to an upright position and sat down too. Soon they were both watching the old cowboy movie on the television. Isabel knew she had seen it before, but she couldn't quite remember what it was. She didn't want to remember, and she didn't want to watch it. She didn't want to be here. She wanted to ask her questions and leave. Al's school picture looked solemnly at them from its place on top of the television.

"Did you have a good winter, Sonny?"

He looked around, surprised, as if he had forgotten about her. "I wouldn't say good, but we got through it. What about you?"

"I'm okay. I've been living with my mother in Cleveland. When I get back, I'm going to work on a farm, for an old couple who live near Aurora. They need some help, and they're going to teach me. They have dairy cows and a big garden."

Sonny didn't say anything. He tried to appear interested, but his eyes kept wandering back to the television.

"They do things the old fashioned way," Isabel said. "Like you."

After a while, without looking away from what he was watching, Sonny nodded politely. "Well, that's nice."

Isabel wondered what he was thinking. Neither of them had mentioned Al, but her presence was there with them in the room. Isabel wondered whether it would be better to say something or nothing. Neither one felt right.

She still hadn't asked the questions she meant to ask, when the door at the end of the house slammed. Raymond shouted, "Hey Gramps, there's a brand new Honda with Ohio plates out front on the road. You seen...." Then he got to the front room and saw Isabel and said, "Oh....hi....excuse me. Is that your Prelude out there?"

"I left it there so I wouldn't block your driveway."

Carol Ann pushed past Raymond and came into the room. "Hello Gramps," she said. She tilted her head toward Isabel and stood there looking puzzled with one arm out of her puffy, pink jacket.

Sonny said, "This here is Isabel from last summer."

There was a silence, and then Carol Ann said, "Oh. That's who you are. I thought I'd seen you somewheres, but I couldn't place you. You look different." She studied Isabel's face. "Your hair's a lot shorter, ain't it? I thought you left town last summer, after...after the funeral."

"I did. I went to Cleveland where my mother lives. I have a sister there too."

"That's good."

"I came over to see if you got through the winter all right." She tried to make it sound casual, not as though she had driven all those miles just to visit them. It was true that she also planned to spend a few days with Joey at his college, but she didn't want to talk about him to Carol Ann. "Did you have a good winter?"

"We still got mud season to go," Carol Ann said.

"I was worried about the mud, but it didn't seem bad. Your road is solid."

"That's because it's cold today," Carol Ann said. "You wait. Them machines over to the old place are goin to tear it up. It's goin to be somethin else. I hope we're goin to be able to get through that mess without a four-wheel drive. There's always been a bad place right out in front of the house."

"I remember that place," Isabel said. "My husband and I got stuck in that mudhole."

"I don't remember that," Carol Ann said. She put her jacket down on a chair in the corner and sat down heavily on the couch.

"Maybe you weren't there. Your Gramps and his oxen pulled us out. It was amazing."

"Oh," Carol Ann said. "Gramps don't do nothin like that no more." They both looked at Sonny, but he was watching the movie again.

"Your new house is really nice," Isabel said after a while.

"We got some problems with it, but at least it's easier to heat."

"It's warm in here now," Isabel said. She was sweating.

"Gramps can't get enough of it. If we'd stayed the winter in the old home place, he probably would've froze to death."

"That's a real nice car you got there," Raymond said from the doorway.

"Take your jacket off, Raymond. You'll roast to death."

"No, baby. I'm goin out to the shed to work." He looked at Isabel. "What kind of mileage do you get with her?"

Carol Ann said, "I tell Gramps if he just got out a little, maybe it would heat him up, and we could turn down the thermostat."

Sonny heard that. "There ain't nothin to do outside. That's

why I don't go out. It's too cold to just stand around."

"You could walk. That's good exercise, ain't it? You could go up through the woods." She turned toward Isabel. "Why, he didn't get out deer huntin even once last year, if you can believe it."

"I told you and told you, Carol. They got posted signs all over up there."

"You could *ask* 'em, Gramps. They probably don't mean you."

"Oh Carol, honey. I *can't* ask. I can't go up to Leroy or one of them other guys he brought in here and say, 'Can I go up in your woods?' Up there where I always went just where I pleased. Up there where Al got killed. I just *can't* ask for that."

Carol Ann sighed and gave Isabel a look that said, "You see what he's like. There's nothing I can do."

When Isabel remembered Raymond's unanswered question and looked around, the doorway was empty, and he was gone.

"Carol, honey," Sonny said. "I do what I can. You know that, don't you?"

"Yes, Gramps."

"I didn't intend to sound like I was mad with you."

"I know, Gramps, but we got company right now. Did you forget?"

"No, I didn't forget. I just wanted you to know I was sorry. That's all."

"I know, Gramps."

There was another awkward silence. Isabel said, "Have they made a lot of changes over at your old place? I saw they cut down the lilac bushes."

"I feel awful about them lilacs. They was over a hundred years old. Gramps' mother planted 'em. I don't think Leroy and them knew what they were. They must've thought we just had brush growin up around the house. Them bushes was somethin to see in spring."

"I remember," Isabel said.

"Two colors of lavender and some white ones by the front door. I feel real bad about them lilacs."

"They dug a big hole up in the pasture."

"That's a mess too."

"What's it for?"

"They say they're goin to put these little cabins all over up in the woods and around, and that's goin to be the recreation center or somethin. It's supposed to be a year-round vacation place for people from New York and Boston." Carol Ann paused and looked at Sonny who had gone back to watching his movie again. "Or so they say."

"I wonder what it will be like to live next door to something like that. Do you think it'll really happen?"

"Maybe. I don't know. Why wouldn't those people go to Florida if they're so rich? Leroy LaFourniere's ridin high right now, anyways. He's up here all the time in his big, black car. Doesn't even wave when we go by. He's got us where he wants us now, I guess."

"I'm sorry."

"I didn't mean to complain. I just hate to see what they're doin over there. It's got to be hard on Gramps, even though he don't say nothin about it."

"It must bother all of you," Isabel said, thinking Carol Ann had never said so much to her before.

Carol Ann shrugged. "We're okay. We've got each other. That ought to be enough. At least it don't bother Raymond. He's happy. He's got a place to work on his engines. That's all he cares."

"Are you still working at the Texas?"

"Oh sure. I couldn't leave May."

"I went by there today."

"Are you livin back in Severance again?"

"Just visiting."

Carol Ann nodded.

"I'm going back to Ohio—that's where my family is."

"That's right," Carol Ann said. "You want to be near your family. You never know....even when you think...."

"I know," Isabel said. "I'm sorry."

Carol Ann looked down at her little, dimpled hands, lying in her lap. "Maybe someday you get used to it."

"I hope so."

Sonny looked away from the television. "We could offer her a cup of tea, couldn't we, Carol?"

Carol Ann looked at her, and Isabel quickly said, "Oh no, thank you. That's very kind, but I really ought to get going." She stood up. "It's been good to see you both. Tell Raymond I said goodbye."

"Stand up, Gramps, and say goodbye." Carol Ann went over to him and gave him a little poke to make him pay attention.

Sonny got slowly to his feet. Isabel held out her hand, and Sonny took it with his lumpy, old one, and they shook, but even then he didn't look at her.

Isabel walked to the door, and Carol Ann followed her. There was an awkward moment in which Isabel wondered whether or not to hug Carol Ann. She almost did, but she was afraid she might have misread Carol Ann's friendliness. She held out her hand instead. "Goodbye," she said. "Take care." She went out quickly into the blowing snow. There was already a thin, white layer on the roof of her car.

She got into her car and turned around and drove back the way she had come, past the new development. This time she didn't slow down to look.

Since graduating from St. John's College, Ruth Porter has spent her life writing and reading in rural Vermont. She has lived on a subsistence farm for thirty years where she raised four children and most of their food. She was born in New York and grew up in Ohio. Porter, Maxwell Perkins' granddaughter, has completed a one-man show about Perkins and has collaborated with her aunt, Bertha Frothingham, Maxwell Perkins' oldest daughter, to edit Perkins' personal letters, *Father to Daughter.* She is working on her third novel about Vermont.